FROM NOB HILL
TO CAPITOL HILL...
FROM THE BACKLOTS OF HOLLYWOOD
TO THE BATTLEFIELDS OF ISRAEL—
THREE GENERATIONS
OF AN UNFORGETTABLE FAMILY

Barbara Lavette—She gave up everything for love. Humiliated, blacklisted, unjustly punished, she would surmount every obstacle to learn an extraordinary truth and the lesson of a lifetime.

Bernie Cohen—Barbara's husband. A reckless soldier of fortune, he gave up adventure for love, until a mysterious mission to Palestine stunned the world and shattered a precious dream.

Sally Lavette—Barbara's sister-in-law, torn between devotion to her husband and a glamorous Hollywood career that was hers for the asking.

Tom Lavette—Barbara's brother. His power was unrivaled in the West. His possessions included a corrupt politician targeted for the White House.

Dan and Jean Lavette—Barbara's parents. They built an empire and gave birth to a dynasty. Now they lived in bold defiance of society's rules.

**A TURBULENT LEGACY AND ITS
GLORIOUS FULFILLMENT**

Books by Howard Fast

*In Dell Editions

THE ESTABLISHMENT

Howard Fast

A DELL BOOK

Published by
Dell Publishing Co., Inc.
1 Dag Hammarskjold Plaza
New York, New York 10017

This book is published by special arrangement with Eric Lasher
and Maureen Lasher

The lyrics quoted on page 122 are from "Masquerade"
by Paul Webster and John Jacob Loeb, copyright 1932
by Leo Feist Company.

Dell ® TM 681510, Dell Publishing Co., Inc.

ISBN: 0-440-12393-3

Reprinted by arrangement with Houghton Mifflin Company

Printed in the United States of America

First Dell printing—September 1980
Sixth Dell printing—December 1982

To Molly

Welcome to this best of all possible worlds

CONTENTS

THE
ESTABLISHMENT

PART ONE

Marriage

Cohen, a large, heavyset man of forty-three, was gradually losing his patience, and that would be a prelude to losing his temper and taking it out on everyone around him, and that had been happening too often. Small things, unimportant things, irritated him and provoked him. He had been through too many large things in his life, things that had failed to provoke him, not to realize that something unpleasant and corrosive was happening to him. He had fallen into a pattern of swallowing anger, frustration, and annoyance, remaining fairly unconscious of what was building up inside him. Now he exploded at the meek little woman who faced him.

"God damn it, Mrs. Melcher, I am trying to explain to you why this happens! You ride the damn clutch! A clutch is not something God made, like a horse's rump. It's a mechanism for connecting and disconnecting the engine and the transmission. There's a spring-loaded pressure plate, which is surfaced on both sides with friction material. Your foot is always on the damn pedal, and it shouldn't be. You have to learn how to drive. It happened before, and it will happen again."

She turned white and whispered, "You have no right to talk to me like that. You have no right to."

He stared down at her. "Oh, Jesus," he said to himself. Gomez, one of his mechanics, was watching him. He dropped his voice and apologized.

"You have no right to talk to me like that," Mrs. Melcher complained, on the point of tears, as if there were no other words she could imagine.

"I'm sorry. We'll fix the car. You'll have it tomorrow."

He turned and stalked through the garage to the men's room at the rear, locked the door behind him, slammed down the toilet cover, and sat there with his chin propped on his clenched, grimy fists. On the door facing him, surrounded by expressions of witless smut, someone had scrawled: "There was an old hermit called Dave, who kept a dead girl in his cave. He said, I'll admit I'm a bit of a shit, but think of the money I save." He stared at the words at first without comprehension. They hadn't been there the day before. Then, suddenly, everything bottled up inside him exploded. He kicked the door open and roared out at his four mechanics, "I want this goddamn toilet painted! Today! And the next one of you mothers who writes on the walls gets booted out of here on his ass!"

With the mechanics staring at him in amazement, he strode across the garage and into the little glass-walled office. A knot of pain swelled in his stomach as he dropped down behind his desk. He breathed deeply and stared at the inkstained blotter and wondered whether he was developing an ulcer. That would be the final ignominy. An ulcer or a heart attack. He was a big, heavily muscled man, and the last time he had undergone a physical examination, the doctor had warned him that he was the physical type that suffered the greatest incidence of early coronary.

Gomez opened the door of the office gingerly.

"Hey, Bernie," he said softly, "something bad happen?"

He stared at Gomez without replying. Gomez, a small, skinny, competent Chicano, was the foreman of the shop.

"You really want the crapper painted, Bernie? We're loaded with work."

"Forget it."

"You let them crazy dames get under your skin. Two guys here, they want to see you."

"Take care of it."

"They want to see you."

"About what?"

"I don't know." Gomez spread his arms. "Bernie, Jesus, what is with you? You got good men working here. We give you a day's work, and you chew our asses off. I stand here arguing with you. These guys, they don't want a car job. They want to talk to Mr. Cohen. Talk to them, huh? Let me get back to work."

Cohen nodded. Gomez left the office, and a few moments later, the door opened, and two men entered Cohen's office. One was a slight, sandy-haired man in his mid-thirties. He had bright blue eyes, a pale mustache, and a scar that ran from his temple to his chin. The other man was younger, twenty-three or twenty-four at the most, Cohen decided, plump, with a round, pink-cheeked, baby face. They came into the office and stood facing Cohen, and the pink-cheeked man said, "That's him?"

"That's him," said the sandy-haired man.

Cohen stood up slowly, staring at the sandy-haired man, who grinned at him complacently.

"He is one big sonofabitch," the pink-cheeked man said.

Cohen came around the desk, stared for a moment

more, and then threw his arms around the sandy-haired man, sweeping him up in an enormous bear hug. The pink-cheeked man watched and nodded.

"You're killing me with affection, you dumb slob," the sandy-haired man managed to say.

Cohen let go of him.

"This is Herbie Goodman," the sandy-haired man said. "Herbie, I want you to meet Bernie Cohen."

They shook hands. "You're a legend," Herbie said. "You are absolutely a legend."

"How in hell did you find me?" Cohen asked.

"We got our ways. You'd be surprised what ways we got."

Barbara Lavette's child was born six months after she married Bernie Cohen and became Barbara Lavette Cohen, or, as the gossip column hastened to point out, Barbara Seldon Lavette Cohen. The reference was pointed, since the Seldon family had been part of the tight, high-walled circle that constituted San Francisco society for almost a hundred years, which now, in 1948, spanned the whole age of San Francisco. Scandal, and the juicy gossip that flows from it, had begun when Barbara's father, Dan Lavette, the son of Italian immigrants, had wooed and won the daughter of the banker Thomas Seldon. Jean Seldon, the banker's daughter and Barbara's mother, had subsequently divorced Dan Lavette, married the very wealthy John Whittier, divorced him, and now lived openly and out of wedlock with her first husband, a condition that provided some of the best dinner table and cocktail party conversation that San Francisco had known in a long while. The marriage of Jean and Dan's daughter, Barbara Lavette, to one Bernie Cohen, a more or less indigent soldier of fortune, a man without family or past or future—and a Jew, to boot—heightened the gossip to a point of delightful titillation. When, six months after this marriage, a son was born to Barbara at Mount Zion Hospital, with no attempt at concealment, the resulting structure of gossip and scandal reached a new level of interest.

To all this, Barbara was indifferent. When she considered the stages of her life, it was always with the sense of being a late finisher. Her childhood had been long and lonely; her adolescence had continued beyond the suggested boundaries, and her age of innocence had extended into her college years. She felt that she had never caught up with a proper calendar of life. In 1946, at the age of thirty-two, she had her first and only child. Dr. Kellman, who saw her through her pregnancy, was not worried about her age; he said that thirty-two was by no means too late to begin childbearing. Barbara was a tall, strong, and healthy woman, and Kellman assured her that the birth would present no difficulties.

She rejected the use of anesthesia. Until the last month, her pregnancy had been relatively easy, and she said to her husband, "I may or may not have another child—"

"Or two more or three more," he put in.

"Another, I said. Never mind about two or three more. The point is that I want to experience this, and experience it fully. I want to know what happens and how it happens."

"So you can write about it? That's crazy."

"I write about what I have seen and experienced, and it's not so crazy at all."

Bernie was with her when her labor began, and he wanted to remain with her in the hospital. After the first two hours, when her moans at each contraction

became screeches of agony, Dr. Kellman persuaded
Bernie to leave the room. Twelve hours later, her
strength gone, her agony tearing her mind apart, they
decided that her pelvic opening was too small and
that the child could not come through the birth canal.
A Caesarean section was performed, and a nine-pound
boy came into the world.

Now, fifteen months later, Barbara was sitting in
the nursery of her home on Green Street, instructing
her son in the proper pronunciation of *dump truck*.
His name was Samuel Thomas Cohen. The Samuel
was for Sam Goldberg, who had been Barbara's lawyer, who had been much beloved of her, and who had
once owned the Victorian house in which she now
lived. Thomas was her Grandfather Seldon's name.
Young Samuel was a large, chubby, healthy child,
with brown hair, blue eyes, and five fingers on each
hand and five toes on each foot—all Barbara had
asked for.

This evening, feeding Samuel his dinner and introducing a modest dose of linguistics, Barbara was listening for the sound of the door downstairs that
would tell her Bernie was back—providing he had decided to come home for dinner and not work until ten
or eleven or midnight. Another part of her mind was
engaged in planning a way to get through the evening
without rancor, acknowledging at the same time that
similar plans had failed dismally on other nights.

Again and again during the past months, she had
told herself that her marriage was going down the
drain; again and again, she had denied it. She had
waited until her thirty-second year before she married, and then, as most of those who knew her put it,
she had married the most unlikely person on earth.

"I have waited," she said to herself. "I have not

plunged into a marriage. I have watched the marriages of almost everyone I know go down the drain. I know the weaknesses of this man, and I also know his virtues. I have no more illusions about marriage. I have seen enough love nests turn into snake pits to realize that at best a marriage is close to impossible. But we are both mature people, and we have each of us been through our own particular hells. We will work it out."

When she said much the same thing to her mother, it sounded flat and unconvincing, and her mother had regarded her thoughtfully and without too much enthusiasm. Jean Whittier, at fifty-eight, was still a very handsome woman. Together, they were no longer taken for sisters, and Jean made no attempt to fight wrinkles and graying hair; but they had the same height and the same good carriage. Jean had seen two marriages wash out, both of them her own.

"You may work it out and you may not," Jean had observed.

"I want to, desperately," Barbara had said.

"He needs the same desperation. Why should he have it? You're a very successful writer. You have a national reputation. Just because you put your money into a charitable foundation doesn't change things too much. You head the foundation. You have money of your own. That puts one damned awful burden on him, doesn't it?"

"I think we've talked that out."

"The question is whether you've worked it out."

Barbara's son said something that sounded vaguely like "dump truck." Barbara finished feeding him and presented him with the dump truck; then she heard the door downstairs. It was only six o'clock. Bernie shouted, "Hey, Bobby, I'm back!" There was a note in his voice that she had not heard in a long time, eagerness, enthusiasm, and excitement.

The day before, it had been almost midnight when Bernie came home. There was never a thought in Barbara's mind of another woman, an extramarital affair. You didn't come home from a tryst in working clothes, hands ingrained with dirt, and a body slumped with weariness. They had their assortment of problems, but another woman was not one of them.

Barbara had been in her room, writing. Hearing the sound of her typewriter, he opened the door and stood there. She had leaped to her feet and turned to embrace him, but he pulled back. "I'm filthy," he'd said.

"I'll draw you a bath."

"I'm too damned tired to take a bath."

"Bernie, you can't go to bed like that."

"Why not? I'm a lousy grease monkey. What in hell difference does it make?"

"Come on. You're not a grease monkey. You run one of the best garages in town and you're making a good thing of it."

"I wish you wouldn't wait up for me. I work late, and we get into these stupid arguments, and I'm just too damn tired to argue about anything."

That had been the night before. There had been other nights precisely like that. Barbara would always feel a chill creep through her, she would fight for control, she would tell herself that all people hurt but all people are approachable.

"I wasn't waiting up for you, Bernie," she had answered gently. "I can't get much work done during the day. I mean, not that I wouldn't want to wait up for you, but it's a good time to work. Sammy is demanding—"

So many other nights, no different; suddenly tonight his voice from downstairs, booming with eagerness and warmth. Barbara put her son and his dump truck into the playpen and ran down. Bernie caught her up in a bear hug. Then he apologized. "Filthy as usual. I'll have a bath. Where's the kid?"

"In his playpen. I just fed him."

"Good. I'll let him know who's boss, and then I'll take a bath. I won't be fifteen minutes. What's for supper?"

"Chicken, potatoes, peas, salad—"

"Great!"

Bewildered, delighted, yet apprehensive, she watched him bound up the stairs. This was not the man she had lived with for the past six, seven, eight months, not the morose, depressed, angry man who felt he was cornered in a trap of his own making. She followed him up the stairs. His time with the child had been brief, for he was already in the tub. By the time she had put Sam into his crib, Bernie was in clean clothes and waiting for her.

At the table, Barbara said gently, "It's been a good day for you, Bernie, hasn't it?"

"The best."

"I'm glad." She waited for him to tell her what had happened.

"I haven't been much fun lately, have I?"

"Not much. No. I think I understand."

"Do you, Bobby?" He stopped eating and stared at her. "I used to say to myself that I love you as much as anyone can love a woman. That's not true. I love you as much as I can love anyone. I've loved you since the day we met in Paris. I've been pretty damn faithful to that love."

"I know," she said softly. A clutch of fear began to tighten in her stomach. In spite of his ebullience, this

was not going to be a good evening. His words
brought back that day in 1939 when he had knocked
at the door of her apartment in Paris. She had opened
the door and there he stood, an enormous figure of a
man dressed in old dungarees and a sweat shirt, unshaven. The Spanish war had ended. The International Brigades had been disbanded. Bernie Cohen,
one-time volunteer in the Abraham Lincoln Brigade,
then unemployed, had made his way across the Pyrenees into France and had walked and hitched to Paris.
She could even remember the first thought that had
gone through her mind: What a strange man, like a
bear with a large nose! Until she saw his eyes. His
eyes were pale blue, large and wide and innocent as a
child's. You looked at those eyes, and there was no
question of mistrust or deception.

Those same eyes were watching her now, wide
open, childish. Her son, Sam, had the same eyes. This
man had never grown up. Women mature; it is in their
glands, their bodies, their life force; but men can experience a host of hells, and still they are small boys
framed in large bodies.

"What happened today, Bernie? Why don't you tell
me about it?"

"Well, sure, sure. But it's one of those damn things
that has a history. It didn't just happen, any more than
you and me, any more than we just happened. You
remember when I left you in Paris?"

"I remember."

"Well, I made my way south. I told you about that,
and in Marseille I teamed up with this kid, Irv Brodsky. You remember?"

"He was with the Internationals too." Barbara nodded. "Just tell me, Bernie. I remember."

He looked at her questioningly. Something in her

tone threw him off. "What was I saying? Oh, yes, Irv Brodsky. A Spanish vet from the Bronx in New York. He got out of Barcelona by boat to Marseille, and we both got jobs with two Frenchmen who were running illegals from Marseille into Palestine. We were scuttled off the coast of Palestine, and we got to shore and made our way inland and ended up in a kibbutz near Haifa."

Barbara nodded. She had heard the story many times.

"Well, I wasn't sure you remembered. We were very close, Brodsky and me. We worked at the kibbutz a few months, and we organized a defense for them. I'm just putting it into perspective," he said uneasily. "I guess I told you how the kibbutz decided that I should enlist in the British army and learn how to be a pilot. I mean that was the last time I saw Brodsky—until today."

"You saw him today? Where?"

"That's what I'm trying to get at, Bobby. Today, around lunchtime, he and another guy, name of Herb Goodman, well, they just walked into the garage and there they were, Irv Brodsky and this fellow Goodman. You can imagine how I felt, seeing Brodsky after all these years."

"You mean they just walked into your garage by accident?"

"No, no. Good heavens, no. Brodsky tracked me down."

"What do you mean, he tracked you down?"

"It's not so complicated. The Lincoln vets have an office in New York, and they keep track of us. I subscribe to their newsletter, you know, and I sent them some money. He got my address from them—I gave them the garage address—and he and Herb Goodman came out here to see me."

"Just to see you," Barbara said after a long moment. "They came all this distance just to see you again. I got the impression that you never met this Herb Goodman before."

"That's right. And I get the impression that you're angry. Good God, for once I don't feel like a hole in the ground and you're angry."

"I'm not angry." And to herself she added, "Only afraid. I'm so afraid."

"I run a garage," he exclaimed. "Do you ever reflect on that fact? That's what I do. I'm a damn grease monkey, whether you want to accept it or not. I work twelve, fourteen, sixteen hours a day trying to meet my payroll and make the mortgage payments. I don't even support my wife and kid. You do."

"That's not true."

"I come home at night and I'm too damn tired to put my arms around you and say I love you. I'm too tired for sex. Or maybe I've come to hate myself so much that sex doesn't work."

"Do you want dessert?" Barbara asked quietly. "We have ice cream."

He leaned back, and a slow grin spread over his face. "You know, I love you, Bobby. I get these crazy fits, but I love you so damn much. It's just that loving you and running a garage don't make it for me. I don't know why. I eat myself up. This morning I was sure I was developing an ulcer. I'm only forty-two years old. That's not old. But I live with the feeling that everything's behind me and nothing's ahead of me."

"Until today?" Barbara asked.

"Yes."

"Do you want ice cream?"

"Sure."

She went to the refrigerator. With her back to him, scooping the ice cream onto a plate, she asked. "Who are they, these two men—Brodsky and—?"

"Goodman. They're both members of the Haganah, which is the defense force of the Jewish settlements in Palestine. They're Americans, but they've been living there. Now they've come back on a special mission."

"What kind of a mission?" She set the ice cream in front of him. He began to eat it, watching her out of his pale, childlike eyes.

"This is very damn secret, Bobby."

"I am your wife."

"All right. With the UN decision for the partition and the creation of a Jewish state in Palestine, all hell will break loose. It will probably happen in weeks, months—in any case it means war with the Arab states, and the most desperate need for the Jews is planes. Somehow or other, they made a deal with the Czechs. They can't get anything out of the States because of the embargo. The Czechs want two million in cash, and the money was put together in New York. It was all very subrosa. They can't go to any of the regular sources. Then there's the question of getting the money to Czechoslovakia, picking up the planes, which will be dismantled, and getting them to Palestine. The FBI has gotten wind of it, and they're watching the whole operation like hawks."

"And why did they come to you, Bernie? Just to renew an old friendship?"

He had finished the ice cream. He got up, went to her, and bent and kissed her. She made no response. She felt that her blood had stopped flowing, that ice

was congealing around her heart. He went to the
stove and picked up the coffeepot. "Can I pour you
some coffee?"

When they got married, he had had about three
thousand dollars, his British army pay, and what he
had picked up shooting craps. He would be a good,
honest, substantial, hard-working citizen. He bor-
rowed five thousand more, and for eight thousand
dollars and a large mortgage, he had purchased the
garage. He went to work each morning; he returned
each night.

He poured coffee for both of them. "There are ten
C-54s on a field down near Barstow. They're the big
four-motor jobs that Air Transport used during the
war. The guy who owns them bought the lot for sixty-
five thousand, war surplus. He wants a hundred and
ten thousand for them. If we can get them, we'll rip
out the seats and use them for cargo. Fly them to
Czechoslovakia, pick up the planes, and fly them to
Palestine." Then he waited, watching her. The silence
built up between them.

Finally she said, " 'We,' Bernie?"

He nodded slowly.

"When did you make that decision?"

"Bobby, haven't you watched me? Don't you see
what's happening to me? I'm turning rotten. I tried.
God, how I tried! For two years I've gone to that damn
garage every day. It's no good. You've seen the way
I've been for the past six months. Do you want me
that way?"

"I want you," she whispered. "I still want you, Bernie. I didn't come to this marriage easily. We took each
other for better or worse."

"I'm not walking out on you. I love you. We got a
kid together. We got blood and grief and agony be-

tween us. We didn't just run into each other and say 'I do.'"

Controlling herself, choosing her words carefully, Barbara said, "You're not walking out on me. Then what would you call it, Bernie?"

"It's something I have to do, Bobby. Sure, this thing with Brodsky came out of the blue. But there hasn't been a day in the past year when I didn't think about what's going on over there. Now I look at it this way. I'll help them find the money to buy the planes, then I'll make the flight. I've spent ten years of my life being a soldier. I'm worth my weight in gold over there, and I'm needed. That's the thing. I am needed. I fought for the Spanish Republic, and for six years I fought for the damn Limeys. And I wasn't needed. There were twenty million others. Here you count heads. I'm a Jew. You forget that."

"You never let me forget it, Bernie."

"And I'm not walking out on you. It may take a few months to work things out over there, but we will. Then there'll be peace, and I'll be in a place that I made. I'll have a function. My life will make some sense. Then you and Sam can join me."

She shook her head. "No. This is my place, Bernie, here in San Francisco. I had my romantic dreams. It's your place too."

"Then I'll come back. I'll do what I have to do, and I'll come back."

"Funny," Barbara said, "so damn funny." She fought to hold back tears, to keep her voice steady. "You don't come to me and say, Let's discuss this. Let's talk about it. Let's weigh this against that. You don't ask me how I feel, what I want. Good heavens, Bernie, we're man and wife. And now you tell me that you're going off to another stinking war like you're going across the street for a pack of cigarettes. Is that what this whole thing means to you? Weren't two wars enough for us? And if you're killed, what then?"

"I won't be killed. A few months and I'll be back."

"Damn you!" she exclaimed. She pushed back her chair and ran out of the kitchen, up the stairs to the bedroom, where she flung herself on the bed. She heard his steps following her, and she closed her eyes and pressed her face into the counterpane.

"Bobby, Bobby," he said, bending over her. "I love you. I don't want to hurt you." He lay down beside her, pressing his head close to hers.

"Don't go away," she begged him. "Please, Bernie, don't go away and leave me alone again."

Eloise was a timid woman. It was one of the qualities that endeared her to her husband, Adam Levy. She was blond, with a peaches and cream complexion and golden hair that fell in natural ringlets. She was small-boned, gentle, and totally vulnerable, and on first encounter she often gave the impression of being entirely empty-headed. The impression was far from the truth; she was not only sensitive and aware, but well educated and on her way to becoming one of the Bay Area's foremost authorities on modern art. Adam and his wife lived in the Napa Valley, in the house he had built for her on the grounds of the Higate Winery, which his family owned, but she spent two days a week in San Francisco, where she acted as curator for the gallery of modern art that Jean Whittier had established in the old Lavette mansion on Russian Hill. For the most part, Adam would accompany her to San Francisco, and they would spend the night in a room that Jean had provided for them in the house on Russian Hill.

Eloise suffered from an ailment called cluster headache, which was little understood in the forties and simply diagnosed as another form of migraine. One of the most painful afflictions known to medicine, it caused her constant and devilish suffering, which she managed to bear without complaint and with surprising cheerfulness. If her husband adored her, it could be said that she worshipped him. Some of the worship was based on contrast. Her first marriage, in 1941, was to Thomas Lavette, Barbara's brother, and that had endured for five years that she remembered as a particularly nasty nightmare. The only positive result of her first marriage was her son, Freddie, who was now six years old.

The day after the two men from the Haganah walked into Bernie Cohen's garage, two other men drove up to Higate and asked for Eloise Levy. They were almost as alike as twins, except that one of them wore gilt-rimmed spectacles. They both wore gray sharkskin suits and Panama hats, although it was only March. They both had even-featured, expressionless faces, and they were both coldly polite. Pedro, a Chicano worker, directed them to Adam's house. Adam was working at the bottling plant and Freddie was at school. The two Airedales, regarded by Eloise as her friends and protectors, greeted them with a flurry of angry barks that brought her to the door. Then they showed her their credentials, which represented them as agents of the Federal Bureau of Investigation.

"I'm sure you've made some mistake," Eloise told them. "I can't imagine anything what the FBI would want of me." Nevertheless, she was frightened, and seeing Pedro standing a few yards behind the two men, she called out, "Pedro, get Adam and tell him to come home, please."

The two men introduced themselves. One, who called himself Agent Williams, said, "May we come in?"

"I think not," Eloise said with surprising firmness, pleased that the two Airedales had ranged themselves on either side of her. "Not until my husband gets here."

"You are Eloise Levy?"

"Yes."

"And you're well acquainted with Barbara Cohen."

"Of course I am. She's my first husband's sister, and she's my very dear friend."

"We'd like to ask you some questions about her."

"Why?"

"Because she's under investigation. It would be in your best interest to cooperate."

"I refuse to say another word until my husband gets here." She had raised her voice, and the Airedales growled threateningly.

Williams spread his hands. "As you wish."

A moment later, Adam came racing up to the house, his father, Jake Levy, lumbering behind him. Adam was a tall, skinny man, with blue eys in a perpetually burned, freckled face, and a long, narrow head topped by a thatch of bright orange hair. Jake Levy, who owned and operated the winery, was large and heavily muscled, a year short of fifty. It was Adam who wanted to know angrily what in hell was going on?

"They want to ask questions about Barbara," Eloise told him.

Jake joined them in time to hear this, and he said to the two men, "Just who the devil are you?"

They showed him their credentials and began to introduce themselves, very restrained, very correct.

"I don't want to know your goddamn names," Jake

interrupted. "You're trespassing. You're on private property, uninvited. So I would ask you to get the hell out of here and off my property."

"That's a surprising attitude to take, Mr. Levy," Williams said. "You act as if you don't know what's going on in this country today, which is very unlikely, or as if you're a part of it."

"What! What in hell are you saying? Are you calling me a communist?"

"The term is yours, not mine."

Jake grinned. "You guys are dolls, aren't you? The last time I had any of you on my place was in nineteen twenty-two. You called yourselves prohibition agents then. In my book, you're still prohibition agents. So get off my land, and get off quickly."

"That's your last word, Mr. Levy?"

"That's my last word, sonny."

They walked back to their car and drove off. Adam watched them, a worried look on his face. "Do you think that was wise?" he asked his father.

"They turn my stomach."

"Why are they investigating Barbara?" Eloise asked. Adam shook his head.

"Communists," Jake said in disgust.

The next day, Bernie met with Brodsky and Goodman at Gino's restaurant on Jones Street. It was the first time in months that Bernie had broken the routine of a sandwich and a container of coffee in his office in the garage. He felt liberated. Just to sit in the little Italian restaurant within sight of the bay was an exciting and exhilarating experience. He had freed himself from the work that was piling up at the garage. Suddenly, he didn't care. All morning he had fed himself with inner dialogues concerning his relationship with

Barbara, his love of Barbara, his resentment of Barbara. Before he left the house, having coffee in the kitchen, he had watched her as she put the breakfast things on the table. She wore a pale blue housecoat, a simple thing of light wool, but she carried it with the grace of an evening gown. No make-up, but then, she rarely used make-up. Her honey-colored hair had been hastily combed, and it fell in light, easy waves around her head. Her wide gray eyes met his occasionally, but without accusation or anger. He knew her that well. She had it out with herself, and now there would be no more arguments or recriminations. It was up to him, and her silent presence was the most telling argument she could present. It wasn't that she was simply a beautiful woman; she was the most remarkable and exciting woman he had ever known. People reacted to her carriage, her manner, her forthrightness, and the feeling of compassion that she conveyed without ever becoming sentimental.

It was this that Bernie found most difficult to deal with. Without realizing it, he had been drawn to Barbara because of her wholeness; he himself was fragmented, an orphaned boy pleading for love and security, a Jew who could only live with his Jewishness by committing himself to a dream of Palestine when he was still a boy, enlisting in the International Brigade in Spain to learn a game of war, then living the game for seven endless years. He never acknowledged that he was a mercenary soldier. "I am not a killer," he had once pleaded to Barbara, which was quite true, yet for seven years he had practiced and mastered the art of killing. "You can't condemn soldiers," he had argued with Barbara. "We did what we had to do." She had accepted that. Men did what they had to do;

it was the only explanation they could offer themselves.

Bernie said to Brodsky, "I'm in this, believe it." Brodsky wasn't sure. Goodman was absorbed in a mound of spaghetti that he was wolfing down.

"I need you, Bernie," Brodsky said. "This operation has become so big and so complex that it's driving me up the wall. Just go find ten Jewish pilots who can fly four-motor planes and who are willing to dump their jobs and go off on this kind of caper. I couldn't. I found seven Jews."

"What about the rest?"

"Two Irish and an Italian. I'm worried about the Italian, a guy named Massetti. He flew in the Italian air force, and he swears he's got a Jewish grandmother. He wants to atone for Mussolini. I think he's maybe O.K., but I don't think he ever flew a four-motor job before. With navigators, it's worse. I only have four, and that means we'll have to fly formation. We don't have co-pilots. Bernie, you're sure you can't fly a plane?"

"I'm sure."

"Back in thirty-nine, the decision was that you'd enlist and learn to fly."

"We've been through that. They put me in the infantry. Now where are these pilots?"

"That's another thing. We got them down in a hotel in Hollywood, and four of the Haganah boys are with them. How long we can hold them there is a question. One of the Irishmen, McClosky, is a drunk, and it's a question of getting out of there before he drinks himself to death. Herbie's going back down there today. For Christ's sake," he said to Goodman, "will you stop eating and pay some attention."

Goodman paused over a fork of spaghetti, a hurt look on his round face. "I'm listening."

"And this guy who has the planes," Brodsky went on. "He's some kind of nut. He says he has an offer from a South American airline to buy the planes for a quarter of a million, but he wants to sell to us because God told him that until the Jews return to the promised land, there'll be no peace on earth. That's what he says. Me, I think he can't get an export license, and I'm not even sure of how he got hold of the planes. There is plenty of hanky-panky in this war surplus stuff."

"Did you see the planes?" Bernie asked.

"We saw them. Herbie here thinks they're O.K."

"Are you a pilot?"

"Navigator," Herbie replied. "I was with the Tenth Air Force."

"And what about an export license? Can you get one?"

"Hell, no," Brodsky said. "This whole thing is illegal. If just a smell of it gets out, we're cooked."

"Then how in hell do you expect to get the planes out of the country?"

"Simple. We fly them out. We got a guy in Bakersfield who deals in aviation gasoline, and he says he can get us the trucks to fuel them. He's Jewish, and he's willing to stake us to the fuel. We got another guy in New Jersey, name of Schullman, who runs an airfield for private planes and freighters. He's willing to look the other way. We fly the planes cross-country and try to match the commercial airlanes, land in New Jersey, refuel, and take off."

"For where?"

"We don't know yet. But we got guys in New York working on it."

"I guess you realize what a harebrained scheme this whole thing is," Bernie said.

"Sure. But what the hell. Everything we do in Palestine is either harebrained or impossible. So we do it. We can muster maybe forty thousand men in the Haganah. We can't even arm all of them. We don't have one plane that's worth talking about. And any day now, we're going to be facing a hundred and fifty thousand Arab troops, real armies with tanks and guns and planes. Do you understand how much we need a guy like you, Bernie. From what I hear, you were one of the best weapons men the British had in Africa—"

"Bullshit."

"Sure. Still, you know your stuff. You got a command personality. You could hold this crew in line—"

"Can it. I'll go."

"Bernie, thanks. Now about the money?"

"I'll try. The thing I don't understand is, why can't you go to regular sources? There are plenty of wealthy Jews here and in Los Angeles. They'll give."

"Will they, Bernie? You can't report this kind of money. You can't claim a deduction. Getting the two million in New York was like pulling teeth out of granite. It took seven months. We can't involve any of the fund-raisers who raise money for Palestine. We can't take chances on questions being asked. It's not simple, and our time is running out."

Jean Whittier, Barbara's mother, had begun life as Jean Seldon, whose father, Thomas Seldon, had founded the Seldon Bank, which already had sixteen branches in California. In the state, the Seldon Bank was second only to the giant Bank of America. Control of the bank had passed to her son, Thomas, and at this time

Jean was living in a rather placid sort of unmarried
sinfulness with her first husband, Dan Lavette. The
legalistic complications caused her to retain the name
of Whittier, her previous husband; as she put it, it
would have been rather pointless to live unmarried
with a man whose name was identical with her own.
She and Dan made their residence in the top floor of
the house on Russian Hill that Dan had built for her
thirty-five years before, soon after their marriage. Jean
had converted the ground floor into the gallery through
which she was none too successfully attempting to
bring to the citizens of San Francisco an appreciation
of modern art. Just now, in the gallery, the doors tem-
porarily closed to the public, Jean had forgathered
with Eloise and Adam Levy, her daughter, Barbara,
and on Barbara's lap her grandson, Sam, who was de-
terminedly attempting to destroy his thumb with his
eight rudimentary teeth.

"I would give him a pacifier," Jean was saying. "I
don't think all that is good for his thumb."

"I know, mother," Barbara said. "I forgot it. I
dashed out of the house, wondering what awful thing
had transpired."

"It is awful," Eloise said. "It's dreadful."

"I don't think it's dreadful at all. Two FBI men
were asking about me. The way things are today, with
everyone seeing communists behind every bush and
wall, they must be asking question about thousands
and thousands of people. It's what they're paid for. I
only wish Jake hadn't been so high-handed with them.
Then you might have found out what they were
after."

"Jake is Jake," Adam said. "I was pretty damn angry
myself. It's the whole look and attitude of them.

They're such cold, malignant bastards. And why Eloise? Why do they come to her?"

"Probably because it's easier to bully a woman than a man," Barbara decided.

"Could it have had something to do with Bernie?" Jean wondered.

"Why Bernie?"

"Well, I only mean he has that kind of a past, hasn't he? Spain, Palestine, smuggling, then the British army. I never did understand what he did during those years."

"He did what most people were doing. He fought fascism."

"Which is not exactly popular these days."

"I think you are all making too much of this. I have nothing to hide and nothing to conceal," Barbara said firmly—asking herself at the same time whether there was any truth in her statement. In fact, she had a good deal to conceal, and she was not very good at dissembling. It was close to lunchtime, and Jean suggested that Adam take Eloise to have seafood on the wharf and that they both take the afternoon in town.

When Barbara rose to go, Jean said, "I'd rather you remained. I have oatmeal and applesauce and all sorts of things to feed Sam, and you and I will talk."

"I'd rather not, mother."

"I'd rather you would."

Barbara sighed and nodded. Adam and Eloise left. "You're very arrogant, mother," Barbara said. "You order people around. You tell them what to do and where to go, and you treat grown folk like children."

"I know. At the same time, we're going to talk. I know you very well, my dear, and I'm not going to lie awake wondering what's happening in your life."

"You never have."

"That's as it may be. Suppose we put together some lunch for your son."

While she fed Sam, Barbara told Jean what had happened between her and Bernie. "I'm trusting you," Barbara said. "It's no matter-of-fact thing to trust one's mother with stuff like this. I do trust you. They would be in terrible trouble if this got out."

"And you think that's why the FBI was asking about you?"

"No, I don't. It's just too soon, and if they were, why wouldn't they ask about Bernie instead of me?"

"I don't know. Bobby," Jean said, "what does it all add up to? Does he want to leave you? Is this crazy scheme an excuse?"

"Anything would be an excuse. It isn't that he doesn't love me. I think he loves me as much as he could love anyone. He's as gentle as a lamb, and you watch him playing with Sammy and you say to yourself, what a happy, darling man—and content. No, he's not content. He's eating out his heart."

"For what? To be in Palestine?"

"That could be what he tells himself. But it's not that. It's to be free, to run after that macho image of a big, heroic man. Oh, maybe not. I don't really know what tortures his soul. He once asked me why I kept publishing my books under the name of Barbara Lavette. Was I ashamed of the name of Cohen? Can you imagine? I tried to make him understand that a writer's name is like a trademark, a record of the work she has done. But the plain fact is that we live on the money I earn. He's so aware of that. Every cent the garage makes goes to paying off his loans and paying the mortgage fees, and he is damn well aware that I clean the house and cook the meals and take care of Sammy and do my own writing as well."

"And how you do it, I can't for the life of me imagine."

"It's no great problem. I have enough time. But I know what it does to him. I've watched the marriage going to pieces for months, and it breaks my heart. He's not cruel or nasty or vicious. He's just dying inside himself, and it's my fault because if I had had an ounce of common sense, I wouldn't have married him. The funny part of it is that I love him so much, almost the way I love Sammy, the way you love a child. You don't know a man until you're in bed with him, and then you know him the way no one else does. And you know, if I plead with him enough I can stop him, I can keep him from going."

"Will you?"

Tears welling into her eyes, Barbara shook her head. "No. That would do no good. That would only destroy both of us."

"Will he come back?"

"If he lives—yes. He'll come back. He thinks he's indestructible. In all those years of war, he was never wounded, never scratched. But that—"

Sammy saw the tears and reacted to the tone of voice, and he began to cry. Jean took him in her arms, and Barbara went to the bathroom and washed her face. When she returned, Jean said, "There's still the money. That must be one of the reasons they came to him. Where could he find a hundred and ten thousand dollars?"

"I think," Barbara said, "I think he'll go to daddy. Would daddy give it to him?"

Jean thought about it for a while. "He might. He just might. I've long ago given up trying to anticipate what Dan Lavette might do."

* * *

Newspapermen who interviewed Dan Lavette frequently described him as leonine. The term amused him. A man is inside himself, and unless he is an actor or a politician, he rarely knows the image he presents to the outside world. It might be said that he generally knows even less concerning his inner self. Long ago, before Dan Lavette's Chinese wife, May Ling, died, he had moments when he felt himself and knew himself at least to some degree, and in those moments he had never seen himself as or considered himself a lionlike character. If anything, he had been as bewildered and confused as the next man. Yet it was quite true that now, in his sixtieth year, he might be described as leonine. He was a large man, six feet two inches in height, and over the past few years he had put on weight. His thick, curly hair had turned white, his face and neck had become heavier, and when he tightened his belt it creased the beginnings of a paunch.

He had become a legend in the Bay Area. When columnists were at a loss for a subject, there was always gold to be mined out of Dan Lavette. They could go back to his boyhood, when he ran his crabbing boats out of Fisherman's Wharf and fought the fish pirates with a double-barreled shotgun, or to the financial empire he had built with his partner, Mark Levy, before the Great Depression, or to his marriage to Jean Seldon, or to his divorce and his subsequent marriage to May Ling, or to his years of poverty when he fished mackerel out of San Pedro, or to the incredible shipyard he had built during the war years on Terminal Island. It was all grist for their mills, and the enticing thing about Lavette was that he never ceased to make good copy. He and his former wife, Jean, scorned to disguise that they were living together, a condition still regarded with censure in 1948. He operated a fleet of tankers that already held a commanding position in the trade, and, true to form, he made the headquarters of his shipping company in Jack London Square in Oakland. The fact that his son, Thomas—to whom he had not spoken for years—was in partnership with Jean's ex-husband, John Whittier, operating the largest cargo fleet on the West Coast, only made the copy more intriguing.

That Bernie Cohen came to him was not solely dependent on their relationship. If there had been no relationship at all and if Cohen had asked for the one man in the Bay Area who might respond to the strange scheme in which he was involved, he surely would have been recommended to Lavette. Now he sat in Dan's office, listening uneasily as Dan said, "I have to get my bearings, Bernie. You're married to my daughter for two years, and you've never asked for a nickel, breaking your ass with that damn garage of yours, and now it's a hundred and ten thousand dollars. I almost like it. Is there any chance of seeing any of that money again?"

"Not much, no. I could give you a note, and Brodsky could sign it as a representative of the Haganah, but I'd be a liar if I said there was any chance of them repaying it."

"So it's charity."

"Not deductible."

"Just to sweeten it. You're a strange man, Bernie, but you're not crazy. At least, not much crazier than most of us. What in hell ever gave you the notion that I'd go for this?"

"Desperation. There's nowhere else to go."

"You don't think I owe you something because you married my daughter?"

"I'm the one who owes you. No."

"And you're walking out on her for a month, two months, six months. Does she know that?"

"She knows."

"Does she like it?"

"What do you think, Dan? No, she doesn't like it. But she won't tell me not to do it."

"What about the garage?"

"Gomez, my foreman, he's a good man. I can trust him. He'll run the garage. If we get the planes and if everything goes according to schedule, I could be back in three weeks."

"You don't really believe that?"

Bernie shrugged. "No, not really. It could take a few months."

Dan reached into a drawer and took out a box of cigars. "Smoke? These are clear Havana." Bernie shook his head. Dan clipped the end and lit the cigar. "Ten C-54s for one hundred and ten thousand. This is a demented world we live in, Bernie. Ford's Willow Run plant cost the government five million and better. They sold it off as war surplus, and someone walked in and bought it for seventy thousand dollars. A part of the plant was filled with cases of sterling silver screws; they were worth ten times what he paid for the plant. No one knew it. I started the first airline out here on the Coast. That was back in twenty-eight. We flew Ford trimotors—tin geese, they called them. One of them cost more than these ten C-54s. By the way, what makes you think they're in any condition to fly?"

"They checked them out."

"I think the whole scheme is totally insane. I don't know whether Barbara ever told you how I feel about war. I made two fortunes out of two wars. It's the filthiest, bloodiest, stupidest rotten game man ever invented. There are no good guys and no bad guys. It's a lousy, rotten scam."

"Sure," Bernie said softly. "I won't argue. I lived in it ten years of my life. What should we do, Dan? Let ourselves be slaughtered? Being a Jew is a unique thing. Other victims are picked at random. We're chosen specifically. Without these planes, the Arabs will slaughter us. Hitler killed six million of us. Doesn't it have to end somewhere? There's just no other way in the world to get fighter planes into Palestine." He shook his head. "I don't know why I'm dumping all this on you. You're not Jewish."

"I'm not. That's true. And let me tell you something, Bernie. If I should take leave of my senses and give you this money, it's not for you or your cause. I don't believe in causes. I'm a hard, cynical businessman, without a bone of idealism in my body, but I had a partner once who was the closest thing to a brother I ever had. Closer. His name was Mark Levy, and I guess maybe Barbara told you about him. He was Jewish, and I have a very large tab that he never collected. I owe him. Maybe this is a way to close a debt to a dead man; maybe it isn't. Let me think about it."

"Our time's running out, Dan."

"I'll let you know tomorrow."

After Cohen had left, Dan sat and brooded and stared at the smoke of his cigar. Then he pressed his intercom and asked his secretary to send in Stephan Cassala. Cassala was the son of Anthony Cassala, who founded the Bank of Sonoma soon after the 1906 earthquake and watched it go under in 1929. Anthony died soon after the collapse of his bank. Stephan, at fifty-three, was now vice president and general manager of Lavette Shipping.

"Steve," Dan said, "sit down and think about this."
Stephan dropped into a leather armchair facing Dan.
He was a tall, slender, dark man, with deepset eyes
and a long, brooding face. "Suppose I were to ask
you," Dan went on, "to get me a hundred and ten
thousand in cash and not have any record of it. Lose
it. Could you do it?"

"You don't want to tell me what you need it for?"

"No."

"It wouldn't be easy. Our cash position is not great."

"What do you draw cash for?"

"Expenses, some bonuses, dock guards on short notice, and bribes. Mostly bribes. You know that, Dan."

"How do you cover the bribes?"

"We lose it. Juggle it—a little here, a little there. But
a hundred and ten thousand will take a lot of jug-
gling."

"Can you do it?"

"If you need the money, I can do it." He stared at
Dan worriedly. "Are you being blackmailed?"

"No."

"You're not paying off? I heard rumours of the Mob
beginning to operate here in Oakland. Dan, if you pay
off, there's no end to it."

"I'm not paying off."

"I'm curious as hell."

"Then stay curious, Steve. If you don't know what
it's for, then someday you can swear under oath that
you never knew."

"That way? Jesus, I don't like it, Dan."

"Don't worry. It's all in a good cause. Or so they tell
me."

At eleven o'clock the following morning, Dan Lavette, carrying a bulging briefcase, rang the doorbell of
his daughter's house. Barbara opened the door, looked

at him in amazement, and then embraced him. "Daddy, what a delicious surprise!"

"I never walked in on you before like this," he apologized.

"Then you should have. Once a week, at least."

He went into the little parlor and put down the briefcase. She helped him off with his coat and asked whether anything was wrong.

"No. Or maybe yes. Depending on how you look at it."

"What?"

"It can wait. Where's my grandson?"

"Upstairs in his playpen, being happy and fat and content, the way no citizen of this world has any right to be. But Sammy's too young and foolish to know that."

"Bernie home?"

"He's at the garage. Come on, what brings you here? Has my mother been talking to you?"

"First I'll see my grandson."

Barbara looked at him for a moment, then nodded. "All right. You want coffee?"

"Sure."

"I'll be in the kitchen." She watched Dan as he mounted the stairs. There was a time when he would have taken them two at a time. Now he walked slowly. Strangely, it was the first time Barbara had ever seen him as an aging man. She did some quick calculations and arrived at fifty-nine. Almost sixty was not old, or was it? There were times when her own thirty-four years felt like the weight of ages. For a moment or two, she listened to his jovial, booming exchange with his grandson, wondering whether he didn't frighten the little boy to death. Then she went into the kitchen and prepared fresh coffee.

"He's crying," Dan said as he entered.

"Well, either you scared him to death or he wants you back there. Either way, he'll stop."

"I don't scare my grandson. He understands me."

"You scare a lot of people, daddy, believe it or not."

"The hell I do. I'm a lamb."

"Yes, I know."

She poured the coffee and they sat down at the kitchen table. "Well," she said, "what brings you here—aside from Sammy?"

"And you."

"Yes. What else? Bernie?"

He nodded.

"He went to see you yesterday?"

Dan nodded again.

"And?"

"He told me the story, and he asked me to give him a hundred and ten thousand dollars."

"Just like that?" Barbara said in amazement.

"No, not just like that. We talked. Tell me, Bobby, what's with you two? Another woman?"

"With Bernie?" She shook her head.

"It's not impossible. That's something no man's immune to."

"Would it sound crazy if I told you he's very much in love with me, and I'm very much in love with him, and our marriage stinks?"

"No. It would sound reasonable. It's happened before. I never asked you how much you make, Bobby. I know the garage is no great shakes. Does Bernie take anything out of it?"

"Not yet, no."

"What do you live on?"

"I'm supposed to head up the foundation when I have the time, which isn't often. I do get to at least one meeting a week. They pay me four hundred and fifty a month."

"Princely."

"It was my decision, daddy. I don't need the money. My last book earned over thirty thousand dollars, and I hope the next one will do as well."

"In other words, you pay for everything."

"Bernie works twelve, fourteen hours a day."

"That doesn't solve anything."

"But it would if he earned the money and I took it," Barbara said angrily. "Oh, I am so sick to death of this idiotic male notion of what is right and what is proper."

"I didn't make it and neither did Bernie," Dan said gently. "We're just the result."

"If that isn't the most self-serving, self-satisfying thing I have ever heard!" She drew a deep breath. "Now I'm getting very angry, and I shouldn't. Not with you, daddy."

"You were right. He did stop crying," Dan said.

Barbara stared at him. Then she began to laugh. "Oh, I do love you. But you're the strangest man."

"I don't know. I've met some really strange ones."

"But what about Bernie?"

"If he can't get the money from me, will that change it? Will he give it up?"

"Bernie? Daddy, if he wants that money, he'll get it. He'll rob a bank. He'll blow up an armored car—or something equally insane. That's the way he is, the way he thinks. But I understand why you couldn't give it to him."

"Did you want me to?"

"I don't know. I just don't know."

"Then you'd better make up your mind, Bobby, because that briefcase out in the living room contains one hundred and ten thousand dollars in cash, and it's up to you whether I leave it here or not."

Moments went by while she stared at him, speechless. Finally she said, "My coffee's cold. Do you want another cup?"

He nodded. She went to the stove, put the gas on under the pot for a few minutes, and poured the coffee. Then she said, "Why?"

"Why? You mean why am I ready to give him the money?"

"Yes, that's what I mean."

"It's complicated."

"I have plenty of time. I have almost an hour before I have to feed Sammy. I'm sure you can explain it in that time."

"Now hold on," Dan said. "I'm not giving the money to him. I'm giving it to you. You will give it to him or not, as you please."

"Great. Oh, just great. That's just what I need."

"All right," Dan said, "I'll try to explain. I've never given you or Bernie a cent, and you haven't asked."

"What has that to do with it?"

"Will you let me talk? I'm not overly bright, but I've watched what's happening to you two. It's no good. Whatever you say about Bernie, he's one hell of a man. You don't find that very often. I guess that's why you married him. I can understand him—maybe not the way you understand him, but in my own way. If he doesn't do this, it's all over between you two. You may stay married; it's still all over. Am I wrong?"

She waited awhile before she answered. "No, you're not wrong."

"All right. Get back to the money. It doesn't mean a damn thing to me. It never has. And I don't know one damn thing about this situation in Palestine except what I read in the papers. But I know something about what the Jews have taken, and the best friend I ever had was a Jew. I owe him. He's dead. All right, this is my way of evening the score. Maybe you don't understand that, but it's the only way I can explain it. I think that if anyone can pull off this crazy stunt, Bernie can. If he does it and he comes back, he may feel that he paid his dues. And one more thing. I like him."

"So do I," Barbara said. "Suppose he doesn't come back? Suppose he's killed."

"I thought of that. That's why I can't make the decision. I'm leaving the money here. It's up to you."

"Why?" Barbara asked almost woefully.

"Maybe because I respect you. Maybe because you always knew a lot more about everything than I did. I sat up with your mother half the night talking about this and trying to figure out what was right. I don't know. I love you very much, Bobby. If you want me to walk out of here with the money and never mention it to Bernie, I will."

"No, daddy," she said. "Leave it here. And thank you."

The foundation that Barbara referred to as the source of part of her income was the Lavette Foundation, with its headquarters on Leavenworth Street in San Francisco. It had an interesting history. Barbara's grandfather, Thomas Seldon, had died in 1928. His will left 382,000 shares in the Seldon Bank to be divided between his two grandchildren and to be held in trust for them by their mother for twelve years. In 1940, after five years of living and working in Europe, Barbara returned to San Francisco and decided to put the whole of her inheritance into a charitable foundation. By then, her share of the stock had a market value of something more than fifteen million dollars, so the gesture was not a small one. Somewhat reluctantly, she agreed to become the nominal head of the board of directors of the foundation.

And it was this foundation that Brodsky spoke about, sitting with Bernie in his office at the garage. Cohen replied that it was out of the question. "I wouldn't even suggest it," he said. "This is a case of something being purer than Caesar's wife. That damn foundation is sacrosanct. God Almighty, Irv, I am married to a very strange and unusual woman, who happens to be married to a sonofabitch. Suppose I didn't go with you. You could still pull it off."

"Not without the planes."

"Why not take the money out of the two million you have in New York?"

"Because the deal with those Czech bastards is for two million dollars. We get ten World War II Messerschmitt fighters and the rest in small arms. You're the best small arms expert I know."

"What are they asking for the Messerschmitts?"

"Fifty thousand dollars each."

"No."

"Yeah, they're our friends. But what do we do? Truman put an embargo on anything here. We could pick up war surplus fighters for five thousand dollars, but we'd never get them out of the country, and if we don't get those C-54s—"

"We'll get them."

"How?"

"Rob a bank if we have to."

"You're kidding," Brodsky said.

"Maybe. I don't know."

*   *   *

Barbara sat in her living room and stared at the bulging brown leather briefcase that her father had left on the floor just inside the doorway. Her house was one of those narrow, two-story Victorian structures that still line so many of the streets that descend from Russian Hill. Sam Goldberg, her father's lawyer and subsequently her own lawyer and friend and protector, had built the house for his bride in 1892. It had survived the earthquake and the fire almost undamaged, and both Goldberg and his wife, childless, had lived there all their lives and finally died there, the wife first and Sam some years later. Barbara bought the house from his estate. It had two bay windows, triptych fashion, one above the other. The doorway, six steps above the street, was framed by wooden columns in a pseudo-Moorish style. The doorway and each of the windows had elaborately carved cornices above them, and each cornice, and the roof too, rested upon rows of dentils, each of which was carved as elaborately as the cornice it supported. The carving on the front of the house was a wonderful, uninhibited mixture of the Ionic, Corinthian, and Moorish styles, sitting upon white clapboard walls.

Barbara loved the house passionately. After her years in Paris and the time she spent in the Far East and Africa as a war correspondent, it was her safe harbor, her refuge and cave. Many people shunned these old houses because of their small rooms, but Barbara enjoyed the feeling of closeness and intimacy. She had redecorated and refurnished most of the rooms and had installed a modern kitchen, but the little parlor, its walls painted a Wedgwood green, was still furnished in the black, horsehair-covered, tufted pieces that had been there since Sam Goldberg acquired them in the eighteen nineties.

Barbara sat on one of these plump, comfortable chairs and contemplated the bag of money, herself, her past, her possible future, and her marriage. She had not opened the briefcase. Money did not fascinate her; neither did it repel her. Aside from its use, she was indifferent to it, which she had puzzled over for a long time and had finally accepted as a syndrome of at least some who are born to great wealth. Years ago, when she was a student at Sarah Lawrence and went to New York with some schoolmates, she had without much thought given a five-dollar bill to a beggar. She would never forget the shocked surprise of her friends. Now she stared at a briefcase filled with money that might or might not change the destiny of some six hundred thousand Jews in Palestine. It had already changed her own destiny. She felt a strange, ominous certainty that if her husband walked out of the house with the briefcase in his hand, she would never see him again.

But she also was quite aware that she had such feelings in the past about people she loved, and that nothing had ever come of her intimations of doom. It was a question of mood and misery. Her mood was bleak, but the misery began to lighten. She was not unused to being honest with herself and facing and accepting her own feelings, no matter how deplorable they were. She had been alone in the past, and she could face the prospect of being alone again without any great qualms. If she had to choose between having a husband who was in a constant state of depression and frustration and having no husband at all, at least for a time, the latter was preferable. Her days were full. She was a mother, a housekeeper, a writer, and the president of a very large and complex charitable foundation. She would not retreat into the hurt of rejection; she had watched and sympathized with the utter terror and hopelessness of women who were rejected, and she had sworn to herself that she would never go that way; in any case, she felt that she understood her husband sufficiently to realize that he was not rejecting her. And in the very back of her mind, deep down where it was pretending to hide from her consciousness, was a tiny flutter of pleasant excitement at the prospect of being in command of her own household and her own time, of not having to plan ways and devices to cope with a morose man who agonized and apologized for not being able to have an erection.

However he conceived of his manhood, it had dried up in the little Victorian house and in the profitless garage. Staring at the bulging briefcase of money, Barbara asked herself, "Have I ever faced what he is? What he truly is? Or have I been unwilling to accept the possibility that a man as gentle and kind and loving as Bernie Cohen, who spent ten years as a soldier, can find his happiness no other way? Or have I been conditioned to believe that a Jew cannot be a professional killer?"

Once the phrase had formed in her mind, she was overcome with guilt and remorse. "No," she told herself angrily, "if I can't understand what a sensitive Jew feels about what has gone on in Europe during the past ten years, then I am a total clod." She was overcome with sadness and tears welled into her eyes, then she told herself even more angrily that this was abject self-pity and she would have no part of it.

"I am a mature, healthy woman," she said. "I am a successful writer. I have had two decently successful books, and I am halfway through a third. I have family and friends and a beautiful son with a voracious appetite, and I have a fascinating husband who is a little crazy. I will not feel sorry for myself. I will do what I have to do and he will do what he has to do. Otherwise this marriage is not worth a damn."

She felt much better after that declaration to herself, and the sound of Sam yelling told her that he had awakened from his nap. By the time she arrived in the nursery, Sam was gurgling with laughter and bouncing in his crib. "You should thank God," she said as she picked him up, "that your mother is descended from a line of oversized fishermen and gold miners. You get heavier and heavier. You're also wet and smelly."

The doorbell rang just as she finished diapering Sam. She put him in his playpen, went downstairs, and opened the door.

A rather stout, red-faced man in a dark suit stood there. He wore a sweater under his suit jacket, and his bulbous nose was heavily veined.

"Are you Mrs. Bernie Cohen?" he asked.

"Yes?"

"Barbara Cohen, maiden name of Barbara Lavette, residing here?"

"Yes. What do you want?"

He reached into his jacket's inner pocket, took out an envelope, and handed it to her. "Killen, United States Marshal. That is a subpoena, Mrs. Cohen. You have now accepted service." With that, he turned on his heel, went down the steps, and walked away.

Bernie returned to the house a little after five o'clock and called out cheerfully to Barbara, "Hey kid, I'm back. Where's the runt?"

She came out of the kitchen and kissed him. "We're

both of us improved, aren't we? Sammy's upstairs. I fed him early."

"What the hell. You win some, you lose some."

To which Barbara responded, "You certainly do."

He went upstairs, and she heard him playing with Sam. "He's wet," he called down to her.

"Well, for heaven's sake, change him! Don't stand there shouting at me that he's wet!"

Pleased, astonished at what she had just said, Barbara stood and waited. A howl of anger and anguish from Bernie. "I'm bleeding!" he yelled. "The damn pin went through my hand!"

Sam was wailing. Barbara nodded with satisfaction. Then she climbed the stairs and diapered Sam while Bernie squeezed blood from his finger and changed his clothes. She put the child in his crib, and when Bernie came down, she had a pitcher of martinis and glasses ready in the parlor.

"I was going to call you and ask you to get a sitter. I thought we might go out to dinner."

"What are we celebrating?"

"Only that I've felt like a human being these past few days."

"I've noticed that," Barbara said.

"Still upset?"

"No. What's to be upset over? Your husband tells you that he's taking off on some lunatic caper—why be upset?"

"Bobby, it's not a lunatic caper."

"And I'm not upset. Maybe a little. Bernie, I've been brooding over this all day. You do what you have to do. Only come back safely and soon, please."

"Do you mean that?"

Barbara sipped her drink and studied him. "Yes and

no. I mean it and I don't mean it. You know, Bernie,
we've always been very honest with each other, very
straightforward, very direct. A lot of folks think we're
the most unlikely couple in San Francisco, but they're
wrong. We're not too different. It's just that I'm a
woman and you're a man. I sometimes think that
being a man in this ridiculous world of ours is more
than any human being should have to bear. But there it
is. If I keep you from going, you'd never forgive me."

"Of course I would."

"Well, perhaps. I don't think so."

"Whose briefcase is that?" he asked, pointing.

"Daddy's. He left it here."

"Oh? Well, as far as this lunatic caper is concerned,
I don't know where we'll find the money. Brodsky has
the names of a dozen Jewish businessmen he can talk
to, but they all give through regular channels. The
guy who has the planes is getting very restless. Herb
Goodman went down to Barstow to talk to him, but I
got a feeling that the whole thing is coming apart at
the seams."

"There's a hundred and ten thousand dollars in that
briefcase," Barbara said casually.

"What?"

"I said the money you need is in that briefcase."

He shook his head.

"Daddy brought it here this morning. He said it was
up to me. I could give it to you or not, just as I
pleased."

"You're kidding."

"Why don't you look?"

He stared at her for a long moment. Then he put
down his drink, crossed the room, picked up the bag,
and set it on the coffee table. He opened it and gazed

silently at the neatly wrapped packages of fifty- and one-hundred-dollar bills.

"Now you don't have to rob a bank," Barbara said gently.

He turned to her. "How the devil did you know I thought of robbing a bank?"

"Only because if there were one impossible, romantic way to go, you'd go that way." He stood there and she watched him. "Did you ever wonder why I love you so much?"

"Now and then."

"I'll tell you. Because now and then you make me feel quite wonderful. I'm trying very hard not to be maudlin. When do you want to go?"

"You can still say no. You're not Jewish and your father has no stake in this."

"Maybe he has."

He sat down, toying with his drink and staring at the briefcase. Barbara waited. Minutes went by. Then he said, "I'll call Brodsky and get him over here tonight. I think it's time you met him. We'll leave in the morning. I'll take my Ford, and we'll drive down. I'll arrange for Gomez to pick it up at Barstow after we leave—if we leave. That should be in two or three days."

"I want you to keep in touch with me."

"Sure. No question. I'll call you from L.A. and from Barstow. And then wherever we stop." He went over to her and drew her to her feet. "I don't know what to say."

"Get back quickly, that's all. We'll work things out. We have a lot of years ahead of us, Bernie."

"When you talk to your father, tell him that someday I'll find a way to repay him."

"He doesn't want to be repaid."

"It won't be long. Two, three weeks. I promise you, Bobby."

"Just do it and get it over with."

They made love that night tenderly, as if they had just found each other, as if they were two people who had met by chance and discovered that each delighted the other. As Barbara lay beside him, naked, his hands touching and caressing her, she remembered the first time, so long ago, and she recalled the same tentative quality that had charmed and seduced her then, as if in each movement he feared rejection, his hands conveying his wonder and pleasure. In a way, his love-making was like that of an adolescent; it was touched with disbelief. His gestures apologized for his huge, hairy, muscular bulk, and she loved it that she was so small beside him, so slender and womanly. She lay in his arms in a strange valley between joy and anger, sensing both emotions at the same time, and afterward, when he slept, she put her face in the pillow and gave way to tears.

There were no tears in the morning when she said goodby to him and to Irv Brodsky. Brodsky was the epitome of the unheroic. He was small and skinny, diffident, vulnerable, smiling shyly as he told her not to worry. "The only thing dangerous about a thing like this," he told her, "is getting nervous, and me and Bernie, we don't get nervous. We been through a lot together from the Spanish war on. And I'll send him back. You can count on that."

They left, and Barbara went back into the house. Through the window, she watched them crossing the street, the big, lumbering man and the small one walking quickly to keep up with Bernie's long strides. They didn't look back.

Barbara went into the tiny room on the first floor where she did her writing. She rummaged through her files and found a letter that Bernie had written to her in 1941. It was a long letter, explaining why he left her in Paris and what had happened to him during his journey to Marseille. She didn't have to read it. She knew its contents by heart; and trying to understand what had prompted her to dig it out again, she had a strange, frightening feeling that this man, her husband, Bernie Cohen, had never really been there and that all she possessed of him was this letter.

Barbara shook off the thought, put the letter back in the file, and went upstairs and dressed Sam to go outside. She felt relieved, as if a great weight had been lifted off her shoulders, and she had a very strong feeling that Bernie felt the same way. She had been married less than two years. She wondered whether any marriage was very different—or whether perhaps thirty-two is past the age where a woman can mold herself into the shape a man demands. Or the man mold himself to what she desired? Hopeless. Yet she loved her husband and he loved her. If either had told the other that it was useless, that he or she wanted a divorce, there would have been a period of emotional agony. This way there was nothing. The thought frightened her. Why was there nothing? Why wasn't she sprawled on her bed, weeping her heart out? Suppose Bernie never returned? Why wasn't she stricken with terror at the years of loneliness she might face? Were all her feelings, all her writings, all her high-minded thoughts a fraud? Barbara did not regard it as a virtue that she was incapable of subjective pretense. She had no gift for lying to herself. She was not grief-stricken. That was the plain fact of the matter.

She put Sam in his stroller and pushed him along Vallejo Street to her mother's house. It was a clear, beautiful morning. The fog had burned off, and a brisk wind set the whitecaps on the bay to dancing. It was one of those mornings when San Francisco appears to crackle with electric excitement and the people on the street share their aliveness, walk with an extra verve and breathe a little more deeply than usual.

"Oh, I do love this place," Barbara said to herself. "But you have to be away for a long time to know it. It's a place you have to return to."

Eloise's brother, Billy Clawson, was at the gallery when Barbara got there. He had come, hoping to find Eloise, but this was not her day to work. He was a tall, attenuated man of thirty, who had entered the ministry, Barbara had heard, to avoid the draft. Now, without a pulpit and with no desire for one, he spent his days doing absolutely nothing. The Clawsons were one of the wealthiest families in Oakland, and they had cast Eloise out of their lives and inheritance when she divorced Tom Lavette and married Adam Levy. The only redeeming thing Barbara had ever heard about Billy was that he did occasionally see his sister. Today he was wearing a clerical collar and explaining to Jean, "I do it as a lark. Of course, I'm a fraud, but aren't most men of God? My virtue is that I don't preach. But one does get the most interesting reactions from people. Do you know, they will stop you in the street to weep on your shoulder."

He greeted Barbara and then departed. Jean picked Sam up from the stroller and hugged him. "He's such a good baby, Bobby. Doesn't he ever cry?"

"He certainly does. Mother, does Billy Clawson do anything?"

"Not that I know of."

"Strange."

"Not really. He's not unique."

"Mother," Barbara said, "can I leave Sammy with you, and will you feed him? I have a lunch date with Harvey Baxter."

"Harvey Baxter?"

"He's my lawyer. You remember, he took over Sam Goldberg's practice."

"Did Bernie leave this morning?" Jean asked abruptly.

"Yes."

"You don't look very disturbed."

"I'm working it out."

"Would you like to talk about it?"

"No. Not now, please."

"I would like to talk about it," Jean said.

"Then perhaps we will, another time."

Harvey Baxter, a stout, serious man of forty-three, was waiting for her when she got to Gino's. He had light brown hair, deep brown eyes, and he wore old-fashioned metal-rimmed glasses and three-piece vested suits of charcoal gray sharkskin. He had been with the firm of Goldberg and Benchly since he got out of law school, twenty years earlier, and with the death of both partners, he had become the senior member of the firm. Goldberg and Benchly practiced civil and corporate law, and the firm had been Dan Lavette's lawyers since 1910. It was now known as Goldberg, Benchly and Baxter. As Barbara had, Harvey Baxter had worshipped Sam Goldberg, and he considered Barbara his personal responsibility, inherited from the senior partner.

Now he asked Barbara why she would not come to his office, and she replied that there they would be constantly interrupted.

"Of course not," Baxter said. "You know I stop all my calls when you come to see me."

"Whereas here, my dear Harvey, we are only interrupted by Gino, who tells me how beautiful I am, and today I need that. It is not absolutely the best day of my life. This was handed to me yesterday." She took the subpoena out of her purse and gave it to him.

Gino hovered over them while Baxter read it slowly and painstakingly. "Shall I order for you?" Barbara asked.

"Anything."

Barbara ordered salad, spaghetti, and veal cutlets. Baxter finished his careful reading and looked at her thoughtfully.

"I read it," Barbara said.

"Then you know what it is. This is a subpoena to appear in Washington ten days from now to testify before the House Committee on Un-American Activities. It's outrageous and, if I may say so, rather disgusting."

"You may say so."

"Did Bernie also receive a subpoena?"

"No."

"That's very curious."

"Why?"

"Isn't it obvious, Barbara? He fought in Spain. That might explain it, the way things are today. But you? That's simply outrageous."

Barbara shrugged.

"I think Bernie should be included in any discussion of this. If you're subpoenaed, it stands to reason that he will be."

"Not really," Barbara said. "From all I've read of

their methods, they love publicity. No one knows Bernie. I'm a reasonably well known writer and I'm Dan Lavette's daughter."

"That still doesn't explain anything. You're not a communist."

"I certainly am not."

"What about front organizations? Civil rights? Committees to free Tom Mooney—that sort of thing?"

"No, I'm not a joiner, Harvey."

"I very strongly suggest we discuss this with Bernie."

"He's out of town."

"Out of town? Where? We'll call him."

"No, we can't, Harvey. I don't want Bernie involved in this."

"Where is he?"

"I'm sorry. I can't tell you that."

"Does he know about this subpoena?"

"No. And I don't want him to know about it."

"Barbara, when you appear before the committee, the whole world will know about this."

"That's ten days from now. By then it won't matter."

"What won't matter? Must I remind you that I am your attorney, that anything you tell me is privileged?"

"I know that, Harvey," Barbara said gently. "I'm not trying to keep secrets from you. But I know how you think, and if I tell you where Bernie is, you are going to be so angry and so upset that we'll never make any sense out of this stupid subpoena. I don't want to talk about Bernie. I want to talk about what I am going to do."

"That's very comforting."

The waiter came with their food.

"Now please eat," Barbara said. "I'm just starved,

and I don't eat out very often these days, and I love the food here, and I won't feel a bit comfortable if I eat and you don't."

"You are an extraordinary woman."

"Not at all, Harvey, just hungry. We'll eat, and you'll explain this ridiculous business to me. I read about the writers and directors in Hollywood. They're going to prison, aren't they? Does that mean that I'll go to prison?"

"No! For heaven's sake, get that notion out of your head! You are not going to prison."

"Harvey, don't be so upset. I shouldn't mind going to prison—for a little while. It would be a fascinating experience."

"One you can well do without. Now let me explain something to you—"

"You're not eating."

"I'm not hungry, you are," he said with some annoyance. "Will you please eat and listen."

"Yes, Harvey," Barbara agreed. She was very fond of Harvey Baxter. He reminded her of Sam Goldberg. He had the same tone of voice and many of the same mannerisms, and she supposed that it came from years of working together.

"The House Committee on Un-American Activities—"

"Harvey," she interrupted, "I don't even know what a House committee is. I'm a writer, but I'm not terribly well educated. I did leave college after my sophomore year."

"I wish you would take this seriously. I wish you were disturbed. I'm disturbed."

"I am disturbed, Harvey. That's why I'm lunching with you today."

"All right. Now this committee is a committee of

Congress. Congress has the right to set up committees to hear testimony, the right to call witnesses on the subject, and then to use the results to frame legislation. Not that this wretched committee has ever framed any legislation."

"But what is the subject, Harvey?"

"Un-Americanism, as they put it."

"That's such a silly, stupid word. Do you think I'm un-American?"

"It doesn't matter what I think. The point is that this nasty little committee has great power. Now in the case of the writers and directiors who call themselves the Hollywood Ten, the committee charged them with using the film for subversive propaganda."

"Is that why they're going to jail?"

"No. And I'm not at all certain that they are going to jail. I want you to understand very clearly that the only crime a congressional committee can charge you with is contempt of Congress, and the only way you can commit a contempt is by refusing to answer a question that is pertinent to their inquiry. Contempt of Congress is a misdemeanor and is punishable by imprisonment of up to a year. Now I have no idea as to whether these Hollywood writers and directors are communists now or ever have been, but they were asked that question among others and they refused to answer. There were other questions that they refused to answer."

"But why?"

"Well, if they admitted to being communists it would be an end to their employment, but they had other reasons, too. From what I've read on the case, the advice of counsel and probably their own decision was to stand on the broad constitutional ground of the First Amendment. If I recall correctly, the First

Amendment states that Congress shall make no law respecting an establishment of religion, or prohibiting the free exercise thereof; or abridging the freedom of speech, or of the press; or the right of the people peaceably to assemble, and to petition the government for a redress of grievances. By virtue of that, I presume that they held that an inquiry into their political beliefs or writing or thoughts was an infringement on freedom of speech and of the press. It's a very broad interpretation and one that I would not advise a client of mine to attempt. But the case is still in the courts, and there is no reason to conclude that they are going to jail."

"My own impulse," Barbara said, "is to tear up this wretched piece of paper and forget the whole thing."

"Which I would hardly advise. That would be a contempt. However, your father and I both know a number of people of influence, and it's possible we could get this subpoena withdrawn. Or quashed."

"How?"

"I'd rather not say how."

"Harvey, you mean you could pay off members of the committee?"

"Your words, Barbara, not mine."

"Harvey, stop being so damn cautious and legalistic. If you are talking about bribing one of those bastards, I will not have it. Not by my father and not by anyone else. Furthermore, neither my father nor my mother is to know anything about this until I choose to tell them."

"I think you're wrong."

"I think I'm right."

"You understand, the alternative is that you must go to Washington and testify?"

"Will you come with me?"

"Of course. But again, let me ask you very seriously, is there any question they might ask that you would refuse to answer?"

"No, of course not. They're not going to ask me who I slept with, are they?"

"Oh, no. No, indeed. The questions must be pertinent. And what about Bernie? Suppose they question you about him?"

"Isn't there something in the law that allows a wife to refuse to testify against her husband?"

"I don't know whether it applies to a congressional inquiry. Probably, but I shall make sure."

"It doesn't matter. There's nothing I know about Bernie that I would be unwilling to talk about anywhere."

"If they ask you where he is?"

"Ten days from now, that won't matter," Barbara replied.

The ten pilots and three navigators who were to fly the C-54s east were staying at the Marypol Hotel in Hollywood, on Hudson Street between Hollywood and Sunset boulevards. It was an old dilapidated firetrap of a structure and catered to unemployed actors and a few transients. Brodsky chose it because it possessed a single virtue: it was cheap, five dollars a day for a single, seven-fifty for a double. Even at that price and buying their own meals, the volunteers had run up a collective bill of over four hundred dollars. Brodsky's resources were down to a hundred and eighty dollars. Bernie emptied the till at the garage to make up the difference.

Driving down to Los Angeles, Brodsky argued that Bernie should take command of the operation.

"Who's in command now?"

"Nobody. That's just it, Bernie. I suppose this could be called a Haganah operation. But the point is that nobody knew just what kind of an operation it would be because nobody knew when and how the Czechs would deal with us. They had to find someone there who could be paid off and arrange for the sale without putting his neck on the chopping block. Then they had to find the two million. That took over six months. Then they had to figure out a way to get the money to Czechoslovakia and get the Messerschmitts to Palestine. When we heard about these C-54s for sale, they sent me out to make a deal. Herbie Goodman and three of the pilots came with me, and the rest we picked up here. We had our leads, and the five of us spent three weeks driving around and talking people into the job. We actually didn't know how many planes we could find. At first we thought it was only three. You see, the way we figure the cargo area, we can't get more than one Messerschmitt inside a C-54, and that's disassembled. It sounds crazy that a country that's going to be at war and fighting for its existence any day now should be waiting for an air force in this kind of crazy way, but that's the way it is. But me, I never thought about it as a military operation, but with the ten planes, that's what it is, wouldn't you say?"

"No," Bernie said emphatically. "You're out of your mind. I don't know what kind of laws we'd be breaking in terms of conducting a military operation here in the United States, but there must be at least twenty. And anyway, we're not armed, so let's forget about a military operation."

"O.K. Then you're boss. How does that grab you?"

"It doesn't. You started this thing. Why don't you finish it?"

"Because I'm half your size, and I don't look like a boss of anything. We got a bunch of lunatics waiting for us down there at the Marypol Hotel. All right, they're good guys, but do you know how crazy you got to be to try to fly those crates to Czechoslovakia?"

"You said the planes are airworthy."

"Sure. Herbie and a guy named Calvin Council—he's a navigator and a pretty good mechanic, he's from El Paso and he's not Jewish—well, he and Herbie went out and spent three days going over the planes. They seem to be all right. What else can I tell you? Bernie, please, take it on. You're the boss."

By the time they reached Los Angeles, Bernie had agreed. It was about half-past seven in the evening when they parked and walked into the Hotel Marypol, Bernie carrying the briefcase of money in a tight grip. Herb Goodman was waiting for them. He told them that six of the men were up in his room, playing poker. The rest were out somewhere or other, except for Seltzer, who was keeping an eye on Mick White, who was in his room getting drunk.

"We'll take Mick White," Bernie said, "him first." He handed the briefcase to Goodman. "There's a hundred and ten grand in there, so don't let go of it. Just stay with us."

Mick White, about thirty, pale, short, and going to fat, looked at Bernie out of glazed, bloodshot eyes. He was pouring vodka out of a quart bottle that was half empty. The tiny room was drab, its paint peeling from the walls, and lit by a single unshaded bulb that hung from the ceiling. "You certainly found the bottom," Bernie said to Brodsky. "I wouldn't put a dog in a place like this."

"Who the hell is he?" Seltzer demanded. He was a tough, hard, streetwise kid with a Brooklyn accent,

and he regarded Bernie with open hostility. He sat back
to front on a wooden chair, with a glass of vodka in
his hand.

There was a small, dirty sink on the wall at one side
of the room. Bernie took the bottle out of Mick
White's hand and poured the vodka into the sink.
When Seltzer leaped to his feet to stop him, Bernie
flung him back against the opposite wall with a
sweep of his arm.

"You sonofabitch," Seltzer began, going at Bernie,
who turned to face him, holding the vodka bottle by
its neck. Seltzer stopped short. Bernie was six inches
taller, fifty pounds heavier, and Seltzer was conditioned to authority. He had spent five years in the air
force.

"My name is Bernie Cohen," he said mildly. "I'm
running this operation. Take one more step, and I
break this bottle over your head. That might cost us a
pilot, but we'll find another. You are a pilot, aren't
you?"

"You're damn right."

"You're Jewish?"

"Yeah."

Bernie nodded at where Mick White sat slumped in
the one other chair the room contained. "He isn't, so
maybe that excuses something. But you, mister, you
take a drink again before this is over and I'll break
you in two with my bare hands." He finished pouring
the vodka into the sink.

"You're real tough," Seltzer said.

Bernie nodded. "Yes. More than you might imagine,
mister. So what do you say we just play it cool and
easy, and no more trouble, right?" He held out his
hand. Seltzer hesitated. Then he took Bernie's hand.

Then Bernie went to White and asked him how he felt.

"Not good enough to beat the shit out of you. That's tomorrow."

"Sure." Bernie put his arm around White and lifted him out of the chair, and with White struggling and swearing, he dragged him to the sink and forced his head under the faucet. "Turn it on," he told Brodsky. For at least two minutes, he held the struggling, cursing White under the faucet. "Get him a towel."

"Motherfucking Jew bastard," White said as he wiped his face.

"You a pilot?" Bernie asked.

"I'll fly your ass off, you lousy, oversized pile of turd."

"Good enough," Bernie agreed.

That night at ten o'clock, the pilots, navigators, and five radio operators whom Goodman had recruited in Los Angeles gathered in what the Hotel Marypol was pleased to call its banquet room. Not having been rented for a banquet these past ten years, the room was half filled with old beds, mattresses, broken chairs, and one-time banquet tables. Three dollars purchased it for two hours. The volunteers sat facing Bernie and Brodsky. The only thing they had in common was that they were all veterans of World War II. Their ages ranged from the middle twenties to the middle thirties. Of the pilots, seven were Jewish, two were Catholic, and one was a Baptist. Two of the navigators and one of the radio operators were not Jewish. What forces impelled them, Bernie did not know. Possibly they bore some of the guilt for the holocaust; possibly they wanted a break in the dullness of postwar life, a chance to travel, an opportunity to put their hands on the controls of a four-motor plane

again. Or possibly the motives of the non-Jews were
as deeply buried and entangled as those of the Jews.
None of them were in it for the money because no one
was being paid; they were guaranteed food and lodg-
ing, such as it was, and passage home from Palestine,
though neither Brodsky nor anyone else appeared to
know just how that would be managed. Three of them
were unemployed; one was a film director who had
just had a notable success, two were actors, one was a
carpenter, one had quit the Los Angeles Police Force,
four were students, two were selling insurance, and
two others had taken a leave from jobs as pilots for
large corporations. Two of the radio operators worked
as television repair men. Oddly enough, nine of the
group were married, and with this information, Bernie
wondered how many of them, like himself, had used
this as an escape hatch, a way to flee, a way to "bug
out," as he put it to himself, of real life. Or was this
real life? Or was anything real life? What had Barbara
said to him once, that no male of the species ever
reaches maturity? Wars were games, politics were
games—deadly, senseless murderous games of children
in adult bodies. Glory, idealism, and courage were the
three mindless labels. "Still and all," he told himself,
"someone has to do it."

Aloud, he said to them, "My name is Bernie Cohen.
As much as anyone is in charge of this operation, I
am, and I intend to see it through. So if any of you
have any second thoughts, doubts, or misgivings,
now's the time to speak up and get out." He waited,
but no one spoke. "All right. We're going to leave here
at five A.M. and drive to Barstow. I say five A.M. because we'll take off if all goes well at five the following morning, and I want the lot of you dog-tired so
you'll sleep. I don't care if you don't sleep tonight as

long as you get a good night's sleep tomorrow. That will give us a whole day to work on the planes. We're flying into a field at Melville, New Jersey, and the weather conditions look good. We've got maps, and we'll lay out our flight plans tonight. Now, how many of you were trained as mechanics?" Eight hands went up. "Good. There is no rank here. Tomorrow, everyone pitches in and works with the mechanics. Tonight, I want you to throw out every question you can think of. Let's have no loose ends."

Tom Lavette, two years older than Barbara, was Dan Lavette's first child. It was common gossip in certain San Francisco circles that the two Lavettes, father and son, had not spoken to each other in almost twenty years. Since San Francisco is not a very large city, and since the group of men who control the wealth and power of the city is even smaller, Dan Lavette and his son were bound to come face to face periodically. On such occasions, they both respected the widening gulf that separated them, and each made no effort to resume contact with the other. Observing this, Jean would press the subject with Dan.

"He is young and insufferable, if you will, but he is still your son."

Dan would simply reply, "That's quite true," and let it rest there.

In time, Jean no longer raised the possibility of a reconciliation. She herself saw her son regularly if not frequently. About once a month, he would call and ask her to lunch with him.

When Jean remarried after her divorce from Dan, she chose John Whittier for her husband. He had inherited the largest shipping line on the West Coast, and during the war years it had expanded enormously.

After his marriage to Jean in 1931, he had developed a growing fondness for Tom, possibly less as a person than as the potential heir to the Seldon Bank. When Tom came into his share of the controlling stock of the bank, Barbara sold him a portion of her share, quite willing to let him have it; then his interests merged with Whittier's to form an entity they called Great Cal, one of the largest holding companies on the Coast.

Through the years, Whittier's position as the dominant force in the corporation weakened. He saw Tom originally as a rather bland, reasonably bright, well-mannered young man, but one without too much ambition and drive. In this, he misjudged him. During the next dozen years, Tom established himself as the major force in the combine. Now, at sixty, Whittier was a petulant, overweight hypochondriac who had already suffered one real heart attack and at least a dozen imaginary ones. Nominally the president and the chairman of the board of directors of Great Cal, he was little more than a figurehead. Problems were brought to Tom and decisions were made by Tom. In western financial circles, he was regarded as one of the most powerful and promising of all the young men who had come into industrial control at the end of the war.

Jean had not heard from him for well over a month when he called and asked her to lunch with him at the Fairmont. When Tom did not lunch at his club, he ate at the Fairmont. Jean once asked him why, in a city that boasts more good restaurants than any other city of its size in America, he always ate at the same place. He had replied, "Mother, I do not eat in strange restaurants."

Jean knew enough about her son to make anyone

else, possessed of her knowledge, dislike him intensely. For her part, she would not judge him and she refused to dislike him. He was agreeable and pleasant to her, and he was also quite handsome. She thought of this as he came across the dining room to join her, more slender than Dan, but with Dan's height and breadth of shoulder and with her own blue eyes, light hair, and fair skin. Jean felt that physically, both children had the best of both of their parents.

He greeted her warmly. "Mother, you look absolutely splendid. Still the most beautiful woman in any room you enter."

"What nonsense! I am fifty-eight years old, and I make no attempt to hide or deny it."

"No need to."

"What on earth makes you this amiable?"

"I always am."

"Except when you're being a beast, which has happened. Anyway, I am glad to see you. Sit down, and we'll have a drink to celebrate. We live in the same city a few streets apart, and we're more or less strangers."

"I've been busy, mother," Tom explained. "Very busy."

"Of course you have. You're a throwback, Thomas. You remind me of your great-grandfather who began as a placer miner in fifty. But he soon discovered that one can't pan gold fast enough to become really rich, and so he became a usurer, lending out his gold at three hundred percent. When I was a child, well, by then he had become a banker and had slipped to twenty or thirty percent, but when I was a child he would give me a ten-dollar gold piece on each birthday. Only it broke his heart to let go of it. You would enjoy seeing the way he fondled it. I think the only time the old goat had an erection was when he was counting his money."

"Mother," Tom whispered, "you do say the damnedest things."

"Yes, I suppose I do. And I do wonder what drives you, Tom. You have enough money to sit back and enjoy life."

"I enjoy what I do. It's not the money. That's just a way of keeping score."

"Not very original. I wonder."

"Then did you ever wonder, mother, who makes this country work, who keeps the wheels turning, who makes it possible for people like yourself to enjoy life, as you put it?"

"Bravo. Now stop snapping at me and order some drinks and lunch, and then you can tell me why I'm here."

After the food arrived, Tom said flatly, "John has been pestering me to get married again."

"Oh?"

"Don't just say oh."

"Is this something we should discuss?" Jean asked kindly. "I'm your mother."

"Does that make it too sticky for you? Who else do I talk to?"

"A psychoanalyst—please, don't be angry."

"No!"

Jean pecked at the food for a few moments. She had not expected anything like this, nor did she know quite how to handle it. Finally she said quietly, "All right, we'll talk about it. As much as I can. I don't know—"

"Neither do I," Tom said. The note of pleading in his voice was something she had not heard in a long,

long time, and it melted her and brought up all the guilt she suffered from a long-standing and deep-seated contempt for this man, her son.

"Very well," Jean said as flatly as she could. "John Whittier wants you to get married. What earthly affair of his it is, I do not know. Do you want to get married?"

"I have plans, mother. That's no surprise to you. I'm running for Congress. I do intend to be elected. Six years from now, in nineteen fifty-four, John and I feel I have a very substantial chance for governor. If I can get the Republican designation, with Earl Warren's record in this state, I am as good as elected."

"And that's what you want so desperately—to be governor?"

"It's a step."

"And then? What then?"

"I'm not sure. The Senate, perhaps. John has his own strange ideas about the White House, but that's what every upright American boy wants, isn't it?"

"Yes, every upright American boy," Jean murmured.

"And why not? I have a decent war record. I have the money and the position, and I'm no fool."

"You certainly are no fool," Jean agreed. "I'm just trying to understand it. You cannot grow up in San Francisco, Tom, and respect politics or politicians. It's a nasty game, played mostly by wretched men. Well, you have your dreams. Tell me, is there someone you want to marry or is it just a general notion?"

"There is. Lucy Sommers."

"Al Sommers' daughter," Jean said, recalling the retired vice president of the Seldon Bank and his single child, a dark, long-legged girl. She had never cared very much for either of them, and she had not seen

Lucy for years. "She's a widow, isn't she, and at least four years older than you, if I remember rightly?"

"Yes, that's so. It doesn't matter—the age, I mean—and a widow doesn't carry the implications of a divorcée. It's bad enough that I have one divorce on my back. When I think of Eloise—"

"We're not discussing Eloise."

"No, we're not. Well, Lucy and I have talked about marriage. She feels, as I do, that there are concrete benefits for both of us. There are no children, and living alone is no pleasure for any woman. She's a very striking and handsome woman, she's an excellent hostess, and thank God, unlike Eloise, she enjoys the role."

Concrete benefits for both of us, Jean thought. My God, what a way to approach a marriage!

"What do you think of her?" he asked Jean.

"I hardly know her. Certainly, she's elegant, and I imagine that is what you want. Does she know?" Jean asked uneasily. "I mean—"

"I know what you mean, mother. I made it very plain to her that I am not interested in sex, that we would live in a civilized arrangement. She agrees."

"And what about her sex life?"

"She has been doing without it. She's apparently content to continue that way."

"I've heard of such things." Jean sighed. "It will take some doing on both your parts."

"It will be a small wedding, just a few people. Will you come?"

"Without Dan?" Jean asked. "I don't think so."

Tom stared at her.

"If I were you," Jean said, "I would take a trip. France or England or even the Islands. Get married there. A sudden, romantic decision, and then there's nothing in the papers to worry about."

That night, Dan asked her about the luncheon, and she told him of Tom's plans.

"Is he in love with the woman?" Dan asked.

"I don't think so."

"Then what in hell is he walking into this marriage for?"

"Your son," Jean said calmly, "is a very rich and important man, as such things are measured in our lives. He's also ambitious. You may think he's a bastard, Dan."

"I never said that."

"Then you've thought it. Well, he isn't—any more than most men are. He needs the form of marriage, if not the function."

Dan stared at her for a long moment before he said, "What are you trying to tell me, that he's a faggot?"

"I hate that word!"

"Then he's a homosexual?"

"You've never suspected it?" Gently, she said, "Danny, don't eat yourself up with this. We have enough horrors in our past. Don't add any more to them. I want so desperately to have a little bit of decent happiness before it's over."

Barbara and Sam went to Huntington Park the same day that Jean lunched with Tom at the Fairmont, a stone's throw away. Barbara went on foot; Sam was pushed in his stroller, facing her and grinning with pleasure at the cool, clean wind that blew in from the Pacific. Barbara never tired of being with her child, and she also never could get truly used to realizing that this fat, alert, and good-natured young man had

come out of her very own loins. She had few of the
discontents of the average mother and housewife, but
then, she had lived a good deal of her life before becoming a mother and a housewife, and to her Sam was
an improbable miracle. She knew she would not have
another child. She often listened with curiosity to
other young mothers in the park, most of them a
dozen years younger than she, but she listened without being a part of it. It seemed that she had always
watched and listened to a world outside her—it was
part of being a writer; and in her new book, the book
she was at work on, she was attempting a story about
just such people as the young mothers she met in
Huntington Park.

She enjoyed listening more than talking, preferring
to talk to Sam. He received the profound and the
mundane with equal placidity. He was infrequently
bored, and when he was, his boredom could be assuaged by either his thumb or a teething ring.

Today, staring at the Fountain of the Turtles, she
informed Sam that it was a gift to the city from the
Crocker family and a copy of a fountain in Rome. Sam
decided that he wanted to sit on the rim and touch
the water. "You know you pee when you dabble in
water. Well, why not? Sooner or later, anyway."

They sat on the rim of the fountain. "You know,"
Barbara informed him, "the Crockers couldn't bear
not to have something in the park here. I wonder if
they were jealous of old Collis Huntington. Do you
know, he was a friend of my grandfather? Grandpa
used to tell me how they would both ride the cable
car up California Street and then walk off to their respective mansions. Truth. Both of them had great,
magnificent old mansions right up here on top of Nob
Hill. Grandpa's was there." She pointed. "Hunting-

ton's was over there. All gone now. I remember when they tore down grandpa's house—twenty-eight, or was it twenty-nine? I was fourteen or fifteen, and it just broke my heart. It was an ugly old place—"

She stopped. A rapt expression had come over Sam's face.

"Ah, yes. And now we go home and change your diaper." She picked him up and put him back in the stroller. "Someday, God willing, you'll learn to talk, and we'll have perfectly wonderful conversations."

Walking back to the house on Green Street, Barbara tried to understand why she was neither distressed nor unhappy. Her husband had gone off on a wild, unlikely adventure and she herself had been subpoenaed by the House Committee on Un-American Activities—in spite of which she was quite content and reasonably happy.

"I must be a very strange and unfeeling woman," she told herself.

PART TWO

Games

I don't like to bargain with Jews," Mr. Kennedy said. He was a large man whose belly lipped over his belt. He wore a broad-brimmed western hat, and his white duck suit was soaked with sweat. "Too grasping." He clenched a fist to illustrate his point. "Money, always money. I'm sticking out my neck to sell you these planes, Mr. Cohen. Suppose you take them out of the country. That's against the law. I been reading up on the law. I had a dream and God said, Sell them the planes. Only I was awake. My wife testifies to that. She says there I was sitting bolt upright in bed with my eyes wide open—bug-eyed. So I say it's the word of God. But God respects a man's right to do business as he sees fit, as long as he don't skin his customers. And I ain't skinning you. Taking a fair profit, but that ain't skinning. Do you know what one of them planes costs new?"

They were sitting under the tin awning in front of Kennedy's building supply store, with the desert in front of them undulating in the heat. Bernie wiped his brow and said softly, "I'm not trying to skin you, sir." He hefted his briefcase. "Right here, I have one hundred and ten thousand dollars in fifties and hundreds, unmarked bills, Mr. Kennedy. Let's talk plainly. You wouldn't take a check. You wanted cash."

"Hell, mister, are you accusing me of illegal dealing?"

"No, no, no. Absolutely not. Still and all, you won't find many customers who can pay cash and not put it on their books. This money is not on anyone's books. You might have to look far and wide to find another situation like this, and meanwhile those planes are sitting out there in the desert sun and deteriorating. Deteriorating. You know, we asked Lockheed what it would take to put them into shape. A hundred and fifty thousand each. Mr. Kennedy, those damn things are flying coffins."

"Appears you're mighty eager to have a funeral," Kennedy chuckled. "What's your proposition, Cohen?"

"We picked up five more radio operators and two more navigators. They'll be here in Barstow before midnight, but they got to be paid. Two hundred each, that's fourteen hundred dollars. Then we got the hotel bill for the rest of my men, and food, and so help me God, we don't have a nickel. Only what is here in this bag. Now if you're going to stick to your price, I'll just have to cancel out, pay out bills, and look elsewhere."

"Elsewhere! Where the hell elsewhere you going to find planes like these at this price? There ain't none."

"There's sixteen C-46 cargo jobs down near San Diego. They don't have this range, but they're a damn sight better for our needs."

"Cohen, you're bluffing."

Bernie shrugged and waited.

"Suppose I said one hundred and nine thousand?"

"Wouldn't do us a damn bit of good."

"Christ, I hate to do business with Jews. How much do you want out of that bag?"

"We need three thousand dollars to cover us. I'll

give you a hundred and seven thousand dollars, take it or leave it."

"Just don't get snotty with me, boy," Kennedy snapped angrily. "How in hell do I know that money's clean? You're in Barstow, not in L.A. Suppose I call the sheriff and tell him you're sitting here with a bag of hot money? Sheriff's a friend of mine."

• "Call him." Bernie shrugged. "I know where the money came from. You want the sheriff to hear where it came from and check it out—that's O.K. with me."

"You are one nasty sonofabitch."

"It's your deal, Mr. Kennedy."

"You really going to fly them planes to the Holy Land, Cohen?"

"Now you know that is illegal, Mr. Kennedy," Bernie said patiently. "You know all about Truman's proclamation number two seven seven six. You told me that yourself. You know that under the law we can't take these planes out of the country."

"That's what my lawyer tells me."

"Right. Now suppose you should be under oath, and they say to you, Did you know where those planes were going? All you have to say is that their flight plans were cleared for Melville, New Jersey. All aboveboard and absolutely legal. Now, do we have a deal for a hundred and seven thousand?"

"Boy, you'd squeeze blood from a stone." He nodded. "We have a deal, boy. You squeezed me, and I caved in. We do have a deal."

The afternoon of the same day, Dan telephoned Barbara and told her that he and Jean were dining out. Would she join them?

"Daddy, I'd love to. I really would love to. But Bernie will call me this evening, and I can't leave the house. I have to wait for his call. And anyway, I don't know whether I could find a sitter this late."

"Too bad. I was counting on seeing you."

He sounded depressed. "Are you all right?" Barbara asked.

"I'm just fine."

"Then look, daddy, I'm housebound anyway. So after you eat, why don't you and mother stop by, and I'll give you dessert and coffee and we'll talk for a while. Would you, please?"

"I'd like that," Dan said.

"Good. Then I'll see you later."

Filled with a sense of unease, Barbara put down the phone. Something in her father's voice—or was it her imagination? A sudden chill shook her, and she ran up the stairs to look at Sam. He was sleeping peacefully. She went back downstairs and dropped into the chair facing the telephone. Why didn't Bernie call? It was only two days since he had left, and suddenly, at this moment, it turned into an eternity. She had not really missed him until now; in all truth it had been a relief to find herself alone with her child and the mistress of her own destiny. Now, for some reason she did not entirely understand, her mood had changed. When she married, people had wondered about her alliance with a penniless ex-army sergeant; but as Dan said to her at the time, "You've found a man, Bobby. I can understand that." Yet it was not the thing of maleness or toughness or ruthlessness; he was none of those things. He was a very open, straightforward person who adored her, and he was unlike almost every other man she had known. "He just is what he is," she told herself. "Damn you, Bernie, call me!"

The telephone rang almost in answer to her request,

and she grabbed it before the first ring had finished.

"Bernie?"

"How are you, Bobby? How is Sam?"

"Both of us are fine. Just fine. Sam's asleep, and I'm sitting here watching the telephone and trying to make it ring. Where are you, Bernie?"

"Barstow. Everything is falling into place. We made the deal for the planes, and the boys have been working on them all day."

"I'm terrified of those damn planes. Will they fly?"

"Like birds. Believe me."

"And how do you feel?"

"I feel great. Hell, I miss you and the kid. I miss you terribly. But I needed this. My soul was rotting away. That has nothing to do with you, Bobby, or with how much I love you, believe me."

"I understand."

"I'm alive again. It's a good feeling."

"I know the feeling, Bernie."

"I'm filled with guilts."

"Oh, damn the guilts. Just get it done and come back in one piece."

"That's my intention," he said. "We're in good shape. We have a radio operator on every plane now, and that was the thing that worried me most. We're only short two navigators, and we'll make out with that."

"When do you take off?"

"Dawn tomorrow. The weather's good right across the country, and we should be in New Jersey no later than four o'clock, Eastern time. Listen, Bobby, I never had a chance to talk to your father about what he did. I was so damn compulsive about this thing that I never even took the time to think about the size of what we asked. God Almighty, the man gave me a hundred and ten thousand dollars without even blinking an eyelash. What a hell of a thing to do!"

"I think so. I think it was pretty magnificent."

"Bobby, why? Do you know why he did it?"

"Sort of, not entirely. He's a strange man and he's had a strange life. He just does things that other people don't do."

"You can say that again. Will you thank him? Make him understand that I won't forget this."

"I'll try, Bernie."

"I love you very much, Bobby. In my own, stupid, neurotic way."

"I'll take that from where it comes. There are things about you that I admire, Cohen. Not many, but some."

"I'll nurse that. God bless you."

Barbara put down the telephone and leaned back and stretched her legs and closed her eyes. Tonight she would thank Dan. "Daddy, I want to thank you for being as idiotic as my husband." No, not quite that way. Then why had he done it? To repay a debt to Mark Levy? That was romantic nonsense. There was no way to repay the dead. There must have been reasons, very deep-seated and compelling reasons. Barbara wondered whether she had ever understood her father or his true motives for anything he did. Did she know him at all? She remembered an incident once, long ago, shortly before his divorce from Jean, when he had asked her to have dinner with him, just the two of them, alone. He was reaching out, desperately, like a drowning man; but Barbara was unaware of that, unaware of anything except that this man, her father, had betrayed her mother and was having an affair with a Chinese woman. Barbara remembered very well indeed how that had horrified her. It was years before she actually met May Ling and came to know her and love her. At that time, she had only a sense of adolescent disgust and outrage; and, adding insult to injury—as she saw it then—her father took her to the same restaurant to which he took May Ling so often, to Gino's, where the proprietor praised her beauty so lavishly, chattering to her father in Italian, bringing out all her ethnic fears and resentments. Then Barbara had turned on her father like a wounded cat, clawing, insulting, demolishing him.

The memory of it brought tears to her eyes. The thought of that strong, magnificent figure of a man, still young, Dan Lavette, who with his two hands and his brain had subdued a proud, intolerant city and made it his own domain, cringing under her anger, the scorn and anger of a witless schoolgirl, was almost more than she could bear. How little she had known and how little she had understood!

It was almost eight o'clock. Enough of this, Barbara decided. What was done was done. There remained at least another hour before her father and mother would appear, and that could conceivably produce a page of usable if not immortal prose. She went into her study and sat down at the typewriter.

It was almost ten o'clock when Dan and Jean arrived. Barbara had rarely seen her mother so relaxed and ebullient. She wore a new dress that Barbara had not seen before, a high-collared, deep blue and black taffeta, with long sleeves and a tiered skirt. The great high collar framed her neck and shoulders. Barbara stared at her in undisguised admiration and said, sighing, "If I could ever look like that!" To which Jean replied, "Oh, my dear, I'm an old woman, pretending. You have no need to pretend. You will never guess where we dined tonight. We just turned the clock back right to the beginning. At the Palace, in the great dining room under the glass dome. Oh, I will admit that the kitchen has pretty well gone to seed, but there it was, and do you know, Dan and I haven't been back there together since nineteen eleven. Can you imagine? Nineteen eleven—and this is nineteen forty-eight."

Dan dropped into a chair. Barbara thought he looked tired, very tired. He watched Jean, a slight smile on his lips, the way one might watch a totally adored child, uncritically, as if to say he asked no more than the right to be near her, to look at her; and seeing him that way, Barbara tried again to understand how her father could love two women so completely and so long, thinking again of the strange, bemusing puzzle that Dan Lavette presented.

"He wore his tuxedo that night," Jean went on. "In nineteen eleven. Dinner jacket to you, my love, but then we called them tuxedos. Why, I wonder? Do you know, Danny?"

"Not a notion. Hell, I'm no authority. That was my first one."

"And the very first time he wore it on a date, Bobby. Oh, he wore it to the house, to a dinner party. That's why he had it made, to come and dine with the very swell Seldons on Nob Hill, and him just a pushy, tough little kid from the Tenderloin."

"Not little. Daddy was never little," Barbara protested. "He was born large."

"Thank you," Dan said, taking out a cigar. "You don't mind?"

"I wish you wouldn't," Jean said. "Well if you must. Anyway, it was our first formal date, and Danny wore the tuxedo and he took me to dinner at the Palace. Dinner at the Palace, my dear, in nineteen eleven would feed a family of five today for at least a week. Seven courses, and each with some silly French name, and there was young Dan Lavette, all of twenty-two years old—"

"I still can't read a French menu," Dan muttered.

"—and being so very sophisticated. I'm sure he decided that if I ate myself into a comatose state, he could have his way with me. Do you remember, Danny, brook trout and venison and quail, and on and on. I will never forget the expression on his face as the courses kept coming. Dinner was not nourishment in those days. It was an endurance contest."

Dan burst out laughing. Then Barbara saw the laughter turn into a grimace of pain. He was trying to light the cigar and he dropped it. He bent to pick it up, stopped, and sat bent over.

"Daddy, what is it?" Barbara cried.

Jean ran to him and put her arms around him. "Danny, are you all right? What is it?"

"I have the most godawful pain," he managed to say. "It's ripping out my gut—and here in my arm. I think you'd better get a doctor."

Barbara had never before seen her coldly beautiful mother—whom May Ling used to refer to as the snow lady—react like this. She appeared to go to pieces completely, overcome with terror and clutching Dan, who muttered, "I'm all right, Jeanie, I'm all right." Barbara called Dr. Kellman and found him at home; after listening to her description of what was happening, he said, "It sounds very much like a heart attack. Don't be too alarmed. Dan is in good shape. I'll order an ambulance, and I'll be there in a few minutes. Where is he?"

"Just sitting here in a chair."

"Help him lie down on the floor. Don't let him try to move. I'll be right over."

Barbara put down the phone. "Mother," she said evenly, "I want you to pull yourself together. Daddy will be all right. Dr. Kellman says we should help him lie down on the floor. Daddy," she said to Dan, "I'm going to hold you while mother pulls the chair away."

"I can get up," Dan said.

"I know. But do it my way." She bent over her father, holding him under the arms, amazed at her own strength. She eased Dan down onto the floor as Jean pulled the chair away, and then said to her mother, who stood there trembling, her make-up smudged with tears, "Mother, go upstairs and get a blanket from my bed, please. Quickly."

Barbara put a pillow under Dan's head. "How do you feel?" she asked.

"Rotten. What did he say? Am I having a heart attack?"

"Or maybe the Palace Hotel is taking its revenge for your low opinion of their food. Come on, daddy, how does he know?" Again Dan's face contorted in pain. He reached out and clutched Barbara's hand.

Jean came down with the blanket, and they covered Dan. About ten minutes went by before Dr. Kellman arrived; the ambulance came a few minutes later. Jean clung to Barbara as they watched Dan being wheeled out in a stretcher, a mask over his face, breathing from the portable oxygen unit.

"I'll take you with me to the hospital," Dr. Kellman said to Jean. "We won't know anything for certain until we've run some tests. I'd guess it's a coronary. I hope it's a mild one, but as I said, we won't know for sure until later."

"I can't leave Sam," Barbara said woefully. "I'll call

Eloise and ask her to come first thing in the morning. But you will call me from the hospital, please?"

"Of course." She hesitated. "Should I tell Tom? I just don't know—"

"That can wait."

"And you'd better call Joe."

"Yes," Barbara said. "I thought of that."

Jean and the doctor left, and Barbara closed the door behind them. She experienced a brief moment of panic—first her husband, now her father, as if some force were intent on divesting her of those she loved, of the men who, as the world informed her, were the wall of protection and security behind which a woman must always crouch. "Well," she reflected, drawing a deep breath, "I have never been one to crouch and my walls have a way of crumbling. As a matter of fact, I have even gotten out of the habit of weeping." She went to the telephone to call her brother Joe.

Joseph Lavette, now thirty-one, was Dan's son by May Ling. When Joseph was ten years old, May Ling, finding the situation of being Dan's mistress and living in a shadow of his life intolerable, moved to Los Angeles. Two years later, Jean and Dan were divorced, but another two years went by before Dan and May Ling were married. Dan did what he could do to be a father to his half-Chinese son. Joe Lavette completed college and medical school, was drafted into the army, did his internship and residency in the South Pacific during World War II, and soon after his discharge married Sally Levy, Adam's sister. They had lived in Los Angeles for the past two years, where Joe worked in a free clinic.

Joe answered the telephone, and Barbara told him what had happened.

"It's after eleven," he said. "If I can still get a plane, I'll be there tonight. What hospital did they take him to?"

"Mount Zion. It's at Post and Scott, not far from here."

"I know where it is. Can you put me up for the night, Bobby?"

"Of course."

"And if I can't get out tonight, I'll call the hospital and talk to Kellman. But I'll be there first thing tomorrow."

Setting down the telephone, Barbara asked herself, "Do I tell Bernie?" But that, she decided, would be pointless, just as she had decided that it was pointless to tell him about the subpoena from the House committee.

Barbara could not face the thought of going to bed; in any case, she was certain that she would not be able to sleep. She sat down with a book, but she was unable to concentrate, and after reading half a dozen pages without the faintest memory of what she had read, she put the book aside and switched on the radio. She twirled the dial until she picked up a news program, wondering whether there might not be something about Bernie and the planes. She listened to a congressman talk about America's need for an uninterrupted flow of atomic weapons and switched it off in disgust. Again and again she reached for the telephone and pulled back her hand. She must have dozed, for it was two-thirty when the telephone rang, its shrill jangle bursting into her sleep.

It was Joe. "I'm at the hospital, Bobby. Pop's not going to die. He'll pull through."

"Joe, are you sure?"

"Pretty damn sure. As much as one can be at this

point. He's still in intensive care and in an oxygen tent, but his vital signs are good. It was a fairly severe coronary infarction, and he'll have to be on his back for quite a while, but he's a hell of a strong man and he'll come out of it. Did I wake you?"

"I'm not in bed, Joe. I'll wait up for you."

"All right. I'll take Jean home first. She's not in good shape, and I'll give her something to calm her; then I'll come over to your place."

"Oh, thank you, Joe. And thanks for rushing up here."

"Not that I could contribute anything. Kellman's a good man, but I feel better now that I'm here."

She dozed off again. It was well after three when Joe rang her doorbell, and they sat in the kitchen, drinking coffee almost until dawn. Barbara told Joe about Bernie and then about the subpoena.

"It never rains but it pours. You poor kid."

"I don't look at it that way," Barbara said. "The marriage wasn't working, and it wasn't getting any better, only worse. It's bad enough to have a marriage go down the drain when you hate the man. But when you love him—and I do love him so much, Joe—well, then it's just awful. And about the subpoena, Harvey Baxter assures me I have absolutely nothing to worry about. Evidently someone on that Un-American Committee is literate enough to read and read my book about what happened to me in Europe, and Harvey says that they go out of their way to pull celebrities down there—not that I'm such a celebrity—and then they make a circus out of it. To tell you the truth, Joe, I'm rather excited about the whole prospect. I feel somewhat the way I felt when I went to Germany in nineteen thirty-nine, a little afraid, yet terribly curious to see the devil in his den."

"Does pop know about this?"

"He knows about Bernie, of course, but not about the subpoena. I don't want anyone to know, and you're the only one who does beside Harvey Baxter. I suppose that when I go to Washington it'll be spread all over the papers, but until then I just don't want to be bothered, and certainly daddy doesn't need this now."

With ten years of intermittent warfare behind him, Bernie Cohen was neither a pilot nor a navigator nor a radio operator. He rode as a passenger in one of the big C-54s as the ten planes took off, one after another, from the desert airfield. They flew into the morning sun, just lifting above the horizon. Bernie's plane was piloted by Jerry Fox, a small, red-headed, freckled young man who looked eighteen but was actually twenty-six, and who had been with the Tenth Air Force. The navigator, who also doubled as radio operator, was Al Shlemsky, a dark, morose man of thirty who had been born in the Williamsburg section of Brooklyn, who had gone to Palestine at the age of sixteen, and who, like Bernie, had enlisted in the British army. After the war, he had gone back to Palestine and joined the Irgun, the underground terrorist organization led by Menachem Begin. Captured by the British occupation forces, he had been held in the Jerusalem Central Prison for seven months. "I was there when they hanged Dov Gruner," he told Bernie, his dark eyes turned inward. "They hanged four of us—Gruner, Drezner, Alkochi, and Kashani. We just didn't believe it could happen. They were soldiers fighting for their homeland, and all our lives we had been fed that shit about the British being civilized. Then, when it happened, when they were taken out of their cells to be hanged, we heard them singing the Hatikvah. Someone yelled to us what was happening, and we began to sing, ninety of us singing the Hatikvah in that lousy jail. I remember that I was crying as I sang. A month later they released me, and I came back to the States to see my mother. She was dying. Funny, she was a nice, plain, little orthodox Jewish lady, and she could never understand what I was doing in Palestine. I could never explain it to her, either. Then I heard that the Haganah guys here were looking for pilots and navigators, and here I am."

Jerry Fox, the pilot, was something else. He was enjoying himself thoroughly. "I never flew one of these cookies before," he told Bernie, "but they're sweethearts. They handle a damn sight better than the 17-G, and there's nobody shooting at me. I did forty-two missions with the 17-G. I tell you, Cohen, this beats West Covina all to hell. You ever been to West Covina?"

Bernie shook his head.

"You are fortunate. Outside of L.A. My folks live there. Pop runs a hardware store. I get out of the service and I'm back in Pomona College, working weekends in the hardware store, getting laid now and then and going crazy. Absolutely going crazy. There is nothing I want to do except fly an airplane, but go find a job with ten thousand pilots scrambling for the few jobs there are. And then this comes along. I'd pay you to let me fly this crate. Funny thing is, I'm not all that Jewish. My father is, but my mother's Irish and I was raised as a Catholic—parochial school, the whole shtick. And here I am on my way to Palestine. If that doesn't beat the shit out of it, nothing does."

Sitting in the copilot's chair, the Rocky Mountains beneath him, the other planes spread out to the left and to the right, it occurred to Bernie that if anyone had told him a week ago that he would be here, he would have dismissed the whole notion as an incongruous dream.

Sally Lavette, Joe's wife, was, as he would have been the first to admit, a very unusual young woman. For one thing, she had decided at the age of thirteen that Joe would be her husband, come what may. He was then working summers at the Higate Winery. At thirteen, she was a skinny, freckled, tow-headed kid who bewailed her lack of breasts and stuffed a brassiere with absorbent cotton to simulate them. By the age of twenty, when she and Joe were married, Sally had become a tall, slender woman, blue-eyed, blond, with no need to simulate anything. At fourteen, she wooed Joe with sonnets copied word for word from Elizabeth Barrett Browning and blithely signed Sally Levy; at twenty, she published her own first book of poems, which was critically acclaimed and earned her all of eighty-six dollars. She was bright, ebullient, caustic, impetuous, and romantic. She informed her husband, once they were married, that she intended to bear him ten children. After the first was born, she reduced the anticipated number to three.

Sally had many dreams, and one of them was to live in San Francisco in a house like Barbara's and preferably within walking distance of Barbara, whom she idolized. She decided that Joe should set up practice in such a house. It was precisely the place and life for a physician that fitted in with her plans. Joe thought otherwise, and this led to their first fight, wildly emotional on her part, stolid on his, and followed by a tearful reconciliation. Joe had his own plans, which he had worked out during the long, wretched years in the

South Pacific. He wanted to operate a clinic in East Los Angeles, an area known as the barrio and inhabited for the most part by poor Mexican Americans, or Chicanos, as they called themselves in Southern California. He would have no part of Russian Hill or a lucrative San Francisco practice. He had no good memories of San Francisco, and he remembered all too vividly the stories Feng Wo, his grandfather, had told him of the virulent anti-Chinese hatred that once infested the city. He had grown up in Los Angeles, and he had an affection for the city that was beyond Sally's understanding.

Joe applied to the Lavette Foundation for a grant, and with it he acquired an old, one-story, brick warehouse on Boyle Avenue in Boyle Heights. He then went into partnership with Frank Gonzales, whom he had known from medical school and who had been with him in the army. They remodeled the old warehouse into a neighborhood clinic, with examining rooms, an X-ray room, a room for minor operations, and a few emergency beds. They charged a very nominal fee, for those who could afford it, and nothing at all for those who couldn't. For Gonzales, a small, dark, serious Chicano, the clinic was the fulfillment of all his dreams, and he looked upon Joe Lavette as one of the Apostles might have looked upon his Master. Sally, who felt that her husband fell somewhat short of sainthood, adapted to the situation and accepted it. Until the baby came, she worked part time at the receiving desk of the clinic. They had purchased a tiny house near Silver Lake, a place in East Los Angeles that was no lake at all but a large, concrete-lined basin filled with water, surrounded by a chain-link fence and rows of dismal, dreary houses. It was the sort of place from which Sally was repelled at first sight and which did not grow on her. Joe felt that they had to live in East Los Angeles, and accepting that decision, Silver Lake was as good a place as any. Sally, having spent most of her life in the Napa Valley, found Silver Lake loathsome, even more so than the barrio where the clinic was.

Sally still covered the receiving desk two days a week; she would take the baby with her and keep her in a carriage beside her desk. She was a casual, unworried mother, and May Ling was a relaxed and easy child. The morning after Joe went to San Francisco to be with his father, Sally put May Ling and her folding carriage into the car and drove down to the clinic. She had written most of her poetry sitting there at the receiving desk. The place fascinated, repelled, and irritated her; but Sally always converted herself into a third person, and the image of herself, still unrecognized as the foremost poet in the country, sitting at the receiving desk in a clinic in Boyle Heights, made a satisfying dramatic entity. She did not know Joe's father too well, but she liked him, and the thought that he might be dying sobered her and depressed her as much as she was ever depressed. She was relieved to hear from Gonzales that Dan would pull through.

"Joe called me," he explained.

"Why didn't he call me?"

"It was the middle of the night. He wanted me to be here early and cover for him. You know how Joe is. He wouldn't call you in the middle of the night."

"I know how Joe is."

"Look, Sally," Gonzales said, "the kid's asleep. I'll put her in the X-ray room. Very quiet. No one bothers her there."

"No, I don't want her in there with all that radiation."

"Sally, when no one's using the X-ray, there's no radiation. It doesn't linger."

"So you say."

Gonzales sighed and gave up. A few hours later, Sally took May Ling into Joe's office to nurse her. When the child was born, her doctor had suggested bottle feeding, which was very much in vogue. But Sally rejected the idea; she felt she had adequate breasts for the first time, and she was going to do nothing to lessen their size. Having finally achieved size 32A, she could relinquish the notion that she was dismally flat-chested.

There was always a rush at the clinic beginning at about nine o'clock and tapering off toward noon, when Sally would be relieved by one of the two nurses, Jessica Tamal or Roberta Syznick. Then she fed May Ling. Today, sitting in Joe's office with the baby at her breast, she heard someone knock at the door.

"Who is it?" she demanded.

"Is that you, Sally? They said I'd find you here. This is Billy Clawson. Can I come in?"

"Billy Clawson? I don't believe it. Sure, come on in."

He came into the room, closing the door behind him, and then stopped short and stared. He started toward the door again. "Maybe I'll come back."

"For heaven's sake, Billy," Sally said impatiently, "haven't you ever seen a baby nursed before? Or is it verboten to clerics? Oh, don't be silly about it. Your sister's married to my brother, so we're practically related. Come in and sit down. I'll be through in a moment or two."

He had to make an effort to tear his eyes away, and then he sat down and pointedly looked across the

room, putting her out of his line of sight. Sally had
never seen him dressed like this before: heavy brown
turtleneck sweater, denim trousers, and old shoes. She
had always considered him somewhat laughable, an
amiable, inoffensive caricature of a man, without hostility and without ambition; now it occurred to her
that she had never actually looked at him before, or if
she had looked at him, she had not seen him. He had
a long head and a shock of unruly brown hair; not
very handsome, she thought, but rather nicelooking,
with dark, lonesome eyes. That was her label—
lonesome eyes—and the notion pleased her. Words, especially adjectives, always fascinated Sally.

Billy Clawson was glancing at her furtively, guiltily.
She looked down at her breast, which May Ling was
finally relinquishing, sucking mechanically and without enthusiasm, her pink face relaxed, her eyes closed,
and she decided that it was well worth a furtive
glance or two, a lovely, well-rounded breast. She covered it now and put May Ling into her carriage.
"After all," she said to Billy, "I never had what you
might call a proper breast until I was almost seventeen, and why on earth women cover up the best part
of them, I'll never know." She hooked her brassiere
together and began to button her blouse. "Of course,
it's something the men worked out. What an unbelievable set of pious, hypocritical bastards you all are!"

"Do you always say such outrageous things?"

"My dear Billy, we've never really talked before.
I'm being absolutely demure. Now what on earth
brings you down here? This is the last place in the
world I'd expect to see you, here in Boyle Heights in
Los Angeles. This is the barrio, Billy, the pits, the soft
underbelly. Do you know, we treat more knife
wounds than any other outpatient clinic in the city?"

"I came down to see Joe, and now I find that he's not here but up in San Francisco. I heard his father had a heart attack. I'm frightfully sorry about that. I only met Mr. Lavette once or twice, but he appeared to be a very interesting man. Very vital. You don't think of such people as being stricken." Sally was smiling. Billy shook his head, confused.

"I'm sorry," Sally said. "It's the way you talk—forgive me. I'm not really lacking in compassion, Billy. I like Dan Lavette, and Joe says he's going to be all right. Have you had lunch?"

More confused than ever, Billy shook his head again.

"Because I have an enormous sandwich here," Sally said, unwrapping it. "Ham and cheese on rye. Please have half of it. I also have a thermos of coffee. I can't bear the coffee they make here, so I bring my own. Please. It's more than I can eat."

It was his first more than casual encounter with Sally Lavette, and he was ill-prepared for it. He accepted half of the sandwich because he could think of no way to refuse.

"Could I help you?" Sally asked. "I mean, if you made the trip to see Joe? I'm sure he'll be back tonight."

"Well, I don't know," Billy said uneasily. "Or perhaps I should talk to you and not lay my burdens on Joe. I just had the notion that I might be of some use here, that there might be something here that I could do that would justify my going on from day to day. Does that sound crazy to you? I'm an Episcopal priest who actually can't bear to set foot inside a church. Now I've never said that before, not aloud."

"And you see," Sally said gently, "God has not struck you dead."

"Sometimes I wish He would. Trouble is, I don't believe in Him very much. I don't belive in anything. I never wanted it, but mother insisted that it was a way to avoid the draft. I ended up as an army chaplain in the Pacific—two long, bloody nightmarish years from Guadalcanal to the end. And since my discharge I've done nothing. Absolutely nothing. I just drift from day to day."

Sally stared at him in amazement. This was not the man she had met half a dozen times, not the man they gossiped about, not the man she had heard Joe refer to with total contempt. "What is wrong with me?" she asked herself. "Why do I see people without ever seeing them or knowing who they are? I'm not a poet. I'm an indifferent and blind fool."

"You see?" he asked uncertainly. "I admire Joe so much, and I think what he's doing is wonderful. It means something. Nothing I do means anything. My father wants me to go into the business with him. I can't tell him why it's meaningless to me. Mother wants me to get a post in a church. She has dreams of Grace Cathedral. I'd be a stevedore on the docks before I'd let them trap me into a place like Grace Cathedral."

"Then why aren't you?" Sally asked him.

"Why aren't I what?"

"A stevedore on the docks?"

"God knows. I suppose I haven't got the guts, and I'd be taking the job from someone who needs it. I thought there might be work I could do here, in a place like this. I don't need the money. I have enough money."

"Do you know what kind of nasty, filthy work it is?" Sally asked.

"Not really, no."

"I mean, what could you do, Billy? You haven't any training."

"I had two years in the Pacific, Sally. Do you think anyone in those hellish islands wanted an Episcopal priest? They wanted a medic, and that's how I spent most of my time, as a volunteer medic. I don't know much of anything, but I do know how to deal with a man whose body has been mangled. It's the only worthwhile training I've had. And here no one knows me. I hate to say that's important to me, but it is."

He waited while Sally stared at him.

"Aren't you going to say anything?"

"I'll talk to Dr. Gonzales. He's Joe's partner."

"Do you want me to talk to him?" Billy asked.

"No. Can you come back later, Billy? Or better yet, call us at home tonight. I'll give you the number. I'd ask you to stay with us, but the house is tiny."

"Oh, no, no. That's not necessary. I'll find a hotel. I'll call you tonight. Absolutely."

After he left, Sally told Frank Gonzales about him.

"Come on," Gonzales said. "You got to be kidding. An Episcopal priest? Anyway, what the devil is an Episcopal priest? Like a Catholic priest? I thought they had ministers."

"I guess it's sort of the same thing as a minister. They can get married and all that. But Frank, this poor guy is at the end of his rope."

"I met him. Come on, Sally, what can he do for us?"

"There's more work here than we can handle. Maybe he can get me off the receiving desk so I'll have time to be a mother and a writer. You know what happens when we have a heavy day. He says he worked with the medics. He must know something."

Gonzales shook his head. "He is just not it. This is the barrio. He'll stay a day, and he'll go."

"He also comes from one of the richest families in Oakland, and you and Joe are running the most poverty-stricken clinic in California."

"Come on, come on. We function. We pay wages. Still, and all, you say he is loaded?"

"His father. I don't know what he's got."

"Sally, you know what we could do with another ten, twenty thousand? O.K., I talk to Joe about it."

"And maybe you're just saving his soul."

"That's another line of work." He paused and looked at Sally. "You're a good kid. Only you push it."

"What does that mean?"

"Think about it."

When Barbara got to the hospital, shortly after nine the following morning, Jean was already in the waiting room. She told Barbara that Dan was sleeping.

"How is he?"

"Better, they tell me. Who is with the baby?"

"Eloise. Was Joe here this morning?"

"Yes. He's on his way back to Los Angeles."

"When can I see him?"

"As soon as he wakes up, I guess." Jean was making an effort to keep her voice light and controlled. "I think he's going to be all right. I've had a bad time, Bobby. I want you to understand."

"I do."

"Yes. Perhaps more than I do, because all I could think about last night is that if he should die, that's the end for me. That's selfish, but then, I've always been selfish, haven't I?"

"Mother, I'm not going to feed self-pity. If a person dies, the living feel it, not the dead. I think you love daddy very much, more than you ever dared admit to yourself, so it's perfectly natural for you to feel that if he died, it would be the end of everything for you. Only it would not be the end of everything."

"You're so damn sure of yourself!" Jean burst out unexpectedly, in a tone she had never taken with Barbara before. "Did it ever occur to you that my life has been no bed of roses, that I've messed it up as much as one human being can mess things up?"

"It has occurred to me, yes."

"One small measure of happiness, having that man back for the last few years. After thirty years of misery. It went wrong from the very beginning, and neither of us knew why or how."

She went on. Real or not, the agony poured out. It was a side of her mother Barbara had never seen before, nor was she ready to believe it entirely. For three decades, Jean Lavette had been, in her circle, the most beautiful woman in San Francisco, again by accolade of her small, tight circle; and she had moved and lived in that circle with relish and pleasure. Or had it been a pose and a game? In all the years Barbara could remember her mother, she had never before witnessed this descent into self-pity. The cool, austere, aloof Jean Lavette was beyond such things— or was she? Now she paraded her unhappiness before her daughter, a thousand nights of unspeakable loneliness, meaningless relationships, joyless gaity. Barbara was cold inside. Suddenly, she wanted to be away from there. Somewhere in the world, there was reality. Jean's plaint disgusted her, which in turn filled her with guilt and remorse. She was grateful when a nurse appeared and told them they could see Mr. Lavette.

Jean changed as they entered Dan's room. Barbara was absolutely astounded at how a whining, petulant, aging woman could suddenly become erect and self-confident and young and attractive. She gave a silent cheer. Jean was amazing. Blessings on her, as she kissed Dan coolly and said, "You never do things by halves, do you, Danny boy? You had me quite terrified."

"That makes two of us," he said weakly. "Hello, Bobby. How does the old man look to you?"

"Not bad, daddy, not at all bad. How do your feel?"

"According to Joe, it was a mild attack. The worst part is that they'll have me in bed here for weeks. But I'll manage."

A few minutes later, Jean excused herself and left the room. "Where is she going?" Dan asked Barbara.

"I think she went outside to cry. I've never seen mother cry. I don't think anyone ever did until last night. It's a pleasure she never permitted herself. I'm going to cry any moment now, but it's never been a problem with me. She's terribly upset. She's very much in love with you. Did you know that? Or is that a dumb question?"

"It's not a dumb question. I've never really been sure. You know, Bobby, when May Ling died, I thought death had lost all meaning for me. I didn't care. Then when I met your mother, after all those years, I began to care again. We've led strange lives, the two of us. Last night I thought I was going to die. I didn't want to. Life was very sweet."

The flight across the country went more smoothly than Bernie had dared to expect. The March weather, so given to unanticipated storms, was as mild as a day in June. The planes stayed within sight of each other in a reasonably well kept wide pattern. They answered queries along the way and met with no interference.

They landed in Dodge City, Kansas, to refuel.

Debts were being collected everywhere. Over thirty years before, a Jew named Glazer and an Irishman named Sweeney had smuggled four crates of rifles and ammunition into Dublin. Now Sweeney's son, reasonably successful in the oil business and bearing a residual hatred of the British as well as an unpaid obligation to his father's partner, had supplied four tanker trucks of aviation fuel at a quiet commercial airport sixteen miles from Dodge City.

Joe Sweeney, a big, slack-bellied man in his fifties, had a bottle of fine old Irish in his car, and he and Bernie each put down a paper cupful. "What I would give to go with you," Sweeney said. "It's purpose you got, sonny, and I got no fuckin' purpose but to get drunk twice a week and pretend I'm a man."

Bernie saw him standing there, waving with both arms, as the planes took off. The flight continued without incident, and late that afternoon they circled the airfield in New Jersey and received their landing instructions.

Bernie's plane came in first, and Jerry Fox brought it in for one of those landings where it is almost impossible to say that you are no longer airborne. "Sonofabitch!" the pilot crowed. "What a beauty, what a daisy!" As they came down, Bernie noticed a cluster of men at the far end of the field, and two of the men came running to meet the plane while it was still in motion.

The airfield, lying in the sandy pine barrens of southern New Jersey, was neither large nor well equipped. It had two X-shaped runways, three hangars, and a wooden control tower. Half a dozen small planes were parked near the hangars. Fox took the whole length of the runway for his landing, then wheeled the plane off onto a parking sheet of asphalt.

The two men were running clumsily but hard to inter-
cept it. Bernie saw another group of men leave the
hangar and start toward the plane. The second C-54
had landed and the third was coming in.

Bernie's plane was still rolling.

"Leave enough room for the others," Bernie shouted
to Fox. Then he ran back through the plane and
opened the door.

The first of the two men was shouting at him, but
he couldn't make out the words against the roar of the
motors. The plane came to a stop, and Bernie dropped
to the ground.

The running man, panting, middle-aged, bald, trying
to get his breath, gasped, "Where's Brodsky?"

Bernie pointed to the planes coming in.

"Who are you?"

"Cohen. I'm running the show, for the moment."

"Bernie Cohen?"

"Right."

The second man joined them. He was small, dark,
dapper, breathless. "I'm Jack Feinstein," said the bald
man, handing Bernie a dollar bill. "Take this. No time
for questions. Trust me."

Bernie took the dollar bill.

"Trust me. No time for questions," Feinstein
gasped. He took a sheaf of folded papers out of his
breast pocket and handed a pen to Bernie. "Sign right
here. Trust me."

The papers fluttered and rustled in the wind raised
by the landing planes. "What in hell am I signing?"
Bernie demanded. "And who are you?"

"Feinstein. Lawyer for the Haganah. Look." He
pointed to the four men walking toward them. "FBI
and Customs. You got to sign before they get here. It's
a bill of sale. For a dollar and other valuable consider-

ations, you are selling these ten planes to Señor Luis Montego. Lineas Aereas de Panama. For Christ's sake, don't stand there! Believe me."

Brodsky was running across to them now. The four men were fifty yards away, walking quickly. "That's Feinstein!" Brodsky yelled. "He's O.K.!"

"Sign it, señor, sign it," Montego begged him.

Bernie took the pen and signed.

"Initial here and here," Feinstein said.

Bernie scribbled his initials. Feinstein handed the papers to Montego as the four men reached them. The last of the ten planes touched down. Brodsky, Jerry Fox, and Herb Goodman joined the group.

The four men, all in dark business suits and unsmiling, faced the growing group of pilots, navigators, and radio operators. One of them displayed a badge. "Fenton, United States Customs. I have an order here to impound these planes. That means they are not to be entered or moved and nothing is to be removed from them."

"Let's see your writ," Feinstein said, still trying to catch his breath.

"Who are you?"

"Feinstein. Attorney."

"Attorney for who?"

"Señor Luis Montego of Panama Airlines."

"I don't know how he comes into this," the Customs man said, taking a paper out of his pocket. "Here's the order. President Truman's proclamation two seven seven six. That puts commercial planes under the Munitions Control Board."

"Only," said Feinstein, "when such planes are taken out of the country for implied military purposes."

Another of the four men showed his badge. "Bently, Federal Bureau of Investigation. According to our information, these planes were purchased yesterday from one Cary Kennedy in Barstow, California, by one Bernie Cohen, to be removed from the United States."

"So much for Kennedy and the word of God," Bernie whispered to Brodsky.

"The sonofabitch!"

"If that is the case," Feinstein said, "the planes are here. You have no right to impound the private property of a United States citizen."

"Don't be cute, Feinstein."

"I'll be cuter. The planes don't belong to Cohen. They are the property of my client, Señor Montego of Panama Airlines. In other words, they belong to a foreign commercial airline, and any attempt to impound them will cause no end of trouble, gentlemen. Señor Montego has with him all the permits and export licenses required by law. Will you show them the bill of sale, Señor Montego?"

Smiling, Montego handed Bently the bill of sale Bernie had just signed. Bently glanced at it, handed it to his associates, and said sourly, "It won't wash, Feinstein. We know damn well what those planes are intended for, and it just won't wash."

Brodsky nudged Bernie. Two men had appeared and were slapping decals on the tail assembly of the planes. The decals read: LINEAS AEREAS DE PANAMA.

"Stop that right there!" the Customs man yelled. Then he said to the FBI men, "Will you take some action? This is a scam. It's a cheap, underhanded scam."

"You know the law," Feinstein said. "You need a court order to void Mr. Montego's export license. When you find a federal judge and get an injunction against the shipment of these planes to Panama and show us that injunction, we will comply with it. Until then, we will resist by every means at our disposal any attempt to prevent the departure of these planes."

"Are you going to let them pull this off?" Fenton demanded of Bently.

"Let's get to a telephone, and we'll see."

When they had gone, Brodsky introduced Bernie to Feinstein. The circle of pilots and navigators were grinning with pleasure. A man called Condon joined them, a thin, worried man who was the field manager. "I got a hell of a lot of sympathy for you," he said, "but this means trouble."

"Being alive means trouble."

"That may be. The point is, can you get fueled and take off before dark? They'll get that court order, believe me."

"I think so. We'll try."

Feinstein led Bernie and Brodsky and Montego across the field to where his car was parked. He explained that Montego had a Jewish grandmother. "Half the world is Jewish, if you look hard enough. By the way, Luis here will fly with you to Panama. He has a crew waiting there to tear out the seats and convert the planes to cargo carriers." At his car, he unlocked the trunk and took out two leather suitcases. "Two million dollars," he said. "Cold cash. Ten Messerschmitts and all the munitions the rest of it will buy. Use it wisely, kids."

"You mean you left it like that," Bernie said, "sitting there in the car?"

"What did you expect, an armored car? The trunk was locked."

Bernie and Brodsky each took a suitcase. "The closest we'll ever get to being millionaires," Brodsky said.

Three hours later, the sun sinking behind the pines,

the planes took off. The Customs men and the FBI had not returned.

Sarah Levy came to visit Dan at the hospital. She brought a jar of nuts, a box of homemade cookies, and a bunch of yellow roses. "Although," she said, looking around the room, "flowers are the last thing you need. You have enough already to start a flower shop."

"I know. A man never knows his rating in flowers until he's dead."

"And you're not dead, Danny. I don't like to see you lying there feeling sorry for yourself. You're a lucky man."

He didn't deny it, aware that she was thinking that it was almost twenty years since her husband, Mark, Dan's partner and best friend, had died of a massive coronary occlusion. That was how it was written for him and his kind; you clawed and scrambled and grabbed and went to bed each night counting another marker of money and power, and then it washed out in the same senseless ending—and for Sarah, the apparently endless years of loneliness and waiting. For what? What did she wait for so patiently? What would Jean wait for? He wondered how old Sarah was now. Seventy? Certainly close to seventy. She was a thin wraith of a woman, her hair white, her face wrinkled, the skin, once so white and pink, having long ago given up the struggle. He could remember clearly the young woman Mark had married, her long yellow hair braided and piled in a crown on her head. Half a century had passed since then. Dan had been only ten years old at the time of Mark's marriage. Mark had been twenty. Dan's father had taken him into the chandler shop on Fisherman's Wharf that was owned and operated by Mark's father, old Moe Levy, who had come across the country with a peddler's wagon, trading grimcracks with the Indians. Sarah had just arrived, nineteen years old, an immigrant girl from Lithuania, alone, without family, tagged and shipped across the breadth of the country to marry a man she had never seen. Frightened, thousands of miles from a home she would never see again, surrounded by the babble of a strange and incomprehensible tongue, she was like a beautiful, terror-stricken young animal.

"You're a lucky man, Danny," she said again.

"I suppose so."

"Just give up the cigars and stop drinking and you have another twenty years."

She spoke in expected clichés. Did she think that way? he wondered. Had she given up all the questions to which there were no answers? How desperately he wanted a cigar! A long, cool, sweet-smelling Cuban cigar.

"Joe was here?" she asked him.

"Came up the night it happened."

"He's a good boy, such a good boy. Do you know how happy Mark would have been, your son married to his granddaughter? On the other hand, my Sally is a very strange girl. She would try the patience of a saint."

"They'll get along."

"I hope so. Jean has been here?"

"She's always here. I chased her out." He knew that Sarah could not reconcile herself to Jean, could not accept that they had come together after May Ling's death. Dan realized that he wanted Sarah to go, to leave him be, and the realization filled him with guilt. What happened to people? He had once adored Sarah. A thousand years ago.

"You're tired," she said.

"I guess so."

"Then I let you rest, Danny. Don't worry about anything. Only get well."

The telephone rang, and Barbara, waiting eagerly, anxiously, grabbed it. The operator wanted to know whether she would accept a collect call from a Bernie Cohen in Panama.

"Yes, yes, of course."

His voice came through, apologizing. "It's just that there was no other way I could call you from here, Bobby."

"I know. Never mind, Bernie. Oh, I'm so glad to hear from you. Are you all right?"

"Just fine. What about you and Sammy?"

"Strong and healthy and lonely."

"Don't be lonely. A few more days and it's done. Say, two weeks at the most before I get out of Palestine."

"Bernie, what are you doing in Panama?"

"I'm at Tocumen Airport here. It's our route, honey. It was all planned and laid out by the guys in New York. We got out of New Jersey two jumps ahead of the sheriff—well, not exactly the sheriff. The FBI and Customs. We're refueling here, and then we fly to the Azores, and then from the Azores to Czechoslovakia, where we pick up our cargo and take it to Palestine."

"Bernie—" She hesitated. "Bernie, do you have to go all the way? Can't it go on without you?"

"I can't drop out now. Look, Bobby, I called because I was afraid you'd get the news on the radio and begin to worry."

"What news?"

"We lost a plane. It went down over the ocean. Three good guys—Jesse Levine, Bob Sanders, and Al

Green. If I stepped out of it now, it would throw them all into a panic. There's just no way I could do it."

"But you said the planes were good?"

"They are good. This one developed engine trouble and came down. It happens."

"And it could happen again."

"It won't happen again."

"But three men are dead."

"We don't know. They may have been picked up. We radioed their position, so there's still hope." Then she was silent until he asked, "Are you still there, Bobby?"

"I'm just so damn miserable. I've never said that before. I just feel you're stretching this beyond luck."

"Bobby, I'll be all right."

Barbara put down the telephone and sat and stared at it. An hour later, when the doorbell rang, she had still not severed the connection between herself and the black instrument she faced. Jean was at the door.

"How is he?"

"Much better, I think," her mother said. "What were you doing?"

"Staring at the telephone. Bernie called."

"Where is he?"

"In Panama." She told her mother what had happened.

"I'd like a drink," Jean said.

"Have you eaten?"

"Sort of. I'm not hungry. Do you have any brandy?"

Barbara watched her mother sip the brandy. "About men," Jean said. "They come in two sizes, you know."

"I didn't know."

"It's time you did. It has to do with games, which is

what differentiates them from animals. Animals don't
play games."

"Puppies?"

"Not really. Consider the lion. The lioness does the
hunting, finds the food, delivers the children, and
raises them. The lion does nothing. Struts and forni-
cates. Nothing else."

"I really don't care to discuss lions," Barbara said.
"My world is very crumbly. Last week I was married
to a sober, worried businessman who ran a garage
that didn't make any money. Now my father is in the
hospital with a heart attack; my husband is in Panama
with nine old airplanes—what do you mean, men come
in two sizes?"

"Not that it matters." Jean sighed and refilled her
glass.

"You're entitled to get drunk," Barbara said. "It's all
right. You can spend the night here."

"Have you ever seen me drunk? And on brandy?
No."

"It matters. I can't stand people who are enigmatic.
Anyway, it's time we had a good talk."

"About men?"

"Yes, by all means."

"They play games. That's a childhood preoccupa-
tion. There are essentially only two kinds of men.
They all begin the same. They play games, and one
kind continues with the games and the other kind
stops. But neither kind ever reaches adulthood. I can
lay claim to being a modest authority, since I married
both kinds. John Whittier was the kind who stops. It
just died inside of him. Men like Dan and Bernie, they
go on with the games. You're like me, which is why
you made the same kind of idiotic marriage."

"Thank you, mother."

"I'm not being nasty," Jean said. "I fell in love with Dan Lavette forty years ago. If he dies, I'll be an empty, worthless old bag. But I don't deceive myself. Anyway, I'm talking a lot of nonsense, am I not?"

"Yes and no."

"Oh, I do wish you wouldn't be so damn righteous and superior. Try being a little girl for ten minutes. Tell me that you love me and that I exist!"

"I do love you, and I'd look silly trying to be a little girl, even for ten minutes. I'm a woman of thirty-four years who has a lot of problems. A week from now, I have to go to Washington and testify before the House Committee on Un-American Activities."

Jean put down the glass of brandy and stared at her. "I don't understand. What on earth are you talking about?" Then she added, "That's impossible. It's ridiculous and impossible. You're a Seldon."

Barbara burst out laughing. "Mother, I love you, I do, truly. I am still a Seldon. My name was Barbara Lavette, and then it became Barbara Cohen, but I am a Seldon. It's so simple. But it isn't."

"Will you please tell me what happened?"

Barbara told her about the subpoena and her meeting with Harvey Baxter. "But this is my thing, mother, not yours and not daddy's. I don't want him to know. In fact, I don't want anyone else to know about this yet, and I think with daddy in the hospital, you'll agree he shouldn't know."

"I still don't understand. Is this because of Bernie and what he's doing?"

"No, it's because of me. I am not a simple housewife who writes books between feedings. Things have happened to me."

"They certainly have. What will you do about Sam?"

"It's only for a few days."

"I'll take him, of course."

"No, you'll be with daddy. I'll take him up to Higate and leave him with Eloise and Adam for a few days. They'll be delighted."

"I won't hear of it!"

"Do you know," Barbara said, "you are an amazing woman, mother. I do patronize you, and that's sheer stupidity on my part. But it's not basic. Basically, I think you're quite remarkable, and I do love you."

To fly at night, Bernie decided, was to move out of man's ordinary reality into another world. Time and space collapsed, and the roar of the four motors obscured all other sounds of life; yet beyond the motors they were ringed by silence, and the sound and the silence coexisted. He must have dozed off, for Jerry Fox was shaking him. "I've got it on automatic, Bernie. Sit at the controls for a while." He pointed out the dials to watch. "Shlemsky's right here next to you, so there's nothing to worry about." Fox relaxed and was asleep almost immediately. Bernie rubbed his eyes and watched the maze of dials. Shlemsky sang softly, "Twilight soon will fade, nobody's left at the masquerade . . ." Ahead of them, the rim of the sea lightened and the first hint of a corona of light appeared. A while later, Bernie could make out the shape of the other planes, stretched across the sky in irregular formation.

"Counting them?" Shlemsky asked.

"We're all here."

"Not all. Only nine."

"Only nine," Bernie agreed.

"Better wake Fox."

The first glowing edge of the sun lifted above the

water as he shook Fox awake. An hour later, one after another, the planes touched down on the great flat expanse of the airport in the Azores.

Phil Kramer, a New York accountant, a round-faced bald man who wore gold-rimmed glasses and who carried two pens and a pencil in his breast pocket, was waiting for them. He was a fussy little man, very neat, very organized, and he kept jotting things down in a little notebook. He shook hands with Bernie and Brodsky, jotted down Bernie's name and address for future reference, and asked about the money.

"Safe in the planes."

"You know, it's not small change. Two million dollars is not small change. It took a lot of crying to come up with two million dollars."

"The money's safe," Brodsky assured him.

"I see only nine planes."

"Haven't you heard? We lost one on our way down to Panama."

"Terrible. That's terrible. What about the crew?"

"We don't know."

"I'll try to find out. I've been here for three days, that's why I haven't heard. Now I've made all arrangements for refueling. Do your men need sleep? I can arrange for something overnight."

"We've been sleeping in shifts. I think it's best that we take off as soon as we're fueled. I don't know how far the hand of the FBI reaches, but this was sort of an American field all through the war, wasn't it?" Bernie could not shake off his uneasiness.

"It's Portuguese now. Don't worry about that. I've spread a little vigorish here and there," Kramer told him. "The fuel is paid for, and I've made arrangements with the restaurant for the food. Just let your boys fill up with whatever they want. Now, does anyone in your gang talk Czech?"

"I doubt it," Brodsky said. "But our French is good; Bernie's is better than mine, but I get along with it. They've got to speak French."

"Probably. The point is, you have to bargain with them. They'll take your blood if you let them." He reached into his pocket and took out a small thirty-eight-caliber revolver, which he handled gingerly and uncomfortably.

"What's that?" Bernie asked.

"You don't have any weapons, do you?"

They shook their heads.

"With two million in cash, we thought you ought to have a weapon."

"That was very thoughtful of you," Bernie agreed, grinning. "Very thoughtful indeed." He put the revolver in his jacket pocket. "But I don't think there's anything to worry about. One suitcase is with me and the other's with Brodsky. There's nowhere to go in an airplane."

When they took off, four hours later, Bernie saw Kramer standing in front of the airport building, jotting entries in his little notebook.

"But you know," Shlemsky said, "he was right, Bernie. When you think of guys sticking up gas stations for fifty bucks, you got to admit that a million is very enticing. We got a lot of wild guys on this flight."

"Like killing someone," Bernie said. "You have to do it on the spur of the moment or think about it a long time. The same with this money. No one came into this to steal a million or two, and we're moving too quickly for anyone to figure out how to do it."

It was dusk as they crossed over into Czech airspace and received instructions to put down at a military airfield near Pilsen. The runway was lit as they landed, and a man in uniform, standing in a jeep and shouting at them in French, signaled for the planes to follow his car to a parking area. The sight of a hundred or so soldiers around the parking area made Bernie nervous. Brodsky had assured him that there would be Haganah men waiting when they put down in Czechoslovakia, but when he finally dropped out of the plane, spotlights blinding him, he felt a knot of fear in his stomach. He had heard every story conceivable about what went on or could go on behind the so-called Iron Curtain, and now it occurred to him how simple it would be for them to impound the planes and the money. He tightened his grip on the suitcase. Brodsky was shouting to him. Soldiers with submachine guns pressed toward him, and the pilots, navigators, and radiomen were gathering in a cluster around him, blinking, shading their eyes from the lights, very nervous now that they were in the land of the enemy—or what might be the enemy. Then Brodsky reached him, clinging, like Bernie, to a suitcase containing a million dollars. Behind him were two stocky men in leather jackets.

"What the devil is it?" Bernie demanded.

"It's all right."

Two uniformed Czechoslovak officers joined the group.

"They're in the middle of a revolution of some kind," Brodsky whispered to Bernie. "I don't know exactly what's going on, but they're suspicious as hell."

One of the Czech officers was saying in French, "We shall have to search the planes."

"Go ahead," Bernie told them. "They're empty."

"We shall see." They shouted a string of commands, and some of the soldiers took off toward the parked

planes. Meanwhile, one of the two men in leather
jackets said to Bernie, "That's the money, in the port-
manteaus?" He had a heavy accent. Brodsky introduced him as Dov Benash. The other was Zvi Kober.
"They're Haganah men," Brodsky explained.

"We meet you here, yes," Benash said. "We take the
money."

"We'll hold on to the money for the time being,"
Bernie said.

Kober's English was better, his accent British. "Will
you tell this bloke who we are, Brodsky?"

"His name's Cohen, Bernie Cohen," Brodsky told
Kober. "He's running the operation, not me. I think
he's right. We'll hold the money until we see the
goods."

"You know us. Don't you trust us?"

"I wouldn't trust my own mother with two million
dollars. Don't worry. We intend to stay close. Everyone stay close!" he shouted to the pilots.

Evidently the Czech officers did not understand
English. They were listening and watching. Bernie
identified himself. "I understand this was all prear-
ranged," he said to them, speaking French. "You were
expecting us."

The Czech officer nodded coldly.

"My men are hungry and tired. They need food and
they need a place to sleep. This is Irving Brodsky. My
name is Bernie Cohen. We're also cold and hungry and
tired. Isn't there a place where we can sit down and
talk?"

Kober said to him in French, "Get off your high
horse, Cohen." Then he said to the officer, "Can we
go to the lounge, colonel? You're not the only one who's
suspicious. He's suspicious too. But we've got the
money and we're ready to do business. And if you can

find some food for these boys, we'd appreciate it."
Then he asked in English, "Got any money, Cohen?
American?"

"How much?"

"Twenty'll be enough."

Bernie took out his wallet and handed Kober a
twenty-dollar bill. The Czech officer was watching
intently, as was his companion. "They come cheap,"
Brodsky whispered. Kober palmed the bill and then
shook hands with the Czech. It was utterly transpar-
ent, and the men from the flight, watching, began to
grin.

"Let's get to the lounge," Kober said. "Look, Cohen,
you got to trust Dov and me. We're all you got here."
He dropped his voice. "Never mind those two clowns.
They're nothing." He led the group of men across the
field. "I don't know you either. There were supposed
to be ten planes. You only have nine out there."

"We lost one at sea."

"Rotten luck."

They walked the whole length of the field. The
lounge, as they called it, reminded Bernie of a cheap
highway lunchroom. Beyond it loomed the hulks of
factory buildings.

"Skoda Works," Kober explained. "This is a very
tense moment. I think the communists have taken
over. Either that or it's in process. Benes' position is
very shaky, and no one wants to go out on a limb. I'm
not even sure whether our deal is on or off because,
the money aside, this is one cold nest of anti-Semitic
bastards."

"Nobody hates two million dollars."

"Cohen, they got the two million. We're here, and
that money is sitting right here in Pilsen. They have
us by the short hair, and don't you forget that."

A file of soldiers had accompanied them to the lounge and remained outside. Except for themselves, the room was empty. The pilots began to badger Bernie.

"Cohen, we're starved."

"What's with those goons outside?"

"Do we eat or don't we?"

"Where do we stay?"

"What gives, are we under arrest?"

"I guess twenty's not enough," Kober said.

Bernie took out forty dollars, which Kober gave to Benash, who left the lounge. A half-hour later, he returned with two soldiers, who carried a case of bottled beer and a basket filled with bread and sausage.

Bernie, Brodsky, and Goodman sat at one of the tables with the two Haganah men. The sausage was hard, the bread stale, and the beer warm, but they were hungry enough to overlook the quality of the food.

"What do we do?" Bernie asked Kober. "Sit and wait?"

"That's right. We wait. They know we're here."

"What about sleeping?"

"God knows. At least this bloody shack is warm. Maybe we can bed down here. There's a toilet out back, so your guys have the convenience."

"And who are we dealing with? The army?"

"We are not sure," Benash said. "Is hard to say. Maybe army, maybe Communist Party, maybe secret police."

"You must have made the deal with someone," Bernie insisted.

"There's a sleazy chap called Lovazch," Kober told them. "He's got a finger in a lot of things. He's a civilian, but the colonels hop to attention when he speaks.

Which makes me think that perhaps he's party, commissar or something of the sort. The army's in on it, because this is a military airport attached to the Skoda Works, which have been taken over by the government. We got to him through Max Selnik, who's a French filmmaker with a lot of contacts in curious places. Max is Jewish, so he went to the trouble of setting this up. The Haganah has been buying arms from the Czechs, but this will be the biggest deal we've had a go at. Brodsky tells me," he said to Bernie, "that you're a weapons expert."

"I've used them. I fought in Spain and then I did six years in the British army."

"Are you a commie?"

"I'm afraid not."

"Pity. They might listen better to one of their own. Do you know the German weapons?"

"A bit. Not a damn thing about Czech guns."

"Don't worry. They won't sell us any Czech guns. They'll want to palm off the German junk they picked up after the war."

"It's not all junk," Bernie said. "Not if it's in decent condition."

"Can you be the judge of that?"

"With the weapons, yes. Not with the Messerschmitts."

"Dov's a mechanic. That's his game."

"What do you need most?" Bernie asked.

"Small arms, rifles, machine guns. And mortars. Small field pieces, if we can get any. But I suppose we'll have to take what they give us—if they give us anything."

They had been in the lounge for almost three hours before anyone appeared to remember they were there. Most of the men were stretched out on the floor.

Some were asleep. A few played cards. A few were still chewing on what remained of the sausage and bread. Most of the men who were awake were smoking, and the small room was heavy with cigarette smoke. A counter across one end of the room had a curious baroque mirror behind it. Evidently, it had once been used as a lunchroom or barroom of some sort; on the wall behind the counter were a number of cardboard signs with words and prices printed on them. There were four tables in the room. At three of them, poker games were in progress. Bernie, Brodsky, Goodman, and the Haganah men sat at the fourth, the two suitcases under the table, each between two sensitive feet. Bernie, half-dozing, was listening to Kober's description of the political situation in Czechoslovakia. There were rumours that Jan Masaryk, the foreign minister, had been murdered by the radical left only two days before. "The story is," said Kober, "that he fell from his window in the Czernin Palace. Bloody clumsy of him, if one is to believe it. I don't. They've been arresting members of the government in the opposition parties right and left—that is, the left is soaking it to the right, and the situation appears to be on the edge of a communist takeover. None of our concern. Ours is to get the bloody planes and weapons and get out of here."

That was when Bernie saw the two men come into the room. One was a very fat man in civilian clothes. His pink, perspiring face sat in collars of fat, and even as he entered, he was wiping his brow. He had thin blond hair, tiny blue eyes, and a curious cupid mouth. He wore a gray suit, white shirt, and black tie, and a black armband was sewn on his sleeve. "That's Lovazch," Kober whispered. "The armband's for Masaryk. Kinky sense of humor they have. He's a shrewd pig." The other wore a uniform with three rows of medals on his breast; he was a tall, gray-haired, military type who walked stiffly and held his spine erect. "Don't know him," Kober said.

Lovazch, spotting Kober and Benash, led the officer across the room to their table. Bernie preempted two chairs from the nearest poker game, and Al Levine, a pilot, wailed, "For Christ's sake, Cohen, you want me to deal the motherfuckin' cards standing?"

"Can it," he whispered. "This is the brass we've been waiting for."

Lovazch bowed stiffly as Kober introduced Cohen, Brodsky, and Goodman. "This is General Anulko," Lovazch said, speaking English with a heavy accent. Then he spoke to the general in Czech. Bernie caught the names of all five of them and the word Haganah.

"Cohen here, and Brodsky—both of them speak French," Kober said.

"We talk in English, so? The general don't speak French."

"Please sit down," Bernie said.

"So? Thank you." They seated themselves. "You have money?"

"We have money," Kober said.

"How much?"

"Two million, American."

"Where?"

"Let that rest for a while," Kober said.

"Oh? Please—don't give me shit, like you say. Either show me money or I walk out."

They looked at each other. "Show him the money," Bernie said. "What's the difference?"

Kober shrugged. Benash nodded. He had a face like a hawk, brown and cold and hard, with blue eyes narrowed to slits. "Unless I've forgotten all I used to know about men like him," Bernie said to himself, "he has a gun in his pocket and his finger on the trigger. He's a killer, and like all killers, a little crazy. He'd like nothing better than to put a bullet into Lovazch, and that would be just dandy."

Aloud, Bernie said, "I am in command of this operation, Mr. Lovazch." Kober and Benash glanced at him, surprised. They remained silent. "May I first express my gratitude to the great people's democracy of Czechoslovakia, and of course to you. The money is nothing. It is merely a symbol. The struggle for liberty is everything." He smiled and nodded and reached under the table for the suitcase. Brodsky followed his action, and they placed the two suitcases on the table. Neither had been opened since Feinstein had turned them over. The thought occurred to Bernie that conceivably neither suitcase contained any money. How long was the chain that had to be trusted? How many before Feinstein? What strange force held them all together in this? He had never really believed that anything superseded human greed, but evidently the will to create something on a parched piece of desert on the Mediterranean took precedence even over greed. He met Irv Brodsky's eyes. Brodsky's thin smile suggested that perhaps he had the same thoughts. Curiously, the luggage was not even locked, only held together with snaps and leather straps. He and Brodsky undid the fastenings, and the others around the table rose as they opened the suitcases. Both were packed with tight bundles of hundred- and five-hundred-dollar bills.

As if possessing a dynamic force of its own, the money communicated itself. The poker games stopped, and the chatter of voices in the room stopped too, and slowly and silently the whole group of airmen gathered around the table.

With awe and respect, someone said, "Holy shit!"

It expressed it completely, Bernie thought. "All right, guys," he snapped at them. "Break it up! You all seen a dollar before. Forget it. We have business to do."

They moved away, slowly, reluctantly, as Bernie closed the suitcases. "Do you want to count it?" he asked Lovazch.

The fat man wiped his brow. "Not necessary." He took out a notebook. "You pay as we decided each purchase."

"Nothing doing!" Kober said curtly.

"Isn't it simpler," Bernie said, "to make the payment when the goods are loaded?"

"You must trust me," Lovazch said. "I trust you, you trust me."

"When the goods are loaded."

"You are making it difficult for me. Do you not know, Mr. Cohen, that you are in Czechoslovakia at very trying time? You must not press me too hard. It is within my authority to impound your planes and your money. That would be unfortunate, no?"

They sat in silence for a while, and then Bernie suggested that he and his friends have a few words. "Of course," Lovazch agreed. "Of course." The five of them went across the room and put their heads together.

"We had a deal," Kober whispered.

"Forget it," Bernie told him. "He's going to skim the cash, he and that sonofabitch general. Suppose we told him to fuck off? Is there any kind of appeal here, any straight people you can do business with?"

"Are you kidding?"

"The question is," Brodsky whispered, "will he deliver?"

"Oh, yes, he'll deliver, at his own bloody price. He has us, we have him. I say, pay his price and let's get the hell out of here. If we insist on paying when they load, that cuts him out, and that fat bastard isn't going to see himself cut out."

They returned to the table. "We'll deal," Bernie said.

"Ah, I see, Cohen, you are a man of sensibility. Then we begin with the Messerschmitts. Ten planes."

"The planes are disassembled and ready to load," said Kober. "But we can only take nine. We lost one of our transports in flight."

"You agreed to ten, you pay for ten."

"We can't take ten," Bernie put in. "God Almighty, you have a handful of people there in Palestine who'll be fighting for their lives any day now. Every dollar we have here means something."

"Please not to invoke God. You contracted for ten planes, you pay for ten, sixty thousand each, all together, dollars six hundred thousand."

"The price was fifty thousand!" Brodsky exclaimed.

"So price changes."

"What is it, Mr. Lovazch? Are you determined to have your pound of flesh?"

"Ah, Shakespeare. *Merchant of Venice.* I am not Jewish, Mr. Cohen." He pronounced it *Youish.* "You are Jewish. You will have your pound of flesh, but not from me. Oh, no. I do not bargain. Very Jewish, bargaining. We offer you life and you bargain." He pursued his little cupid-bow mouth and made a sour face. "Disgusting. No more bargaining or I walk out of here and tell you and your Jews to go to hell. Do you understand me?"

Bernie nodded. Benash's face became even colder

and tighter. Kober was smiling pleasantly. Bernie whispered to Kober, who sat beside him, speaking an inadequate Hebrew, "No trouble from Benash, please." Still smiling, Kober said to Benash in Hebrew, "If you do something crazy, Dov, I'll kill you, I swear."

"I only have a gun," Benash replied in Hebrew. "If I had a knife, I'd cut that fat pig's heart out."

"You will speak in English," Lovazch said.

"Yes, of course," Bernie agreed. "We accept the price."

"Then the money," Lovazch said, making marks in his notebook.

"Now?"

"Of course, now. We make a deal, money passes hands."

"Irv," Bernie said, "count out six hundred thousand."

Brodsky counted out the money. The very fact of the enormous sum of money changing hands brought the listening airmen to their feet. Now they moved closer to the table.

Lovazch consulted his notebook. "I have Russian rifles, very good, three thousand, two hundred twenty."

"No Russian guns," Bernie said flatly. "I hear you have German guns."

"Russian guns are excellent."

"Close that goddamn suitcase, Irv," he shouted at Brodsky. "The hell with it! We came to do business, not to be robbed! You can take this money from us, but you'll have one hell of a fight. Most of here are American citizens. If you think you can kill or jail thirty American citizens and get away with it, Lovazch, then go ahead and try! You're going to load those nine Messerschmitts and we're going to take off—and you just try to stop us!" His voice had climbed to a snarling roar, and Brodsky and Goodman were staring at him in amazement. Kober was smiling, and for the first time, Benash's lips parted in a thin smile. The airmen were grinning with pleasure.

Lovazch spread his hands. "Who is talking of robbing?"

The general was speaking in Czech. Lovazch answered him, and for a few minutes they held a dialogue. Then Lovazch said again, "Who talks of robbing? I suggest Russian weapons. The Red army is the greatest army in the world. You think they fight with pitchforks? You want German guns? Fine. We talk about German guns. What do you want?"

"Volksturm Geschuss," Bernie said.

"Ah, Volksturm Geschuss. Why not Mausers? I sell you five thousand Mausers."

"What the devil is a Volksturm Geschuss?" Kober asked.

"Light carbine type. Nine and a half pounds. Forty-four-caliber, and takes a magazine of thirty rounds. It's a hell of a weapon. That's what I want," he told Lovazch.

"Cost you, Mr. Cohen. It will cost you." He consulted his notebook. "Two hundred we sell, no more. A hundred dollars each."

Bernie nodded at Brodsky, who counted out twenty thousand dollars.

"Ammunition?"

"Sixty rounds for each gun."

"We need more—double that, at least."

Again, Brodsky counted out money.

"I want Schmeizers," Bernie said.

"Schmeizers, Schmeizers!" Lovazch exclaimed. "Ask me for diamonds!"

Brodsky nudged him. "Machine pistols," Bernie said. "The damnedest weapon that was ever made. Seven hundred and fifty rounds per minute."

"No Schmeizers," said Lovazch. "Schluss. No Schmeizers."

"Why not?"

"You pay a thousand dollars each, yes?"

Kober shook his head. "Buy the Mausers," he whispered to Bernie.

The bargaining went on for another hour. Twenty-two MG-42 light machine guns, the five thousand Mauser rifles, an assortment of Lügar pistols. The money was heaped in front of Lovazch and the general. The general could not keep his eyes off it. He sat with his cold gaze fixed on the piles of American dollars.

"I want fifty thousand dollars' bond," Lovazch said finally, "for airport privileges, fuel, loading."

"Fifty thousand dollars!" Brodsky exclaimed.

"How do you say?" Lovazch smiled. "A pound of flesh, yes. We will load the planes tonight. You are to take off at dawn. You will tell your Jews in Palestine that we are good businessmen too. Because we are Marxists, it does not mean we don't understand capitalist techniques." The general was putting the money back into the suitcases as Lovazch spoke. He had a penchant for neatness. He piled the bundles of bills carefully, caressing them with his long, thin, carefully manicured fingers. "I do not press you," Lovazch continued. "Our country is in a state of revolution. I am a friend of the Jews. Others are not. So the sooner you get out of here, the better for you."

"When will you start loading?" Bernie asked.

"In an hour."

"We want to check what you load."

"You don't trust me?"

"That's two million dollars," Bernie said. "We want to check the loading."

He shrugged. "As you wish." He and the general rose, each picking up a suitcase. Lovazch smiled and nodded. "As you wish. I see you at the planes." They turned and marched out of the room.

There was silence for a long moment after they left, then came an outburst from the airmen, a barrage of curses and epithets until Bernie was forced to shout, "Will you all knock it off!"

"We've been had!" someone yelled.

"Maybe yes, maybe no. I want you to try to sleep. If we're taking off at dawn, you've got to get some sleep."

"Where? On the floor?"

"On the floor. That's right. We never promised you a picnic. If today was bad, tomorrow will be worse. So get some sleep. And keep it down. If you can't sleep, maybe the next guy can."

Kober was humming to the tune of "I've got six-pence, lucky, lucky sixpence." Benash had taken a Colt forty-five out of his jacket pocket, and now he was checking the cylinder.

"Going to shoot your way out?" Bernie asked him.

"Maybe."

"What do you think?" Brodsky asked Bernie.

I think they'll deliver and load the planes," Bernie said. "He wants us out of here in the morning because he's taken us like Grant took Richmond. But there's not a damn thing we can do about it except try to check him as he loads."

"You're an optimist," Kober observed.

"No. Look, Kober, he's running a scam. I don't know who else is in on it beside the general, but it stands to reason that if we make a fuss or if he does, it's going to louse up his take. We paid double for everything, but we still got a hell of a lot of stuff, and we got the nine Messerschmitts."

"If he delivers."

"We'll see." He turned to Goodman. "You get some sleep, Herb. You're a navigator. The four of us, we're just passengers, so we'll check the loading. How about that?" he asked the others.

Benash put the gun back in his pocket. The four of them left the lounge and walked across the field. The place where the planes were parked was lit with portable lights. Two trucks, loaded with parts of the disassembled Messerschmitts, were already backing into the area. There were at least a hundred men there, half of them in uniform, the others in work clothes.

"Well," Kober said, "it looks like our Lovazch is a man of his word."

"That dirty anti-Semitic bastard," Brodsky said.

"A fine way to show your gratitude."

Lovazch appeared a few minutes later, and the loading went on almost until dawn. Kober and Benash remained with the planes. Bernie and Brodsky made their way back across the field to the lounge. It was predawn, a gloomy gray under a clouded sky that began to drizzle lightly. The airmen, unshaven and aching from their night on the floor, were ill-tempered and bitter.

"Come on, guys," Bernie said gently. "We'll be in sunshine tomorrow. Soft beds, decent food, and you can spend the day lying on the beach."

They filed back across the field through the rain. Sitting in the copilot's seat, next to Al Shlemsky, Bernie managed to stay awake through the takeoff. A few minutes later, even before they broke through the clouds into the sun-drenched sky, he was asleep. He didn't wake up until they were making their approach to the airport outside Tel Aviv.

The same day she received a cable from Bernie, informing her of his safe arrival in Tel Aviv, Barbara had lunch with Jean at Jack's on Sacramento Street. The wire from Bernie, in the few words it contained, fairly bubbled with satisfaction. "A great story for you and for Dan too. Kiss him for me. Back soon, and never another gripe about being a grease monkey." But no word as to when, precisely, he would be back. That day, also Barbara had a morning meeting with the board of directors of the Lavette Foundation and an afternoon session with Harvey Baxter, her lawyer.

Barbara was first at the restaurant, and when Jean entered, Barbara did not have to inquire about Dan. Jean was her old self, statuesque in a pearl gray Chanel suit of French mohair, her blouse a blue that matched both her eyes and the lining of her jacket. "Of course, daddy's much better," Barbara said. And Jean agreed. "His old self. He pleaded with me to smuggle in a cigar. I told him he'd have to give them up forever, and he repeated that stupid, disgusting bit about a woman is just a woman, but a good cigar is a smoke. He began as a hoodlum kid from the Tenderloin, and he's reverted. Perhaps it's lying in bed that makes him so tough. If men weren't so totally pathetic I could very easily despise them all. What on earth is that you're wearing, Bobby?"

"Just what it appears to be, mother. A sweater set and a skirt."

Jean shook her head. "The sweater is practically falling apart, and that skirt is ancient. Will you ever learn to dress properly?"

"I doubt it. Do you want a drink?"

"I do. I want a stiff martini. I want to celebrate that I am not a widow, a hideous state. What have you heard from Bernie?"

"I do love the way your mind moves. I had a cable from Tel Aviv. He got there safely with the nine planes, mission accomplished. If one can judge from a cable, he's high as a kite."

"Then we'll both have a drink and celebrate. You know, he is a remarkable man. How did you ever come to meet him, Bobby? You were never very clear on that."

"Didn't I tell you?" She paused to order the drinks. "No, I don't suppose I ever did tell you. It's not the sort of thing one tells one's mother."

"I don't know what you could possibly tell me that would shock me. It's the illusion of each generation that the previous one lived in a kind of childish innocence. Of course there are innocents in every generation, but I was not one of them. By the way, I saw Tom yesterday and told him about Dan's heart attack. I think it touched him."

Barbara doubted that. It was not difficult for her to follow her mother's train of thought. It was easier to have a homosexual brother than a homosexual son.

"He's getting married, you know," Jean said.

"I didn't know." Barbara hesitated. There were things one could not discuss with one's mother. "Lucy Sommers, I suppose."

"How did you know?"

"They've been around together. Do you know," she said after a moment, "I can forgive Tom most things, but not to go around and make his peace with daddy now—well, that's unforgivable."

"It takes two, and Dan hasn't helped." The waiter

came, and they were occupied ordering food; Jean
tried to recall where the conversation had started.

"You were asking me how I met Bernie. Of course I
can tell you. I can't believe I never did, but I was a
good deal younger then. You know he worked for the
Levys at the winery—"

"No, I didn't know that."

"Long ago. Nineteen twenty-two or twenty-three.
He was just a kid then. He kept in touch with them,
and eventually he joined the Abraham Lincoln Brigade. He always had his own strange reasons for what
he did. He went to work at the winery to learn to
grow grapes, because he believed that one day he
would grow grapes in Palestine. He was an orphan
who created his own dream place where everything
that had been wrong in his life would be put right.
That place was Palestine. He studied agriculture because that would be his life in Palestine. He joined the
brigade to learn how to fight. When the Levys wrote
to me that they would be coming to Paris, they mentioned that Bernie was in the Lincoln Brigade. Of
course, I hadn't met him then. It was just a name. But
when Marcel, this French journalist I was in love
with, was assigned by his paper to go to Spain and do
a story on the Lincoln Brigade, I mentioned Bernie's
name to him. Just as a contact. He found Bernie, and
when the terrible retreat across the Ebro took place,
Bernie saved his life—he swam the Ebro with him and
practically carried him on his back for miles. Marcel
wrote all this to me in a letter from the hospital in
Toulouse. Before he died," Barbara finished slowly. "I
don't think I ever told you that either. His leg was
badly mangled, and he wouldn't let them amputate
until I got to Toulouse. I talked him into it. It was too
late. He died of gangrene."

"You don't have to talk about it."

"I don't mind. I can talk about it now. Marcel was a beautiful man. Quite ugly, with a long bony face, but very beautiful. I never met anyone else like him. He was full of joy, and it was always joyful to be around him. He picked me up on the Champs-Elysées, saw me and followed me and insisted that if I walked out of his life, he would be utterly devastated. Well, that was only the beginning. We were together for a long time, and we were to be married. But I think you knew that?"

"I knew it," Jean said softly.

"So different from Bernie. That's odd, isn't it? But you wanted to know about Bernie. Well, it was months later. The Spanish Civil War was over, and the international brigades were disbanded. Bernie walked over the Pyrenees into France, sold his rifle for a few francs, and hitched his way to Paris. To see Marcel, strangely enough. You see, Marcel had talked of nothing else but this wonderful American girl he was going to marry. Bernie didn't know he had died, and since Marcel was the only person in Paris he knew, he went to the offices of *Le Monde*, where Marcel had worked. They told him about Marcel and gave him my address. And there you have it. My doorbell rang, and when I opened the door, there was this enormous, hulking brute of a man, in a sweatshirt and blue jeans, with two days' beard on his face. Well, we talked, I took him to dinner, and then he came home with me and used my shower and shaved, and I washed his very dirty clothes, and then we went to bed. And that's it. I think I fell a little bit in love with him, the moment I saw him at my door, so woeful and sad and inarticulate—or maybe I simply had a desperate need to love someone and to be loved by someone, or maybe he was all that remained of Marcel, or maybe his saving Marcel's life joined him to me in some way. He was so gentle and so kind. God, I needed someone to be gentle and kind to me. But that's it. That's how I met Bernie Cohen."

The waiter brought their food. Jean toyed with hers. It occurred to Barbara that she had never actually seen Jean eat, certainly not with the gusto and pleasure that food brought to so many people. But that perhaps was the reason for her mother's slender figure, for the smooth, tightly drawn skin that covered the bones of her face.

"I was never clear about how long he was with you then," Jean said.

"He was gone the next morning. Before I woke up. Left a note that he was broke, he loved me, and he didn't intend to sponge off me. And I didn't see him again until he turned up here one day more than six years later. He got to Palestine, where he joined the British army. Six years of it."

"And you still loved him?" Jean asked.

"No, I loved a romantic dream I had. But then I got to know him. He's not hard to know. He's rather simple and very direct. And also terribly complicated. Not an intellectual; his complication is different."

Jean nodded.

"I wish you would eat something. I wish you wouldn't sit there and just cut up your food. I'm hungry, and watching you fills me with guilt. Was I a fat child?"

"You never were. I hardly ever eat at lunch, Bobby."

"There's a fat, guilty child somewhere inside of me. Have you ever seen a psychiatrist, mother? I mean, have you ever been psychoanalyzed?"

"What on earth ever gave you that idea? No."

"Don't be upset. We are both being highly personal, aren't we? I was only thinking of how much you've changed."

"Have I? I don't know. I've always been the spoiled daughter of a very rich man. When all that was going on in Spain, I had only the vaguest notion of what was happening. I was always concerned for myself. Even during the war, I was hardly involved."

"Yet you can say that."

"What?"

"I mean, you look at yourself. Whether you're right or wrong about what you are, you're making the judgment."

"Is that a virtue?"

"I don't know," Barbara said uneasily. "I keep trying to look at myself, but I can't get away from it. From me. As if something is missing from us. I keep asking myself, will I grow up and when?"

"You're very grown up," Jean told her. "You're the most mature person I know."

"That's a lovely illusion. I think it's remarkable to fool one's own mother. We're both of us the spoiled daughters of very rich men. Only you seem to have made your peace with it. I'm afraid I haven't."

Irv Brodsky pleaded with Bernie to remain in Palestine and join the Haganah. "You don't know how much we need you. Since the UN declaration, the Arabs have gone mad, and the British aren't doing one damn thing about it. Just hands off and get ready to leave. They've killed more Jews in the past few months than in the past twenty years. Bernie, we prepared for this, both of us. There aren't ten men in Palestine who know what you do about tactics and mod-

ern war. How in hell can you walk out? How can you
walk away from it? You remember Hyam Kadar?"

Bernie remembered the name vaguely, a slight,
dark boy with curly black hair.

"He was at the kibbutz with us in thirty-nine. He
was killed three days ago. He was with a convoy
trying to break through to Jerusalem. The Arabs put a
log blockade across the gorge below Bab el-Wad, and
then they slaughtered them. Maybe three thousand
Arabs and a handful of our guys. And that's every
day. How in hell can you walk away from it?"

"I was never in it," Bernie said. "I'm not in it now.
I'll be forty-two next birthday. I'm a middle-aged garage operator from San Francisco. I'm married. I have
a wonderful wife who isn't Jewish and who puts up
with my insanity for reasons beyond my understanding. At this point, I don't even know exactly how I got
into this. I guess I couldn't face the thought of spending the next ten years running a garage. But I paid my
dues. I got up the money for the planes, and I stayed
with it. I'm done. I got a wife and child to go back to. I
had enough of war to fill my gut."

He and Brodsky and a woman called Lena Polda
were sitting at a table in an outdoor café on Dizengoff in Tel Aviv. The sun was shining. The air was
warm and gentle. Men in shirtsleeves and women in
summer dresses walked by. Children played in the
street. There was no sound of war, of guns firing.
Lena Polda was a dark, intense woman in her middle
twenties. She was a fourth or fifth cousin to Brodsky
and worked as a bookkeeper in Tel Aviv. Brodsky's
mother, who still lived on the Grand Concourse in the
Bronx in New York, had telephoned her to find out
whether her son was alive or dead; surprisingly, she
had gotten through, something of a miracle in Pales-

tine in March of 1948. Lena had gone to the airfield and was there when the nine planes landed; two days later, she met them for lunch, and until now she had said very little. Her English was adequate but heavily accented. She had been born in Poland, in Vilna, put in a concentration camp by the Nazis when she was seventeen, watched her mother and father, in the same concentration camp, go to the gas chamber, and had then been used as a prostitute by the camp officers. She had survived and had come to Palestine in 1945.

Now, somewhat unexpectedly, she said to Bernie, "What dues have you paid, if I understand you, Mr. Cohen, if dues are like, like an obligation?" It was her first contribution to the conversation.

"More or less. It's just an expression."

"So tell me."

"What Bernie meant," said Brodsky, "is that he fought in two wars, in the Spanish war and in the last war."

"Oh?" She stretched out her hand to reveal the number tattooed on her forearm. "So. Have I paid my dues?"

Bernie nodded slowly.

"Should I go home?"

"This is your home. It's not my home."

"No? No, I am sure not." She rose. "I must go back to work. Thank you for the lunch."

After she had left, Brodsky said, "Don't let that get under your skin. She's strange. They all are after they've been in the camps."

They sat in an uneasy silence for a while. Then Bernie said, "It's funny, but when I was a kid, all I ever dreamed about was coming here. I hated Hitler, but I didn't join the brigade because I was antifascist. I joined to train for this, and even when we got here first in thirty-nine, it was 'Home is the sailor, home from the sea.' And now all I want is to get back with Barbara and the kid. I can understand the way Lena feels. It's not the way I feel, so it's no use arguing with me, Irv."

"Well, what are you going to do? You can't get a plane out of here this week. It's impossible."

"I know. I booked passage on a ship out of Haifa for Naples. I can get a flight from Naples to London, and from there home."

"When?"

"Three days from now."

"All right. Look, we're driving up to Haifa. They're dropping me off at the old kibbutz, so come along, and you can spend an hour at the place and see all the improvements, and then get to Haifa in plenty of time."

"Who are they? Who's driving you up there?"

"Dov Benash and Zvi Kober. They're both attached to a Haganah unit up there. They're leaving tomorrow morning."

Waking the following day in the small room he shared with Brodsky in the rickety stucco house on Allenby Road that called itself the Hotel Shalom, Bernie had a momentary difficulty recalling where he was. The room was hot, the windows uncurtained, the sunlight pouring in, and some twist of memory flung him back to the months he had spent in North Africa. He had a moment of panic; life and time reversed itself, and for that moment all of his life with Barbara was a dream. Still not fully awake, he moaned in agony.

"Are you all right?" Brodsky called out. He was at the sink, shaving.

"Yeah, I'm all right."

Too much had happened too quickly. It was like a dream—the airfields in Kansas and New Jersey, the airfield in Panama, the airfield in the Azores, the fat Czech, Lovazch, cheating them on the price of the guns, and then the end, so flat, so unemotional, a man called Yigal Allon, tall, slender, blond, youthfully aloof, shaking his hand in an almost noncommittal manner, "Good work, Cohen," and then seeming indifferent, as if it were a perfectly ordinary and expected thing that a man in San Francisco called Dan Lavette should put up a hundred and ten thousand dollars to buy ten old airplanes, and that he, Bernie Cohen, should direct their flight across half the world and bring them into Palestine loaded with guns and Messerschmitts. But it fitted in with the rest of it. Where else in time or place would two million dollars packed in two suitcases be treated in such a manner, as if the suitcases held shirts and pants and coats? There was a convulsive thing of the spirit happening here, and it reached out to touch people in every corner of the earth, and for a day or a week it changed them, the way he had been changed, or perhaps regressed to adolescence and catapulted off in search of romance and all the golden dreams of youth. But now he felt used up and let down. His necessity to the adventure was of his own invention. It was true that Brodsky had pleaded with him to head up the operation, but he could have refused, and Brodsky could have carried it off just as well. What had he expected of Yigal Allon, who commanded the Palmach, the front-line striking force of this tiny, desperate nation that would soon be fighting for its very existence? That Allon would embrace him and make a speech, declaring that they had been rescued by Cohen the savior?

"Are you sure you're all right?" Brodsky asked. "Better get your ass out of bed, because they said they'd be downstairs at seven, and it's almost seven-thirty now."

He dressed and shaved and packed the flight bag that contained two shirts, both of them dirty now, underwear, and socks. Brodsky saw him pause, holding the revolver that Kramer, the accountant, had given him in the Azores. Then he handed it to Brodsky.

"What's this?"

"Kramer gave it to me. The little guy who met us in the Azores. He felt the money needed protection. I have no use for it. Out here, any weapon's something."

Brodsky put the gun in his pocket. They went downstairs, and while Brodsky settled their bill, Bernie went outside. The jeep was parked in front of the hotel, and Benash and Kober sat in the front seat, eating fried fish out of a greasy paper bag and breaking pieces off a loaf of bread.

"Have some," Kober said. "Fish and chips without the chips. Not as good as London, but quite worthy. The bread is first rate."

Bernie reached into the bag, and Benash tore off a piece of bread for him. With his first bite, he realized he was ravenously hungry. "Enough for all," Kober said. The fish was cold but good. Brodsky came out of the hotel and joined them and accepted fish and bread. Bernie pointed to four wooden boxes in the jeep.

"Our share of the boodle," Kober said. "Forty Mausers and two cases of ammunition. We deliver it to Haifa. We may have a bit of trouble along the road, so I suggest you both take guns and fill your pockets with ammo." Benash had two rifles in front and a pistol in his belt. "That case is open."

The started off, Kober driving, Bernie and Brodsky in the back seat. The Mausers were thick with grease. Bernie took a T-shirt out of his bag, and he and Brodsky wiped the guns and loaded them.

They drove north along the coastal road, turned inland at Natanya, and continued north to Hadera. So far, the day had been peaceful beyond belief. They did not even encounter a British patrol; the only signs of war were three burned-out trucks on the wayside. To the east, the hills were still hazy in the morning mist. Men and women working the fields with guns slung across their shoulders waved to them, and burnoosed Arabs tended their goats and sheep, lazily indifferent. The whole aspect of the land, so calm, so peaceful in the sunshine, filled Bernie with a sense of déjà vu, a feeling that he had never left this strange, haunting place. Once out of the stucco turbulence of Tel Aviv, it became timeless.

They stopped at Hadera for lunch, then they turned northeast on the dirt-surfaced road that led through the foothills of Carmel to Nazareth. From where they crossed the rail line it was no more than fifteen miles to Kibbutz Benyuseff, where both Brodsky and Bernie had worked in 1939, and where Brodsky had lived since then. In 1942, Brodsky had been briefly married; a month later, his wife was killed by an Arab sniper, and he had not married again. He spoke about it now for the first time. "She said once," he told Bernie, "that she knew you like an old friend. Just from what I had told her. We talked about you a lot. She was sure she'd meet you one day. Well, that's the way it goes. Anyway, you won't recognize the place. Two hundred orange trees, seventy acres of wheat and barley. And cows, we got over forty cows. Nursery, school. And me, I'm the agronomist. Would you believe it—Irv Brodsky, Grand Concourse and One Hundred and Sixty-third Street in the Bronx, the agronomist? They sent me to school in Tel Aviv for six months, but mostly I get it out of books. Sit up half the night reading Weber and Batchelor."

"Who are Weber and Batchelor?"

"Top experts on citrus growing, from your part of the world, California."

"And what, pray, is the Grand Concourse, old chap?" Kober asked him. "Sounds like one of those debutante affairs they have in the States."

"Just a big, ugly street in the Bronx."

It was slow going after they crossed the railroad. The road was rutted, washed out by the spring rains. At times Kober had to put the jeep into low gear and crawl almost at a walking pace. The countryside had changed to a region of low, rolling hills dotted here and there with Arab villages of mud and stone huts. The land had not been reclaimed here. White rocks jutted out of the stony hillsides. Goats had eaten the vegetation to the roots, and the starkness of the hillsides was relieved only by an occasional olive grove. They passed the ruins of some ancient building, a single pillar jutting from the pile of stone. When they were seen from a village, men, women, and children disappeared into their houses.

"I don't like it," Brodsky said. He picked up his Mauser, worked the bolt, and checked the load.

"Can't you go any faster?" Bernie asked Kober.

"Not without wrecking this job. It's old and venerable. Just keep your eyes peeled for snipers. We're four of us and armed, so I don't imagine they'll try anything rash. How much farther?"

"Ten miles or so."

They didn't hear the shot. A hole with a spider web

of cracked glass radiating from it appeared in their windshield. The bullet rang off the metal between Bernie and Brodsky. Kober braked to a stop.

"Why are you stopping?"

They heard the second shot. It whined past, missing the jeep entirely.

"Dead ahead," Benash said. "Eight, nine hundred meters." He pointed to the hole in the windshield.

"Any closer, it wouldn't crackle," Bernie agreed. "Rotten shooting."

"They may get better." He pulled the jeep off the road to the right, lurching into the shelter of a rocky spur of hillside. They heard at least five more shots, only one of which found its mark in the jeep. Then they were sheltered. Kober turned to face Bernie. "Well, old chap, you're the mavin on tactics. They're bloody poor shots, but who isn't at eight hundred meters? That one"—he nodded at the windshield—"could have taken your head off. Mostly these beggars have old single-shot Lee-Enfields or Martinis, so I'd say there's at least half a dozen of them, and that's only the beginning. Every nasty within hearing will come prancing in for the kill."

"Then I'd say we turn around and head back to that last kibbutz."

"And how do I get home?" Brodsky demanded.

"You come to Haifa with us," Kober told him. "I'm glad Cohen is more sensible than heroic. I detest arguments." He turned the ignition key. Nothing happened.

Bernie leaped out of the car and raised the hood. "Oh, Jesus," he said. A bullet had pierced the radiator and found the battery. The radiator was draining, the lead on the battery shattered.

"Can you fix it?"

"Two or three hours, maybe."

"Can we start the damn car?"

"No way." He looked around. On top of the rise of the hill, about a hundred yards from them, was an Arab herdsman's shelter, a tiny hut of mud and stone, roofless, abandoned. "Up there, that's defensible."

"We might beat them back to the kibbutz on foot," Brodsky speculated. "They're on foot. It's a long run, but we've still got a lead."

"Never!" Kober snapped. "After that shooting, every beggar with a gun will be out potting at us. All it takes is a couple of gunshots. Trying to make a run for it, we'd be sitting ducks."

"I don't leave the guns," Benash said. "Do what you want; I don't give them these guns."

"Then let's do it," Bernie said, "before they're on top of us." He slung the rifle over his shoulder and hefted one of the boxes of ammunition. It weighed at least a hundred pounds. He picked it up and started off for the hut. The others followed. Brodsky managed the second box of ammunition, but it took both Kober and Benash to carry one case of the Mausers, leaving the other case in the jeep. The moment they were out of the shelter of the hill, bullets began to kick up the dust around them. With their load, they couldn't quicken their pace, and it was all uphill. Bernie felt that his feet were weighted. An eternity seemed to pass before he had climbed the hundred yards and dropped, panting, inside the ruined hut. The only casualty was Benash. A bullet had torn a shred of flesh from his arm. He protested that it was nothing. Bernie made a bandage of his handkerchief and stopped the flow of blood, then Benash started out of the hut.

"Where the devil are you going?"

"Twenty guns left in jeep."

"They're not eight hundred meters away anymore. Will you use your head and look."

Two Arabs had rounded the fold of the hill, and as Bernie pointed, they saw the jeep and raced toward it. Benash raised his rifle and fired. One of the Arabs dropped. The second man stopped in his tracks, stared at Benash, standing in the doorway of the hut, and flung a wild shot from his gun. Benash fired a second time. The man's head whipped back and he crumpled to the ground.

Benash said something in Hebrew, then snapped at Bernie, "I go get guns now."

"No!"

"Fuck you, Yankee," Benash said, and he flung himself down the hillside in wild, sure-footed leaps.

"God willing, there's only two of them," Kober said.

The three men crouched in the door of the hut, watching. Benash reached the jeep, loaded himself with the Mausers, and started back up the hillside. Another Arab rounded the protecting fold of the hill. Hardly thinking of what he was doing, Bernie raised his rifle and fired. The man fell. Somewhere deep in his mind, the thought raced, I've killed a man. God help me, I've killed a man. Stone chips splattered from the edge of the doorway. Kober and Brodsky dropped flat. Bernie stood there. Now there were Arabs firing from both flanks, and three of them topped the ridge behind which the jeep was sheltered. Benash was about thirty paces from the hut when he was hit. He stumbled for three or four steps, the Mausers falling from his shoulders and leaving a trail behind him; then he collapsed and fell face down. Bernie raced to

him and heaved him up on his shoulder in a single
convulsive movement. Leaving the shelter of the hut,
picking up Benash, and getting back with him could
not have taken half a minute, but to Bernie it felt like
an eternity, slow, slow steps back to the hut, where
Brodsky and Kober crouched in the doorway, empty-
ing the magazines of their rifles. Bernie felt the shock
of bullets against Benash's body. Benash had been hit
twice more, but the first shot, through his body from
the side, would have been the fatal one. He was dead
when they laid him down in the hut.

Brodsky and Kober lay flat in the doorway, main-
taining a steady fire through a haze of smoke. "Dov is
dead," Bernie told them.

"Poor pigheaded bastard!"

"What the hell are you shooting at?" he demanded.
"Do you see any of them?"

"No."

"Then stop wasting ammunition."

They stopped shooting and rolled out of the doorway into the protection of the walls.

"Plenty of ammunition, old chap," Kober said to
him. "It will outlast us, you know."

The hut was roofless, low-walled. Standing erect,
Bernie could see over the walls. There were Arabs in
the distance, tiny figures. He could count at least
thirty of them.

"Our own stupidity," Kober said. "You're an outsider, but Brodsky and I should have known better."

"I came through here six months ago," Brodsky remembered. "They were gentle as lambs."

"They're not very gentle now, are they?"

"Will they rush us?" Bernie asked him.

"In the daylight? No. Why should they? They'll
come at night and toss a few grenades. *Finis*."

"They have grenades?"

"Oh, yes. Between the Mufti and the British, they're well supplied. The curse of being Jewish, Cohen. Nobody really likes us."

"Then we have to get out of here before it's actually dark. I imagine they'll wait until it's damn good and dark."

"I'm beginning to like you, Cohen," Kober said. "I put you down as just another arrogant bastard. But I must say, I like your style." He turned to Brodsky. "Cheer up, Irv. The best or the worst is yet to come. Either way, it'll be a change. And gratefully. Notice the smell in here? Sheep dip. They gather it and use it for their fires."

"What about poor Benash?"

"What about him? We can't bury him and we can't take him with us. Our own chances are so thin, we can't even properly weep over him."

"Do you mind if I say the Kaddish for him?" Brodsky asked bitterly.

Regarding him strangely, Kober shook his head. He took his rifle and lay down in the doorway. The Arabs were shooting again. It was late afternoon now, and the hills cast long, dark shadows. The Arabs were invisible in the cover of those shadows. There was a velvet quality to the landscape, the hills becoming softly rose where the sun struck them. Bernie closed Benash's eyes, and Brodsky spread his handkerchief over his face. Bernie felt that they were both thinking the same thing, that the Arabs castrated the Jewish dead, disemboweled them and frequently cut off their heads. The fierce hawk had fled from Benash. His face in death was like a small boy's. An occasional bullet struck the doorway, sending chips flying from the stone. "Irv, step back," Bernie said gently. Brodsky moved out of the line of the doorway and began to intone the prayer for the dead, swaying slightly, the way Bernie had seen Rabbi Blum sway so many years ago. Rabbi Blum had taken Bernie out of the orphanage and raised him. Rabbi Blum had never killed a living thing, not even an insect. He was an outsider. He lived on earth as an outsider. What was it Kober had said to him only moments before?" "You're an outsider, Cohen." Filled with overwhelming sadness, he listened to the Kaddish. It was too late. Everything came too late.

"Say ye amen," Brodsky said in the ancient Aramaic in which the prayer was composed.

"Amen," Bernie whispered.

Kober was very still. The firing outside picked up, increased; it was still at least two hours to sunset.

"Show the flag," Bernie said to Kober, his voice thick and harsh. "Lay down some fire. They're getting bold."

Kober didn't move. Brodsky crawled to him, then said to Bernie, "He's dead." The bullet was in his forehead. He had died instantly and silently.

"They're all around us," Brodsky said tonelessly. "There's no way out of here, Bernie."

With the butt of his rifle, Bernie pounded a stone out of the back wall. "Take the back," he said to Brodsky. "I'll take the doorway. Keep up a constant fire. Maybe Kober was right and they won't attack until dark. We'll try to slip away before then."

When Bernie's Mauser stopped firing, Brodsky listened for it to start again. He was shooting through the loophole Bernie had made, only shooting; there was nothing to see, only smoke and the deep shadows of twilight. But Bernie's gun remained quiet.

"Oh, my God," Brodsky whispered. He yelled, "Bernie! Bernie! Don't leave me alone here!"

He ran over to Bernie, who lay quietly in the doorway, and shook him. Then he rose and faced the three Arabs standing in front of the doorway. It took just an instant for the sight of them to register before they fired pointblank, and his body fell across Bernie's.

PART THREE

Inquisition

There were those who described Lucy Sommers as an austere person. She was a dark, intense woman of forty years, the only child of Alvin Sommers, once president of the Seldon Bank and now retired at the age of seventy-nine. People have a rhythm in their lives, and some live in their early years and some in their late years. Sommers became president of the bank at sixty-five, and at seventy-nine, he was a hard, dry specimen who promised to go on forever. Lucy was tall, handsome, and possessed of a good figure. She rarely smiled, and she did nothing in the way of make-up or hairdo to enhance her looks. She was the sort of person about whom fashionable women were wont to say, "It kills me to think of what I could do for her in two hours with the proper face and the proper clothes." But no one ever did it or even suggested it.

When it became known to the few hundred people in San Francisco who composed what they considered "the city" that Tom Lavette was to remarry and that Lucy Sommers would be his bride, there were many and vociferous expressions of disbelief. In fact, there was no one in that entire circle who was more the total opposite of Eloise Clawson, his first wife, than Lucy Sommers.

Tom, on the other hand, felt comfortable with
Lucy, a feeling he had never experienced with Eloise.
In some ways, she reminded him of his mother, although the only physical resemblance was in their
common height. Eloise had been shy, retiring, and always uncertain with Tom. Lucy was calm and firm,
and at this point she knew precisely what she desired
in a marriage.

"They say one doesn't speak ill of the dead," she
once said to Tom. "I don't know why. I think it's much
more damaging to speak ill of the living. My husband
is dead, but there is nothing good I care to say about
him. He was an animal. I think you ought to know
that, Tom. I don't know whether I would ever have
enjoyed sex if I had married someone else. Whatever
the possibilities were, he spoiled them. After a year of
marriage, we separated, but I must say that the memory lingers on. You have asked me to marry you. I
want to be specific about the kind of arrangement
you would be entering into."

"I have asked you to be my wife, not my bed partner."

"And you don't consider that rather strange?"

"No stranger than a dozen marriages I know about,
where that arrangement exists. The only difference is
that we are putting our cards on the table."

"Do you have a mistress?" she asked bluntly.

"No."

"I wouldn't object to it, but I would object to it becoming known. I will not be an object of laughter or
contempt. I respect you and I think you respect me.
We are both of us very wealthy and we are both ambitious. My father owns three acres on Pacific
Heights, which he has promised to me. I think you

know the property. It has a magnificent view. I want you to understand what I will ask of you."

"I already have a house on Pacific Heights," Tom said rather lamely.

"I know. It's not the sort of house I contemplate, and it also happens to be another woman's house. I am marrying you, Tom, because I like you. I am also marrying you because I feel that between us we can be successful. Success to you means wealth and political power; I understand that. However, I am a woman, and I have my own dreams. I intend to be the most fashionable and successful hostess on the West Coast, and when the time comes, in Washington as well. I don't know whether you realize how much you need a person like me. I know that our circle has a certain impression of me. I could not care less. When the time comes, an invitation to our home will be like an invitation to the White House. Politics is something more than the formalities of the governor's mansion and the legislature. Politics is a question of power and the cultivation of people who have that power."

After that conversation, Tom changed his opinion of Lucy Sommers. He almost retreated from the marriage, caught between fear and admiration. He was torn between a sense of impending danger and the desire to give himself into the hands of a very strong woman. The need for security won out.

After speaking to his mother, he told Lucy of her suggestion that they be married abroad.

"What nonsense!" Lucy exclaimed.

"I don't think so. My mother will not show up without my father."

"Then it's high time you made your peace with your father. We will have sufficient enemies without having them in the family."

"Oh, no. Lucy, I have not spoken to the man for twenty years."

"He's in the hospital now. What better time is there? If you don't do it now, you never will."

Harvey Baxter's assistant was a young man with the unlikely name of Boyd Kimmelman. He was very bright, had served with the judge advocate's office during the war, finished law school a year later, and displayed an aggressive sharpness of thought that disturbed Baxter as often as it pleased him. Now he was violently disagreeing with a position Baxter had taken.

"As sure as hell," he said to Barbara, "they're going to ask you are you now or have you ever been a member of the Communist Party."

They were meeting in Baxter's office, the two lawyers and Barbara, the morning of the day before she was due to leave for Washington. Young Sam, in his stroller, sucked a pacifier and good-naturedly observed the proceedings.

"That doesn't bother me," Barbara said. "I am not and I never have been. All I have to do is answer truthfully."

"Exactly," Baxter said.

"Oh, no. No, sir, if you will permit me. It's just not that simple. Those cookies hold all the cards. Suppose you were at some meeting, some civil liberties meeting, maybe a meeting in defense of the itinerant farmworkers. From what Harvey says, you go for that kind of thing. Am I right?"

"You may be right, Mr. Kimmelman."

"Call me Boyd, Mrs. Cohen. As Harvey will tell you, I'm too pushy to be entitled to respect."

"All right, Boyd. Yes, I've been to meetings. I've been to civil liberties meetings, and just two months ago I went to a meeting in defense of the Hollywood writers. I think that's my right, isn't it?"

"Today? Who knows? The point I'm making is this. Those creeps on the Un-American Committee, they have access to information, they have access to the FBI files, and you may be sure that every one of those protest meetings is covered by the FBI. You're not exactly unknown in this town, Mrs. Cohen. So let's say that you deny under oath that you ever have been a member of the Party. Then one of their paid informers stands up and swears he saw you at a communist meeting."

"He'd be lying."

"Can you swear it was not a communist-organized meeting?"

"For heaven's sake, Boyd," Baxter broke in, "that doesn't make her a communist."

"Can she prove she's not? How? Suppose an informer swears that she is."

"But I am not," Barbara said. "How could anyone swear that I am? What proof could they offer?"

"You're old-fashioned," Kimmelman said impatiently. "Those babies are not running a court of law. They're not interested in proof or the rules of evidence. They're running a Star Chamber. All they're interested in is headlines, and they make headlines by nailing you. I know you're not Jewish, Mrs. Cohen, but your name is, and they're going to suck on that for starters."

"Come on, Boyd," Baxter said with annoyance. "You see anti-Semitism everywhere."

"Only where it is."

"And Barbara can't refuse to answer a pertinent question. That's contempt, and I will not subject her to a contempt."

"Contempt is only a misdemeanor, punishable by a year in prison—if they cite her. Perjury is a felony—a five-year offense. Would you subject her to that?"

"Now just hold on," Barbara said. "This whole discussion is beginning to sound like a scene from Kafka, the two of you arguing about a one-year versus a five-year jail sentence. I am not a criminal. I have done nothing illegal. I am a San Francisco housewife with a baby, and I have no intentions of going to jail."

"Nor shall you," Baxter assured her. "I think Boyd here is raising ridiculous ghosts. I cannot conceive of anyone testifying that you are a member of the Communist Party."

"I can," Kimmelman said.

"Suppose I were a member of the Communist Party?" Barbara asked. "Would that send me to prison? I seem to have been laboring under the quaint and old-fashioned illusion that we live in a democracy."

"We still do," Baxter affirmed. "Absolutely, and I will not let a handful of bigots in Washington convince me otherwise. If you were a member of the Communist Party, Barbara, and they asked you that question, you would simply admit it. That is, if you wished to. They cannot punish you for a truthful answer to a question."

"Oh, my word," Kimmelman said.

"Boyd," Baxter said, "we differ in our attitude toward the law. I regard it as a shield that man has erected through the ages as a defense of the best of civilization. You regard it as an antagonist, to be anticipated and outwitted. No, hold on," he said as Kimmelman began to protest. "Those are precisely the qualities that I treasure in you, but you are young and cynical. Whenever I encounter a situation of this sort,

I ask myself what Sam Goldberg would have done. I have absolutely no doubts on that score here. Sam would have advised Barbara to answer every question truthfully and forthrightly. I simply do not share your fears about informers and entrapment. For Barbara to refuse to answer a question because she feared entrapment would be folly."

"So be it." Kimmelman sighed.

"We sit and talk about this ridiculous committee," Barbara said, "and the only thing that really disturbs me is why I have not heard from my husband. For two days I've tried to call Tel Aviv, and I simply cannot get through. I send cables and receive no answer. There must be some way to reach Bernie."

"It's a very disturbed situation," Baxter said. "You realize that, Barbara. Palestine is in a turmoil, practically a state of war."

"I know, and that worries me so. Harvey, there must be some way. You must know people who can make inquiries and get answers."

"Mrs. Cohen," Kimmelman said, "my own feeling is that your husband may have sent you several cables. They are not getting through. The telephone lines are tied up with priorities. I know someone in the local Zionist organization who may be able to swing a priority, and I'll be happy to see him this afternoon and see whether we can get a call through. Trouble is, it's almost midnight in Tel Aviv, so we'll have to wait a bit. I have a cousin who's some kind of officer in the Haganah—that's the Jewish army—and if I can reach him, I may have some news for you.

"On the other hand, it may take a few days, and then there's the possibility that your husband's on his way home. I doubt that he could get a plane out of Palestine, so he may have had to take a ship to Italy or France. If he sent a cable, it may be lost or delayed. Why don't you let me get into this while you and Harvey are in Washington?"

"I'd be so grateful," Barbara told him. "And you will let me know the moment you hear anything?"

"Of course."

The baby's mood changed, and suddenly Samuel Thomas Cohen filled the office with the wailing sound of a healthy pair of lungs.

"I'll get him home," Barbara said. "That's almost indecent in a law office."

"It's a fine sound of life," Baxter protested. "I'll pick you up tomorrow morning at seven, Barbara, and we'll drive to the airport. I don't think we'll be in Washington more than a day."

At home, Barbara fed Sam and then put him in the car and drove to the Higate Winery in the Napa Valley. It was early afternoon when she arrived, turning off Highway 29 and climbing the dirt road that led to the cluster of old, ivy-covered, stone buildings. A visit to Higate always gave Barbara a feeling of warmth and security. For one thing, it was old, as such things are measured in California. The original stone buildings had been put up by Italian masons in the eighteen seventies and had been added to and refurbished by the Levys. And the warmth of the Levy family made her feel that she was always welcome.

After Barbara had arranged with Eloise to take care of Sam for the next few days, Clair Levy persuaded her to remain at Higate for an early dinner. Sarah Levy, Jake's mother, had sold her big house in Sausalito and was now living with her son and daughter-in-law at Higate. She was at the table with Jake and Clair, Adam and Eloise, Sally, who had come up from Los Angeles with her daughter, and Barbara. Sally's

ostensible reason was to allow Sarah to feast her eyes
on the infant May Ling; but in all truth, Sally could
not bear for Barbara, whom she worshipped, to go to
Washington without seeing her.

They sat around the big deal table in Clair's high-
ceilinged, beamed, and tiled kitchen, the table heaped
with food—platters of fried chicken, bowls of potatoes,
asparagus, broccoli, stewed apples, tomatoes, and
three kinds of pickles—as if this vast amount of food
was a testimony to the existence of normality and sanity. Barbara did not know whether to laugh or weep.
She had no idea what Jake Levy had been long ago,
but now he was totally a farmer, a big, sunburned
man with the farmer's narrow suspicion of and anger
at people outside, people in Washington, people who
tilled no earth and grew no crop, but sucked the
substance of America. The thought of Barbara being
handed a subpoena, of Barbara hauled to Washington,
of Barbara before an inquisition, enraged him. Clair
was calmer but equally indignant.

Strangely, Barbara found herself on the defensive.
"Nothing is going to happen to me. In fact, I look
forward to the experience. I tell myself that it is part
of being a writer, part of the price one pays for the
trade. And it's a very positive thing that I am being
shaken up a bit. When I take Sammy to Huntington
Park and sit there in the sunshine with the young
mothers, I begin to forget that any other world exists.
So this is good for me, and if I could only get some
word from that crazy husband of mine, I would relax
and allow myself to be delighted with the experience."

"It wouldn't delight me," Jake said. "It's a damned
outrage!"

"But I know exactly what Bobby means," Sally told
them. "If Oscar Wilde had not gone to prison, how

could he have written *The Ballad of Reading Gaol*,
and if Bunyan had not gone to prison, then no *Pilgrim's Progress*, and Cervantes and *Don Quixote*—and
do you know, Thoreau was put in prison because he
refused to pay taxes to support the Mexican war, and
when Emerson saw him there, he said, 'Henry, what
are you doing in there?' and Thoreau said, 'Waldo,
what are you doing out there?' So I know exactly what
Bobby means, but I still think it's a stinking shame."

"I am not going to prison, and I do think there are
more pleasant matters to discuss, and this wine is so
good! What do you call it?"

"Pop calls it a Chablis," Adam replied, "which it is
not. There is really no such thing as a Chablis in California."

"Damn nonsense!" Jake snorted. "It's as fine a
Chablis as ever came out of France."

"Which is just the point. Chablis is the generic name
for the white Burgundies that come out of the Chablis
region in France. This is better than any Chablis I
ever tasted. It's more delicate, and it has a better bouquet. Just hold it in your mouth a moment before you
swallow, Bobby. No tartness, or almost none. It's a
California wine, pure California. In fact, outside of
the Napa and Sonoma valleys, no one grows a grape
that can do this. We can make the best damn wine in
the world, but we have such an inferiority complex
about it that we give them French names and pretend
we're making French wines. We're not."

"It's hard enough to sell it as it is," Jake said. "Without calling it Chablis, we wouldn't sell a hundred gallons."

"What would you call it, Adam?" Barbara wanted to
know.

"I don't know. Any local name. I'd call this Eloise."

"Oh, thank you," Eloise said. "I prefer not to become a wine, if you don't mind. One glass of it gives me a splitting migraine. If you name it after me, heaven knows what would happen."

"You mean you never drink wine?" Barbara asked.

"Never. I don't dare. And I do love it. Isn't that an awful irony, to be married to a winemaker and not be able to drink it?"

Sally grabbed her hand as they left the table. "Bobby, I must talk to you. Are you going home now?"

"I'm afraid I must. I'm leaving for Washington in the morning."

"Just a few minutes, please?"

They went up to Sally's old room, and Sally sat with May Ling in her arms. "Isn't she absolutely darling, Bobby?" Sally said. "And for a one-year-old, she's brilliant—I mean for twelve months, you can't expect too much, can you? I think she looks very Chinese, but Joe insists that Chinese children do not have sandy hair. But with seven or eight hundred million people, such a generalization is ridiculous—"

"Sally," Barbara interrupted, "that's not what you want to talk to me about."

"No. My marriage. My marriage stinks. And I want to weep, because how can I be married to your brother and have it turn into such a rotten mess?"

"It has nothing to do with being married to my brother. You're married to Joe. Now what has happened?"

"I've disappeared. I don't exist. We've been married two lousy years, and I don't exist."

"Oh, Sally, come on. What do you mean, you don't exist?"

"I'll tell you exactly what I mean. He's up at six-thirty and off to the clinic at seven. At ten he goes to the hospital to operate. Then back to the clinic. Then back to the hospital. Then back to the clinic. If I'm lucky, he's home at eight. Otherwise, nine, ten—just early enough to stuff some food into himself and fall into bed. Oh, I don't mean he's cruel to me or nasty or mean. You know Joe. He couldn't even be mean to Adolf Hitler. He'd just examine him and prescribe pills for his craziness."

"Have you tried to talk to him?"

"Of course I have. He doesn't hear me. I have my poetry and I have May Ling. He considers that a full life. The only thing he leaves out of his thinking is marriage. I do love him, Bobby, and this thing is driving me right up the creek."

"Sally, darling," Barbara said, "I don't have any quick answers. Perhaps there aren't any, but I don't think your marriage is breaking up. It won't unless you want it to. Let me get through this stupid committee business, and I'll be able to sit down and talk with both of you. Perhaps that will help."

"Will you? Will you, Bobby?"

"I promise."

Sam was asleep in his crib. Barbara kissed him lightly, thanked Eloise and Adam profusely, and then drove back to San Francisco alone. The cable was pushed under her front door. She tore it open, and saw from the date that it had been delayed five days. It read, "No way to get through on the phone. Flight successful, goods bought, and all planes safe in Tel Aviv. Flight out of here impossible. Booked passage from Haifa to Naples. Then to London, and hopefully flight home. Ten days at most. I love you. Promise never to leave you again." It was signed "Bernie."

* * *

Jean was standing in the corridor outside Dan's hospital room when Tom appeared. Her surprise was more than she could cope with; she simply stared and said nothing.

"Well, I'm not a ghost, mother. I'm real," Tom informed her.

"Yes, I know you're real," Jean said slowly.

"How is he?"

"Much better."

"Can I see him?"

"I don't want him upset," Jean said. "I don't want him hurt. He's been hurt enough. What made you come here?"

"That's a hell of a note," Tom complained. "Instead of admitting that I might be doing a decent thing, you're being hostile."

"I'm not hostile. I'm just worried. You haven't spoken to your father for twenty years."

"And he hasn't spoken to me."

"All right, Tommy. This is no time to rehash anything. If you go in there, I don't want any of that. Are you concerned for him?"

"I think so," Tom replied uncertainly. The truth was, he didn't know.

"Then if you go inside, you must forget the past. I don't want you to talk about anything but your concern for him."

"I'll try."

"That's not good enough. I want you to promise me."

Tom nodded.

"I'll go in first and tell him. He doesn't need a shock." She turned to the door. "Wait here. Don't lose your nerve and run."

"I'll be here," he answered, thinking that she still treated him like a small, willful boy.

Dan, propped up in bed, was reading an old, battered copy of Masefield's *Salt Water Ballads*. May Ling had bought it for him thirty years before, and it had her inscription inside the cover: "For a loving and gentle saltwater man." Jean had found it among his things and had brought it to him, not mentioning the inscription. That puzzled him, but there were any number of things about Jean that puzzled him. Now he put down the book and said, "I wish you liked small boats."

"That depends on how small they are. I could learn."

"I've been thinking of something about thirty feet, sloop-rigged, something that the two of us could handle. I'd build it myself—well, not with my own hands, but I'd design it and watch it every step of the way. Build it of teak—none of this rotten plastic they're using now. I'm not thinking of anything ambitious. There's enough water and shoreline in the bay to keep a man occupied for years. I'd teach you to sail. You know, that was something I planned to do from the first day we were married, and believe me, you'd learn at the hand of a master."

"It's a thought."

"Come on, Jeanie, would you?"

"Get well first. I'm not saying no. Meanwhile, there's a visitor outside. I thought I'd tell you before he comes in."

"Who?"

"Tom."

"Tom?"

"Our Tom. Your son."

Softly, Dan said, "No. Well, I'll be damned. He wants to see me."

"That's right. Do you want to see him?"

"I want to see him. Yes."

"All right, Danny. But the past is over. Otherwise, there's no use seeing him at all."

"I'll buy that."

"I'll send him in and stay outside," Jean said. "I think it's best if you see him alone."

Dan waited apprehensively. His heart was beating more rapidly, and he wondered whether that was good or bad after what had happened to him. It would not be literally true to say that he had not seen his son for twenty years. San Francisco is not a large city, and three times during the years he had caught sight of Tom, most recently in the distance, and before that twice in the same room at public functions. His feelings about Tom were a complex maze of contradictions. On one level, Tom was an unmitigated bastard; on another level, Dan blamed himself and softened the characterization; on still another level, he tried to grapple with the fact that his son was very possibly a homosexual, but since his notions of what constituted homosexuality were rather primitive, he dealt with the possibility by negating it and putting it down to an incorrect conclusion of others or as a temporary aberration from the normal. With all his faults, Dan Lavette was not intolerant; he was not given to hatred or grudges. After all, two generations ago, when the Chinese were an anathema to almost all of the white population of San Francisco, he had hired May Ling's father as his bookkeeper and had subsequently made him the manager of all his enterprises. His judgment of himself was so unsparing that he hesitated to condemn others. And as far as Tom was concerned, he had lived with an aching desire, a dream that one day the boy would lay aside his hurt and bitterness and return to him, for Dan had never denied Tom's right to despise him. By the measure of his own coin, he had failed his children, and if Barbara and Joe chose to forgive him that failure and to love him in spite of it, the virtue was theirs, not his. When he had given the hundred and ten thousand dollars to Bernie Cohen, his excuse that he was paying debt to Mark Levy was an empty apology and no more; the truth was that a child of his, through her husband, had come with a plea. At that point he was allowed to give, and that was all that mattered to him. His was the peculiar anguish of a once poverty-stricken child whose family now was of the establishment. He still measured giving by the thing that was given.

So when Jean asked him to put aside the past, she was controlling her own ghosts. There was no thought of the past in Dan's mind as Tom entered the room. He was unaware of his slight smile, thinking only that his son was a fine-looking man, tall, well built—his father's frame and his mother's color and good looks. He was thirty-six years old, one of a half dozen of the wealthiest and most powerful men in California. Dan made no obeisance to wealth and power, but they were the measure of the game he had played for most of his life.

"Hello, dad," Tom said tentatively. He, too, was apprehensive. Dan held out his hand, and Tom took it. His grip was firm. "How do you feel?"

"Not bad," Dan replied. "You know, this is a Jewish hospital. They have a funny expression about a coronary. They say, now you're bar-mitzvahed." The words came out, and Dan didn't know why he had said them. What a stupid thing to say, he thought. What a stupid way to begin! Why couldn't I keep my mouth shut? "I guess you don't know what that means," he said lamely.

"Sure I do. Only it doesn't apply. You were a man when you were still a kid. It's people like me who have to do the growing up."

Dan stared at him, wondering whether he meant it. He remembered a boy's voice. This voice was strong, well modulated, the voice of a man who was listened to.

"I'm glad you came," Dan said. "It's been too long."

"I know it has."

"Pull over a chair. Sit down."

"I should have brought flowers," Tom said.

"Who the hell wants flowers! I'm not dead. The flowers keep coming and I send them down to the ward. You know what you should have brought me? A cigar."

"I wish I had thought of that. But mother would have killed me."

"I suppose so. She prowls around here like a cop. You look good. Taking care of yourself?"

"I try."

"How's business?" Dan asked, unable to think of anything else to say, or unable to say any of the hundred things he thought of, unable to ask whether he had been missed, loved, cherished, hated, unable to ask whether his son was happy, lonely, fulfilled, resentful.

"Well, the chaps in Washington say we're going to own the world, that it's our century. I used to think that business was a matter of making money. But then money becomes meaningless, and the whole game becomes something else."

"I know the feeling," Dan agreed.

"I suppose we own a very substantial part of the world already. The question is, where do I go from here?"

Dan waited. He mistrusted the words on the tip of his tongue.

"I'm going to run for Congress," Tom said.

Dan nodded. "I heard."

"What do you think of the idea?"

Dan nodded again. "I think you'll make it. Does that mean you'll leave Whittier in control?"

"Not on your life," Tom said. "I know you don't like John. I guess you have your reasons. He's no one to like or dislike. He's an old fool and a hypochondriac. I've been pressing him to retire, and I imagine he will. You know, I'm getting married."

"Yes, Jean told me."

"Lucy Sommers."

"I knew her father, but I never met her. I'm sure she's a fine girl."

"She's a fine woman, dad. A year or two older than I. But that makes no difference."

"Of course not."

At that point Jean entered. Tom rose, explaining that he did not want to tire Dan. He shook hands with his father and kissed Jean, then left.

"How did it go?" Jean asked Dan.

Dan shrugged. "All right."

"He was pleasant?"

"Oh, yes."

"What did you talk about?"

"Nothing."

"You were pleasant, weren't you, Danny?"

"I was so damn glad to see him—"

"Then what happened?"

"Nothing. Absolutely nothing." Then Dan added, almost woefully, "He was a total stranger, Jeanie. I suppose I anticipated everything else, everything except that. But how could I expect anything else?"

The next day, when Barbara was already on her way to Washington, the story about her subpoena broke in the San Francisco press. The headline in the *Chronicle* read: SAN FRANCISCO WRITER SUBPOENAED BY HOUSE COMMITTEE. The *Examiner*'s headline said: BARBARA LAVETTE COHEN TO BE UNFRIENDLY WITNESS AT SUBVERSIVE HEARING. Jean, realizing that Dan would have the news sooner or later, told him about it before she showed him the newspapers, assuring him that neither Barbara nor Harvey Baxter was greatly concerned. "No doubt it's her experience in Germany that they wish to make the most of, but that's no secret. Barbara wrote about it, and thousands of people know about it. It's their wretched way of making headlines, and you are not to become angry, please, Dan."

"Those filthy sons of bitches," Dan said. "What in hell is happening, Jean? What's happening to this country? And why didn't Barbara tell me? When did all this begin?"

"About ten days ago. And it's perfectly obvious why she didn't tell you."

"Did you know?"

"Yes, Barbara told me."

"And you didn't tell me?"

"Danny, you can understand that."

"She ought to have the best damn legal advice in the city."

"She has Harvey Baxter with her."

"Harvey Baxter is a damned old woman. You should have told me. I know people in Washington. I probably could have had this squashed."

"You were in no condition to do anything, Dan. I spoke to Harvey, and he's not worried."

"Where's the baby?"

"At Higate with Eloise and Adam. Don't worry, please." It was easier to tell him that than to keep her own fears down.

John Whittier entered Tom's office and put the *Chronicle* on his desk. Whittier, a stout, red-faced man, looked sick.

"I've seen it," Tom said. "Are you all right?"

"I don't know. It's either my stomach or a heart attack. This is terrible. This is absolutely terrible, Thomas."

"Yes."

"With the primaries three months away."

"I can count, John."

"Well, what do you intend to do about it? That damned sister of yours has been nothing but grief and aggravation since the day I met your mother."

"I know. We don't pick our relatives."

"Did you know about this?"

"No, not until today," Tom replied. "I am as upset and angry and frustrated as you are."

"Why on God's earth didn't she tell you? We might have done something about it."

"You'd have to ask her that."

"Has the press been in touch with you yet?"

"Not yet. But they will."

"How the devil can you sit there like that? Have you called her? Spoken to her?"

"I imagine she's on her way to Washington. I called her home. There's no answer."

"Well, what are they after? Is she a commie? I've always suspected she was."

"John, don't be an ass."

"Or is it that Jew husband of hers? I've heard all sorts of wild stories about him."

"John, I don't know any more about this than you do. I've been on the phone with the county chairman and the state chairman, and there was nothing I could tell either of them. I told Janet to hold all my calls so that I could think about this. Now I suggest you go back to your office and do the same."

After Whittier left, Janet Loper, Tom's secretary, buzzed him and said that Mrs. Carter was on the phone. Carter was Lucy Sommers' married name; after her husband's death, she had resumed her maiden name. Tom had to think for a moment before he made the connection.

"I'll talk to her," he said. He tried to pull his thoughts together. "Since when are you Mrs. Carter?" he asked her.

"Did I say that? Well, that shows you where my mind is. Tom, have you given any statement to the press?"

"Not yet, no."

"Don't. Get out of the office. I'll meet you at Casper's for lunch in half an hour. It's a quiet place, and probably no one we know will be there. We must talk before this goes any further."

"I can't leave now. Everyone and his mother is trying to reach me."

"Precisely why you should leave. Please trust me."

At Casper's, a tiny French restaurant tucked away on Leavenworth Street, Lucy was waiting for him, well hidden in a booth at the rear. Tom dropped down on the bench facing her and stared wordlessly.

"Poor dear," she said. "I ordered a Scotch for you. I had to get you out of there. I can imagine." She appeared so competent, so cool and self-contained, that Tom found himself relaxing. "You know," she went on, "I'm rather glad we can face this together. I don't think it's the end of the world by any means, but we must sort out things before this goes any further. First things first. Is Barbara a communist?"

"John asked me that. I told him not to be an ass."

"But now you're not so certain?"

"How does one know? I talk to Barbara three or four times a year. We're not exactly loving siblings. She has done some damn strange things."

"The *Examiner* calls her an unfriendly witness. What exactly does that mean?"

"I called my lawyer and asked him. Apparently they subpoenaed her, after which she made no gesture of cooperation."

"Perhaps she has a clear conscience."

"Lucy, Barbara has done some crazy things in her time, like giving away the fortune she inherited to set up the Lavette Foundation, but I've never had an inkling of her being a red."

"And suppose the worst came out? How would the Republican party people feel about that? Would they still give you the designation?"

"They're shaky."

"All right, Thomas. Until we hear what happens in Washington, we make no statements and speak to no one. I have a lovely little cottage at Nicasio up in Marin. Suppose we go there and hide out for two or three days. It will give us a chance to think and plan— and to know each other a little better."

Tom stared at her. Her use of "we" unsettled him; on the other hand, no one had ever taken responsibility for him or his fate before; looking at this strong-featured, handsome woman who sat facing him, he experienced a sense of relief. For the first time that day, someone had proposed an affirmative action.

"I have my car outside. Shall I order lunch?"

Tom nodded.

"One of my larger regrets," Harvey Baxter said to Barbara, "is that I never joined the Masonic order. Not that Sam Goldberg didn't urge me to. He was a Mason for forty years." They were in the plane, flying east to Washington, when Baxter voiced his regret, apropos of nothing that Barbara could think of; she asked him why on earth he should think of that just then.

"It might help. I'm trying to think of anything that might help. There might just be a Mason on that committee, although it's not too likely. Anyway, I should have joined. My wife talked me out of it. Said I had enough things in my life that kept us apart. Never met my wife, did you, Barbara?"

"I'm sure she's lovely, Harvey."

"But possessive, Barbara. Possessive. Women are possessive. With the exception of a few like you. If I had ever proposed going off as your husband did, my wife would have had a case of hysterics. Not that I see myself embarking upon anything as ill-advised. As your attorney," he apologized, "I must state that I considered it ill-advised. You do understand?"

"Of course, Harvey."

"Even a trip like this worries her. I suspect it's the thought of the two of us traveling alone."

"Well, Harvey, you are an attractive man."

"Do you think so? I assured her—"

"Of course you did. Now let's talk about what to expect. Will this be anything like the Hollywood

writer hearings, with the publicity and the cameras
and all the rest of it?"

"I don't think so. I spoke to Donald Jay. He's the
counsel for the committee, and he'll do a good deal of
the questioning. He indicated that the session will be
held in chambers."

"What does that mean?"

"It means no press and no publicity during the
hearing. They'll meet in the committee room in the
House Office Building, just you and the committee.
You see, they're not too sure of themselves. I think
they're fishing. I think they'd like to have a go at a
whole slew of writers, and they chose you because
they feel you're vulnerable."

"But why? Why me?"

"The Nazi business, probably. But I am stating
their position. I do not think you're vulnerable. Possibly they have something entirely different in mind. It
doesn't matter. I feel quite secure about you."

"Well, I'm glad you do. I don't. Tell me, Harvey,
isn't this precisely what Boyd calls a Star Chamber
hearing? If I remember correctly, historically, the Star
Chamber was a place in England where the accused
was tried without benefit of defense counsel or jury.
Isn't this the same thing?"

"Oh, no, no. Not at all, Barbara. Congress functions
through committees. Theoretically, this committee
was formed to frame legislation to defend the United
States against internal subversion. As such, they have
the right to subpoena witnesses and take testimony
that will aid them in framing such legislation. Not
that they have ever offered any legislation. I have
nothing but contempt for their methods. But their
function is within the law. They are not a court, simply a committee of inquiry, and so long as you answer

any pertinent questions forthrightly and honestly, there is absolutely nothing they can do to you. I do not share Boyd's qualms."

"Will you be in the room with me?"

"They have the right to exclude me, but I don't think they will. Jay was very polite when we spoke on the telephone, very cooperative."

"And just what is pertinent?"

"That's hard to anticipate. They operate under a very broad spectrum. We'll decide that on specifics. I know this is unpleasant and time-consuming, Barbara, but it's a fact of life in these times."

"I suppose it is."

Because of the three-hour time difference, it was almost dark when the plane landed in Washington. They took a cab to the Shoreham Hotel, where Baxter had booked rooms for them. Barbara pleaded tiredness and begged off dinner with Baxter, saying she would have a sandwich and coffee in her room. She felt that another hour of Harvey Baxter's observations on history and politics was more than she could tolerate.

In her room, she unpacked her things, then drew a very hot bath and soaked in it for almost an hour. She lay there, up to her neck in the deliciously warm water, now with her eyes closed, drifting off into fantasy, then with her eyes open, observing and measuring herself. The scar of her Caesarean, once so raw and ugly, had faded to a modest pink. Her body was still good, her breasts firm, her waistline only an inch more than it had been ten years before. Needing reassurance, she accepted the pleasure that came from observing herself. She was still a well-formed and attractive woman. She visualized a second scar on her body. She could still have another child, and Dr. Kellman had assured her that a second Caesarean section was no more dangerous than a normal birth. Very easy for him to say. He did not have to be sliced open. Still, she was rapidly approaching an age where the decision would have to be made, but not tonight. It would wait for when she could discuss it with Bernie—and from Bernie, her thoughts drifted to Marcel. More and more, as time passed, Barbara found it difficult to accept the fact of Marcel's death. It was so easy to drift into the fantasy that it was simply a separation and that one day she would see him again. Was it because France was a world away and Paris almost like a dream that had never happened? In her dreams, Paris was always soaked in sunlight, a dream city of wonderful romance. How would it be now, she wondered, after the war? Would she ever go back there? Did she want to? Marcel was buried in Toulouse. Strange that she had no desire to go back to Toulouse, to see his grave again. She was not the type who put flowers on graves and who wept on tombstones. The past lived in her mind. It was there whenever she wanted it.

After her bath, she called room service and ordered a sandwich, salad, and coffee, then read a copy of the Washington *Post* that she had bought at the airport. Her appearance before the House Committee was front-page news, and the story described her as the "attractive San Francisco heiress-turned-novelist." The story was noncommittal. Even the liberal newspapers were cautious about taking sides, and Barbara had the feeling that no one was totally exempt from the pall of fear that had cast its shadow over the country. Was it indeed like Germany in the time of Hitler? She cast back to her own memories of Berlin in 1939. No, she would not accept that. She could not.

It was not yet ten o'clock, and she was not ready for

bed, for what would probably be a sleepless night. She sat down at the writing table and decided to write to Bernie. She had nowhere to send the letter, but it was pleasant to imagine that he might well be back in San Francisco when she returned, in which case she would simply hand the letter to him. There it is; you can read what I felt the night before I faced the tiger in his den.

"My dear oversized husband," she began; then she tore the sheet up impatiently. Why did she always dwell on his size? Was it because she saw him as a small, frightened boy who had spent his life attempting to overcome his fears? "Bernie, dear one," was better, and she went on: "Here I am in a hotel in Washington, D.C., trying to understand why I deceived you. At first I thought it was very noble of me not to tell you about the subpoena, which arrived before you left on that nutty mission of yours, because if I had told you, then you might have decided not to leave me to face the House Committee on Un-American Activities all alone; but upon due reflection, I have come to the conclusion that I withheld the fact because I was afraid that you would never forgive me for aborting your adventure. Believe me, I know you and love you well enough to know how much you wanted to take that flight of planes over to Europe and save the brave Jews whom you felt you had deserted by marrying me and settling down to run a garage in San Francisco. But don't think I didn't have some very bad moments when days went by without a word from you. Happily, I received your cable yesterday, so I could come here with no more to worry about than two days of Harvey Baxter's legal advice. Why, why do lawyers talk the way they do? Ah well, you will not solve that one.

"As to why I have been subpoenaed, we have not the faintest notion, except to guess that it concerns my own harebrained adventure when I undertook my mission to Berlin. But since I put that in a book for the whole world to read, I am not concerned about repeating the story to these local anthropoids. Anyway, here I am in Washington, and today we made the front page in both the San Francisco *Chronicle* and the Washington *Post*. I really am notorious. And it just occurs to me, as I write this, that poor Tom will have no end of explaining to do to his Republican sponsors. What will they think of a conservative candidate whose sister is redder than a rose? I think I shall clear Tom by making a public statement to the effect that we disagree about everything. After all, Booth's career was not ruined simply because his brother shot Lincoln. Or was it? I shall have to check that.

"Anyway, just as you must assuage your soul by such dumb escapades as the present one, so must I as a writer poke my nose into this and that. It did occur to me that daddy, with all his kudos from the War Shipping Board, might do something about quashing this silly subpoena; but the poor man had a mild heart attack, and right now he's in the hospital, and this is hardly something to annoy him with in his present condition. He is going to be all right, but still, I did not want him to know about it until he was much stronger. And I must confess that I am filled with curiosity as to how our local brand of repression functions, and also, believe it or not, it's my first trip to Washington. I am to appear before the committee at ten A.M. tomorrow, and if they don't keep me too long, I intend to spend the rest of the day sightseeing, since I don't have to be at the airport until five.

"Also, you must not worry about Sam. Our beautiful son is up at Higate, where Eloise is taking very good care of him. We do have good and dear friends. Harvey Baxter is a very nice gentleman, but I think he is a dunderhead; if you ask why I didn't find another lawyer, the answer is that one doesn't. He was Sam Goldberg's partner, and he must know something. Anyway, I have my own common sense to fall back on, so I am not really worried, just quite curious to see what faces me.

"Now to bed, and please, please be home when I arrive tomorrow, so we can resume our sensible, plodding lives. It should please you that I am ready to be so content in a world that is so packed with discontent. I love being a housewife and I love being a mother, and if you have gotten all the maggots out of your system, I am ready to discuss having a second child. I know I can't produce the half dozen you originally desired, but two are a nice round number. *Get home!*"

She underlined the last two words.

Stephan Cassala opened the door of Dan's room tentatively. He had been a daily visitor since the heart attack, and today he came with a briefcase and his son, Ralph. Ralph, a short, slender boy, much like his father, was twenty-one and a senior at Stanford. He was Stephan's only child, a fact of considerable sorrow to Stephan's mother, whose daughter, Rosa, had presented her with five grandchildren.

"Come on in," Dan called out; Stephan was relieved at the strength and vigor in his voice. Dan's bed was tilted up, and half a dozen newspapers were spread out over the counterpane.

"I had dinner in town with Ralph," Stephan explained. "I thought I'd bring him along. He wanted to see you."

"Glad you did." Dan shook hands with the boy. It was two years since he had seen him. "You look fine."

"How do you feel, sir?"

"Good. What are you up to, Ralph?"

"Well, sir, you know I'm in my last year at school. They've been allowing me to do some independent work on the Wilson cloud chamber method, and I think I've found a way to improve it."

"Physics?"

"Well, it's all I ever really wanted."

The boy shook hands with Dan again and left. When he had gone, Stephan shook his head. "I try, Dan, but he's beyond anything I understand. Would you believe it, there's a good chance he's on his way to a Nobel Prize. Twenty-one years old, two generations out of a Sicilian hole of ignorance and superstition. We didn't do too badly."

"We sure as hell didn't. How's Joanna?"

Stephen shrugged. "How long can an empty marriage survive? She lives, I live. There's no point in talking about that. How do you feel?"

"Pretty good. Another week, and Jean takes me home—but how I'm going to stand another week of this, I don't know. Tom came to see me."

Surprised, Stephen made no comment.

"It wasn't too bad. It's time."

"Yes, it's time," Stephen said.

"I've been reading about my daughter," Dan said, pointing to the newspapers.

"I know. I saw Senator Claybourne. He happened to be in town yesterday, and I pulled all our rank to get to him. He gave me ten minutes."

"We gave that sonofabitch ten thousand dollars."

"Well, it's a thousand dollars a minute. It didn't buy much. The truth is, Dan, he's scared. So help me God, McCarthy and this committee has the whole damn country running scared. He says there's not one blessed thing that he or anyone else in the Senate can do about the House committee. He won't touch it. This business of guilt by association has become a disease with us."

"Did you get anything from him?"

"Nothing. He suggested that you might call the President. You do know him, don't you?"

"I met him once. So did ten thousand others."

"I spoke to Judge Fredericks. His feeling is that you should relax and simply let events take their course. They will question Barbara and she'll answer their questions, and they'll make their headlines and that will be the end of it. Whatever damage it may do to her career—well, that has already taken place, and she'll survive it. I had the crazy notion of a lawsuit against the committee—"

"That's not so crazy."

"Well, it's out of the question, Dan. You can't sue a congressional committee."

"I'd like to corner the lot of them in a dark alley. That's all in the head. I indulge the luxury of talking tough, and there isn't a damn thing I can do for the kid. What's all that?" he asked, pointing to Stephan's briefcase.

"I thought we might go over some things."

Dan shook his head. "No. No, forget it, Steve. Business is the last thing in the world I give a damn about right now. I've been lying here trying to make some sense out of being alive sixty years on this earth, and in my present state of confusion, you'll get nothing

sensible out of me. By the way, have you been able to
reach Bernie?"

"No. Nothing at the house, and at the garage,
they've heard nothing."

It was almost three o'clock in the morning before Barbara finally fell asleep, and she was awake at seven,
wide awake with no feeling of weariness, cheered by
the thought that after seeing this long day through,
she would be back home in San Francisco before midnight, California time. Jean had been very insistent
about Barbara's clothes, having always regarded her
daughter as a prime enemy of fashion; so in deference
to her mother's wishes, Barbara had agreed to appear
in a navy blue suit, black pumps, and a white shirt.
Her light brown hair was just wavy enough to present
no difficulties. She wore it parted on the side and cut
evenly just above her shoulders, and it took her only a
few minutes to comb it out. Her complexion was
good, and after a brief glance in the mirror, she decided that the occasion did not warrant make-up.

Before breakfast, she walked in the lovely gardens
of the hotel. She was alone except for a black man
who was trimming rose bushes and who bid her good
morning.

"It's a beautiful morning," Barbara agreed. "Do you
have many days like this?"

"Some. Not so much at this time of the year as in
another month. You ain't from here?"

"California. San Francisco."

"That's a long way."

"It is. It is indeed."

She walked back to the hotel dining room, hungry
now. Harvey Baxter was already there, hunched over
bacon and eggs. He jumped to his feet.

"Oh, don't get up, Harvey. I feel wonderful. We shall tilt against Mr. Drake's committee and conquer them. Onward and upward!"

"Barbara, I do wish you'd be serious. It's not Mr. Drake's committee. He's simply well known locally because he's from our state. Not that I wish to defend him. I find most of his practices deplorable. But you must take this seriously. I just had a call from Congressman Hood's office. He's the ranking member. The hearing will be public. It will not be filmed or televised, but they will have a press table."

"What made them change their plans?"

"I don't know, and that worries me. They must have dug up something. Barbara, are you sure that we've discussed everything?"

"I think so. Harvey, please don't worry."

"One slight ray of sunshine. With this kind of hearing, I shall be sitting next to you, and you can consult me whenever you wish."

"Good. Now let the condemned woman eat a proper breakfast."

They took a cab to the House Office Building, and Barbara, looking about her, observed, "It is a rather nice city, except that one has seen so many pictures of everything."

"I keep thinking that Sam Goldberg would have been more thorough," Baxter said worriedly.

"I suppose it's why I'm here that keeps me from being thrilled. You've been here before, so you're not thrilled. That's the Capitol, Harvey." The truth was that Barbara was simply impatient with the whole thing. Her mood of a few hours before was washing out, and now she was irritated that a handful of men in Washington had the undisputed power to summon her across the country and ask her questions—with the

threat of punishment hanging over her head if she refused to answer. The guard at the desk in the House
Office Building took their names and told them what
room to go to. It was on the main floor, down a corridor to where a cluster of men stood smoking and waiting. They examined her with their eyes as she and
Baxter entered the room, but no one spoke to her, and
she wondered whether they were reporters.

There were five men already in the room. Three of
them sat at the press table. One sat in front of a raised
platform that held a long table and fiddled with a
stenotype machine. The fifth man, tall, cadaverous,
and gray-complexioned, came to them as they entered.
He had small, dark eyes under bristling brows, sunken
cheeks, and a long hatchet chin; he introduced himself
as Donald Jay, counsel to the committee. Barbara noticed that his fingernails were clogged with dirt. He
shook hands with Baxter. She told herself that if he
offered a hand to her, it would go untouched.

"You can both sit here, Mr. Baxter," he said, indicat-
ing a small table in front of the press table and to one
side of it.

There were only six chairs at the press table, but
Barbara noticed a dozen additional chairs behind it,
either for additional press or for some small section of
the public. The room itself was no more than forty-
five feet long and twenty-five feet wide. On the long
table on the raised platform, five small placards
spelled out the names of the congressmen who would
make up the quorum: Arthur Hood, Norman Drake,
Lomas Pornay, John Mankin, and Alvin Bindle. Of the
five, Barbara was familiar only with Drake, who represented a district in the Bay Area.

A few minutes after Barbara and Baxter were
seated, people began to drift into the room—a United

States marshal, a fat man in a dark suit, his badge pinned to his jacket; additional members of the press, until all the seats at the press table were filled and four more seats behind it; and finally the congressmen: Hood, short, tight-lipped, pale blue eyes behind gold-rimmed glasses; Drake, expressionless, his puffy, round cheeks giving him an air of innocence; Pornay, fat, rolls around his neck, a bright pink complexion, a sort of Tammany Hall caricature; Mankin, the oldest of the lot, his face drooping in folds of flesh like a hostile basset hound; and last, Bindle, good-looking, youngish, smiling nervously. They took their respective seats, picked up the pencils at each place, surveyed the group, and waited, for the most part expressionless.

Then, after what he apparently considered a suitable amount of time, Mankin, speaking in a heavy southern drawl, said, "Meeting of the House of Representatives Committee on Un-American Activities, sixteenth day of March, nineteen forty-eight. Let the record show that a quorum is present."

"So noted," Donald Jay said.

"Is the first witness present?"

"Yes, sir."

"Let the witness be sworn," Mankin said.

The marshal walked over to Barbara and held out a Bible. "Put your hand on it," he said. "Do you swear that the testimony you give here will be the truth, the whole truth, and nothing but the truth?" The words ran together, blurred and meaningless.

"I do," Barbara said.

"Let the record show that the witness has been sworn," Jay said. He had moved to one side of the room so that he would not block the view of any of the congressmen, and he stood there with his arms folded.

"Will the witness state her name?" he asked Barbara.

"Barbara Cohen."

"Is that Miss or Mrs.?"

"Mrs."

"Is that your only name?" Dixon snapped suddenly.

"I don't understand you."

"Are you known by any other name?" Jay asked her.

"Barbara Lavette," she replied uncertainly.

"Is that a pseudonym?"

"No, it's my maiden name. I use it for my writing."

"Why?"

"Because I began to publish before I was married. I had a circle of readers who knew me as Barbara Lavette. I saw no reason to change my literary name." Then she whispered to Baxter, "This is idiotic. Must I answer any stupid question they ask me?"

Baxter nodded. "Please—you must, Barbara."

"Will you state your profession," Jay said.

"My profession? But I just told you."

"Please answer the question."

Barbara sighed. "Very well. I am a writer. I am also a housewife. I am also a mother. I practice all three professions, and I suspect that all of them are professions more constructive in the life of this nation than that of being a congressman—"

"The witness," Hood interrupted, "will confine herself to answering the questions asked of her!"

"For heaven's sake," Baxter whispered, "don't antagonize them."

"I see the witness has a sense of humor," Jay acknowledged. "This is hardly the place for it. Now I want you to consider my next question thoughtfully.

Are you now or have you ever been a member of the Communist Party?"

Barbara did not pause to consider it. "I am not and I never have been a member of the Communist Party."

"I see," Jay said. He turned to Drake, who took a sheaf of papers out of his breast pocket and spread them on the table in front of him. He studied the papers for a long moment, pursing his lips.

"Mrs. Cohen," Drake said, "where were you residing in the month of May nineteen thirty-nine?"

Here it comes, Barbara thought, almost relieved. "I was living in Paris."

"I see. And what was the nature of your residence there? I mean, were you a tourist, a student?"

"I was journalist. I was the Paris correspondent for *Manhattan Magazine*."

"And what were your duties in that position?"

"I wrote a weekly newsletter. I commented on styles, on new books, on plays that opened, art exhibits—that sort of thing."

"Then you say you were not a political reporter?"

"I'm afraid not."

"Now is it not true that in May of nineteen thirty-nine, you were persuaded by two French communists, Claude Limoget and his wife, Camille Limoget, to undertake a communist mission for them?"

"The way you put it," Barbara replied, "is an obvious attempt to turn my previous answer into a lie."

"Will you answer the question!"

"And your information comes from my book," Barbara cried, almost shouting. "I made no secret of it. My book was widely read. It was a book club selection. Thousands of people know exactly what happened."

"Are you going to refuse to answer the question?" Dixon insisted.

"Barbara, please," Baxter whispered, "Answer the question."

"I am not refusing to answer the question. I shall answer it. But since you are making a record, I do not want the record to indicate that you have discovered some secret in my life." She felt herself getting angry and excited, and she told herself, No, that's no good. Very calm, Barbara, very calm.

"Please answer the question," Jay said.

"Yes, I undertook a mission for them. But it was not a communist mission."

"How would you characterize it?" Dixon demanded. "According to your own book, you went into Germany to contact the Communist Party."

"Claude and Camille Limoget were communists. They made no secret of it," Barbara said quietly.

"Will you speak up!"

"I said that the Limogets were communists. I was not. That is why they came to me. They told me that the Communist Party in France had lost all contact with the Communist Party in Germany, that it was desperately important to have some kind of contact, and that as a journalist with no communist connections, I could safely enter Germany."

"You say you were not a communist, yet you were willing to enter Nazi Germany at the risk of your life to attempt this contact?"

"I did not consider that I was risking my life. I was a journalist, and my editor was delighted at the thought that I might send some stories out of Germany."

"But you undertook this mission for the Communist Party of France?" Dixon insisted.

"Yes."

"And was it successful?"

"No," Barbara said softly. "The man was dead."

"Please speak up!"

"No."

"And still you deny that you were ever a member of the Communist Party?"

"I was never a member of the Communist Party."

Dixon leaned back and smiled slightly.

"It's all right," Baxter whispered. "They're just making smoke. It's all right."

Donald Jay unfolded his arms. "Do you know Harry Bridges?" he asked Barbara.

"I know who he is. I don't know him personally."

"In nineteen thirty-four, Mrs. Cohen, during the incident on the San Francisco waterfront that is remembered as 'Bloody Thursday,' did you work at a communist first-aid station?"

"No. I know of no communist first-aid-station. I had first-aid equipment in my car, bandages and that sort of thing, and we helped longshoremen who were hurt and bleeding."

"What do you mean by *we?*"

"Myself and a longshoreman."

"What was his name?"

"I can't remember. That was fourteen years ago."

Jay walked to the table and picked up a sheet of paper. "I have here a sworn deposition by one Manuel Lopez, a San Francisco longshoreman. I will read it for the record. 'In July of nineteen thirty-four, on the day known as "Bloody Thursday," I helped to set up a unit field hospital in a station wagon on Second Street in San Francisco. The station wagon was owned by Barbara Lavette. She worked at the unit hospital. I was then a member of the Communist Party, and I ac-

cepted the fact that she was also a member of the
Communist Party.' Will you comment on that, Mrs.
Cohen?"

"I certainly will," Barbara said. "It's a bare-faced
lie. I never knew a Manuel Lopez. There was no unit
field hospital, as he calls it. It was a station wagon
with some bandages and iodine and peroxide. It had
nothing to do with the Communist Party, and I was
certainly not a member of the Communist Party, not
then or ever."

Jay walked over to the table to confer with the committee members, and Barbara whispered to Baxter,
"Harvey, what is this crazy thing with this Lopez?"

"You're sure you never knew anyone by that name?"

"I'm absolutely sure."

"Then for some reason they got him to lie and invent this. I hate to think that they would suborn a
witness, but it's possible that they've done just that.
Please don't worry. Your answers are frank and straightforward, and I want you to continue that way. As for
this Manuel Lopez, if we have to face him in court, I
can tear his story to shreds."

"Court? Harvey, I am not a criminal. What on God's
earth is happening here?"

"Barbara, please, please do not get excited. And
don't worry. None of this is as bad as it sounds."

"Oh, Harvey, that is great comfort," she said bitterly. "None of it is as bad as it sounds."

Jay stepped away from the table and paced slowly
back to his former position. He took a small notebook
out of his pocket and studied it thoughtfully. Then he
snapped it closed and said, "Mrs. Cohen, did you
know a man named Marcel Duboise?"

"Yes."

"What was your relationship with this man?"

"I loved him. We were to be married."

"Then you were never married to him?"

"No. He died before we were to be married."

"I see. What was his occupation?"

"He was a newspaperman. He worked for a French newspaper called *Le Monde*."

"Did you and Marcel Duboise share the same living quarters in Paris?"

"Do I have to answer that?" she whispered to Baxter.

"It's in your book, Barbara, so it's a matter of public record. You could refuse on the grounds that it isn't pertinent, but why not answer it?"

"Yes," Barbara said to Jay, "we did."

"Was Marcel Duboise a member of the Communist Party?"

"No, he was not."

"Was he a member of the International army in Spain, the Fifteenth Brigade, I believe it was called?"

"No, he was not. He was in Spain as a reporter for *Le Monde*." She felt a tightening in her chest. She closed her eyes and breathed deeply.

"Could we have a brief recess?" Baxter demanded. "My client is under great stress."

"I think we could recess for fifteen minutes," Mankin said magnanimously, "if the lady requires it."

Sitting in a small visitors' lounge, the door closed against reporters, Baxter suggested that they might have the hearing put off to the following day.

"No! Absolutely not," Barbara declared. "I want to get it over with and get out of this wretched city."

"Are you sure you're all right?"

"I'm all right, Harvey. But what are they doing to

me? They've twisted everything and turned me into some kind of insane red agent. And this Lopez thing. Who is he?"

"I don't know and I don't want you to be disturbed by it. As of this moment, they have no way of connecting you with the Party. That deposition is meaningless. You are telling the truth, and we will stick to the course. I don't think there is much more to this hearing."

It was small comfort to her, and she was beginning to lose what faith in Harvey Baxter she still possessed. "There is no point in provoking them," Baxter told her. "Drake is a vindictive man. I should play it very gently, Barbara, and fall back upon the privileges open to you as a woman facing gentlemen."

She stared at him, wondering whether he had lost his mind. "Gentlemen?"

"Only in a manner of speaking," Baxter tried to explain. "The more you resist them, the more aggressive they will become. Are you sure you are in a condition to continue?"

"How much longer?"

"A half-hour at the most. I imagine this Lopez was their ace in the hole, so the worst is over."

The reporters watched her curiously as she walked back to the hearing room with Harvey Baxter, but no one spoke to her or asked her any questions. Their aloofness chilled her. The congressmen were already seated and waiting.

"You are still under oath," Donald Jay reminded her.

Pornay, she realized, was leafing through a copy of her first book, the account of her experiences in France and Germany. Jay looked at Pornay, and Pornay nodded.

"Your husband's name is Bernie Cohen. Is that right?" Jay began.

"Yes."

"He fought in Spain with the Abraham Lincoln Brigade?"

"Yes."

"Was the Abraham Lincoln Brigade a communist organization?"

"I don't know."

"Is your husband now or has he ever been a member of the Communist Party?"

"You don't have to answer that," Baxter whispered to her.

"I wish to." And then, raising her voice, she answered, "No, my husband was never a member of the Communist Party. My husband is and was a dedicated Zionist, which is hardly compatible with membership in the Communist Party."

Jay walked over to the long table, and for a few minutes he and Drake and Pornay talked in whispers. Then he spoke to Mankin. Then he returned to his former position, folded his arms, and said, "You are the chairman of the board of the Lavette Foundation. Is that correct, Mrs. Cohen?"

She whispered to Baxter, "Is that pertinent? Does the foundation come into this?"

"I don't know how. But if you refuse to answer, Barbara, it will just give them a peg to hang something on. Why not?"

"Yes, I am," Barbara said.

"And what is the purpose of the Lavette Foundation?"

"It is a charitable, nonprofit organization that gives financial grants on a broad spectrum, medical, scientific, and artistic."

Again Jay consulted with the congressmen. Then he turned to Barbara, stared at her thoughtfully, and then asked almost indifferently, "What is the Hospital of the Sacred Heart?"

She exchanged glances with Baxter, who was evidently as taken by surprise as she was. He shrugged and nodded.

"It's a hospital in the city of Toulouse, in France," Barbara replied.

"What is your connection with this hospital?"

"Marcel Duboise was taken there after he was wounded in Spain. He died there," she said softly.

"Will the witness speak up!" Drake snapped.

She repeated her answer.

"Let me phrase the question differently," Jay said. "What is your connection with this hospital at the present time?"

"What is this all about?" Baxter whispered to her. "How does the hospital come into this? Do you want me to ask for another recess? Perhaps we should talk about this."

"No, Harvey," she whispered back. "Let's finish it. The hospital thing is very simple." And to Jay she said, "The Lavette Foundation made a grant of one hundred thousand dollars to the Hospital of the Sacred Heart in nineteen forty-five. The foundation has also made two subsequent grants to the hospital."

"And what was the purpose of these grants?"

"To establish a wing of the hospital that would care for the wounded survivors of the Republican army who made their way over the Pyrenees and their families." Then Barbara added, "And since this goes into your record, I would also like the record to show that before these grants were made, we consulted with the proper authorities, and we have written statements to show that the grants were in the proper purview of the foundation." She got that out without being interrupted, and she was pleased that she had thought of it. She was in control of herself now, very calm, and to some extent relaxed. Her heart no longer raced. She raised one of her hands and looked at it. It was quite steady.

"Did all of these so-called grants come from the Lavette Foundation?" Jay wanted to know.

"Yes."

"Were you involved in the raising of any additional funds for the Hospital of the Sacred Heart?"

"Yes. A sum of something over twelve thousand dollars was raised through private subscription for the purchase of penicillin and other medical supplies."

"Was this an action of the Lavette Foundation?"

"No. The Lavette Foundation does not raise money from private sources. I undertook this personally."

"And how many persons contributed to this private subscription?"

Barbara thought for a moment, trying to remember the people she had gone to. "Eighteen—or nineteen."

"Were any of these people members of the Communist Party?"

"I have no idea. It's the last thing in the world I would have thought of asking any of them."

Again Jay consulted with the congressmen. Then he walked to one side, and Drake took over.

"Mrs. Cohen," Drake said, "please give the committee the names of the people who contributed to this private fund of yours."

It was the question Barbara least expected. Afterward, she realized that she should have anticipated it from the very beginning. A tortuous, twisted road of questioning had finally led to it; still, she should have

known. It had always been the same. Every investigation ever undertaken by this committee led to the
same goal: names. Names were all they were interested in, names that could be used to spread an ever-
widening network of fear and suspicion. She thought
of one old lady in San Francisco, a woman of eighty-
two years, who had given her a thousand dollars because, as she put it to Barbara, "these people fought
for our values, my dear. And now they are sick and in
need. You don't desert such people." Barbara thought
of the same old woman brought here to Washington
by subpoena, sitting before this committee. She
thought about a professor at Berkeley who had given
her a hundred dollars. She only had to name him and
he would work no more, not at the University of California, not at any other university. She thought of Dr.
Kellman, who had given her two thousand dollars.
Would the hospital close its doors to him, refuse him
operating privileges? She had read of such cases. She
had read the newspaper accounts of all the hearings
before this same committee, read them with that fine
air of detachment and security that the average citizen has reading the morning newspaper. And now she
was no longer an average citizen. She was sitting in
the House Office Building in Washington, and the
question was put to her.

Harvey Baxter was watching her. "Why doesn't he
say something?" she asked herself. Jay was watching
her. Drake was watching her, his tiny eyes fixed on
her.

"No!" she said.

Jay said, "You were asked to name the people who
contributed to this private fund for the Hospital of the
Sacred Heart. Will you please name them."

"No," Barbara said, "I will not."

"Could I have a moment?" Baxter asked. He whispered to Barbara, "You can't refuse to answer, Barbara. It constitutes a contempt. We can't even cite the First Amendment, as the Hollywood writers did. It simply doesn't apply here. You opened the door, and now you must supply the names they want."

"And become an informer? And turn people who trusted me over to these pigs? Are you out of your mind, Harvey?"

"You are my client, and my duty is to my client. I will not allow you to walk into a contempt citation over a ridiculous matter like this."

"Harvey, please shut up," she whispered; she said to Jay, "No, Mr. Jay, I have no intention of naming the contributors."

"You realize that we can subpoena your books and records?"

"The only books and records of these contributions are in my head. But if there were books and records, rest assured that I would destroy them before you got your wretched hands on them."

"Oh, my God," Baxter whispered. "Don't say any more."

"Mrs. Cohen," Drake said, "do you realize that by refusing to answer this question you are placing yourself in contempt of this committee?"

"I don't fully understand what that means," Barbara said slowly. "I would like to think it means that I have contempt for you and your associates. That would be correct."

"We are through with this witness, Mr. Jay!" Drake shouted over a ripple of noise and laughter from the press. "Get her out of here!"

* * *

On the plane back to California, Barbara realized she was actually feeling sorry for Harvey Baxter, and she found herself saying, "Do cheer up, Harvey. It's not the end of the world, not by any means. We were both of us equally dense in never imagining that it would go this way."

"Why didn't you tell me about those contributions? I'm your lawyer, Barbara."

"Because it never occurred to me, Harvey. Not in a thousand years could I have guessed that they would care that a few friends of mine gave me money for medicine. Who could imagine that such a thing would be frowned upon, even by those creeps?"

"We should have anticipated it."

"And if we had, what difference would it have made? I wouldn't give those bastards the names under any circumstances. Oh, let's forget it. Washington! Never, never have I been so happy to be out of a place! I would not go back there if they decided to make me the first woman President. I would shift the capital to Omaha, Nebraska, or to Tulsa, Oklahoma. Those dreadful, stupid, bigoted men! Well, it's over, and God willing, Bernie's craziness is also over. Wouldn't it be nice if he were home, waiting for me when I get there? He might even be at the airport. Mother knows what plane we're taking. That would be a very nice surprise."

"It's not over," Baxter said unhappily.

"You mean the contempt? I'm not going to worry about that."

"I'm afraid I must, Barbara."

"Very well. What will they do? Put me in jail? Flog me?"

"The first step is for them to cite you, and I'm sure they will. Jay said as much. Then it goes to a vote of

Congress. If Congress
citation, it goes to the j
issue a warrant for your arre

"As a master criminal? As a h

"It's not a laughing matter, Bar
guilty at the trial, they can sentence you to as much as
a year in prison. Of course, I don't expect it to come to
that, but we must look the whole process in the face.
The one ray of sunshine is that the contempt can be
voided at any time right up to the point when the
judge pronounces sentence—and even after that."

"Harvey, you are impossible," Barbara declared.
"Will you stop being a lawyer for a moment and be an
ordinary American citizen. They do not put people in
jail for what I just did. I know these are stinking
times, but it is still the country I was born and raised
in."

"Yes, I suppose it is," Baxter said bleakly.

"Now just what do you mean by voiding a contempt?"

"It's very simple, Barbara. The contempt consisted
of refusing the names. I don't think you would have to
give them all eighteen names. Perhaps even if you
gave them three or four—with the consent, of course,
of the people involved—they might very well void the
contempt. I spoke to Jay about that, and he appears
inclined—"

"Harvey!"

"No need to get angry."

"I will be angry, very angry, if you mention that
again. If I must go to jail, I'll go. I don't think it's in
the cards, but if I must, I will. Right now, I don't
want to think about it. Or talk about it."

"Would you consider giving me the names?"

"No!"

ust me?"

ind," Barbara said more
Harvey, and I think you've
ct me and help me. I do appre-
something I must do alone and
share with no one, not with you and not with Bernie.
You must stop thinking of me as a helpless woman.
I'm not helpless and I'm not weak. Now I want you to
do me a favor. I want you to read your copy of the
Washington *Post* for the next hour and just let me sit
here and think. I have a good deal of thinking to do."
She patted his hand. "And you're not to worry."

Jean was waiting for them at the airport in San
Francisco. Until they dropped Baxter off at his home,
Jean spoke only of Dan, of his rapid improvement,
and of the two days of rain they had just experienced.
She had telephoned Eloise, and Barbara's son was
doing fine, eating his fill, and apparently not missing
her a great deal.

When they were alone in the car, Jean said, "Was it
awful?"

"While it was happening, yes. It was nasty. They
brought up the past, things that had happened to me
in France, and I'm afraid I reacted very emotionally.
Now it's over, and I don't want to think about it."

"Was Harvey helpful?"

"Not very. No. Poor man, he did the best he could."

"Dan thinks he's an idiot."

"No, he's not an idiot. It's just that he refuses to believe what is happening. Most of all, he can't believe
that it is happening to a Lavette or a Seldon or however he thinks of us."

"Well, neither can I. My house or yours, baby?"

"Mine, mother. I want to get out of my clothes, and

there might be something from l.
haven't heard because you would ha

"No, I haven't heard."

At the house on Green Street, Ba.
through her mail. Nothing from Bernie   on
cables under the door. "Do you know," sh   a to her
mother, "I talked myself into believing that he would
be here or at the airport, waiting. I sat on the plane
rehearsing to myself how I would tell him about my
day in Washington. I planned to be so clever and
bright about it. I was thinking about how Dorothy
Parker might tell it if it had happened to her. I do
love Dorothy Parker. Why can't I write the way she
does?" She plopped into a chair, put her face in her
hands, and began to cry.

"Honey, are you crying because you don't write like
Dorothy Parker or because you haven't heard from
that silly husband of yours?" Jean stood in front of
her, watching her helplessly.

"I'm all right, mother. I'm just dog tired. I hardly
slept at all last night. You would think that with all
I've been through in the past, this wouldn't matter so
much. But it was so rotten, so absolutely rotten."

"How did it come out, Bobby?"

"Have you a Kleenex?" Jean handed her a tissue,
and Barbara dried her eyes. "I thought I was over the
tearful syndrome. I still don't dare use eye make-up
for fear I'll have black gullies running down my
cheeks. Oh, I was doing fine until the end, and then
they began the business of names. They wanted to
know who contributed to the medicinal fund for the
hospital in Toulouse, and when I refused to tell them,
they found me in contempt."

"I gave you money for that. Why didn't you tell
them? I couldn't care less."

...ther," Barbara said, "be an angel and don't dis-
...ss it any further. All I want now is a bath and my
bed. We'll talk about it tomorrow. I'll pick up Sammy,
and I'll bring him with me to the hospital. About four
o'clock. Will you be there then?"

The Associated Press had covered the committee hearing in Washington, and the leading San Francisco papers, the *Chronicle* and the *Examiner*, ran the story on
the front page. For the past four decades, the Lavettes
were news and had made news in San Francisco, and
from nine o'clock in the morning, Barbara's telephone
rang intermittently. She had already left the house
and was on her way to the Napa Valley, so she was
spared the newspapers' calls until she returned early
in the evening with Sam.

John Whittier was less fortunate. After he had explained to several callers that he had absolutely no
idea where Thomas Lavette could be found, he
stopped all calls and spent the best part of the day
reflecting on the grief the Lavette family had brought
him since he decided to marry Jean Lavette seventeen
years before. A telephone call from Tom at Nicasio,
which his secretary decided he should accept, did
nothing to ease his anger.

"That damn sister of yours," he shouted at Tom, "is
totally irresponsible!"

Tom tried to calm him. Whittier then wanted to
know what on earth Tom thought he was doing, hid-
ing up there in Marin County.

Tom repeated the conversation to Lucy. It brought
a smile to her face, and Tom found himself smiling in
response. "Whittier," Tom said, "is a horse's ass of the
first water. He's terrified of Ronny Brinks, who runs
the Republican organization in the city."

Sally had decided to remain at Higate until Barbara returned from Washington. Her excuse to her mother, if she needed one, held that it was no more difficult to take care of two babies than one, and that Sally plus her one-year-old could therefore be of great help to Eloise. Actually, Clair needed no excuse. She was totally delighted with the company of both her children and her grandchildren. It had been only a few years since her son Joshua had been killed in the Pacific; her recovery from that had been slow and painful, and for a large part of her being, there was neither recovery nor hope of recovery. Time, which is said to heal most sorrows, left her memory undulled; and even after the passage of years, there would be moments of sharp, awful remembering—a vision of the bright, beautiful boy whom she had given birth to and raised and who had bled out his life somewhere in the Pacific, buried at sea, with not even a grave to remind her that he had ever lived. When such moments came, she would lock herself into her room and give way to an emotional burst of tears.

No one in her family knew this. Clair Levy was not given to tears, and her husband, Jake, could not remember her weeping, not even when the news of their son's death arrived. She was a strong woman, both physically and mentally, large-boned, competent, not very stylish after twenty-eight years of living and working on a farm, and given to blue jeans and work shirts, but still lean and shapely at forty-eight and in Jake's eyes as beautiful as ever.

Yet delighted as she was with even a few days of both her children, Clair told Jake that she was worried about Sally and Joe and what was happening between them. "I think it's less a desire to be with Barbara and her baby than a desire to get away from Joe.

I think the marriage is sour as hell, Jake, and it worries me."

"How do you know?"

"I smell it."

"That's great. That's true perception. Why don't we leave it alone. If the marriage goes sour, it goes sour. How many decent, working marriages do you know about? Our daughter is pretty damn crazy."

"Wonderful. That's the way you see it. And Joe is a sterling, Christ-like figure."

"Joe is a decent, solid, hard-working physician."

"And Sally is a lovely, bright, and sensitive child, whatever you may think."

"She's not a child. She's a woman with a child of her own."

"She's twenty-two years old, and to me she's still a child. I'll tell you what's wrong with you, Jake. You're building a damned empire here. You don't see anything else or give a damn for anything else. I can remember when you were ready to cut your father's heart out because he and Dan made money out of the war. We once grew a few grapes and bottled a few thousand gallons. Now you're bottling a hundred thousand gallons and becoming a damn commuter to Montgomery Street!"

"Hey, wait a minute. What have I done? What have I said? I said Joe is a decent, hard-working guy—"

Clair turned away in disgust and strode off, leaving Jake to shake his head in bewilderment.

Clair's assessment was more than a smell. Sally had always been ebullient, given to endless pseudo-literary declarations, high-spirited to the point of explosiveness, and free to say anything she pleased, which she frequently was pleased to do. Now she had turned quiet, had become subdued.

She telephoned Joe the night Barbara left. She found him at the hospital, between operations.

"What is it? I don't have much time, Sally," he said to her.

"I'm still at Higate."

"Don't you think you should come home?"

"What difference will it make?"

"That's a peculiar thing to say."

"You're not there, so what difference does it make?"

"I try to be there as much as I can," Joe explained impatiently. "I have work to do."

"I know."

"What does that mean? You know, I'm not out with some dame. I'm here at the hospital."

"I know that."

"When will you be home?"

"I'll wait for Barbara. Then I'll leave. That will be in two or three days. I'll help take care of Sam."

"They don't need you for that. They have a whole damn institution there at Higate."

"It's to take care of wine, not babies."

"That's not funny."

"I'm not trying to be funny," Sally said. "I'm trying to stay alive. I'm twenty-two years old, and I'm trying to stay alive."

"Will you please make sense."

"All right, Joe. Don't worry. I'll be back as soon as Barbara returns from Washington."

"O.K.," he said. "Take care."

She put down the phone, thinking that he hadn't even asked how his own daughter was.

When Barbara returned home after picking up Sam at Higate and then stopping to see her father at the hospital, it was already on to evening, and she was hardly overwhelmed with delight to find a reporter from the *Examiner* camped on her doorstep. He was an aggressive young man who would not accept the excuse that she was tired and that she had a wet baby to diaper and feed. He tried to be ingratiating by admiring the Victorian décor of the outside of her house.

"If that's the case," Barbara said to him, "you can sit right here and admire it for the next hour. If I've finished everything I have to do, I'll talk to you then."

"Hey, come on, why can't I sit inside and wait?"

"Because I don't want you there," Barbara said.

When she opened the door over an hour later, he was still waiting. "I admire your persistence," she admitted. "Come inside."

"You're a tough lady, Mrs. Cohen. I'm not out to get you. I want to be helpful."

"I can do without the *Examiner*'s help."

"Yeah, but I can't do without yours. I'll get clobbered if I don't come back with something. I tried to find your husband at his garage. They tell me he's out of town. Where?"

"I don't think that enters into it. You'll have to ask him when he returns."

"O.K., I'm not pushing. After your experience, what is your opinion of the House committee?"

"Low, very low."

"Low opinion." He made notes. "You know, I agree with you. I read your first book. Overseas—you know, the armed services editions, those little paper books. I liked it. I haven't read the second one yet, but I'm going to. What about the names?"

"What about them?"

"Are they local people?"

"Mostly, yes."

"I guess it wouldn't do any good to ask you who they are?"

"No."

"Suppose Congress cites you for contempt. Will you go to jail?"

"I hope not."

"What is your opinion of the Communist Party? I mean, do you think they're subversive, I mean, do you think they're dedicated to the overthrow of the government by force and violence?"

"I haven't the vaguest notion."

"Would you describe yourself as an anticommunist?"

"You're cute," Barbara said. "If I say yes, I'm lumped with those cretins in Washington, and if I say no, you've got a wonderful hook for your story. Do you know what I think? I think you'd better go."

"Aw, come on. You're an old newspaperman yourself. I've got to try. Just another question or two. What about your brother?"

"What about him?"

"I hear he may get a Republican designation for Congress. What does this do to his plans? Are you friendly?"

"Good-night, dear boy," Barbara said. She ushered him to the door, ignoring his fervent pleas. "Well, my love," she said to herself as she closed the door behind him, "the hayride is over. You are no longer girl guide. You have pink spurs, and the trouble is, you've really done nothing at all to earn them."

Finally she had a chance to go through her mail. There was a letter from her publisher, which was cheerfully supportive, but in the final paragraph he voiced the hope that her new novel would not be "too political." She went upstairs and gratefully found young Sam sound asleep. Downstairs again, she positioned herself in front of her typewriter, guiltily reviewing the days lost, but the words would not come. She sat for a whole hour staring at the keys, and her thoughts were everywhere but on the page of white paper that confronted her. Only two weeks before, sitting in Huntington Park with Sam in his stroller, she had engaged in a conversation with a French nursemaid. Barbara had been delighted to find someone to speak with in French, and after they had chatted away for fifteen minutes, the nursemaid had asked her what part of France she came from. At first she refused to believe that Barbara was an American, and then, when she had accepted it, she wondered whether Barbara was a nursemaid. "In a manner of speaking," Barbara told her. "The truth is that I dearly love to come here with my boy. I'm a writer. I write books." "And you waste your time with this?" the nursemaid asked unbelievingly.

Barbara did not try to explain the past fifteen years. She had lived three lives, and now she confessed to herself that she desperately wanted the third life to continue. She wanted her world to remain just as it was, no wider than the narrow Victorian house on Green Street. She wanted her large, moody husband to be sitting in the next room, listening to recordings of the *Well-tempered Clavier*. His lust for Bach was as incongruous as everything else about him. He had over three hundred recordings of Bach's music and could follow most of it in an off-key da-da-da. She no longer had any desire to travel, and she did not want to forage in the past. She loved her tiny study, the walls lined with books. She had paid her dues, as she saw it, and the guilt that had come with an inheritance of fifteen million dollars had been assuaged by her creation of the Lavette Foundation. She was romantic enough to appreciate her action of renouncing the inheritance, and she considered herself to be a very decent, normal human being. There was hardly one of her girlhood friends who had not been psychoanalyzed or divorced, and she was fiercely possessive and protective of her own unshaken castle, the little wooden house that was her home.

All of which only went to make the past two weeks more unbelievable. She was essentially a cheerful person, rarely given to depression; now, unable to write, she set about paying the bills that had accumulated since Bernie's departure. At eleven o'clock, she turned on the radio and listened to the news.

She and Bernie had discussed the purchase of a television set. Most of her friends already possessed one, but Barbara was uncertain about taking the step. She looked upon it as a sort of intrusion, images of people coming into her home uninvited. Bernie had argued otherwise. "Good golly, Barbara," he had said, "how different is it from radio? I can remember when there was no radio, and so can you. I remember building a crystal set when I was a kid. The whole thing cost seven dollars, and I remember the first time I asked Rabbi Blum to try the earphones. I expected him to be annoyed, but he was as excited as a kid. He said he had always tried to imagine on what level God communicated, and now he finally knew. Of course, he didn't say who the sponsor would be. He didn't think that way."

Now she hadn't expected her own voice. It was impossible for her to think of herself as a news item, and here she was listening to herself being asked questions and answering them. She was far more interested in the news from Palestine, which had taken on an ago-

nizing sameness. The Mufti's men had ambushed a
bus with grenades and machine-gun fire. Twelve Jewish children and four adults had been killed and
twenty-two others wounded. War loomed on the horizon. The Arab nations were poised for a four-pronged
invasion of the tiny Jewish state. A kibbutz had been
wiped out, with the loss of thirty-seven settlers, men,
women, and children. There was was no emotion in
the announcer's voice, and Barbara reflected that the
world had become inured to the killing of Jews. It was
a matter of course.

"God help me," she whispered. "I'm taking it that
way myself. All I can feel is relief that Bernie is on his
way back. Why don't I cry out with their agony? Why
don't I weep? My husband is Jewish. How can I just
sit here and listen so calmly?"

She turned off the radio, put out the lights, and
went upstairs. In the luxury of a hot bath, she found
herself relaxed and dozing, but when she crawled between the cold sheets of her bed, she was wide awake
again.

For a time she made a conscious effort to find
sleep; then she gave up and allowed fancies and images to crawl around in her mind. The thought that
something might have happened to Bernie had always
lurked there; it surfaced now. In all the years of war,
he had never been wounded, never even scratched,
and he had told Barbara of how an Indian soldier in
North Africa had ascribed it to his karma. Self-
consciously and feeling somewhat foolish, Barbara
once made a trip to the library to read about karma,
but she could make no more of it than that Buddhists
considered it to be the record of past existences acting
upon the present one; since none of it was within the
scope of her belief, she had dismissed it from her

mind. She had not thought about it for years, but tonight she clung to it as some of her friends clung to the convolutions of their horoscopes. She was not a person who enjoyed sleeping alone. The male body in bed alongside her was an assurance of wholeness; a single sex was a fragmentation. To awaken at night and reach out and feel a body, the swell of muscles, the pressure of a body against hers—this was night as it should be. The night was lonely and empty, filled with shadows and anxieties.

In the morning she called Jean and said, "Mother, would you be a dear and baby-sit for a few hours. I have to meet Dr. Kellman at the hospital, and I can look in on daddy while I'm there."

"You're not ill?"

"No, I'm fine. It's not medical, it's something else."

"They're letting Dan come home tomorrow, so that doesn't have to take you to the hospital. You did see him yesterday."

"I know. It's just that it's convenient for the doctor."

In the hospital room, Dan was sitting in bed, growling over the *Examiner*'s treatment of his daughter. "Those bastards!" he exclaimed. "I'd like to buy the rag and fire the lot of them!"

"Mr. Hearst's not selling," Dr. Kellman told him, "and unless you learn to stay calm, I'll just keep you here."

"How is he, really?" Barbara asked the doctor as they walked down the corridor to his office.

"He's good for another twenty years if he takes it easy. Now what is it, Barbara? If it's about that money I gave you for Spain, for the medical supplies— well, I don't give a damn whether you give them my name or not."

"No, it's not that, and I won't discuss this business

of the names with anyone, including people like you.
That's my problem, and only mine."

"I'd just like to make it easier for you." Sitting in his
office, he lit a cigarette and looked at Barbara inquir-
ingly. He was a thin, bald man of about fifty. His
smile was reassuring, a nice smile, Barbara thought,
for a doctor, very reassuring. "Well?" he asked her.
"You're not sick. You look worried but healthy."

"Have you ever given money to help the Jewish settlers in Palestine?" she asked bluntly.

"Well, there's one I didn't expect. Yes, I have. Some.
Not enough."

"How do you do it? I mean, is there an organization
of some sort here that has connections with Palestine?"

"Why, Barbara?"

"Please, I have my reasons."

"It's no secret. It's called the United Jewish Appeal.
Yes, I'd say they have connections in Palestine."

"Do you know the man who runs it?"

"I know him. His name's Alex Denaman."

"Could you call him and ask whether he'll see me
now? As a favor, please."

"No problem." He picked up the phone and made
the call. Then he said to Barbara, "He'll see you in
half an hour. It's over on Market Street. I'll jot down
the address."

When Barbara walked into the office on Market
Street, a small, plain room about ten by ten, half of it
taken up with files, she was greeted by an affable,
plump man who apologized for the condition of the
place. "I'm looking for a secretary," he explained. "Not
that there's any place to put her, but my typing . . .
We use volunteers. Volunteers—draw your own conclusions, Mrs. Cohen. Welcome. Any friend of Doc Kell-

man's. What can I do for you? Have you come with a checkbook?" And seeing the expression on her face, he said quickly, "Sorry. That's a joke. Please sit down." He pulled an old wooden chair into place for her. "Joke—yes, no. We're desperate for money. We're always desperate, but these days . . . That's my problem, not yours. How can I help you? Or how can you help me?"

"I'm not Jewish," Barbara said.

"I suspected as much."

"My husband is. I want to tell you what he's done, and then perhaps you can help me. I'd like to tell you this in confidence, if I may, simply because my father is involved."

"All right, in confidence. You're not only pretty, you have an honest face. Wait a minute—of course, you're the Barbara Cohen I've been reading about."

Barbara nodded. "Yes. Does that change anything?"

"No, no. Go ahead."

He listened attentively without comments while she told him the facts about Bernie and the ten C-54s. When she had finished, he said with feeling, "That is a story. That is something. Do you know, this is the first I've heard of it. Just great. And you mean they actually got the planes to Tel Aviv, with the guns and the Messerschmitts inside?"

"Yes. I had a cable from my husband that said so."

"He must be quite a man," Denaman said.

"He is, yes. But this cable was sent nine days ago. According to the cable, he had made arrangements to take boat passage from Haifa to Naples, a plane from there to England, and then a plane home. But I've heard nothing, not a word, and I'm worried sick."

"Perhaps he was held up in Haifa, delayed. Those ships have no regular schedule."

"Then he would have telephoned me. I know him."

"Ah, but it's not so easy, young lady. I've had to wait three, four, five days to get through to Haifa. Maybe I don't get through at all. The same with cables."

"But it's been nine days."

"What would you like me to do? You tell me the way your father takes out a hundred and ten thousand dollars—my goodness, I am speechless, absolutely speechless."

"Can you try to find out what happened to my husband, whether he's all right and where he is?"

"Look, I can do this. I'll call our New York office, and I'll make a big mystery out of it. I'll tell them it's double-A-one priority. If it's humanly possible, I won't take no for an answer. So maybe I'll have something for you. Only don't worry. A man like your husband—well, don't worry. It will be all right."

"I'm sure it will," Barbara agreed. "I don't know how to thank you."

"Don't thank me yet. We'll see what I can do."

Barbara gave him her address and telephone number, and when she left, she felt better. On the cable car, mounting California Street, she was able to smile at her own fears and frustrations. If Bernie were on his way home, why should he bother to communicate with her? It would only be a matter of days, and then he could have the pleasure of ringing the doorbell and seeing her face when she opened the door. What a dramatic nuisance she had made of herself, both with Dr. Kellman and with Mr. Denaman!

She told Sam about it that afternoon as she trundled him over to Huntington Park. She had read somewhere that mothers who take refuge in one-sided conversations were demonstrating a highly neurotic pattern of behavior, but then, Barbara was not given to chattering. Unlike her sister-in-law Sally, she did not indulge in what she thought of as verbareah, a word she had invented to describe Sally's condition; and since Sam did not yet possess any critical facilities beyond gurgles and two words, one of which was "mama" and the other in all probability "cookie," he remained an appreciative audience. He good-naturedly accepted her apologies, and she considered that one day he might make a useful diplomat. "Or a garage mechanic," she told him. "That's nothing to sneeze at. The ability to fix a car is becoming just about the most useful skill in our society, and both branches of my family made it with their hands. Daddy began as a fisherman—crabs, which is why he never eats them now. He was responsible for the death of heaven only knows how many thousands of crabs, and naturally with all his guilt he couldn't face one today. It's true that mother was born with a golden spoon in her mouth, out of what San Francisco loves to refer to as the highest echelon of its society, which freely translated means two generations of money—and after all, her daddy, my Grandpa Thomas, was president of the Seldon Bank. But the deep, dark family secret is that Grandpa Thomas' father was a placer miner, although it is rumored that he owned a dance hall, which was a large tent and not really a dance hall at all, if you get my drift, which I will not go into any deeper in light of your youth. But he soon discovered that usury paid even better than the oldest profession, and here we are today, only a hundred years later. Grandma, on the other hand, came from a very posh Boston family and her name was Asquith. I don't remember her too well, except that she was a tall lady with a long, thin nose. We all of us seem to run to long bones. But on Daddy's side they were all fishermen, which makes it much simpler—"

She broke off in deference to the two old ladies who had seated themselves on the bench facing her and who were regarding her uncertainly. "He's very young," Barbara explained, "but he has an amazing vocabulary. I mean, he's older than he looks."

She wheeled Sam off, and when safely out of sight, she burst into laughter. She couldn't understand why her talk with Mr. Denaman had made her feel so lightheaded, but it had, and after she took Sam home and bathed him and fed him and put him in his crib for the night, she scrambled two eggs for herself, toasted two slices of bread, and read the first chapter of Sinclair Lewis' new book, *Kingsblood Royal.* One chapter was enough. She could not share her father's enthusiasm for Lewis.

She then went into her study and sat down to attempt her evening stint at her own book; she had not yet begun to write when the doorbell rang. She had not been expecting anyone, and she was pleasantly surprised to see Alex Denaman. She welcomed him enthusiastically as he stepped into the house until she saw his face.

Then she knew. She would always remember the look on his face. Denaman was not capable of concealing emotion.

"Please come in," she said. It doesn't matter what you know. One part of the mind turns off the other part, and death is not a part of anyone's experience. Only life is a part of experience. Death is what exists without being imagined, which cannot be imagined. For all her familiarity with it in the past, it was still the malignant stranger who comes unbidden. All doors are closed to him; he walks through doors.

Denaman stood facing her in the little parlor, his hat in his pudgy hands, an old gray felt hat that he kept sliding through his fingers. His topcoat was worn, and his shoes were cracked under their polish. Evidently there was not much money in being the executive officer of the United Jewish Appeal in San Francisco in 1948.

"Please tell me what you found out," Barbara said. He would remember afterward how gentle and kind her voice was, as if she pitied him.

"I found out about your husband, Mrs. Cohen." Each word was edged with pain. "I felt I must come here myself."

"Is he dead?" she asked slowly. "Is that what you have to tell me?"

"Yes."

For a long, long moment the two of them stood there, looking at each other in silence. Barbara was aware that as yet nothing had happened to her; inside her, from head to foot, there was emptiness, as if she had been turned into a fragile, hollow shell of being. She took a step back and sank into a chair.

"Can I get you something?" he asked. "A glass of water?"

"No," she said softly. "No, thank you, Mr. Denaman." She formed each word carefully and slowly, as a child might. "Please sit down and tell me what you learned. You might be mistaken." She thought how odd it was of her to say that, to decide that he might be mistaken.

He sat on the edge of the chair facing her, fingering his hat nervously. "Are you sure you're all right?"

"Yes."

"I got through to Tel Aviv. I found out that your husband and another man whose name was Irving Brodsky and two Haganah men had set out to drive from Tel Aviv to Haifa. That was on the day or the day after he sent you the cable. Maybe," he interrupted himself, "I should call someone, your mother? You're all alone here?"

"Please go on, please."

"They drove in a jeep. And they were attacked by Arabs, and all of them were killed. The bodies were found the next day by the Haganah, but they could not be identified. Then, only yesterday, they took some Arabs prisoner and found the things they had taken from the bodies. Your husband's wallet and some cards. Today, just a few hours before I got through, a man called Goodman made a positive identification. He was one of the men who traveled with your husband to Czechoslovakia, so he could not be mistaken."

The thickness in her chest came again. She struggled for breath. "I think," she said, "that if you go into my kitchen, Mr. Denaman, you will find a brown paper bag—"

"I know, I know," he said, relieved to be able to act in some way. Barbara pointed. He ran to the kitchen and then returned with the paper bag. She put it over her mouth and breathed into it for a minute or so.

"I'm all right now," she said. "I have heard—" She swallowed and began again. "I have heard that the Arabs torture their prisoners. Do you know how my husband died?"

"I asked. He was shot through the head. He died instantly."

"Yes."

PART FOUR

Trial

On the fourteenth of May, 1948, the same day that the British officially ended their mandate over Palestine and a Jewish state came into being for the first time in two thousand years, the Congress of the United States paused in its awesome task of legislating for the most powerful country on earth and sandwiched in, among other earth-shaking duties, a vote of contempt against one Barbara Lavette Cohen for failing to answer a proper question put to her by the House Committee on Un-American Activites.

Harvey Baxter phoned Barbara with the news. "It's not easy to tell you this on top of everything else, Barbara, but I thought you should know immediately. I had hoped Congress might reject it, but the vote went through."

"What exactly does it mean, Harvey?"

"It puts the contempt citation in the hands of the Justice Department. The crime is a federal misdemeanor, which means that if you should be found guilty, the sentence cannot exceed a year's imprisonment. Now don't jump to any conclusions. I am not saying that you face a year in prison or even that this will go to trial. All that remains to be determined. I think you might drop by one day very soon, and we'll talk about it."

Barbara was tired of talking about it. Still, she agreed. "Tomorrow or the next day, Harvey."

She was unable to come to any sort of terms with the notion of trial and imprisonment. These were words, and words, which had once been so important, had now lost all their meaning. Dr. Kellman had spoken sympathetically of the effect of depression. "It will pass," he had assured her.

What would pass? "The hurt will go away and I'll be as gay as a lark," she said to herself. But there was no more hurt, only emptiness. Everything was empty.

It was not the first time. "I have buried two men," she told herself. "I have buried everything good that has happened to me." Only one was a grave she might never see. Bernie was buried somewhere in what was now, this day, the State of Israel. Denaman had made inquiries, and he told her that there was a way to bring the body back to the United States. It would be very difficult and might take a long time, but it could be done. Barbara said no, let him lie there. It would have been his wish. It was the place he had given his life to. She was not the type who worshipped graves or brooded over them. She had never returned to Toulouse to look at Marcel's grave. Whatever was left of him and of Bernie was inside her.

Life went on. She knew this out of past experience. Life doesn't pause for death. Sam peed in his diaper, gave in reluctantly to toilet training, gobbled his food, ate and slept and played in the wonderful world of his infancy and shed tears only over wet diapers and an empty belly. He existed in a totality of life, in a world where there was no death. Of his father he would know nothing except the pictures Barbara showed him and the stories she told him. What kind of an image would he have of the big, easygoing gentle person who had fathered him? He would carry a Jewish name, but Barbara knew that according to Jewish law he would not be considered Jewish. The burden or stigma or pleasure of being Jewish comes through the mother's line.

After the first awful night, she cried very little. Jean, never very good at coping with death, suggested a memorial service, but Barbara refused. She was the only person on earth who had known the man who had been her husband, and she would not suffer others to speak maudlin, empty phrases of adulation. She herself had no feelings of adulation; she had known Bernie for what he was. It was only that of all the men she had known, there were only two that she had wanted to live and be with.

She had been raised as an Episcopalian within sight of Grace Cathedral, but to her, formal religion was as meaningless a memory as the fairy tales of her childhood. The chapel at Sarah Lawrence College was the last church she had attended. She had no bias against religion and no bias toward it, and she had no real belief in or desire for an afterlife or an existence without a body. Her own body had always pleased her; it was strong, healthy, and good to look at. It was a body men loved and admired, and she had reacted to that love and admiration. When Barbara's first book had been published, the account of her experiences in France and Nazi Germany, a critic had written: "One should not expect profundity from Barbara Lavette. She is not a deeply profound person. Essentially, she is a very ordinary, amiable, and cheerful person confronting a nightmarish world gone mad, which is precisely what gives her writing its excitement and meaning." The critic, seeking profundity, found an absence of gloom and pessimism. The two are often confused.

Barbara wallowed neither in gloom nor in profundity. There were weeks of total, devastating misery, but throughout she functioned, took care of her child, and presented a calm front to the family and friends who came to see her. Even that first night she had been able to say to herself, "Bernie is dead, but I am alive and Sam is alive."

It was only after weeks had passed that she became aware that a part of her was unable to accept the fact of Bernie's death. Not that she doubted the report. In due time, a package had arrived, containing his wallet, some cards, and, curiously enough, keys to a car, possibly the keys to the jeep they had been driving. There was also a letter from Herb Goodman, in which he said, in part: "I hate to write about this because it seems cold and callous, but I feel that I must tell you about the identification. There is no question that it is Bernie. His face was not disfigured. It was very peaceful, so I don't think he suffered. I had come to know your husband and to love him. He was a brave, decent man. We could never have done what we did without him . . ." So the fact of his death was not to be doubted—and still a part of her waited for him to return.

She spoke to Clair Levy about this, and Clair said, "I know, Bobby. I still feel that way about Josh. I find myself wondering when he will come back and calculating how old he will be now. Maybe it happens to us because there is no grave—no grave that you can look at. You have the advantage of me there. Someday you will go there and see the grave."

"And then I'll know that he'll never come back?"

"I think so, yes."

"And until then, each time the doorbell rings—"

"I'm a strong woman," Clair said to her. "I think you

know how I was raised. I've had whores as baby sit-
ters—for myself—and by the time I was twelve I could
swear as well as any sailor on the Redwood Coast, and
if pop disappeared for a week, as he often did, I survived very nicely. But when Josh was killed in the Pacific, I died too. I don't know what is worse than for a
mother to lose a son. I remember thinking then, as
much as I love Jake, why couldn't it have been Jake—
or me? So I died. I was empty. I had no will to live or
laugh or speak or to wake up in the morning."

"I know the feeling," Barbara said.

"And I didn't think it would ever change or that it
could ever change. The thought of joy, any joy, had
become obscene. But do you know, it changed. I
changed. Not that the grief isn't there, but I live with
the grief, the way Eloise lives with those monstrous
headaches of hers. And I'm happy, very happy. And
that will happen to you, believe me."

"It has happened to me," Barbara said. "I've been
through this twice. I know because when Marcel died,
a part of me died. I'll be all right, Clair."

Bit by bit, Barbara picked up the threads of her
life. To begin writing again was a slow, painful process, a form of self-torture, for the very sight of her
typewriter forced her into introspection and memory.
No writer, she realized, truly invents. He takes from
here and there, shapes, changes, contrives, but always
with something that had touched his life. So much
had touched her life! She remembered a day in 1946,
soon after she had returned from her two years of
overseas reporting in North Africa and in the China-
Burma-India theater and had purchased Sam Goldberg's house on Green Street. Her mother had come to
see her and had found her engaged in an article on
Spode china for the *Woman's Home Companion*.

"Spode china!" Jean had exclaimed in amazement. But that kind of flight from reality was exactly what she had needed then, and now she needed it no less. But none of the women's magazines, which until the committee hearing had plied her with endless requests, wanted anything now.

She tried to continue with her novel, but it was almost impossible. The words were empty. She could communicate nothing of herself to the paper. She found herself attending much more seriously to the work of the Lavette Foundation. The Treasury Department, not to be outdone by the House committee, sent a team of auditors to examine the books of the foundation, and for two weeks they pried, examined, added, subtracted, and checked. When Barbara asked Harvey Baxter what they were looking for, he replied that he had no idea and that in all probability neither did they. He told her not to worry. "We have been meticulous," he said, "absolutely meticulous."

Bernie's garage also made demands on her time, for which she was grateful. She had no desire to keep the business, and she made arrangements that permitted Francis Gomez, the chief mechanic, to assume ownership and to pay her out of the profits, assuming there should ever be any. She was touched by his gratitude, just as she was touched by the very deep and sincere feelings that he and the other mechanics expressed at Bernie's death. "He was a good man," Gomez said to her. "Believe me, Mrs. Cohen, he gave a man a fair shake."

Barbara felt that he could have had worse epitaphs.

When Barbara went to Harvey Baxter's office the day after the contempt vote, she took Sam with her. One of the side effects of Bernie's death was a feeling that she must never leave Sam alone again. She knew that this feeling would pass, but just now it was very strong. He was agile enough to climb out of his stroller, and his desire for freedom and exploration was increasing by leaps and bounds. At Baxter's office, she requisitioned the secretary to keep Sam occupied while she met with the lawyers.

"I am now in contempt," she said to Baxter. "Wasn't I in contempt before? What difference does all this charade make?"

"It makes a difference, Barbara. The Un-American Committee cited you for contempt. The House voted the actual contempt. Until that step was taken, there was no indictment, so to speak."

"And now?"

"And now, as I said, it's in the hands of the Justice Department. In the ordinary course of things, they will serve a federal warrant for your arrest."

"Oh, no, you're kidding," Barbara said.

"I wish I were. But please understand that this is merely a formality. You'll appear at the federal courthouse here, and then you will either be released on your own recognizance or some nominal sum will be set for bail—for example, five hundred dollars. You are not to be alarmed by this. The moment the warrant is served, if it is served, you telephone us, and either Boyd or I will take care of matters. You will not go to jail for even an hour. Please understand that."

"I'm trying to. I am also trying not to go insane. Here I am, a housewife and mother and a widow living in these United States in this year of nineteen forty-eight, and I am being told that I shall be arrested by the government. Doesn't it sound crazy to you, Harvey? What have I done?"

"Mrs. Cohen," Kimmelman said, "I would like to get

a word in here, because this can be as confusing as hell. What you have done is very simple. You protected the eighteen people who gave you money to buy medicine for the hospital in Toulouse. That was a decent and courageous act, and in normal times you would be applauded widely, and nothing else would come of it. And what you did, both raising the money and protecting your people, is not a crime. There is nothing criminal about it. But these are not normal times. This country has gone crazy, and we're embarked on some kind of lunatic witch hunt. You are caught in the middle of it. Why they chose you is obvious to me but perhaps less obvious to you. I read through the record of your hearing very carefully. This Manuel Lopez whose deposition Donald Jay read is either a stool pigeon of the committee or of the FBI, or else he's a criminal who's buying his way out by feeding the committee names. Those crumbs are insatiable. If Lopez ever was a communist, he would soon run out of names. Then he has to invent. He was a longshoreman, so he would know that you were mixed up in the thirty-four strike. What better name than Barbara Lavette, daughter of Dan Lavette, granddaughter of Thomas Seldon, the cream of West Coast class, right up there with the Crockers and the Hearsts and the Huntingtons and the Gianninis—and then with the neat little twist of her married name being Cohen. They couldn't resist that. They haven't had headlines like this since the Hollywood writers."

"And is that what they're going to arrest me for—for being a communist?"

"Oh, no. No, indeed. When they threw that at you, you replied under oath that you were not and never had been a communist. If they were to get you on that, it would have to be perjury, not contempt. You

answered that question about being a communist, so
there was no contempt, and they're smart enough to
know that they could never get a charge of perjury to
stick. It would be thrown out of court, and I don't
think they'd dare put Lopez on the stand. They just
kept trying until they pinned a question on you that
you were unwilling to answer. That's the contempt—
the refusal to answer."

"But you can vacate it," Baxter put in. "That's the
door that's always open, Barbara. Surely three or four
of those people would not be hurt if you revealed
their names. Probably they would not even be subpoenaed."

"Harvey," Barbara said coldly, "I told you once that
I will not discuss that."

"Mrs. Cohen," Kimmelman said, "I don't think we
should rehash that. The point is, if we do go to trial, it
will be a very important trial. The fact that it is a
misdemeanor won't lessen its importance. And if we
do go to trial, I don't think we should be your trial
counsel. I don't mean that we should step out of the
case, but I feel that your courtroom representation
should be by a very distinguished counsel, someone
who will impress the court and give the judge reason
to think twice before he imposes any sentence."

"Do you agree with him, Harvey?" Barbara asked.

"Yes, I think I do. I think Boyd tends to leap to
conclusions. I am not at all sure that this will ever
come to trial, but if it does, we should have distinguished counsel to act in court."

"Do you have anyone in mind?"

"I was thinking of Judge James Fredericks. He's
your father's friend. He retired after a very distinguished career on the bench."

"And he's damned impressive," Kimmelman added.

* * *

When Sally Lavette's baby, May Ling, reached the age of thirteen months, Joe convinced her to halt breast feeding and to start the child on regular milk. Sally agreed reluctantly, feeling that for the first time in her life her breast development was adequate in terms of what every American girl should have. She had read somewhere that removing a child from the breast would reduce said organ to a size even smaller than the original. Joe convinced her that this was quite unscientific, but the process of convincing led to a bitter and one-sided argument.

Such arguments had become increasingly frequent. They were one-sided because Joe would not fight back verbally, would not lose his temper, and thereby would not give Sally an opportunity to scratch at the roots of what was bothering her. It was an odd match in any case. At the age of thirteen, when Joe, nine years older, was working at Higate Winery during the summer, Sally specified that if he ever married anyone else, she would kill him. She was an unusually bright, unusually romantic little girl. As much as a woman may create a man, she created Joe—only the creation never matched the reality.

Joseph Lavette was serious, sober, and unimaginative, which is not to say that he lacked intelligence. In medical school, he had been among the top five in his class. In the hospital where he operated, he already had a reputation for skill and probity. In the Pacific theater, he had crammed a lifetime of experience into three years of front-line surgery, but in exchange he had given away his boyhood, his fancies, his romantic images, and practically all of his illusions. He did not possess his sister Barbara's joyous optimism, her deep, unshakable appreciation of simply being alive; when he returned from the Pacific, the only thing that remained to cling to was Sally Levy. It was not unreasonable that a young man who was half Chinese and half Italian, dark, and given to brooding should be enamored of Sally. She was a natural golden blonde, in spite of her constant reference to her long, straight hair as being straw-colored. She had never been pretty—she had her mother's large bones and wide shoulders—but at a point in her maturity she became suddenly quite beautiful, her pale blue eyes deepset under straight brows, her high cheekbones framing a face that was exciting and different. She existed with one foot in the world and one foot out of it. Her imagination was wild and unrestrained, and with the publication of her first book of poems, *Songs of Napa*, she was very warmly recognized if not enriched.

Joe accepted her only partially for what she was. He did not want her to be different, yet he did not want her the way she was. Instead of coming out of his war experience as a cynic, or as a brutalized, self-satisfied medical thug, or as a heartless, success-oriented surgeon, or even as a reasonably compassionate physician, he emerged as a sort of selfless saint who had taken a vow of poverty. In the beginning, Sally had been impressed and filled with admiration; in due time, the admiration became tinged with frustration and eventually with irritation—which was compounded by her inablility to press him to a confrontation. Anger on his part might have cleared the air. He never permitted himself real anger.

Sally had taken no vow of poverty. She disliked the clinic, she disliked working there, and she disliked Boyle Heights. She was not insensitive to the poverty and misery of the people who lived there; she simply felt that she had the right to her own existence. At first she attempted to make herself a part of Joe's life at the clinic. She worked at the admissions desk. She cleaned rooms. She boiled instruments. She consoled mothers with sick children and put her own child aside to comfort the sick and battered children who were brought there. But all of this was motivated by a romantic view of Joe's work, and when the romance washed out, as it of necessity had to, the work turned into pointless drudgery.

There was one night in particular that she would never forget. She was in the sixth month of her pregnancy, helping Joe at the clinic. It was one of those nights of torrential tropical rain that come during the Los Angeles winter, blinding sheets of rain, and a few minutes before midnight, three Chicano boys, one of them sixteen years old, two of them seventeen, were brought into the clinic by friends. They had been in a gang fight and had been badly hurt. Frank Gonzales had already gone home, and only Sally and Joe were at the clinic.

Joe told her to telephone for an ambulance, which she did. Not until the next day did she learn that the ambulance had crashed head-on into a truck. Meanwhile, Joe took the three boys into his examining room. The other boys vanished—understandably, since there would certainly be a police investigation. Sally finished telephoning and heard Joe calling for her. She ran into the examining room, cried out in horror, and pressed her hands over her mouth to keep from being sick. There were two examining tables holding two of the boys, both covered with blood. The third boy lay on the floor, the handle of an ice pick sticking out of his chest, the ice pick quivering and moving with his breath. His eyes were open, and he was pleading in Spanish, "Help me, please. I am going to die."

Sally turned toward the door, and Joe's voice hit her like a whiplash. "Stay here! I need you! I can't handle this alone!"

"I can't."

"You damn well can and you will!"

The following day, Sally read Joe's notes on what had happened. "Fortez, knife wound, entrance subcostal on the left side, hand's breadth from umbilicus. Deep and not clean. Debris on inner aspects. 1½ inches in length. Immediate question: puncture of spleen. Aguila, gunshot. Clean hole located on chest wall approx. at 2nd interspace on right-hand side. No exit wound. Conscious. Complaint of pain in right axilla—with paresphesias of fingers and hand of right arm. Should have X-rayed, but no way. Luck. Bullet in axilla close to brachial plexus. Decent vital signs. No name for third. Ice pick in heart, conscious. Puncture wound parasternal on left side at third intercostal space." That was the following day. Now Joe pleaded with her, "I need you, Sally."

"I can't do this. You know that."

"Hand me that scissors. Did you call the ambulance?"

"Christ, I'm in my sixth month."

"Hand me the damn scissors!" he yelled at her. "And that kid on the floor. I don't want him to move. Talk to him," he said as he took the scissors from her. "Did you call the ambulance?"

"Yes."

"Well, talk to him. Get down there and talk to him. Tell him to lie still, not to move. Go on, your Spanish is better than mine."

She knelt by the boy with the ice pick sticking out of his chest. She felt that she was going to faint, and afterward she had nightmares about that moving, bobbing ice pick that went up and down with the boy's heartbeat. While Joe cut away the clothes of the boy with the knife wound, she knelt on the floor, whispering in Spanish, tongue-tied at first and saying "*Lo compadezco*" inanely, and then, "Please. Lie still. You will be all right."

His hand went to the ice pick, and Joe snapped, "No! He mustn't touch it! Make him understand that! He dies if he pulls out that ice pick! Make him understand that!"

"Why can't you help him?"

"Because I have a kid here with a punctured spleen, and he's going to die if I don't remove it. Anyway, I can't do anything about that one. If the ice pick's in his heart, and it probably is, I need a heart-lung machine. God damn it, I need a hospital. Where the hell is that ambulance?"

She told the boy, "Please, please, you must lie still and don't touch that thing in your chest. You'll be all right, but only if you lie still."

He was crying and he clung to her hand.

"Call Frank," Joe said suddenly. "Tell him to get his ass over here." His voice softened. "And then come back, baby. Please. I need help."

She fled from the room and telephoned Joe's partner. Frank was asleep. "There are three men dying here!" she shouted. "Please get over here!" Then she went into the bathroom and threw up. She stood at the toilet for a few moments, hugging her swollen belly, trying to stop shaking, trying to halt the convulsive heaving of her stomach. Then she went back into

Joe's office and called the hospital again. The ambulance, they told her, was on its way. She called the police.

Then she forced herself back into the examining room. "Frank will be here in ten minutes," she said almost primly. "I called the cops."

"How do you feel?"

"I think I'm all right."

"This one can't wait. His spleen is punctured, and if I don't get it out, he'll die. As soon as Frank comes, we'll operate. You know how the sterilizer works. Frank will do the anesthesia, but we need your help, Sally."

She helped. No ambulance came until it was too late. The boy on the floor with the ice pick in his chest died. Sally got through the next two hours without fainting or being sick again, but the horror of that night remained with her. She had no feeling of achievement, of succoring human suffering. Intellectually, she could create such an attitude within herself, but it always crumbled. She felt no triumph at the miracle of two successful operations conducted in the limited facilities of the examining room. She could not share that with Joe. She could only recoil in horror at the waste of the senseless gang fights and at the misery that poured into the clinic.

"You and me," she said to Joe, "we are different people, different bodies."

"I understand that."

"No, you don't. You don't understand it at all. You only see me as your wife."

"Well, you are my wife," he said placatingly.

"I am not your anything. You don't own me."

"Have I ever said that I own you?"

"Yes, in a hundred different ways, and the main way is that whatever you do is of great importance and whatever I do is silly nonsense."

"I don't look at it that way at all," Joe protested.

"Of course you say you don't. If you could see it the way I see it, it wouldn't happen. But you just look at me with that damned superior, condescending manner of yours, and you don't even respect me enough to blow your top at me?"

"Would it indicate that I respected you if I lost my temper and called you names?"

"I think it would, yes! At least I would be here. I would know that I existed."

"Sally," Joe begged her, "I admit that I get lost in my work. It's not only that I love my work. It's also a part of me. It's the reason I exist. I know there's too much of it, but what can I do? Frank Gonzales works just as hard as I do, and his wife doesn't complain."

"Of course not. She's a Chicano."

"Oh, great! I never expected that from you."

"All I mean is that Chicano women have every shred of independence kicked out of them. I'm not being anti-Mexican when I say that they kick the life out of their women. Oh, I give up! What's the use?"

A few days after that specific argument, Billy Clawson telephoned and asked Sally whether he could drop by the house and see her. Since his first visit to the clinic, he had been working there without pay and living in a furnished room on Boyle Heights. Sally was not sure she liked him, but neither could she bring herself to dislike him. She told herself once that he and Joe were the two polarized ends of what she thought of as the Jesus Christ complex. "Joseph," she said to herself, "is a strong, assertive, pain-in-the-ass saint. Billy is a gentle, obsequious, pain-in-the-ass saint. They are a fine pair. Though obsequious," she added to herself, "was perhaps not the precise word." Billy was gentle, bewildered, always giving the impression of having stepped into life accidentally. Thirty years old, he had the diffidence of a young man ten years his junior; like his sister, Eloise, he appeared always to be saddled with a conviction of his own worthlessness.

When he arrived at the house on Silver Lake, Sally was tucking May Ling into a carriage. "We're going for a walk," she said to Billy. "Why don't you come along."

He wore the same turtleneck sweater that she had seen weeks before, the same kind of shapeless corduroy trousers and heavy work shoes.

"Oh, fine. Surely. A walk would be nice."

He ambled along beside her in silence until she began to wonder whether this was the reason for his visit, silence. She said the weather was nice and that May Ling was healthy. "But what can I do for you, Billy?"

"Well, nothing for me exactly. But I have felt so guilty about Barbara."

"About Barbara? But why?"

"Well, you know, she has gone through a bit of hell, losing her husband and having that rotten experience with that committee in Washington. Well—well, you know, she is an Episcopalian and here I am an Episcopalian priest, and we are friends—well, not close but friends—and I was wondering whether you thought it might comfort her if I went up there to San Francisco and spoke to her"

"Barbara?"

"Oh, yes Barbara."

Sally stopped wheeling the carriage and turned to

face him. "Billy," she said, "you're a very nice man and very kind. But no, I don't think it would be a good idea. I think the last thing in the world Barbara needs at this moment is to be comforted by a minister."

"I'm glad you said that," he admitted. "I'm not much good at comforting."

"Oh, I think you are. But not Barbara. You know, you're a very strange man."

"Yes, I suppose I am."

"Are you a homosexual?" she asked bluntly, and then she added as he stared at her, "Don't look so dismayed. It's better to ask straight out than to have lots of little whispers going around. For my part, I really don't give a damn whether you are or not."

"No," he said slowly, "I'm not. I can see why you might think so, but I'm not."

They continued to walk. "What I don't understand," Sally said, "is the way you are about your life."

"What way am I?"

"I mean this business at the clinic, being half a male nurse and half a janitor and not taking any pay."

"I don't need the pay. I have enough money."

"Do you like what you're doing?"

"Yes."

"But don't you ever wonder," she insisted, "where your life is going?"

"But where does any life go?" he asked, apparently puzzled. "Where is yours going? Not that I want to pry. But it's an odd question."

"I don't think it's an odd question at all. It's a question I ask myself all the time. I used to feel that being a poet was a good direction and that I knew where my life was going. But there's no respect or money in poetry, and I can't feel that I'm alive or independent unless I have enough money to do what I want to do. Now I've taken a new direction. I'm writing a screenplay. There's money in that, and what's the use of living a hoot and a holler from Hollywood if you can't take advantage of it."

"If you need money, Sally—"

She burst out laughing. "Oh, Billy, I don't believe you. You're not real."

"Why?"

"You were going to offer me money?"

"Yes, if you need it."

"My turn. Why? Why the devil should you offer me money?"

"Because I like you," he said. "Because you're a wonderful woman. Because you're Joe's wife," he finished lamely.

"You did it!" she snapped.

They walked on in silence. She was annoyed, and he had no idea why. Finally she said, "Why don't you give the money to the clinic?"

"I gave them some. I gave them five thousand dollars. I didn't want to mention it."

"Of course not," she said sourly. "That's the fifth rule of sainthood. Don't mention your damned good works."

Even before Dan came out of the hospital, Jean decided that her dream of creating a viable museum of modern art in San Francisco was a dream and no more; she also decided that she wanted the house on Russian Hill to be solely a home for herself and Dan. She would soon be fifty-nine years old. She reminded Eloise of this when she told her that she was closing the gallery for good and refurnishing the house. "I want it ready when Dan leaves the hospital. I don't

know how long he will have, but I want a few good,
ordinary years."

"I understand but I'm miserable," Eloise said. "It
meant so much to me—not just the gallery, but the
whole world of art. And you gave it to me, Jean. All
I've learned, all the courses I've taken. I know it's
silly, but I always pretended to myself that someday
there would be a great, splendid modern art museum
here, and you would be the curator and I'd be your
assistant, or one of your assistants. I was sure you'd
have at least half a dozen."

They were sitting upstairs in Jean's breakfast room
in the house on Russian Hill. Already, decorators and
painters were at work downstairs. Jean's decisions
were always followed by immediate action, and now
she was intent upon refurbishing the house before
Dan saw it again.

"At least half a dozen," Jean agreed, laughing. "No,
no, dear. Rich, pampered ladies do not become cura-
tors—indeed, they never become much of anything.
We are cursed with dilettantism, as much a disease of
the rich as gout was in old England. But there are
good loose ends, aren't there? You've learned so much.
I doubt that there are five people in this city who
know as much about the moderns as you do."

"Even if I do, I don't know how to use it. I feel so
lost, and worst of all, I'll no longer have an excuse to
come into the city. I love the valley, but coming
here—Jean, you're the dearest person in the world."

It was accolade enough for Jean. She had heard
through the years so many descriptions of herself—
cold, icy, arrogant, aristocratic, snobbish, incapable of
a human reaction—so much and so often that Eloise's
simple statement almost brought her to tears. How
very fond she was of this gentle, timid woman who

had been so loyal to the gallery since the beginning!

"My dear," she said, "I want you to have your pick of the paintings, any one of them, as a gift from me to you."

"Oh, no, you can't do that, Jean. They're priceless, every one of them."

"Nothing is priceless."

"But I can't."

"Then I'll be very hurt, and I'm sure you don't want to hurt me."

"Jean I couldn't, I wouldn't dare."

"Well, I would, and I shall do it for you. Come downstairs."

Eloise followed Jean downstairs to where the paintings were stacked in the old kitchen, now an office, soon to be a kitchen again. Jean selected a splendid twenty-four-by-thirty-six-inch Mondrian. "This is something that doesn't have to be understood, just the most direct and charming arrangement of color and space that man can devise, and I think Adam will like it better than a Klee or a Kandinski or any of the others that require a philosophical headstand before they can be really seen."

Eloise shook her head hopelessly. "Jean, it's the only one. There is no other Mondrian in San Francisco—or in California, for that matter. I won't take it. It's worth thousands of dollars."

"Then we'll have a frightful argument, and we'll end up not talking to each other. Do you want that to happen?"

"No," Eloise said weakly.

"Then no more words. Take it."

By the time Dan was released from the hospital, much of the decorating had been done. The stark plaster white of the gallery rooms had been replaced by wallpaper and molding, and Jean led Dan with slow steps into a house not too unlike the one they had lived in thirty years before. Dan stood in the living room, still only half-furnished, looking around him with the odd feeling that time had indeed reversed itself. The room was lit by soft lamplight, and Jean, a few paces away and facing him, her face half-shadowed, might just be mistaken for the young woman he had fallen so hopelessly in love with an eternity before. He had never been very good with words, and now there was nothing he could think of saying. Jean waited. Then, almost foolishly, Dan pointed to the couch and said, "It's the same one. It's the same damn sofa." As if she had done a marvelous trick of magic.

"Danny, no. I had it made. It's the same style, a Lawson, but I will say this. If you go through that door into the room that used to be your study—no, come. I want you to see it." She led him into the study. She had furnished it in comfortable, over-stuffed, leather pieces, and over the mantel was the rather primitive painting of his first ship, the *Oregon Queen*.

"I'll be damned," Dan said softly. "Where did you find it?"

"Sarah Levy had it, and when she heard what I was doing, she insisted that you have it."

"Wait a minute. Hold on," Dan said. "This is your house. I don't live here."

"I know. It's very proper. You have your own apartment in Oakland, and you only use this as a sort of private cathouse."

"You are learning the language. That's a hell of a way for an old lady to talk."

"Oh, I have a few good years left, Danny. How would you like to move in?"

"What do you mean, move in? Is that why you gussied the place up, to tempt me?"

"Sort of. I'd like you to marry me."

"What?"

"You heard me. I'm making a formal proposal of marriage. I'll admit I'm past the childbearing age, and I suppose that with all your money you could find a young filly if you want one; but on the other hand, I've still got a pretty good figure, and you've been sleeping with me on and off for almost forty years, and we've put the worst of it behind us, and I think I love you, sort of—"

"Hold on," he said, dropping into a chair. "Just give me a moment to think."

"All right. You want a drink?"

"I do. Scotch and water. You didn't happen to include a box of cigars with the furnishings?"

"Cigars are out, Danny, forever, according to Dr. Kellman. He says you're as good as new, providing you stay away from cigars and a few other things."

"Does he? We'll see about that."

Jean left the room to get his drink, and Dan sat there, staring at the picture of the *Oregon Queen*. In a few minutes she returned with his drink.

"You're not having one?"

"No. I want a clear head. What is it, Danny? Ghosts or too much past?"

"Some of each."

"Man is given three score and ten."

"If he's lucky."

"We've used up the three score."

"The hell with that! Maybe we can work the next

ten. Maybe. I've had a heart attack. I'm half a man.
You're sure you want to marry me?"

"The half is better than anything else I've seen
along the way. Yes. I've thought about it long enough.
I would have liked the proposal to come from you,
but I'm tired of waiting."

"What kind of wedding?"

"City Hall."

"Joe's too damn busy to come up here for a wedding, and Tom would only be a pain in the ass," Dan
said. "We'll have Barbara for a witness."

It was then that the telephone rang, and Barbara,
her words coming slowly, her voice low and controlled, told them that Bernie was dead.

Two months later, at City Hall, with Barbara as the
only witness, Jean and Dan were married for the second time, and Jean Seldon Whittier once again became Jean Seldon Lavette.

Thomas Lavette and Lucy Sommers were married a
month later, on the last Sautrday of June in 1948. Both
Tom and Lucy had an active ten days before the wedding, but since they planned to leave for a honeymoon
of two weeks in Europe, they felt it was vital to clear
the decks and depart with the assurance of a place for
everything and everything in its place. John Whittier
was first on the agenda.

He greeted Tom petulantly when Tom came into
his office, pointing out that he had barely passed the
time of day with him for the past two weeks. "Decisions without me, meetings without me, and that Milton ship contract. That's a ten-million-dollar contract,
and I wasn't even shown the final specifications. First
thing I know of it is a letter from Leonard Milton,

"I've heard."

"Barbara is making her own bed. She has to sleep in it, Tom."

He nodded.

"You do understand what I'm driving at?"

"You don't have to convince me. That stupid display in Washington caused me enough grief."

"That is only the beginning, believe me. These are very interesting times we live in. I don't think there's ever been anything like this before in these United States. But they're not bad times for us."

Norman Drake was next on the agenda. Tom's secretary called him in Washington, and upon learning that he was due back in Berkeley the following day, wondered whether he might be inclined to come to San Francisco and join Mr. Lavette for dinner. When she told Tom about that, he smiled and shook his head.

"Don't go on. He said that I could damn well come to Berkley if I desired to see him."

"Yes," Janet replied. "How did you know?"

"That little bastard is cock of the walk right now. You told him I'd come?"

"Yes."

"Good. Suppose we say day after tomorrow for dinner. Call him back and tell him, and be very sweet. And make reservations for three, or four if he wants to bring his wife."

"In Berkeley? Where?"

"At Frederick's. Where else in Berkeley? Mention his name when you make the reservation and tell them we want a good table."

Lucy had some second thoughts about Drake. "I don't trust him, and his involvement with Barbara makes it tacky."

"We're not exactly searching for an honest man," Tom said.

"He's depressing. Just to look at him is depressing."

"The point is that he plays the game. Everyone who knows him agrees on that score. He plays the game."

Tom and Lucy were first at the restaurant. Tom handed the head waiter twenty dollars, impressing him with the charge that Mr. Drake was to be treated as visiting royalty. Lucy's knowledge of Berkeley was hazy. She had never been to Frederick's before, and she smiled dubiously as Tom explained to her that their table, near the front of the restaurant, was one of the three or four most desirable.

"I suppose so," Lucy agreed, "as such things go. It's a deplorable place."

The head waiter brought Drake over. He was in his middle thirties, slender and plump at the same time, with a small round paunch and round puffy cheeks. He seated himself dubiously. He had come alone, ignoring the invitation to bring his wife. He was wary; his handshake was without enthusiasm.

"My fiancée," Tom said, introducing Lucy. Congressman Drake's expression questioned her presence at what was certainly intended as a business meeting. "She is also my associate," Tom explained. He successfully covered the contempt he felt for this small, fox-like man. Lucy was right about politics. This man, who had a seat in the House of Representatives, was shabby, shabby in his manner and shabby in his pretenses. He had no idea of the relationship between Tom and his sister, and with an ounce of pride or integrity, he would have avoided the meeting. Tom wondered what he was expecting. A payoff? What would it take to buy Barbara out? Or was it too late? Lucy felt it was too late since Congress had already voted the contempt. What then? Respect for money? That certainly was a part of it. He knew the wealth and the power Tom represented, and Tom realized that he himself was only beginning to understand the extent and potency of that wealth and power. Lucy understood it much better.

He felt a surge of possessive pride that Lucy was sitting next to him. To hell with those who didn't think she was attractive! He did. She was a strong woman, and to his way of thinking, a very handsome woman. They had never been to bed, never made physical gestures toward each other; but the thought of such gestures excited him, and no other woman had excited him in a long time.

All this went through his mind as Lucy engaged in chitchat with the congressman. Tom ordered drinks, Scotch and water all around.

"Now let's understand this," Drake said, flatly and unexpectedly. "There's nothing I can do for your sister now. It's too late. I just want you to know that when the committee subpoenaed her, I didn't know she was your sister. The name was Barbara Cohen. Then I found out who she was. She was insolent and hostile, but that's not to the point. The point is that she can vacate the contempt citation any time she pleases to. All she has to do is to answer the question and name the names we asked for."

Tom stared at Drake thoughtfully for a long moment before replying. Lucy observed him with interest, wondering just how Tom intended to proceed. Finally he said, "That's up to my sister, isn't it?"

Drake was taken aback. He simply nodded.

"I'm not terribly fond of my sister," Tom went on, his voice cool and without emotion. "She's a grown woman, and she has never consulted me about any action of hers. I was going to wait until we knew each other a little better, congressman, which two or three drinks might accomplish, but since you have plunged in, I'll swim with you. I didn't ask for this meeting to plead my sister's case. I wish to talk to you about the Lavettes, because it seems to me that when you took this step of subpoenaing my sister, you knew very little about us."

On the defensive now, Drake again stressed that he had not known Barbara's identity.

"Of course," Tom said. "That's water under the bridge. But let me make this plain. I am the president and I control the majority stock of the fifth largest corporation in this state. I am not speaking only of the Seldon Bank, but of a conglomerate of interests that reach into every corner of California and a few corners outside it. I don't think I have to say much more than that. You come up for reelection in the fall. I have also heard it bruited about that you'd like to be governor. I doubt that the Republican party could elect a governor in California without our help."

"I don't know what I could do at this point about your sister," he said helplessly.

"Nothing, I'm sure. It's unfortunate that my sister stepped into the middle of this. Now suppose we talk about your own plans, Mr. Drake."

For the next hour, Tom and Lucy listened to the pompous self-importance of Norman Drake. They fed him food and Scotch and praised his acumen and patriotism, and he in turn became wet-eyed in his apologies for his ignorance.

Finally, Tom and Lucy drove him home—he was too drunk to drive himself—to his place in San Pablo; then, too exhausted to face the drive back to Pacific

Heights, they registered for the night at a local hotel, registered separately, and took adjoining rooms.

Excited, stimulated by his and Lucy's manipulation of Drake, nervous as a college boy with an illicit date, his exhaustion gone now, bathed and in shirt and trousers—since they had no luggage—Tom nerved himself to go to Lucy's room. She solved his curious struggle by knocking at the door to his room. She carried a handful of magazines.

"Just something to read if you can't sleep." She stood facing him, reagarding him with fond interest.

"You look very beautiful," he said.

"Thank you—not for the truth but for saying it. I was very impressed with the way you handled that little swine."

"Come on, Lucy, not so harsh. I think he's our little swine from here on in."

"And you really don't give a damn about what happens to Barbara?"

"Does that shock you?"

"No. I'm not fond of your sister. To be truthful, I think she's a sentimental ass. But I must say that my opinion of Drake doesn't bear repeating. What an unctuous, dreadful little man he is! Do you really imagine that he's destined for great things?"

"If we help to destine him. That's not really a word, is it, but it fits."

"Perfectly good word."

"He'll be very obedient, and I don't think he'll bite the hand that feeds him. He's very guilt-stricken about Barbara at this point, and I can't convince him that I don't actually give a damn. I'm not sure that I want to convince him."

Lucy sprawled on the bed. "Come over here, Thomas," she said.

"Oh?" He walked to the bed and stood looking down at her.

"Has a woman ever made love to you?" she asked.

"Lucy, I'm thirty-six years old."

"Ah, and you've made love to women. That, dear boy, is not what I am talking about. Has a woman ever made love to you?" She reached out and took his hand. "Don't answer that. Take off those ridiculous trousers and lie down here beside me."

Suddenly, as he tried to undo his pants, his hands were shaking like those of an adolescent confronted with his first sexual opportunity. Lucy was smiling at him, her long, angular face almost pretty. She kicked off her shoes and slipped out of her dress and underthings. It was the first time Tom had ever seen her naked. She had a strong, muscular body, narrow hips, flat breasts. He was shivering with excitement. No woman had ever acted upon him like this before, excited him this way. He finished fumbling with his clothes, and now he was naked.

"Lie here," she said, moving over and making room for him. "Just lie down here and forget that anything in the world ever troubled you." He stretched out next to her, and she began to caress him, touch him, stroke him, his body shivering under her hands. When he tried to respond on his own part, she whispered, "No, no, this is mine."

"Don't you want the lights out?"

"No. Better this way."

When he touched her, she pushed his hands back down on the bed. In his mind, he was her prisoner, her plaything, her pet, and the thought gave him a wild, erotic pleasure; and when finally she straddled him, her dark hair falling on his face, her small breasts hanging loose from her body, her lips parted in a kind of triumphant grin, he climaxed with a violence that shook his body and left him limp and mindless.

Afterward, Lucy said to him, "I think we will be good for each other, Thomas, but I shall not play the jealous wife and you will not play the jealous husband. I think we make an interesting match."

Three days later, they were married in San Francisco at her father's house. Since it was a second marriage for each of them, the wedding party was very small, restricted to members of both families—Alvin Sommers, the bride's father, very old and withered, an aunt and uncle of the bride, Dan and Jean Lavette, and Barbara. It was understood that Joe, Tom's half brother, would be left out of the festivities. In actual fact, he and Tom had never met each other. Alvin Sommers, who had taken over the presidency of the Seldon Bank after Jean's resignation, was smugly delighted at the match, chuckling with geriatric glee that his family would once again control the swelling Seldon fortune. But aside from the old man's financial joy, the little wedding party was curiously cold and subdued, kisses confined to small, polite pecks. It broke up early, Dan and Jean taking Barbara home with them for a drink and a few minutes of relaxation.

Just the week before, Barbara had hired Anna Gomez, the nineteen-year-old daughter of Francis Gomez, the mechanic who had taken over Bernie's garage. Anna would live in at the house on Green Street, do the housekeeping, and take care of Sam when Barbara had to be away. She was a pleasant, honest young woman, and Barbara liked and trusted her; now, as her recognition of Bernie's death passed from grief into an accepted and permanent reality, Barbara realized that she must have more time, not only for her work but for the necesssary business of living as a single woman.

"We are a strange family indeed," Barbara said to Jean. "What a loveless, cheerless occasion! I don't think I could love Tom, but I do pity him, and mostly during his moments of exultation."

Dan brought them brandy, and they sat in front of the fire in the living room of the house on Russian Hill.

"I would hardly call it a moment of exultation," Jean said. "But I suppose it's no worse than most marriages."

"The woman's a barracuda," Dan said. "Not that Tom doesn't have piranha qualities of his own—"

Barbara burst out laughing. "What a beautiful piscatorial equation! You will always be my own very dear fisherman, daddy."

"I'm afraid I agree with Bobby," Jean said. "I feel sorry for Tom."

"He'll hold his own. You haven't heard about John Whittier?"

"No. What about John?"

"Tom dumped him. Came in with the voting rights to Al Sommers' stock and threw John out on his ear. Old Grant Whittier must be turning over in his grave."

"What on earth are you talking about?" Jean asked.

"Just what I said. John Whittier has been tossed out of Great Cal Shipping, which is now the GCS Corporation. Tom's the new president."

"How do you know all this?"

"Word gets around."

"But Tom was his protégé. John adored him."

"I don't think John Whittier ever adored anyone but John Whittier," Barbara said.

"I know you disliked him, Bobby, but he was fond

of Tom. It was his notion to combine the bank with his own company. Why on earth would Tom do it? John is old and sick."

"And Tom is impatient," Dan said. "I wouldn't weep for John Whittier. He still has his minority hold-ings and enough millions to live in luxury."

"Do you think it was Lucy's idea?"

"Possibly. She got him the voting rights. But don't sell our boy short, Jeanie. He's quite an operator on his own."

Playing with her son one day in Huntington Park, trying to get him to realize the potential in tossing a large, soft ball, catching it, and tossing it back, Bar-bara found herself giggling with delight in the simple joy of the game.

It had happened. The wave of guilt that followed soon passed. "There is no sin in laughing," she told herself, feeling nevertheless that there was a deeper sin in being so joyously and completely alive. But it had happened, and she was not the type who could consciously plunge back into depression. What might have been her condition without the presence of Sam, she did not know, but just the thought of something happening to him filled her with terror. Sam repre-sented the only sanity, the only reason, the only valid-ity that remained in her world. She knew now that she would never have another child. She was approaching her thirty-fifth birthday, and even if her childbearing years could be extended, even if she could bring her-self to face a second Caesarean section, she could not cope with the thought of a second marriage. Jean had tried, very gently, to open the subject, but Barbara re-fused to discuss it.

In any case, come what might, she had her son, a

year and a half and a month, weighing thirty pounds,
walking with a tight hold on her finger as she pushed
the stroller, which already he disdained. Life resumed
itself, renewed itself. The sun rose each day; the cool
wind blew from the Pacific; it was a cliché to say that
life belonged to the living, but it was also an unadorned truth. The cable cars lumbered past, and Sam
watched them with joy. When she took him out with
no stroller, just the two of them on foot, and then,
with him in one arm, swung onto a cable car, he was
transported into the seventh heaven of delight. She
thanked God that she was a large, strong woman;
thirty pounds is no small weight. They would ride the
cars from one end of the line to the other, Sam gurgling with pleasure as the car slid over the lip of a hill
with the precipitous slope down to the bay in front of
them; and then she would return home, content to
turn him over to Anna while she went to her typewriter.

She was writing again, and she felt a new depth, a
new strength in what she wrote. Barbara was not unimaginative, but as a writer she felt incapable of dealing with things she had never experienced, and when
she engaged in sheer invention, she felt that her writing became listless and meaningless. Though she
found it difficult to believe that one day, sooner or
later, she mght be arrested and forced to stand trial
for what still struck her as a bit of impossible lunacy,
the thought was never entirely out of her mind, and
she felt a tremendous need to finish her book before it
happened—if indeed it was to happen.

This book was a departure from what she had pre-
viously written. Her first two books dealt with her
own experiences in Paris and Berlin before the war
and then in North Africa and India and Burma during

the war years. Her new novel was a deceptively simple love story about a returned soldier who married
and settled down in San Francisco—certainly nothing
to trouble her nervous publisher, who had begged her
not to make it too political. It was a much harder writing task than either of her previous books, the more so
since Bernie's death had happened when she was halfway into it. For weeks afterward, she could not face
the thought of writing; now she could work on it each
day, and she had a feeling that it was good.

Early in July, Barbara received a letter from Herb
Goodman in Israel. He enclosed a shapshot of a grave,
one of many graves that Barbara could see in the
background, spaced in the neat, geometrical rows that
define a military cemetery. Her eyes misted and her
throat choked up as she looked at it, and for a long
while she sat holding the photo, unable to read the
letter.

It was not long: "Dear Mrs. Cohen I thought you
would like to have this picture of Bernie's grave. He is
buried in a military cemetery on a hillside outside of
Jerusalem. He lies with other men who fell in the
struggle for Jewish homeland, good, brave men. Next
week, I am being married to a Sabra, which means
that my wife-to-be was born here in Israel. We have
decided that we will name our first child, no matter
whether it's a girl or a boy, Bernie, not only because I
liked him but because he was one of the best. The
second child will be named Irv after Irv Brodsky, who
died with Bernie. I don't know how much this will
mean to you, but I thought you would like to know. I
am enclosing, with the snapshot, a sort of map with
exact directions on how to find the grave if you
should ever come here and want to see it. Now that
the war is over, care will be taken of the military cem-

eteries, and the grave will be kept in good condition. I don't know what else to say except to wish you all the best. I can imagine your sorrow, because my girl's brother was killed in the war, and almost everyone you meet lost someone. We just hope this will be the end of war."

Anna came into the room and saw Barbara holding the letter and crying. "Is it bad news, Señora?"

Barbara shook her head. "Just a letter from a friend of my husband."

A few days later, Sally came to San Francisco to visit Barbara. She had left her baby with Lola Gonzales, the wife of Joe's associate at the clinic. "I had to get away," she said to Barbara. "I felt I was choking, drying up and dying. I'm a terrible person, Bobby. I have no patience and I'm a rotten housewife and I make poor Joe miserable, and he's the most wonderful, decent kind of human being, and he deserved better than me. I'm miserable too. Can I stay here overnight? Then I'll drive back in the morning."

"Aren't you going to Higate to see your folks?"

"No. I can't bear to go there. They're happy and content, and all they care about is that precious wine of theirs, and I can't bear to be with Eloise because all she wants out of life is to be a service organization for my dumb brother, Adam—oh, Bobby, I'm miserable."

"All right," Barbara said. "Of course you can stay overnight. Go up to the guest room and put your things away and then take a hot bath, which is the best medicine I know for most varieties of misery. Then we'll have dinner together and we'll talk, just the two of us."

At the dinner table, Barbara said, "Sally, why don't you stop trying to explain that Joe is some kind of tin-horn saint and tell me what's wrong. Joe is my brother, but I love you very much, believe me."

"Do you, Bobby, truly?"

What a strange girl, Barbara thought. She has the most astonishing face of anyone I have ever known. One moment it's a mask of utter tragedy, and the next moment it's like the face of some divine clown, with that wide mouth and those incredible pale blue eyes and that long yellow hair. I do wish she wouldn't wear her hair like that. But to cut it, she'd have to grow up. "Yes, I do," she answered.

"You know how madly, divinely in love with Joe I used to be—"

"I don't think you were."

"Bobby!"

"You were in love, yes. But with Joe, Sally? Or just in love?"

"Bobby, I don't know. I am bored, bored to tears. I do love my baby—most of the time. She's darling. But who am I? What am I? That house we live in depresses me so. Joe comes home, and he's too tired even to talk, and when we do talk, there's nothing for us to talk about. When I read him my poetry, he pretends to listen but he doesn't. He fell asleep once right in the middle. And he never does anything mean or cruel, and I know he's giving his whole life to the clinic, because if he were in private practice he could make all the money in the world. They say he's one of the best surgeons in Los Angeles, and there are surgeons who don't have half his skill, and they make a hundred thousand a year and live in those big, posh homes in Beverly Hills—"

"Is that what you want, Sally, the money and a big house in Beverly Hills?"

"Oh, you know I don't, Bobby. Yes, enough money

to hire someone to take care of May Ling and to have a decent car instead of the old wreck I'm driving That's why I wrote the screenplay."

"Did you, a screenplay?"

"Being a poet is like a public service. I was so excited when they published my book of poems. My royalties amounted to exactly eighty-six dollars, and when I sell a poem to a newspaper or magazine, it's ten or fifteen dollars, so that's no way to get rich, is it? And I see all those dreadful movies and I'm sure I can do better. So I wrote this and I brought it with me. Would you read it, Bobby? It will only take you an hour or so."

"I'll read it, yes, I'd love to," Barbara agreed.

"And then, you know, I remember years ago Joe telling me how your father built a yacht for a director who was very important in Hollywood?"

"Yes, his name was Alex Hargasey. As a matter of fact, I saw a picture of his about four months ago. It was called *Fretful Desire*, or was it?"

"That's the man. Now if Dan could call him up and make an appointment for me to see him with my screenplay . . . ?"

"I'm sure daddy would," Barbara said. "I'll read it later."

Barbara was not impressed with the screenplay. She felt that it was mawkish and sentimental, with very little dramatic impact. But as she said to Sally, "I simply don't know about such things. Truthfully, it's the first screenplay I've ever read, and I have no idea what the limitations and the standards are."

"But did you like it? You, just as a reader?"

Barbara could remember how once, long ago, when she had been living with Dan and May Ling in Westwood and attempting to write her first book, she had given some pages to May Ling to read, and how May Ling had been truthful and merciless. The pages were torn up, and after a brief spell of fury at May Ling, Barbara had begun the book again and more rewardingly. Yet she could not do that with Sally. It was not only that she was unable to judge a screenplay in any professional sense, it was also quite evident that Sally was disturbed.

"I liked it," Barbara lied unhappily.

"Oh, did you? I'm so glad, Bobby. And you will ask Dan to speak to Mr. Hargasey?"

"Yes, I will."

Sally leaped up, ran over to Barbara, and kissed her. "Oh, I do love you. Bobby, what about Billy Clawson?"

The question was totally unexpected. "What about him?"

"I think he's in love with me."

This time Barbara was capable of no response. She sat and stared until Sally said uneasily, "You did hear me. I said I think Billy Clawson's in love with me."

"You are the most amazing young woman."

"I know what you're thinking," Sally said. "Everyone thinks that Billy is absolutely brainless and worthless, and I guess some people think he's a homosexual. But that's only because he can't really communicate with anyone, and because he's on this Jesus kick. I mean, sometimes I think he thinks he's Jesus Christ, and he lives in a stinking little furnished room down in the barrio and cleans the floors and acts as a male nurse in the clinic—"

"Hold on!" Barbara cried. "Sally, will you just stop talking for one minute and let me put my head together. Just stop."

Sally took a deep breath and said, "O.K., if that's what you want. What did I say?"

"Nothing. Just nothing. Look, I know about Billy Clawson. Joe told me. I know what he's doing in Los Angeles. About Billy as a person, I know nothing. I've never said more than ten words to him. But he is Eloise's brother, and I feel about Eloise as I do about you. I love both of you, even though I must admit that you are absolutely insane."

"That's not fair."

"Perhaps not. Now tell me, Sally, are you having an affair with him? Or tell me it's none of my business. I just don't know how I got into this."

"For heaven's sake, no. Absolutely not."

"What then? Did he tell you he's in love with you?"

"No. He's a scared jackrabbit. He'd never tell me anything like that."

"Are you in love with him?"

"No."

Barbara rose and paced back and forth restlessly. "Sally, I don't know why you came to me with this. I'm not rejecting you, but look at the position you put me in. I'm Joe's sister. I don't know how to talk to you. The truth of it is that I don't know Joe very well anymore. We were very close before he went into the army, but he changed. I can understand the position you're in, but I can't help you."

Sally went to Barbara and put her arms around her. "Poor Bobby, I'm the most selfish person in the world, and with all the terrible things that have happened to you, all I can think of is to dump on you."

"It's all right," Barbara whispered.

"No it isn't. Nothing's right. The whole world is screwed up. You find Bernie again after all those years, and he goes off and gets killed, and now those bastards are doing their number with you. Nothing's right." She plopped into a chair and began to weep, and Barbara looked at her hopelessly.

Stephan Cassala was amazed at how fit Dan looked the first time he returned to his offices in Jack London Square in Oakland. He had lost weight and his hair was white, but his skin was burned brown from the long hours of lying in the sun on the terrace in back of the house on Russian Hill, and he looked trim and healthy. He had put off coming back. For the first time in his life, he was content to sit around and do nothing. Being with Jean was enough. He said to her once, sitting there on the terrace, "You know, Jeanie, I look at you and I'm still not sure of you."

"That's as it should be, isn't it?"

"Oh? Maybe. Only after forty years—"

"Not quite."

"Almost. After all that time, I ought to figure I know you. No. I still look at you and find myself conniving how to get up there on the hill and marry Tom Seldon's daughter."

"You did, twice."

"So I did, so I did."

Now he was back in his office, reluctant to take the place behind his desk, pacing restlessly, while Steve Cassala watched him and asked cautiously, "How do you feel, Dan?"

"Pretty good. Maybe it makes you a little more alive to shake hands with death. And then you screw the old bastard, and you say to yourself, I'm lucky. I guess I am pretty damn lucky. How are we doing?"

"We're making money."

"That's the name of the game, isn't it? I just wish to hell I cared." He sat down behind his desk and stared at Cassala. "The trouble is, Steve, it doesn't make sense anymore. I don't care. I don't have to tell you what kind of a life I've lived. You were there every step of the way."

"Yeah, we were both there, Danny."

"What did I want? You know, these past few weeks, most of the time I'd just be lying around on the terrace, reading, with Jean there most of the time. I'd tell her to get out and do her thing, but most of the time she was right there. I'd try to work something out— who the hell is Dan Lavette? What does he want? Well, I wanted Jean, and I had her, sort of. I wanted May Ling, and I had her for as long as she lived, and now I've got Jean again, and I give a damn about that, but not much about this company."

"You can walk out, Danny, if that's what you want. I can run it."

"You've been running it." He stared at the desk calendar in front of him. "What's this?"

"Tom called to see whether you were back. He wants to come by this afternoon and see you. I made it for three o'clock. We can have lunch and talk about things."

"Senator Claybourne?"

"Congress adjourns at the end of the week, and then he'll be back in San Francisco. He says he'll be happy to talk to you."

"How did he sound?"

"Friendly. We put ten thousand dollars into his last campaign, so he owes us."

"I wouldn't give you ten cents for what an obligation by one of those political bastards is worth. They sell when the price is right and when no one can check their moves. In the old days, when we shipped out of New York and Jimmy Walker was mayor, they ran the fix out of Tammany Hall. It was strictly a no-shit thing. They had a mimeographed price list, starting with manslaughter at five hundred dollars, and right down the line, every crime you could think of. Of course, those were Depression times and prices were low. But there was something damned honorable about a fixed, calculated payoff. Or does that make sense, Steve?"

"I suppose so, in a way."

"Did Tom say what he wants?"

"No."

"What do you think of him?"

"I think he's a power, Dan," Cassala said.

"You're being careful."

"He's your son."

"Yes, he is, isn't he."

After lunch, Dan felt tired. He had eaten too much. Kellman had warned him about his diet, but away from Jean and sitting with Cassala in an Italian restaurant, his resistance broke down. He stuffed himself with spaghetti and veal, and then his morale collapsed so completely that he asked the waiter to bring him a cigar. Fotunately, the restaurant carried only a single box of the ten-cent local weed, and Dan was able to wave it away without too much of a sense of sacrifice. He was back in his office at two-thirty. His first day, and he was bored, disinterested.

He found himself sketching the design of a boat on his date pad. In the hospital, Jean had agreed to his dream of building a boat and exploring the bay. Now he wondered whether her willingness would hold up. She had never liked small boats—or perhaps that was because small boats were symbols of the fisherman she had married. Perhaps that would change, as other things had changed. He sketched a yawl, then eliminated one of the masts. Something with a single mast until he could teach her to sail. He closed his eyes and envisioned Jean in white ducks, rolled high to the knee, a striped jersey T-shirt, her hair blowing in the wind. It still made him half sick with desire when he thought of her. She is fifty-eight years old, he thought, and it's like I saw her this morning for the first time. His guilt began to float to the surface. He knew that through all the years with May Ling he had never surrendered Jean, never let go of her. He had read somewhere that the unadorned truth of what was called romantic love was simply the illusion that the loved one possessed what the lover lacked, and that could be said of both women who had been part of his life. He wondered whether other men were like himself, half alive without women to complete them.

He must have dozed, for he came awake to the intercom's buzz, and his secretary informed him that his son had arrived.

"Send him in," Dan said.

Tom entered the office with assurance. After all, Dan thought, we're no longer strangers. Three times in twenty years, once at the hospital, once at the wedding, and now here. They shook hands.

"How do you feel?" Tom asked him.

"Pretty good. No different than before. From the way I feel, I wouldn't know that I had a heart attack."

"That's good."

"How was the honeymoon?"

"Too short. I can't stay away. The truth is," Tom said, "that there's more excitement in doing what I do than in running away from it. Lucy feels the same way."

"Well, a man should enjoy his work," Dan agreed. "Do you?"

"Do I? Do I enjoy my work?" Dan studied his son thoughtfully. So far, in all their meetings, there had been no term of address beyond the pronoun, not "pop" or "father" or "dad" or even "Dan," as if Tom had drawn a careful line beyond which he would not encroach—or had there been? Not at the wedding, but the first time Tom came into his hospital room. Dan tried to remember, staring all the while at the tall, handsome man who was his son. He took after Jean and the Seldon line, no question about that; and just surveying the physical image in front of him, Dan found himself thinking, If I had a son like that—no, it was too late. Too late for anything except courtesy, and that at least was something.

"What were you saying?" Dan asked him.

"Do you enjoy your work, running this shipping line?"

"It's the only thing I do well; hell, it's the only thing I know, ships and shipping. I've had the threescore years, as they say, without learning much about anything else. It's not the Cunard Line. We operate seven tankers, four of them under Liberian registry. They're good, sound ships and we have good contracts."

"But do you enjoy it?"

"No, not much. I'm bored with the whole damn thing, Tom."

"I'm glad you said that."

"Why?"

"I'd like to buy you out," Tom said bluntly. Then he relaxed in his chair, watching Dan and waiting.

For at least a minute, Dan stared at his son without replying. Tom's statement was totally unexpected. He was not prepared for it. He had not thought of anyone buying him out, least of all his son. Finally he said, "Are you serious?"

"Let's see if I am," Tom said calmly. "You operate seven sixteen-thousand-seven-hundred-deadweight-ton tankers. They were built for the Maritime Commission in nineteen forty-five, so they're practically new and damn good ships. You have contracts with Orpheum Oil and Coonstown Oil. You have docking facilities here in Oakland, in Honolulu, in Galveston and in Long Beach. You own this building and you have three storage tanks in Honolulu. I'm particularly interested in your conversations with Freeway Oil in Hawaii. I brought them out last week. I think there's the nucleus of the biggest oil operation in the Islands, and I imagine you agree with me because you proposed a merger with them."

"You sure as hell did your homework," Dan said.

"I like to know where I'm going. There's only one game today that's worth anything, and that's oil. Whittier never had enough wits to see it. All he could ever see was dry cargo. We had one tanker, and it went up in flames, and that scared the very devil out of him. It's true I want the tankers, but that's only the beginning. I got a lead into Germany. They're putting their shipyards into shape, and they sent me the plans for a thirty-thousand-deadweight-ton tanker, six hundred and sixty feet long, overall, eighty-five foot beam, and she draws thirty-four feet loaded to capacity. What do you think of that?"

"That's one hell of a ship," Dan said. He felt the prickles rise on his skin, a moment of seeing himself with a fleet of such tankers, and then the feeling was gone. "That's the size of one of the passenger giants. Is it practical?"

"I think so. I've ordered two of them, and I have leases on twelve thousand acres of land in Texas. Exploratory. So you can see why I want those tankers of yours."

"I think I can." Again he was silent.

"Well?"

"What are you prepared to pay?" Dan asked him.

"I know what you paid for you ships. You got them for a song. But that day is over. I'm prepared to pay ten million for everything. You can have it in cash or in GCS stock or partly in each. I think it's a fair price. What do you think?"

"It's a fair price," Dan said slowly. "Let me think about it. I'll let you know in a few days."

They shook hands, and Tom left. For the next fifteen minutes, Dan sat at his desk and stared at the sketch of the yawl. Then he called Cassala and asked him to come in.

"How did it go?" Cassala asked him.

"Do you know why he came here, Steve? He wants to buy us out."

"I'll be damned."

"For ten million dollars. My son is quite an operator."

"What did you tell him?"

"I told him I'd think about it. Now look, let's get this straight. When you came into this, I gave you ten percent of the deal. If this goes through, you will get a million clean."

"For God's sake, Dan, you can't be serious. What will you do?"

"Nothing, maybe. Collect stamps. Travel with Jean. Build the kind of boat I always dreamed of owning. I'm bored with this, Steve. I've lost interest. I don't give a damn. I have enough money. I just don't care. Now understand me, our mortgages and loans come out of my nine million. I'll still be left with three mil-

lion in cash, and even after taxes, it's more money
than I know what to do with. On top of that, Jean isn't
poor. You'll still have three quarters of a million after
taxes, and that's enough of a stake for anything you
want to turn your hand to. Or just to sit on your ass
and enjoy life. I know I'm pulling the rug from under
you, but hell, I want out of it."

Cassala dropped into a chair and stared at the floor.
When he looked up, he was fighting back the tears
that clouded his eyes. "You didn't pull any rug from
under me, Danny. Three years ago, when you brought
me into this, you saved my life. I'll be rich, if that
means anything. Only—I don't know. I remember,
when pop was alive in the old days, he'd say to me,
'Stephan, Dan is your brother.' I figured we'd be together at least a few years more."

"Steve," Dan said gently, "we'll still be that way.
You're the only one of the old crowd that's left. All the
rest are gone."

Derick Claybourne looked like a United States senator, or at least what a United States senator had
looked like in the twenties and thirties. In the postwar period, he was going out of style. By and large, sen-
ators no longer were hugely overweight; they no longer
sported string ties and wide-brimmed hats and black
serge suits, but these were Claybourne's trademark
and he clung to them, as much a trademark as his
sandpaper voice and his cigar. He offered a cigar to
Dan now. "Seventy-five cents' worth of pure Havana,
Danny boy. Go ahead."

"Thank you, senator. I'm off them. Doctor's orders."

"What the hell do they know! I had my coronary six
years ago. Do I look any the worse for it? These little
beauties keep me alive."

"I don't have your constitution, senator."

"Hell, you don't live right, you don't think right. Now look, Danny, I like you, always have. I guess it's twenty years since Al Smith told me to look you up. So you don't have to argue your case with me. The plain truth of it is that I can't do a damn thing. Your daughter's picked herself a peck of trouble. Damnit, I don't like those puffed up little bastards on the house committee any better than you do, but they are the wave of the future. Don't ask me how in hell it happened. It started with that damn fool executive order of Truman's—loyalty oaths for every federal employee. Then they all ran hog wild. Every pisspot bureaucrat began to run off loyalty oaths on his damn mimeograph, and then the schools and colleges and the big hoopla in Hollywood, and God Almighty, we've just about reached a point where those little assholes on the commieee and Mr. J. Edgar Hoover are running the country. There is a climate of fear," he said slowly, leaning on each word. "A climate of fear, Danny."

"What are you trying to tell me, Derick, that you're afraid?"

"What in hell have I got to be afraid of? I'm a United States senator. But I don't run a fix, Danny, you know that. Hell, I'm not trying to kid you. Sure there's a fix, and more than one. I know a congressman who clears ten thousand a week, runs the whole scam out of the House Office Building. But they won't touch anything red. They are afraid. Senator McCarthy is running hog wild, like some lunatic bull on a rampage, and no one has the guts to stop him, myself included. Anyway, there's no way to fix this. You'd have to get to the attorney general, and Tom Clark is not approachable. Not on this subject."

"He's an old friend of yours, isn't he?"

"Not on this subject, Danny. We might have moved something before the House voted the contempt, but now it's in the hands of the Justice Department. And don't you think there isn't plenty of soft-shoeing right there. They are all scared shitless of Mr. J. Edgar Hoover, and they watch their step careful as mice. My word, Danny, I know Barbara's no communist, but why on God's earth doesn't she name those contributors of hers and vacate the contempt?"

"We just didn't raise her right," Dan said bitterly.

"She has notions of honor," the senator agreed magnanimously. "The truth is, Danny, we can't afford notions of honor today. You know how I stand on these so-called witch hunts, but damnit, boy, internationally we are in a life and death struggle. A life and death struggle."

"And what happens to my daughter promotes the national security? Is that the way you see it?"

"Danny, I told you how I see it. There is just not one damn thing I can do."

Dining with Dan and Jean at their home, Barbara was far more interested in the dinner Jean had cooked than in Dan's failure with Senator Claybourne. "It doesn't matter, daddy," she said. "I love you, I appreciate what you are trying to do, and I wish you would stop. This is my very own mess of porridge. I cooked it. I will eat it. I admit it will taste no way as good as this. What is it?"

"Pasta with ricotta—spinach, ricotta cheese, eggs, parsley, and pasta. Very fancy Italian food."

"Not so fancy," Dan said. "I've had it at Gino's."

"I don't believe that," Barbara told him. "It's absolutely delicious. You are an incredible woman," she said to her mother. "You keep amazing me. In all the years we were kids, did you ever cook anything?"

"It's really none of your business," Jean said. "No, if you must have an answer. The first time I ever tried was the night your father got the award from the Maritime Commission. I took him home with me, and I scrambled eggs for him. I toasted bread too. It's no great trick. You buy a book and you follow directions. Of course, you have to be rich."

"Why?"

"Because you throw it away the first three times, and the fourth time it's edible. Bobby, I haven't reformed. I hate cooking, and next week I am going to find us a cook. I'm not so different from the girl your father chased up Nob Hill thirty-eight years ago. I wish I were; then perhaps I'd understand why you're doing this."

"We've been through that."

"Yes, and I think I can guess who those eighteen people are. Nothing will happen to them. They did no wrong. They gave some money to what they felt was a good cause."

"It has very little to do with them, if the truth be told," Barbara said. "It's a matter between myself and my God, whoever my God is. In my own peculiar way, I have to go on living with myself."

"Was Tom one of them?" Dan asked.

"Are you serious, daddy?"

"I suppose so."

"No, Tom was not one of them. He is my brother, and I'm sure I have some feeling for him, but I don't think he'd bleed even if he cut an artery."

"Aren't you being a little hard on him?"

"I try not to be. It isn't easy. In a way, Tom is a new aquaintance of yours. He's been your son only since you got sick. He's been my brother for a long time. It's not that he's bad or nasty or rotten or anything like that. He just has the good fortune to be utterly devoid of any sense of right and wrong. Perhaps that's what they call a psychopathic personality. Anyway, it's a popular syndrome in America today."

"I would hate to think you're right," Dan said unhappily.

"Bobby's had a hard few months," Jean said to him. "I can understand the way she feels. On the other hand, my dear," she said to Barbara, "it's not all black and white. Tom bought Dan's shipping line. He made him an offer Dan couldn't refuse, and the deal has just been concluded."

"You mean you gave it all up?" Barbara asked her father. "Why?"

"Because the whole thing bored me to hell and back. I just stopped caring. And he wanted it. You may be right about him, Bobby, but he's my son, and it's the first time in my life he ever came to me for something he wanted. He wanted those seven tankers the way a kid wants a new bike. Hell, that's a stupid analogy, but it sort of fits the case."

"What will you do now?"

Dan shrugged. "I'll find things to do. Maybe I'll get to know your mother. It's about time we bummed around together for a bit. We're not too old for that."

Barbara had just fed Sam, and she was dressing him for a morning's stroll in the park when the doorbell rang. "Finish up, Anna," she said. "I'll get the door." She left Anna to pull on his sweater and went to the door and opened it.

A stout man in a dark suit stood there. "Are you Mrs. Barbara Cohen?" he asked her.

"Yes."

He took out his wallet and opened it to show her a badge and an identification card. "Simmons, United States marshal. I have a warrant for your arrest."

For weeks now, from day to day, Barbara had been expecting this, yet it still came as a shock. It took a long moment for her to gather her wits and to face the fact that it had actually happened. "Please come inside," she said as calmly as she could. "I'd like to make a telephone call, and then I'll go with you. I have a child, so I'll have to make some arrangements about him. Where will you be taking me?" Listening to her own voice, it was all very strange and improbable. Everything was so matter of fact. Was this indeed the way people behaved when they were arrested? "Won't you sit down," she said to the marshal.

He looked at her strangely and shook his head, then looked around the room and at her again. "I guess you can take a few minutes. Then we'll be going down to the federal courthouse at Seventh and Mission."

Barbara went upstairs and told Anna that she would be gone for a few hours. "Take him to Huntington Park, Anna, but for heaven's sake, hang on to him. He's getting very frisky and cocky. I think you'd better use the halter. He hates it, but it's good for my peace of mind. If I'm not here when you come back, give him his lunch—one boiled egg, a slice of bread, and some fruit." She then went downstairs and called Harvey Baxter's office.

Baxter was not there, but Boyd Kimmelman got on the phone and said, "Stay cool, Mrs. Cohen, and for heaven's sake, don't get frightened. This is just a formality, believe me. You go with him, and I'll be at the courthouse when you get there. You're not going to prison or anything like that, and I expect you'll be home by noon."

She thanked him. Simmons was looking at his watch. "Do you want to handcuff me, Mr. Simmons?" Barbara asked him.

"That won't be necessary. This is the arrest order," he said, offering her a folded document.

"I'll take your word for it. Let me get a sweater."

The marshal's car was parked outside; it was black, with a government shield on the license plate, causing Barbara to wonder whether black was *de rigueur* for government service, suit and car and tie, simply a symbolic way of letting the victims know what they were in for. It was only a few minutes' drive to the courthouse, and as they pulled up in front, Kimmelman jumped out of a taxicab and ran to meet them.

"I'm Boyd Kimmelman," he said to the marshal, "Mrs. Cohen's attorney. I spoke to Judge Fremont about this last week, and he agreed that when it happened, we could go directly to him and arrange for bail. He's in chambers now."

"Well . . ." The marshal hesitated. "That ain't regular procedure. She should be booked on regular procedure."

"Marshal, if Judge Fremont says so, it is regular procedure. If I tell him you flouted a court order—"

"Is it a court order?"

"The judge is the court, marshal."

Reluctantly, the marshal allowed Kimmelman to lead them into the building and to Judge Fremont's chambers. Fremont was a pink-cheeked, white-haired-impish man in his sixties who stared at Barbara with undisguised masculine delight. He waved the marshal out. "Leave the warrant," he said. "I'll see to it that the prisoner doesn't escape." After the marshal had gone, he said to Barbara, "You know something, if I were twenty years younger—nah, ten years younger— I'd work out the escape myself. That is, in return for favors. Don't look at me like that. I'm an unregenerated, evil old man. Matter of fact," he said to Kimmelman, "this lovely young lady is no stranger to me. I clerked with Sam Goldberg and Adam Benchly way back before the earthquake. Goldberg and Benchly— they don't make lawyers like that today." And to Barbara, "Sam told me all about you, Dan Lavette's wild daughter. That was back in thirty-four, when you were mixed up with Harry Bridges. Sam worshipped the ground you walked on—the old man's last love. Didn't know that, did you?" he said in response to the expression on Barbara's face. "Well, if a man has juices at thirty, he's still got them at seventy. Now I'm off the record. I like you, young lady. You have piss and vinegar, if you will forgive the expression, and it's in short supply these days. It reminds me of the old times, but the old times are gone, aren't they?" He turned to Kimmelman again. "She can go home, Boyd. Bail!" He snorted. "Bail, my eye! What the devil has happened to them down there in Washington? Have they all gone crazy? I'm releasing her on her own recognizance, and if and when this idiocy comes to trial, you'll notify her and she can appear."

Outside in the corridor, Kimmelman said, "Well, Mrs. Cohen, what do you think of him?"

"I think he's absolutely darling. And Boyd, it's time for you to start calling me Barbara."

"O.K.—Barbara."

"I could weep, he was so sweet and kind. But Boyd, I really don't have anything to worry about, do I?"

"How do you mean?"

"I mean that when I'm put on trial, no matter what

happens, I can't see Judge Fremont sending me to prison. Can you?"

"No, I can't. But you might as well face it, Barbara. The trial will not be held in this federal district. It will not be held in California at all. It will be held in the District of Columbia, because that's where the crime took place, in Washington."

"Oh, no!"

"I'm afraid so, Barbara."

"So much for deliverance. When will I have to go there and for how long?"

"When is difficult to say. It might be tomorrow, though that's not very likely, and it might be a month from now. It depends on how they schedule it and how full the docket is. How long? I shouldn't think the trial would last more than three days, conceivably four. But that isn't the end of it. I mean, you mustn't think that you are tried and sentenced, if you lose, and off to the slammer. There's still the Court of Appeals, and if we can find a good constitutional issue here, there's the Supreme Court—and all that could take another year or so. And that is all predicated on your losing. We don't go into court to lose. We go in to win. And one more thing. We agreed that you ought to have distinguished counsel and that Judge Fredericks is the likely choice. He's an old friend of your father's, and I think it would be a good thing if Mr. Lavette talked to him and brought him into the case. Will you ask your father?"

"I'll ask him," Barbara agreed.

Judge James Fredericks, retired, was of that small circle in San Francisco still known as the First Settlers, which meant that his grandfather, Big Bo Fredericks, had been a peace officer in the San Francisco of 1852.

He had arrived there three years before on the Pacific Mail Steamship Company's sidewheeler *California*, having picked up the ship, along with several hundred other eager gold hunters, on the Pacific coast of Panama. He had no luck in the gold fields, so he settled for a regular wage as a peace officer in the burgeoning city that had grown in three years from eight hundred souls to over forty thousand. Now, almost a hundred years later, his grandson resided in an ivy-covered Tudor house on Pacific Heights, collected Chinese ceramics, lectured occasionally, and was unhurriedly engaged in writing a history of the California legal system. He was a slender, aristocratic-looking man, his thin white hair combed sidewise over a long, narrow skull. He had long been involved in maritime law, and he had met Dan Lavette through Admiral Land when Dan was building cargo ships on Terminal Island.

He tried to appear pleased to see Dan. They talked about old times and one thing and another, then about Barbara's case. "You see, Dan," he said, "if I took this case, I'd be taking it under false pretenses. I simply don't have the credentials. I haven't done any trial work in thirty years. Sure I'm a specialist in maritime law, and I've sat on the bench there, but I don't know beans about federal or constitutional law. You may respect me, but in Washington I'd just be a puffed-up California lawyer parading his title. They don't like us. It wouldn't make it any better, only worse."

"I don't know," Dan said. "I just don't believe all this. Everywhere I turn, I come up against a blank wall. No one wants to get involved, no one. My God, this isn't the Lindbergh kidnapping. This isn't an ax murder. This is the case of one decent woman who will not be turned into a stool pigeon. Is that un-American? Is that a crime? What in hell has happened to us?"

"I can appreciate your feelings, Dan," Judge Fredericks said, "but if you're intimating that I'm afraid, you're wrong. I am no longer on the bench and I no longer practice, and I am independently wealthy. I have absolutely nothing to be afraid of, and I have nothing but the most profound contempt for that committee. I am trying to be honest with you. I wonder whether you've been completely honest with me?"

"What does that mean?" Dan asked coldly.

"It means this, that you come here after the fact, and that passes my understanding."

"I think you'd better explain yourself."

"You don't know what I'm talking about?"

"No, I do not."

"Very well. That piece of human flotsam that our state has inflicted upon the nation, namely, Congressman Norman Drake, has been bought and paid for by the Lavette interests. He belongs to you, body and soul—that is, considering he has one. He not only could have prevented this matter from coming to a vote of Congress, he could have stopped it even afterward. He could have let it be known in the Justice Department that the committee did not desire it to come to trial, and that would have been the end of it. So to put it mildly, you confuse me."

Dr. Kellman had warned Dan against anger. "Anger," he had said, "is uncontrolled violence done to your own body. There are other ways. Breathe deeply, think, consider."

Now Dan remembered and fought for control. He managed to keep his voice even and quiet as he said, "You say that Drake has been bought and paid for by the Lavette interests. It's conceivable, sir, that you can't slander Drake. You can slander me, and you do. I have never met or seen or spoken to Congressman Drake, so I think, Judge Fredericks, that it is incumbent upon you to explain yourself, because if you do not there will be hell to pay. I don't think you know me very well. If you did, you would not dare stand there and say what you said."

There followed a long, uncomfortable silence. Dan rose to his feet, and the two men stood facing one another. Finally Fredericks said, "I want you to accept my apology."

"To hell with your apology! I want some explanations!"

"All right. I have been told by two people, both of them trustworthy, that Drake has been meeting with your son. One such meeting took place in Berkeley at Frederick's, and I was informed of this by a person who was there on the occasion. Another meeting took place here in San Francisco. On that occasion, your son gave Drake an amount of cash—how much I do not know. The person who supplied the cash to your son only told me that it was a substantial amount."

"What in hell do you have, a private spy service?" Dan burst out. "What are you telling me?"

"The truth. I have friends. I hear things. I am sorry if you feel that I insulted you. I apologized. That's all I can do. I thought you knew about this, and that's why I was shocked to hear that your daughter was arrested and faces trial. Frankly, I thought there had been a payoff, but now I realize you had no knowledge of what your son is up to, whatever that may be. You see, there are more reasons than one why I cannot take your daughter's case."

Dan took several long breaths before he trusted

himself to speak, and then he said, very slowly, "I think it's my turn to apologize. I thank you for the time you have given me. I'm sorry this all had to come about."

"As I am," Judge Fredericks agreed.

Outside, Dan got into his car and then sat behind the wheel for a while with his eyes closed. "There's one thing I can't do," he told himself. "I can't go through life as a cripple." His rage had passed, but the anger was still with him; it burned like a low, cold fire.

He drove downtown and parked his car next to the towering pile of steel and glass that housed GCS. A bright new colophon in shining stainless steel, each letter five feet high, was fixed over the entrance. Dan went into the building and took the elevator up to the executive floor. Here, too, were the marks of the time—specially woven carpeting on the floor, nonobjective paintings on the walls, a receptionist whose yellow hair was as burnished as the chrome-plated telephone on her desk.

"I want to see Mr. Lavette," Dan told her.

"Do you have an appointment?"

"I'm his father."

Unmoved by this information, she told Dan that she would tell Mr. Lavette's secretary. The blood relationship counted, and he was passed through to an inner office, where a dark-haired woman introduced herself as Miss Loper. "So you're Mr. Lavette's dad. I wouldn't think so, you look so young—" Finding no response on the face of the big white-haired man, she added quickly, "He'll see you in a moment. He's on a call."

Tom opened the door to his office. "Come in, come in," he said to Dan. "You've met Janet—my good right arm. I'm glad you decided to drop in. I should have asked you weeks ago, but I've been snowed under." He closed the door. "Sit down. Would you like a drink?"

Dan remained standing. Tom circled to his place behind an enormous, ebony-topped desk and seated himself slowly. "Something wrong?" he asked, puzzled.

"Tell me, have you been seeing Norman Drake?"

Tom hesitated. Then he said, "Is that what you've come here for, to ask me about Drake?"

"I asked you. Have you been seeing him?"

"Yes, as a matter of fact. I met with him two or three times."

"Did you give him money?"

"That is a personal matter. I don't intend to discuss my relationship with him."

"Did you ask him to drop the charges against Barbara?"

Again Tom hesitated, but for a longer interval. "No."

"Why not?"

"Because Barbara can drop those charges anytime she wants to. All she has to do is stop being a goddamn Joan of Arc and answer the question they asked her."

"Do you know that she was arrested yesterday?"

Tom shrugged. "She's digging the hole for herself."

"All right," Dan said, "you're my son. I find you a contemptible sonofabitch, but you are my son. If you weren't, I think I'd kill you here on the spot. As it is, I don't want to see your face ever again." He slammed the office door behind him, strode past the astonished Miss Loper, and left the building.

That evening, he told Jean what had happened,

leaving nothing out. "What in hell did we do wrong, Jean? How did this happen?"

"That way lies madness, Danny, so let it be. No one in this ridiculous society is equipped to raise children, the rich least of all. I don't like the notion of closing the door on Tom forever, but I am far more worried about you putting yourself through this kind of an emotional explosion. It's no good for you."

"I'm all right. And if you want to see Tom, see him."

"I certainly don't want to see him now. How I'll feel in six months or a year, I don't know. More to the point, what about Barbara? Do we tell her?"

"I have to tell her why Fredericks wouldn't take the case."

"Tell her the other reasons. Don't drive any wedge between them, Danny. She has enough misery."

One morning, about an hour after Joe had left for the clinic, Sally's telephone rang. The woman at the other end informed her that she was Alex Hargasey's secretary, and that if it were possible, Mr. Hargasey would like to see Mrs. Lavette at his office at three o'clock that afternoon. "Can you be there?" she asked Sally.

"You bet! Absolutely!"

"The Paramount Studios. The gate is at Marathon, just east of Gower. If you come down Melrose—"

"Yes, I know where it is."

"We'll leave a pass at the gate. The guard will tell you where to go."

Trembling with excitement, Sally put May Ling in her restraining chair in the car and drove to the clinic. Her car was an eight-year-old Ford that had fits of temper and whimsy, and now she prayed that it would perform through the day.

At ten o'clock, the clinic was overflowing, and she waited impatiently for Joe to come out of his consulting room. She sat at one end of the row of chairs, looking at the Mexican women and children and a sprinkling of men, all of them sitting listlessly, hopelessly, the way people sit in the waiting room of a free clinic, displaying a sort of subdued, sad patience.

Billy came out and saw her, and his face lit up. "Why didn't you tell us you were here?"

"Because Joe gets so angry when I interrupt him."

"Ah, no. Joe doesn't get angry."

"Billy," she said, "will you be an absolute darling? You know that screenplay of mine. I sent it to Alex Hargasey at Paramount, and now he wants to see me. His secretary called, and I have an appointment at three. You talk to Joe, please. I need a baby sitter—just for a few hours. If you can come by at two, that will give me plenty of time."

At that moment Joe came out, and Sally repeated her story. "Aren't you pleased?" she asked. "Isn't it exciting?"

"We have a terrible day. I need Billy here."

"Is that all you can say? I don't believe you!"

"Come into my office," Joe said. "I can't discuss it here."

Billy had said nothing, only watching Sally in a kind of dumb admiration. In his office, Joe said, "You could have telephoned. You didn't have to drag the baby down here."

"I thought you'd be at the hospital and I'd have to talk Frank into letting me have Billy for a few hours. This whole thing is crazy. Do you know what the chances are of selling an original screenplay—maybe one in a thousand—and they pay tremendous sums, sometimes twenty or thirty thousand dollars, perhaps more. And I finally get this chance, and it doesn't mean anything to you."

"Of course it means something to me, Sally. All right, I got a little up tight. There are times when this place drives me insane. Our patient load gets bigger and bigger, and the city doesn't give a damn. No one gives a damn."

"I know. I'll take May Ling with me. They'll survive the sight of a baby."

"Forget that. I'll send Billy over."

When Billy arrived that afternoon, Sally was still trying to come to terms with her face and hair. She applied lipstick and then wiped it off; she applied rouge and then wiped it off. She stuffed Kleenex into her brassiere and then removed it in disgust. She stared at her hair, thinking that it was straw, it had always been straw, and it would always be straw. She stared at her face—the high cheekbones, the deepset, bright blue eyes, the wide expressive mouth—and decided that nothing would help. She had changed clothes three times, deciding finally on a gray pleated skirt, a white blouse, and a gray cardigan. "I'm dowdy," she told herself. "Always have been, always will be." Then she said to Billy, "How do I look? Perfectly horrible? Go ahead, you can tell me."

"I think you're the most beautiful woman I have ever known," Billy said seriously.

"I think you're nutty. I should have known better than to ask you. Do you know, Billy, you have an absolutely crazy notion of what I am. I am not pretty. I am selfish, I am vain, and I'm slowly driving my husband out of his mind."

"Oh, no, no. You mustn't be upset about the way Joe acts. You can't imagine what it's like these days.

After you left, they brought in two kids who were in a knifefight, both of them bleeding like pigs. It took us two hours to stop the bleeding and sew them up, and then they needed blood, and we couldn't find a place to admit them for transfusions—"

"Do you know," Sally interrupted, "this is all my life has been for two years now. Look, Billy, about May Ling. She's still napping. When she wakes up, she'll be wet. Can you change a diaper?"

"I think so." He smiled.

"Then put her in the living room. Give her the teething stuff. She'll be fine, only keep an eye on her. She walks, you know."

"I like her. We'll be all right."

Sally put her arms around him and kissed him. "I like you. You're absolutely an angel, only you're too good to be true."

Billy shook his head. "No, I'm hopeless."

At the studio, the guard at the gate regarded Sally's car dubiously. "What can I do for you, miss?"

"I have an appointment with Mr. Hargasey. I'm Sally Lavette."

He checked his board, then nodded. "You turn right, Miss Lavette, and then park anywhere along that wall. Then just follow the yellow line and you come to a kind of half-timbered building on your right. There's a receptionist there who'll show you where his office is."

After she parked her car, it was still only ten minutes to three. Sally walked slowly through the studio grounds, treasuring each step. It was the first time she had ever been in a film studio, and she found herself utterly enchanted by the place—the great sound stages, the people in costume hurrying by, cowboys, Indians, lovely women in evening gowns and men in tails walking through the hot sunlight, two pretty blondes in Little Bo Peep dresses. Oh, I do love this place, she thought, and wouldn't it be wonderful to work here! A sign on a building to her left caught her eye: WRITERS BUILDING. I'd be there, she thought, right in there doing my own work and feeling that there is some reason for me to be alive. Well, we'll see . . . we'll see what Mr. Hargasey has to say. Who knows? Maybe I'll be in there tomorrow, revising my script.

She found the half-timbered building, and the receptionist told her that Mr. Hargasey was down the hall, number four. Her hand was trembling as she opened the door of number four. The room appeared palatial enough to house Mr. Hargasey, but it was evidently the habitat of his secretary, a well-rounded, pretty woman with bleached hair and heavy make-up who conformed to Sally's notion of what a desirable woman should look like.

"You're Mrs. Lavette," she said, smiling mechanically. "Please sit down. Mr. Hargasey will see you in a few minutes. Would you like to look at the trades?"

Sally had not the vaguest notion of what the trades were, but she nodded, and the secretary handed her copies of *Daily Variety* and the Hollywood *Reporter*. She leafed through them, feeling more and more a part of this wonderful world of filmmaking. Then the phone on the secretary's desk rang, and Sally was informed that she could now see Mr. Hargasey.

"Through there," the secretary said, pointing to a connecting door.

Hargasey's office was large, about twenty by twenty-five feet, all of it carpeted in oyster white. There was a couch, two overstuffed chairs in black leather, and an enormous desk. Hargasey rose from behind the desk as she entered, a totally bald, stocky man in his late fifties. "Sit down, sit down," he said, smiling and pointing to the chair beside the desk.

He spoke with an elusive foreign accent, explained perhaps by a brass placard on his desk that read: "It's not enough to be Hungarian. You must also have talent."

"So you're Danny's daughter-in-law," he said. "By God, I am glad seeing anyone related to Danny Lavette. That is one hell of a man. How is he? Tell me."

"He had a heart attack."

"Oh—no."

"But he's fine now, just fine. My husband—that's his son, my husband, he's a doctor—he tells me Dan made a fine recovery." She was chattering nervously, foolishly.

"And that beautiful Chinese wife of his, she is still just as beautiful?"

"May Ling? No. Poor May Ling was killed at Pearl Harbor, almost eight years ago. My baby is named after her."

"Ah! Such a damn shame! Such waste! You tell Danny my heart goes out to him, yes?"

Sally nodded. She waited. Hargasey was studying her with interest. The silence dragged on. Finally Sally said, "Can we talk about my screenplay?"

"Your screenplay?"

"The one I sent you."

"Oh, yes. Positively. It stinks."

"What?"

"You ask me about the screenplay. What's to say? It stinks. Darling, there is such a thing as a way to write for the screen, a manner, a technique. You don't know any of them. Forget it."

Sally stared at him for a moment, then leaped to her feet and, leaning across the desk, said, "Is that what

you called me in here for, to tell me that my screenplay stinks?"

"I call you because you are Danny's daughter-in-
law. I love Danny."

Her voice rose. "You love Danny! That really gets to
me! You love Danny enough to get all my hopes up, to
put me through this wretched charade, and then you
can't spare the time to tell me what was wrong with
my work! Oh, no! Only that it stinks! Well, you may
be Dan's bosom friend, Mr. Hargasey, but I can't help
returning the sentiment! You stink, sir!"

She stood in front of him trembling with anger, her
pale eyes flashing; behind his desk, Hargasey stared
at her intently, not annoyed, not provoked, simply
staring intently.

"You—you—" The words choked off.

"Go on, go on," Hargasey said.

Sally swallowed, breathed deeply, and clasped her
hands together to stop their trembling. "I'll take my
manuscript and go," she whispered.

"Walk across the room," Hargasey said.

"What?"

"I said, walk across the room. It's possible, yes."

"Why should I?"

"You want your manuscript. Walk across the room,
I'll give you the manuscript."

"Are you crazy?"

"Maybe. Who knows?"

She took two paces and then turned on him, her
eyes blazing. "Damn you, no! You can't make a fool of
me! You can tell me my writing stinks, but that's all
you can do."

"Take off your sweater."

"No! Give me my script!"

Hargasey rose and came around the desk. Sally

backed away. "Now look," she said to him. "I may be skinny, but I'm strong. And I'm taller than you. I was raised on a farm with two brothers—so just don't try anything."

He burst into laughter. "Oh, Sally, little darling, all the stories about Hollywood! You believe it all, yes? That's what's wrong with your screenplay. How old are you?"

"Twenty-two."

"Beautiful. You could be my granddaughter. There are men my age who play with children. I don't. Take off the sweater. I want to see you without it."

His whole manner had changed. He was gentle, cozening, intriguing. She found her anger dissipating as she pulled off the sweater, at the same time asking herself why she was doing it, why she was obeying him? He studied her for a few moments, appraising her from head to foot.

"You ever acted, Sally? Anywhere? Amateur theatricals, anything?"

She shook her head.

"It don't matter." He went to his desk and picked up a manuscript. "Sit down over there and look at this. There's a part in there for a woman. Lotte. That's the name of the woman. You read it and think about that woman."

"I can't act. I never acted in my life. Anyway, I can't sit down and read. I have a baby at home. I have to get back."

He pointed to the phone. "Make a call. You want me to get a nurse to go to your home and sit with the baby? Or I'll send my secretary. Whatever you want."

"I don't know what you're thinking," she said plaintively.

"So just let me think. You call your house."

"I'm not even pretty," she said woefully.

"Sally, pretty is what this town stinks from. On every corner is pretty. Outside there is fifty girls who are pretty. Means nothing, positively nothing. They are the same, like cut out of cardboard. You got that thing Garbo had. I know, you don't look like her, thank God. She ain't my favorite. I won't even call you beautiful, but you got a face like you don't see. And with passion, that's it. Positively. All right, so I'm crazy. Outside on the lot, fifty girls come crawling with tears, I should tell them to read that script. Do me a favor. Call your house."

She walked to the desk, picked up the phone, and began to dial.

"No, first nine. Then dial."

She dialed again. Billy answered. "Billy," she said, "will you be a dear and stay an extra hour or two—or until I come back?"

"Sally, what's wrong? You sound awful."

"No, it's not awful. I'm fine."

"I guess I can stay," he said. "What shall I tell Joe? Will you be back in time for dinner?"

"Oh, yes."

"And I'm good with the diapers. Don't worry."

"And Billy, if I'm not there by five, there's a bottle in the fridge. You warm it to skin temperature. And with it, a bowl of Pablum. The directions are on the box, and just let her eat as much as she wants."

She put down the phone and turned to Hargasey. "I don't know what I'm doing. I think I've lost my mind."

"So you lost your mind." He handed her the script. "Read it."

She took the script, dropped into one of the leather chairs, and began to read. Hargasey picked up the telephone, and Sally heard him say, "Get me Mike Bordon." And then, after a moment, "Mike, I think I found our Lotte. I want you to set up a screen test." Pause. "I know it don't happen, but it happened. You got to see her. Tall, wide shoulders, yellow hair that ain't from a bottle, looks like she just climbed out of a covered wagon. And a face like an angry angel. And she is valid." Pause again. "Can she act? Mike, tell me, who the hell can act in this lousy industry? This one, I think of Lauren Bacall, only she has a quality Bacall should give her eyeteeth for. What can I tell you— you'll see her. In an hour."

It was almost eight o'clock when Sally got home. Joe had been sitting in the kitchen, and he leaped up when he heard her at the door, then embraced her and held her as she came into the house. "I was so worried," he said. "I was just about out of my mind. I tried calling the studio, and all I got was an answering service that told me they had closed for the day."

"Then you're not angry at me?"

"I'm never angry at you, Sally, I love you so much. Don't you know how much I love you? I just couldn't imagine what had happened to you."

"Oh, Joey, the most wonderful, crazy, impossible thing happened to me. You know, I went over there to Paramount because this man, Hargasey—you remember him, your father built a yacht for him—had his secretary make an appointment for me to see him. I thought he would tell me that my screenplay was wonderful. He's a funny little man, fat and bald as a billiard ball, and he didn't tell me that at all, but he just wanted to see me because he's so crazy about your dad—"

"Slow down, slow down," Joe begged her, laughing in spite of himself. "Come on into the kitchen. I made coffee. I'll pour you a cup."

Sally held it in until they were sitting at the kitchen table. "Just listen, Joey, and don't laugh at me and don't be angry, but almost the first thing he said to me was that my screenplay was rotten, that it was worthless, and that I didn't know the first thing about writing a screenplay. Well, I got so angry, I began to scream at him and call him names—I guess I was never so angry before—and he just sat and stared at me. He kept looking at me and telling me to walk back and forth, and then he asked me whether I had ever done any acting, and I thought he was making passes and I was so nasty to him, but he's really a darling little man. Well, he gave me a script to read, and he arranged for a screen test right there—"

"Wait, wait," Joe said. "What are you telling me, Sally? You didn't fall for that kind of thing? It's a racket."

"Won't you listen to me, please? It's not a scam. I'm not a fool, Joe, or some little babe in the woods. Now listen to what happened. I spent an hour reading the script. It's a Western, and I don't think it's any great shakes, but it's all right. It's called *Purple Sage*. Then Hargasey took me to this huge sound stage that had about four different sets in it. They were just using one of the sets because it was there, a western saloon, and the part they wanted me to read happened in a western saloon, but they haven't any sets for the picture yet because they haven't even started. But the set was lit up with all these big klieg lights, and there was a cameraman, and this man—his name is Mike Bordon and he's Hargasey's production manager— well, this man read a few lines as cues, just a page, but I memorized my lines on the page. I read along with him, and they filmed it. Then they had me do some other things that they filmed, and then we talked, and they were both of them so nice and kind, and they asked me to come back tomorrow, when they'll have the developed film, which they call the rushes, and Mr. Hargasey says that if I film all right, he'll give me the part, because he's sick and tired of looking for someone to play the role who doesn't exist. I mean, that's the way he talks. He's a Hungarian, but very nice. And he said not to worry about acting, because he'd find me a coach, and he thinks I'm a natural actress, whatever that is."

She stopped and waited. Joe looked at her and said nothing, his brows knit, his face tight and worried.

"Joe?"

"I love you so much," he said.

"Joe, you haven't looked at me in weeks. Sometimes I wonder if you know I exist."

"That's just the way I am," he said unhappily. "You know that, Sally. That's the way I've always been. It doesn't mean I don't love you. You're the most important thing in my life."

Impulsively, she leaped to her feet, ran around the table, and cradled his head in her arms.

"You used to say I was dumb. I'm dumb," Joe said.

"Oh, no, no, you're not dumb. You're the kindest, best man I ever knew. Joey, don't you want me to do this?" She let go of him and stood by the table, staring at him wide-eyed. "If you don't want me to—"

"You want it, don't you?"

"It's like a dream. Oh, Joe, I would love to be the kind of person you want me to be, and stay here and have children and keep the house for you and always be here when you want me—but I can't, and I'm not that person, and I've been so miserable."

"You want this a great deal, don't you?"

"More than anything in the world." She closed her eyes and stood still for a moment, her hands clasped; looking at her, Joe could understand what had happened at the studio. She was like some wild, strange creature, raised in captivity but never civilized, never truly tamed or subdued.

"We'll work it out," he said. "Don't worry, Sally. You go ahead and do it, and we'll work it out somehow."

When Sally returned to the studio the following day, Hargasey introduced her to a Mr. Jack Lesser, a neatly dressed, bespectacled man in his forties. "Lesser here," Hargasey said, "is from the William Morris Agency. That's a very respectable agency for actors, makes sure they shouldn't be cheated by people like myself. I had him meet us here. I'm going to make you an offer, and he'll tell you what I offer, it ain't enough. That's his work. I could hire you for peanuts, but you're Danny's daughter-in-law, and anyway I like you. But," he said to Lesser, "you should be paying me. I got to teach her to act, to walk, to talk."

"My heart bleeds for you," Lesser said, and to Sally, he added, "I work for an excellent agency, Mrs. Lavette, but you can't let Hargasey inflict me on you. You have to engage me of your own free will, because I'll ask you to sign a contract with our agency. The money you earn will come through our agency, and we deduct a ten percent commission. Now, do you want me to represent you?"

"Yes. I've heard of the William Morris Agency. Yes, of course, I'd like that." Then she added, "If Mr. Hargasey feels I need an agent."

"You will need one," Hargasey said. "Believe me."

* * *

Dr. Kellman called Barbara and asked her whether she could see him at his house the following evening. "I would ask you to dinner, Barbara," he said, "but I can't get home much before nine. Would nine-thirty be all right?"

"Yes, certainly," Barbara said. "Is it about daddy?"

"No, not really. But let's talk when you get here."

Kellman lived within walking distance, in one of the new apartment houses on Jones Street. It was a cool, lovely summer evening, and Barbara enjoyed the walk. She had been spending too many hours at her desk, and she thought longingly of the horse she had once kept at Menlo Park, of rides on shaded hillside bridal paths, of the heated gallop around the track, the wind rushing in her face. She had sold the horse, Sandy, a gift from her father, in 1934, just as she had sold everything she owned then to buy food for the soup kitchen in which she worked during the long-shore strike. It had been fourteen, almost fifteen years, and she had never been on a horse since. Had there truly been a time in her life when Sandy had been the most important object in the world? She recalled the endless hours of currying. What had happened to Sandy? What had happened to her whole wonderful, aimless, untroubled girlhood? Or had it ever been wonderful or untroubled? And by what right did she complain? She had been loved and she had given love, and she had known heights of exultation as well as depths of despair. It was deep in Barbara's nature to emerge from despondency almost the moment it found her, and by the time she reached Dr. Kellman's apartment, she was quite relaxed and cheerful and only moderately interested in the reason for his summons.

From all her mother had told her, Dan was not be-
having as a convalescent patient should, and she was
sure that Dr. Kellman was going to ask her to bring
her influence to bear in that direction, although it did
seem a bit odd that he should turn to her. So all the
more her astonishment when she entered the Kellman
apartment and walked into a living room crowded
with people. It took only moments for Barbara to realize what the occasion was.

Here were the eighteen people who had contributed
money toward the medicine for the hospital in Toulouse: Dr. Kellman and his wife; Professor Brady from
Berkeley and his wife; Mrs. Seligman, eighty-nine,
doyenne of the old San Francisco society; Dr. Montrosa and his wife; Dave Appelle, an accountant;
Eloise and Adam Levy; two old friends of her childhood, Ruth and Leslie Adams, sisters, with their husbands; Professor Gladstone, the historian; Arnold
Dell, who worked on the *Examiner*; Mrs. Gifford, a
widow; Mrs. Abramson; Jed Kenton; Stephan Cassala;
Dr. Murphy; Fred Cooper; and Carl Anson from the
longshore union—all of them here, crowding around
her, embracing her and telling her how delighted they
were to see her.

It was very moving, and Barbara fought to hold
back her tears. Finally Dr. Kellman clapped his hands
for silence and said, "All right, ladies and gentlemen.
The greetings are over, and now find chairs or places
on the floor, because this is a meeting, not simply a
social occasion, and as a meeting, I have to call it to
order. I suppose I tricked Barbara into coming here
this evening, and for that she'll have to forgive me.
Will you, my dear?"

Not trusting herself to speak, Barbara nodded and

spread her hands. Blinking, rubbing her eyes, she sat down on a chair someone offered her.

"Drinks and refreshments later," Dr. Kellman told them. "Right now, the business of the night—a night, I may say, which was no easy matter to put together. You are certainly as busy and preoccupied a group of people as I have ever known. But since this meeting was Mrs. Seligman's idea, I'll give her the floor and let her explain. Please, don't bother to stand," he told the old woman, who sat in one corner, leaning on her cane. "You can talk to us from right there."

"Not that I can't stand," Mrs. Seligman said. "This ridiculous bias against old people—first, that they're feeble, and second, that they've taken loss of their wits. Well, you might as well know that I personally tricked Barbara into giving me your names, every last one of them. I invited her over for tea, and trusting me, as she should not have, she discussed the whole thing. Then I put my head together with Milt Kellman here, and we decided that we would get in touch with each of you. You see, my dear," she said, turning to Barbara, "there are five persons here tonight who might put themselves and their jobs in jeopardy if their names were revealed. That leaves thirteen of us who just don't care, and we have come here tonight to tell you how proud and grateful we are to you for trying so hard to protect us. But that is over. Tomorrow we shall release our names to the press, and that will be the end of it and, we trust, the end of your difficulties."

There was a ripple of applause, and all faces turned toward Barbara. She rose uncertainly.

"You have the floor," Dr. Kellman said.

"Only it's hard for me to speak, because what I

would truly like is to sit down somewhere in a corner and have a good cry. You are so good and dear and brave. I guess this is one of the nicest things that ever happened to me. But you can't do it."

"But we certainly intend to," Mrs. Gifford called out.

"No, please—I'll try to explain. You see, this stupid thing, this contempt of Congress that they are accusing me of, well, it's something that I did, and only I can void it. It would do absolutely no good for anyone, not for me and not for you, to have your names in the press. I would still be in contempt."

"Then you will give our names to the committee," Dr. Montrosa said. "Is there anyone here who would object to that?"

When the heads had stopped nodding agreement, Barbara said, "I'm afraid I would."

"Barbara, why?" Dr. Kellman asked.

"You're all so kind about this, and you feel that I have been trying to protect you. Well, there's a little truth in that, because I do have an obligation to each of you. I came to you and I accepted money from each of you, and that makes it my obligation, not yours—"

There were cries of "Oh, no!" "You're wrong." "We all share it."

"Please, listen to me. That's only a part of it, and whatever you think about it, whether or not I have an obligation to you, I do have an obligation to myself. That's something only I can decide, because I have to live with myself. And I have decided. I will not give the names of innocent people to that wretched committee. I will not do it, and there's nothing you can say that will make me change my mind. I know I sound stubborn and inflexible, but this is something I have thought about a great deal. And it doesn't mean I don't appreciate what you've done in coming here tonight. But that's the way it is."

The arguments went on for another hour, but Barbara would not give an inch, and in the end it was agreed that there would be no public announcement of the names. Barbara left with Adam and Eloise, and once outside, Eloise said, "Bobby, I am so proud of you. I know that in your place I would just cave in."

"I don't think you would."

"Just remember," Adam said, "that we're here whenever you need us. We're only an hour away."

They dropped Barbara at the house on Green Street. It was almost midnight. Whenever Barbara came home late at night and let herself into the house, she had a sense of depletion, of emptiness. Not that the house was empty; Anna was there, and so was Sam. The feeling of emptiness was inside herself, and the feeling communicated itself, like a ghostly presence walking in front of her. She switched on the lights in the living room and stood and looked around her. The hooked rug, the old black horsehair sofa that had been Sam Goldberg's, the two leather chairs in front of the fireplace—the only chairs, Bernie would say, that fit his bulk—the pile of magazines on the coffee table—all of it soaked up the emptiness inside her.

She fairly ran up the stairs, fleeing from it, then tiptoed into Sam's room. The night light burned. In his crib, Sam was happily asleep, fat and untroubled, pink-cheeked and healthy. She tiptoed back out of the room and went downstairs, thinking what a wonderful placebo a well-fed little boy could be, aware that the moment of misery had slipped away, and wondering whether there was not something deeply wrong with her nature, so easily did she shake off depression. If I were normal, she thought, I would be deeply sorry for myself right now, but I don't feel sorry for myself at all. What nice people!

She was not sleepy. She made herself a cup of tea and put the Bach Inventions on the record player. She dropped into the big leather chair that had been Bernie's favorite, sipped her tea, half-closed her eyes, and listened to the marvelous ripple of sound. She dozed off and was awakened by the scraping sound of the record changer.

Chilled, she went up the stairs to her bedroom. Anna always turned down the heat before she went to bed, and the summer nights in San Francisco were cold and damp. Barbara stripped off her clothes and then stood for a moment, naked and shivering, looking at herself in the mirror. She touched her breasts, still high and firm, and ran her hands over the flat surface of her belly. The scar was almost invisible.

"What a waste!" she whispered. "What a stupid, stupid waste."

Then she pulled on her nightgown and crawled between the icy cold sheets. Lying there, waiting for the heat of her body to warm the bed, she said aloud, "What about it, Bernie? Am I right?" Laughing and crying at the same time, she said, "How alike we were! Why didn't I ever see how alike we were? I know exactly what you'd say—fuck them, in your own inimitable style. You crazy bastard, to go off and get yourself killed!"

Boyd Kimmelamn called and said, "Barbara, they've finally set a trial date, first week in September, the federal courthouse in Washington. Now you are not to lose any sleep over this. Remember what I told you, even if it goes down the river and we lose hands down, there is still the Court of Appeals and the Supreme Court."

"Boyd," she said, "by now this has become a normal function of my life. The truth is, I'm happy the waiting is over. Much better this way."

"Harvey and you and me, we'll want to sit down and hash this over a bit—you know, lay out a line of approach. When can you come by?"

"Soon, Boyd?"

"The sooner the better. How about tomorrow afternoon?"

"I can make it."

"Good. We'll clear the decks for you and push it around all afternoon if we have to."

Barbara began to giggle. A part of her mind had been occupied in counting the clichés. In the two minutes or so since she had picked up the phone, she had reached a count of seven. "Boyd," she said, "you're great."

"Why? Did I say something?"

"See you tomorrow."

She put down the telephone, went into her study, and wrote in her daybook: "Three o'clock, lawyers for the defense." She shook her head at the sight of it, looking so sinister and important. She had committed a misdemeanor. Returning home from Washington after the hearing, she had looked up the word and found it explained variously as ill behavior, petty misconduct, less than a felony. Spitting on the sidewalk was in many places a misdemeanor. Smoking in a no-smoking area. Using foul language in certain places. Walking naked on San Francisco streets. "And refusing to answer a question put to you by ill-mannered boobs," she added.

But now the ten writers and directors in Hollywood, who had also refused to answer questions, had been sentenced to prison, most of them for a year less a day, so one did not take it too lightly. Kimmelman had called just as she was preparing to leave the house with Sam. She had finished the working draft of her novel the day before. It was now almost five months since Bernie had died. During the first weeks after she received the news, she had felt she could never write again, never think coherently again, but now the book was done. She planned to spend the day with Sam at Golden Gate Park. Jean had promised to pick them up, and then the three of them would lunch somewhere, Sam's first restaurant lunch at the age of twenty months.

The doorbell cut through her reverie. Jean was there, and Sam welcomed her with delight. "Hand in hand," she told the little boy, taking his hand and leading the way to her car. "You are a handsome young fellow. And a great walker." Her car was a new Cadillac convertible, pearl gray and loaded, as she explained to Barbara, "Dan's present for my birthday. It has everything, does everything except talk. Isn't it a love?"

Barbara held Sam in her lap as they drove off. "What a great big wonderful world we live in," Barbara said. "Daddy gives you a Cadillac convertible as a birthday gift, and Tom tosses John Whittier out of granddaddy's business, right on his ear, which is practically patricide—"

"You heard about that?"

"Is there anyone in the city who hasn't? I have the most amazing brother there. He reminds me of the Emperor Caligula, only with a certain lack of restraint that Caligula may have practiced."

"I'm thankful I know nothing about this Caligula of

yours. I do think you and Tom should maintain some kind of relationship."

"But we do, mother, only I don't enjoy myself in the role of Red Riding Hood. And to go on with the family catalogue, my brother Joe is studying to be a saint or Father Damien or something down there in Los Angeles—"

"Who on earth is Father Damien? I think your problem, Barbara, is overeducation. It comes of too much time spent alone reading. Where the rich are concerned, my love, a minimum of education is all that is called for, a light touch of Princeton, for example, such as your brother Tom was exposed to. Anything more than that can awaken something called conscience. About Father Damien?"

"I'm not rich, mother. I actually earn my own living writing books and articles for ladies' magazines, except lately they avoid me like the plague."

"Well, you will be when Dan and I die, unless you give it away again; and in any case, we're not rich. We're comfortable. Tom is rich. The difference, Bobby, between my son and daddy and me is best defined by the British. They have a word we don't use at all: establishment. It's used to draw a line of separation between fairly affluent people, like myself, for example, and those who are so enormously rich and powerful that they control the state. The British call them the establishment, and Tom is right in there with the best of them. And I still don't know who Father Damien is."

"He was a priest who went to live and work with the lepers on Molokai in Hawaii."

"You mean Joe is working with lepers?"

"No, mother, with poverty, which is a worse disease, and now Sally is going to be a movie star or something of the sort, and just before you arrived, my lawyer called and informed me that the trial date has been set. One petty criminal to complete the roster. On the whole, we haven't done too badly, have we?"

"We won't have Judge Fredericks. He turned us down," Harvey Baxter told her.

"Does Barbara know why?" Kimmelman asked.

Out of the corner of her eye, Barbara saw Baxter shake his head sharply.

"We don't need him," Kimmelman said. "I was always dubious about that notion of distinguished counsel. I mean, not that we can't hire distinguished counsel, Barbara. I can name half a dozen men who would come in on this, and if you want one of them, Harvey and I will go along with you completely. Right, Harvey?"

"Oh, yes, quite. The point is, Barbara, are you satisfied with us as your attorneys?"

"Harvey, I must ask you quite flatly. Will it help me to have another attorney?"

Baxter nodded. "Tell you what, Barbara. I'm going to let Boyd answer that question. He's had his nose in the books, and he is dedicated to your case."

"Absolutely," said Kimmelman. "But I am not looking for anything exclusive, believe me, Barbara. Now let's look at it this way: I have been calling Washington, where I have a few old army buddies, and I think that the judge who will sit on the case is Lansing Meadows. I dug up all the stuff on him that I could. He's sixty-two, a Republican, appointed to the bench by Herbert Hoover, born in Richmond, Virginia. They say he's tough, rigid, and conservative. No California Democrat is going to impress him, and I don't think we could find a prominent Republican to go with us.

Now this is a very funny case, Barbara. Before the war, very few contempt cases went to trial, and when they did, jail sentences were rare. Usually it was a suspended sentence and a stiff fine. Judge Meadows has sat on five contempt cases, the most recent one in forty. In every case, he suspended sentence and leveled a fine. Now, it's a whole new game. Every court case that stems from the House Committee on Un-American Activities ends up in a jail sentence. It seems insane that a misdemeanor should put you in this kind of position, but that's what things have come to. Now Harvey and I think this case can be fought and won, but it's up to you."

"And if we lose, Boyd, what's the very worst that can happen?"

"A year in jail. But that's the very worst. I don't look for that under any circumstances."

"All right," Barbara said. "I'm quite content to go along with you and Harvey. I really don't want any other lawyers."

"Good. Now here's the way it shapes up. I've read the record of your hearing a dozen times, and there's no doubt in my mind that the question they asked you was pertinent. Let's say that the whole inquiry lacked pertinence. That's another point. But if we accept the inquiry, the question was pertinent. They asked it. You refused to answer. *Ipso facto*, contempt of Congress. Now if that is the case, it would appear that the whole thing is open and shut, with no way out. But I don't think so. I think there are two lines of defense we can take. First, a line that holds that the subpoena was invalid, that you, Barbara Cohen, had engaged in no action that could be construed as un-American, and therefore you were wrongly served and summoned. I've found a case in the record to support that, and that will constitute my first move—or, I should say, Harvey's, because he'll try the case, and he'll go in immediately with a motion that the case be dismissed. There's just an outside chance that we might succeed, but I wouldn't want to get your hopes up on that first ploy. If the motion is rejected, we'll make a second motion on the basis that any inquiry calling you as a witness is not pertinent to the function of the committee. That won't hold up, but we'll get it on the record."

"I don't understand, Boyd. Where is the actual courtroom defense?"

"All right, we get to that now. You see, Barbara, in an ordinary criminal case, the accused is presumed innocent and the state must prove guilt. But here, because there is no actual crime involved, the House of Representatives has already voted a charge of guilt, and the defendant must prove his innocence. It is insane, but try to follow me. You are guilty of contempt by a vote of the House. How can we establish your innocence? Only by invalidating the action of the committee. It's a procedure that violates every canon of common Anglo-Saxon law, and it is also a procedure that I believe to be unconstitutional. I believe it's in violation of the sense and implication of the Fifth Amendment, which declares that no person shall be forced to be a witness against himself. Now Harvey feels that we lost the opportunity when he failed to advise you to invoke the Fifth Amendment, and he's been beating his breast over that. But there was no reason for him to tell you to invoke the Fifth Amendment. I'm going to try a new approach and claim that the amendment holds in the case, whether invoked or not. You see, Barbara, not only is this the only foot we can put forward, but it raises a constitutional issue, and I want that desperately. Then, if we lose, we can appeal this right up to the Supreme Court with some hope that they'll hear it. That has to be our ace in the hole."

"But Boyd wants to do it," Baxter said, "by putting you on the stand. As the accused, you don't have to take the stand. I'm afraid of that."

"But Harvey," Barbara argued, "if I don't take the stand, who will? I'm in this alone."

"We'll have character witnesses."

"Come on, Harvey," Kimmelman said, "look at the reality. She is our one and only witness. There's no case without her."

The discussion went on almost until five o'clock. Boyd Kimmelman walked downstairs with Barbara, and she said, "When we first started this afternoon, you asked whether I knew why Judge Fredericks had turned down this case, and then Harvey did some frantic signaling to shut you up."

"You don't miss much, do you?"

"I try not to. Why did Judge Fredericks turn us down?"

"I think you ought to ask Harvey."

"Boyd," she said, "don't turn cute on me. I'm a grown woman, up to my knees in a sewer. I damn well want to know why."

"It's just a rumor we heard."

"Then it's a rumor I should hear too."

He sighed and said, "Are you going to insist that I tell you?"

"Of course I am. What is a lawyer for? And if you don't tell me, I'll find out elsewhere anyway, and there goes a very important question of trust."

"All right. It stinks, but when you put it that way, I have no choice, do I?"

"That's right. You have no choice."

"The rumor is that your brother, Tom, has been playing footsie with Congressman Drake all along."

Barbara stopped walking and turned to face him. They were in the entranceway of the building, in front of the door that led to the street. She felt a lump of ice forming in her stomach.

"I don't believe that," she said.

"Neither did we. Harvey went to see Judge Fredericks, and the judge says it's true."

"Does my father know this?"

"Apparently, because he was the one who spoke to Fredericks first. I'm terribly sorry, Barbara."

"I'm the one who has to be sorry, Boyd," she said unhappily. "What a stinking mess. All right. Try to forget about it now. There's no need to tell Harvey you told me."

Barbara sat between Harvey Baxter and Boyd Kimmelman, watching the selection of the jury. A large, heavyset black man had been called to the stand. Well dressed in a black suit, white shirt, and black tie, he stared unperturbed at Peter Crombie, the government attorney. Four fat cigars poked out of his breast pocket.

"Name?" Crombie asked.

"Ephraim Jones."

"Occupation?"

"I am an undertaker," Mr. Jones replied.

"Excused for cause. Step down, please," Crombie told him.

"Well, that was short and sweet," said Barbara. "How could they know so quickly that they didn't want him?"

"He's an undertaker," Kimmelman answered. "This

is the age of intimidation. How do you intimidate an undertaker?"

How indeed, Barbara wondered? Alice had seen a white rabbit, and when the white rabbit popped into a hole in the ground, Alice popped in after it. From that point on, two and two ceased to make four. With Barbara as with Alice, it was a process of constantly reminding herself: I am Barbara; I am thirty-four years old, well, almost thirty-five; I am five feet eight and a half inches in height, and I weigh one hundred and twenty-nine pounds. I am a widow, I have a small son, and I have just written a novel that the critics will call saccharine and sentimental. Based on the rather unsubstantial data, here I am in Washington, District of Columbia, capital of the most powerful nation on the face of the earth, in this splendid federal courthouse, where all the forces of the mighty have been arrayed to put me in jail.

"Do you know," she said to Kimmelman, "all this nitpicking with the jurors is absolutely meaningless. I know you told me, but it just sank home. I have been found guilty. First the verdict and then the trial. Did you ever read *Alice in Wonderland?*"

Judge Lansing Meadows was regarding her sternly. She smiled at him but he did not smile back. He has a ferret face, Barbara decided. She had never seen a ferret, but having looked up the word in her dictionary once, she remembered that the ferret is a weasel-like animal found in Africa and Europe and used for the hunting of rabbits. Judge Meadows had a thin, almost lipless mouth, a pointed chin, a thin nose, and hair combed sidewise to cover the bald top of his skull. On the bench in front of him, he kept a glass of water, and sitting on top of the glass, shaped so that it dripped ice water into it, was a large piece of ice, almost twice

the size of the glass it rested on. Whenever the judge
felt the pangs of thirst, he glanced at the black attendant who stood nearby. The attendant leaped to the
bench, raised the miniature iceberg while the judge
eased his thirst, then replaced the ice so that the
dripping might continue. The process fascinated Barbara, and she felt it was both eccentric and unique in
this era of electric refrigeration. She found it difficult
to keep her mind focused on the course of events; her
thoughts tended to wander. Nothing that happened
here was as important to her as her separation from
Sam. She would be four days, possibly five days away
from him. Jean was staying in the house on Green
Street so that the disruption in Sam's life might be
minimal. Eloise had begged Barbara to leave the child
at Higate, but Barbara felt that it was easier to keep
Sam at home.

Barbara had always been intrigued by her mother.
Her father was more understandable. She could look
at him and still see the big, wild, hotheaded boy who
had run a string of fishing boats into one of the largest shipping and transportation empires of the nineteen twenties. Jean was something else entirely, the
one-time arrogant beauty—and then the changes, the
growth, the mellowing, the comprehending, each
stage beyond Barbara's comprehension.

There is really no connection between parent and
child, she thought. No way for one to understand the
other. Mother is astonishing, but she bewilders me.
One day, Sam will ask me why I did all this. Mother
only asked once; after that she worried about my
clothes.

"I don't want to hurt your feelings, Bobby," Jean
had said, "but don't think the judge and the jury won't
be influenced by the way you dress."

"What's wrong with the way I dress?"

"At your age, darling, a plaid skirt, a cardigan, and saddle shoes are not exactly *de rigueur.*"

"Mother, I am not going to wear saddle shoes in court."

"I hope not. Let's go through your wardrobe and select something that will help and not hinder. And if we can't find it, we'll spend a day shopping."

Well, Barbara reflected, it was perfectly normal. When one's daughter goes on trial, one sees to it that she is properly costumed.

"For heaven's sake, Barbara," Baxter whispered to her, "what are you laughing at?"

"My mother."

"Well, not here. It makes a rotten impression."

The image Jean had arrived at was that of a middle western schoolteacher. Barbara's thick honey-colored hair was drawn back and fastened in a demure bun. She wore a suit of dark blue wool, a white cotton blouse, and dark blue shoes. Her own instinct was toward no make-up at all, but Jean said that would look suspicious.

"Mother, suspicious?"

"Bobby, the kind of a woman who doesn't wear make-up—"

"What kind of a woman?"

"Well, if I were sitting on the jury, and there you were with no make-up, I'd say to myself, That kind of a woman with no make-up—obviously a radical."

"Mother, I almost never wear make-up."

"And you're a radical. There you are."

"I am not a radical. I am an ordinary housewife."

"My dear Bobby," Jean said patiently, "the last thing in the world that anyone would call you is an ordinary housewife."

Late that afternoon, they finished picking the jury, seven women and five men: three housewives married to government employees, four women who were government employees, and among the men, a bus driver, a telephone company repairman, and three more government employees.

"I don't get it," Barbara said. "The jury's packed with government employees. Who's on our side?"

"No way out of it. We're in Washington."

The reporters were waiting for her as she left the courtroom. By now, the Washington papers had pegged her as "the San Francisco heiress." It did not matter that almost every penny of her inheritance had gone into an irreversible foundation almost ten years before. An heiress she had been and an heiress she would remain. And that her mother had divorced and subsequently remarried the same man was also grist for the mill, as was Tom Lavette's vast holdings in the GCS Corporation. Only in America, Barbara realized, is wealth worshipped and deplored at the same time, the same Puritan work ethic that makes the gathering of wealth a holy mission stigmatizing the possession of wealth as self-confessed moral depravity.

Back at the hotel—the Mayflower this time—sitting down to dinner in the dining room, Barbara barely tasted her food, in spite of Baxter's insistence that this was one of the best restaurants in Washington. "You know, I'm bored," Barbara said, "the way I'd be bored at some stupid orgy. Petty wickedness, stupidity, evil mediocrity—it's boring because it shrinks the soul. When I was in Hitler's Germany, it was naked and brutal and disgusting. Here it's all wrapped in germ-proof containers."

"Come on, Barbara," Baxter said, "you're not comparing us to Hitler's Germany. It just won't wash. You

know that. Here at least we have due process. You are
free on your own recognizance. We don't have a Gestapo here."

"Then why am I here?"

They both stared at her. She shook her head and
smiled. "I'm sorry. You've both been so good and patient, and here I am whining like some spoiled brat."

"I think you've earned yourself a good fit of hysterics," Kimmelman said, "and if it will make you feel
any better, go ahead and let it out."

"No, it's not my style, Boyd."

"O.K., then let's talk about tomorrow. Harvey and I
have been working over the material, and Harvey
wants me to do the opening remarks and the examination if that's all right with you?"

"The point is," Baxter said, "that I'm no trial lawyer.
I think Boyd has a natural gift that way, and he thinks
better on his feet than I do. I'm stuffy," he admitted.

"No, Harvey, you're not stuffy, but if you want
Boyd to do it, that's fine with me."

Harvey Baxter's two opening motions for the dismissal
of the contempt citation were both summarily rejected. Judge Meadows was annoyed. Barbara realized that he had a low threshold of annoyance. "You
should know better, Mr. Baxter," he said. "There is no
citizen of the United States outside the purview of
congressional authority. As for pertinence, that is established during the examination of a witness, as you
well know."

"I am still down there with Alice," Barbara whispered to Kimmelman.

The courtroom was smaller than she would have expected and darker, with only a dozen seats for spectators. Two reporters watched the proceedings drowsily.

There were four other people who, she guessed, might have been spectators, although why anyone would willingly choose a federal courtroom on a sunny September day, she could not for the life of her imagine. The judge's lump of ice dripped water, and with the regularity of a clock, he nodded at the black attendant to lift the ice so that he might drink.

The government called a single witness, Donald Jay, counsel for the House Committee on Un-American Activities. The questioning was brief and uninspiring. Barbara watched the jury. They sat with blank faces, as if this happening in the court was the last thing that concerned them.

"What is your name, sir?" Crombie, attorney for the government, asked Jay.

"Donald Jay."

"And you are counsel to the House Committee on Un-American Activities?"

"That is right."

"And on the occasion this past March, when Mrs. Barbara Cohen came before the committee as a witness, did you conduct the examination of the witness?"

"I did."

"And was she properly subpoenaed and sworn?"

"She was."

"And is it true that subsequently, the aforesaid House committee voted to cite this witness for contempt of Congress, and that subsequent to that vote, the motion was put before the entire House of Representatives, here in the nation's capital, and that the entire House voted to uphold this citation of contempt?"

Kimmelman objected. When the vote was taken, only a bare quorum of the House was present. The record should not give the impression that the entire House voted the contempt.

Meadows agreed and instructed Crombie to re-phrase his question, which he proceeded to do. Barbara could not see that it mattered very much.

"Do you have the stenographer's record of the hearing of the aforesaid House committee to which we are referring?"

"I do."

"I would ask the bench's permission for this witness to use the aforesaid record to refresh his memory."

"Granted," Judge Meadows said.

"Now, Mr. Jay," Crombie said, "in the light of this citation of contempt, would you repeat the question that led to Mrs. Cohen's contemptatious action?"

Barbara began to giggle. Kimmelman nudged her and objected. "It is taken out of context, your honor. Let him read the whole record."

"Since the record is in evidence, you can request that when you cross-examine. I see no need for it now."

"Barbara," Kimmelman whispered, "don't laugh. Those characters in the jury box are watching you like hawks."

"Contemptatious, really. It's not a word. It's as unreasonable as all the rest of this."

"It's a word here in court."

"Go ahead, Mr. Jay," Crombie was saying.

"Congressman Drake speaking: 'Mrs. Cohen, please give the committee the names of the people who contributed to this private fund of yours.'

"Her answer: 'No.'

"Donald Jay speaking: 'You were asked to name the people who contributed to this private fund for the

Hospital of the Sacred Heart. Will you please name them?'

"Her answer: 'No, I will not.' Then the witness, Mrs. Cohen, consulted her lawyer. Then she added to her answer the following: 'No, Mr. Jay, I have no intention of naming the contributors.'

"Donald Jay speaking: 'You realize that we can subpoena your books and records?'

"Her answer: 'The only books and records of these contributions are in my head. But if there were books and records, rest assured I would destroy them before you got your wretched hands on them.'

"Congressman Drake: 'Mrs. Cohen, do you realize that by refusing to answer this question you are placing yourself in contempt of this committee?'

"Her answer: 'I don't fully understand what that means. I would like to think that it means I have contempt for you and your associates. That would be correct.'

"Then the witness was dismissed."

Crombie turned to Kimmelman. "Your witness, sir."

Watching Boyd Kimmelman, Barbara realized that his twenty-nine years weighed heavily upon him. The fact that this was his first important court case did not bother her. He was a small, compact young man, with bright blue eyes and a thatch of sandy hair that tended to stand upright regardless of how he pressed it down with hair dressing. He was innately theatrical, and Barbara was sure he had practiced every movement for hours. Now he asked his first question without rising:

"Mr. Jay, according to the record you have just read, Congressman Drake warned Barbara Cohen that she was placing herself in a position of contempt by refusing to inform on her friends—"

"Objection!" Crombie snapped. "The implication is insufferable."

"Is it?" Kimmelman asked mildly.

"You will rephrase the question, Mr. Kimmelman," the judge said. "And I must warn you that I will not have this courtroom turned into a political platform."

Kimmelman nodded. "Nevertheless, the congressman warned Mrs. Cohen that she was committing a contempt. Is that correct, Mr. Jay?"

"It is."

"Would the stenographer read her reply?"

The stenographer read, "I don't fully understand what that means—"

"That's sufficient," Kimmelman said, rising and walking over to Jay. "And when she said that, Mr. Jay, you did not feel it was incumbent upon you to explain what contempt of Congress means?"

"No, sir, I did not. A question was asked, and she refused to answer."

"But you had been at many such hearings. This was her first. You didn't feel it necessary to explain the gravity of the situation, the meaning of a congressional vote of contempt, that one day she could sit here in court and face the possible punishment of this court? You didn't see any necessity to inform her of that?"

"She had counsel beside her. The answer is no."

Kimmelman turned to the jury. "What is the purpose of the House Committee on Un-American Activities, Mr. Jay?"

"Objection!" Crombie said.

"No, I'm going to allow that," the judge said.

"He has to allow it," Baxter whispered to Barbara. "He wants a clean record that won't be reversed."

"To frame legislation to protect the people of this country against subversion."

"Very laudable. As I understand it, the committee was established in the month of May, in the year nineteen thirty-eight."

"I think so."

"You think so. Don't you know when the committee you work for was established?"

"Yes, nineteen thirty-eight."

"Ten years. A long time. We were in a depression, we emerged from a depression, and we fought a long, terrible war. Which incidentally took up four years of my own life."

"You can spare us the biographical detail, Mr. Kimmelman," Judge Meadows said sourly.

"Yes, your honor. Now, Mr. Jay, in those ten long, busy years, how many pieces of legislation did the House Committee on Un-American Activities frame and offer to Congress? Was there one, two, ten, or none?"

Before Kimmelman had finished speaking, Crombie was on his feet objecting. Meadows asked both attorneys to approach the bench.

"What do you hope to accomplish by this line of questioning, Mr. Kimmelman?" the judge asked softly.

"I intend to show that this committee has aborted the purpose for which it was created, and that now, in defiance of the Fifth Amendment, it acts as a Star Chamber, the only purpose of which is to entrap witnesses into self-incrimination or to make them victims of the misuse of the committee's power of contempt."

"Not in this courtroom, Mr. Kimmelman."

"I think I stand on constitutional grounds, your honor. May I respectfully ask why not?"

"Because the House committee is not on trial here, Mr. Kimmelman. Your client is on trial. I'm sure you are aware of that."

"But still, with the greatest of respect, your honor, my duty is to defend my client, and that's my only constitutional line of defense."

"I'm sure you're clever enough to find another approach, Mr. Kimmelman. You must remember that when an attorney licensed to practice in another state, in your case, California, pleads a case in a federal court in the District of Columbia, he does so as a privilege granted him by that court. I am sure you will do nothing to cause me to question that privilege, Mr. Kimmelman."

"No, your honor."

Crombie smiled and returned to his table.

Kimmelman had no further questions of Jay, and Crombie magnanimously waved away redirect. "The government rests," he stated, as if offering the simple testimony of a single witness was all that the occasion required.

The judge then announced that the court would reconvene at two o'clock.

At lunch, Boyd Kimmelman wept without tears. "Oh, I am something," he said. "The boy genius, all ready to inscribe a page in the history books, the brilliant California lawyer who destroyed the House committee. Brilliant—I am an idiot, an unredeemed idiot! And I sold you down the river, Barbara. That miserable, tight-lipped sonofabitch!"

"There was no way you could have anticipated this," Baxter told him. "You did the right thing, Boyd."

"No, no. Oh Jesus, I should have seen it. So simple. Why didn't I see it?"

"But Boyd," Barbara said, "it's not over. I know how you feel, but you are going to put me on the stand—"

"I don't know."

"Why not? You say that what happened this morning blows our chance for a constitutional issue. Well, there must be some way you can work a constitutional issue into my testimony."

"It's not quite that easy, Barbara," Baxter said. "No matter how this trial works out, we will try to bring it before the Supreme Court on a constitutional basis. It doesn't have to be a part of the court record. Boyd's scheme was to force Meadows to face up to the constitutional issue right here and either make him accept it or put him in error. But he's too old a hand to step into such an apparent trap, and he scotched it neatly. I must say, I don't like the notion of you taking the stand."

"If I don't, what will the verdict be?"

When neither of them replied, she said, "Guilty, am I right? But at least I have a chance if I take the stand."

"Yes, you have a chance," Kimmelman agreed. "But, face this. Crombie will ask you whether you're a member of the Communist Party."

"But you said he can't."

"He can and he can't. He'll ask it, and I'll object, and the judge will sustain my objection. But the jury will hear the question."

"Is that so terrible?"

"I think so."

"There's also the record," Baxter said. "Crombie will bring up the deposition of Manuel Lopez. We'll object, but the jury will hear it. There's also a chance that the judge may allow it."

"I can't believe," Barbara said, "that out of a jury of

twelve men and women, there isn't one person whom we can convince that I've taken a course of common decency. If that's the case, what on God's earth has happened to us?"

"A climate of fear," Baxter murmured.

"They're government employees for the most part, Barbara. But I think the choice must be up to you. If you don't take the stand, I don't think we have much chance. If you do, well, maybe. I don't think you can make it any worse."

"We'll give it the old school try," Barbara agreed, smiling. "Come on, cheer up, both of you. Somewhere under Lansing Meadows' icy exterior, we hope, there beats a heart of flesh and blood."

But as she sat on the witness stand, the judge's cold, expressionless face turned toward her, she doubted her assessment of flesh and blood. Anyway, she thought, I have always wondered what this feels like, and now I know. It feels idiotic, and as for that jury—

She looked at the jury. It was amazing that not one of the twelve would meet her gaze. They stared into the distance.

"Mrs. Cohen," Kimmelman said to her, "according to the testimony of Mr. Donald Jay, you were asked to provide the House Committee on Un-American Activities with the names of eighteen persons. You refused. Is that correct?"

"Yes."

"Who were these eighteen persons? Not their names. I am not asking for their names. I am asking a general question—how you are related to them and the type of persons they are in social terms?"

"They are my friends. They are people I have known in the course of my life in San Francisco and in the course of my work with the Lavette Foundation.

Some professional people, physicians, businessmen, teachers, housewives, trade unionists."

"I see. And you know all of these people personally?"

"Yes, I do."

"Do you believe on the basis of your knowledge of these people that any of them are subversive or pose a threat to the government of the United States or to our institutions?"

Crombie was objecting before Kimmelman had finished his question. "Calls for a conclusion!"

"You will not answer that question," the judge told her.

"Very well. Now according to your testimony before the House committee, the Lavette Foundation has made several grants of funds to the Hospital of the Sacred Heart in Toulouse, a city in France. Will you tell us something about this hospital?"

Crombie objected.

"I'll allow this. You did open the door, Mr. Crombie." And to Kimmelman, the judge said, "Rephrase your question. I'll have no speeches or declarations here. We'll save that for your summation. Ask your questions specifically."

"When did you first come in contact with this hospital, Mrs. Cohen?" Kimmelman asked her.

"In the spring of nineteen thirty-eight, my fiancé, Marcel Duboise, was brought to that hospital with a bad leg wound that he had suffered in Spain. He was a correspondent for the French newspaper *Le Monde*. I was in Paris when news of this reached me, and I went immediately to Toulouse. He died there in the hospital."

"Was he well treated at the hospital?"

"Yes. The doctors and the sisters there were skilled and kind and good."

"You say sisters. Is it a Catholic hospital?"

"Yes, in that it has connections with the Catholic Church."

"I see. Now how did the Lavette Foundation become involved with the Hospital of the Sacred Heart?"

"Dr. Charles Lazaire, the surgeon who tried to save my fiancé's life, wrote to me in San Francisco, telling me of the enormous problem the hospital was having with refugees from Republican Spain and of the lack of facilities. It's not a large hospital. I put the matter up to the board of the Lavette Foundation, and it was agreed that we would make funds available to the hospital for the specific purpose of caring for Republican refugees and their families."

"I see. Now according to your testimony, a sum of some twelve thousand dollars was raised from among this group of eighteen people for the purchase of penicillin and certain other medical supplies. Why couldn't this purchase have been made through the Lavette Foundation?"

"It was a question of time. The medicine was urgently needed. There's a great deal of red tape connected with a foundation grant, and when it goes to a foreign organization, that complicates the matter even further."

"Then exactly how did you raise the twelve thousand dollars?"

"I telephoned friends and put the problem to them, and the money was subscribed that same evening."

"Now, is it true that three weeks ago these same eighteen men and women whose names you refused to give to the House committee gathered together at the apartment of one of them in San Francisco?"

"Yes, it is."

"Were you aware of that gathering in advance?"

"No, I was not."

"Then you came to this gathering unaware of its purpose?"

"That's right."

Barbara had expected Crombie to object, but he was listening intently. His assistant, a younger man sitting beside him, whispered something to him. Crombie shook his head. Evidently he was intrigued by the material and wanted to see where it would lead.

"What was the purpose of the gathering?"

"These friends knew of my dilemma. They decided that they would make a statement to the press, revealing their names."

"And what did you say when you heard this?"

Again Barbara noticed the young man next to Crombie whispering fiercely, and again Crombie shook his head.

The judge said, "Don't answer that question, Mrs. Cohen." And he went on to Crombie, "Mr. Crombie, I'll entertain an objection here if you wish."

"I'd rather hear the witness' answer," Crombie said.

"You may answer," the judge said.

"I refused their offer. I said that the only way out of my difficulty was for me to supply the names, and this I would not do. I thanked them and persuaded them not to reveal their names."

"Why did you refuse to give the names to the House Committee on Un-American Activities, since the sense of this gathering would indicate that the persons involved were not afraid of reprisal?"

"Because," Barbara said quietly, "I must continue to live with myself as a woman and as a human being. If I am turned into an informer, then I lose a very precious thing, my self-respect. No one can ask this of me—not Congress, not any committee of Congress. As for these eighteen men and women, their jeopardy was for me to judge. I had asked them for money. The responsibility was mine, not theirs."

"Thank you," Kimmelman said. "I have no further questions."

He walked back to his table. Baxter whispered, "Splendid, Boyd, just splendid."

"Yes. God help us now."

Crombie rose and stood looking at Barbara.

"Watch this now," Kimmelman whispered.

"Are you a member of the Communist Party, Mrs. Cohen?"

"Objection!" Kimmelman shouted.

"Strike that question," the judge said to the stenographer.

"Could we approach the bench?" Crombie asked.

The judge nodded. Crombie, Baxter, and Kimmelman went up to the bench.

"The question was asked during her testimony," Crombie whispered. "We have opened the testimony. I think the question is allowable."

"She denied it," Kimmelman argued. "She denied it under oath. If there is any question of proof, why doesn't the government bring a charge of perjury?"

"I ask it only to lay a foundation. The question comes up again and again in her testimony before the House committee."

"May I see the testimony?" the judge asked.

Crombie handed him the printed record, and he leafed through it. The lawyers waited. Then the judge said, "I'm afraid I shall have to allow the question, Mr. Kimmelman. You can deal with it on redirect."

"Then I respectfully request that my objection be on the record."

Crombie walked slowly around Barbara, and, facing the jury, he asked, "Mrs. Cohen, are you now or have you ever been a member of the Communist Party?"

"No, not now, not ever."

"Did you, in nineteen thirty-nine, undertake a mission for the Communist Party of France into Nazi Germany?"

"Objection," Kimmelman called out.

"Overruled."

"It was not a mission—"

"Would you answer yes or no. Did you, in nineteen thirty-nine, undertake a mission for the Communist Party of France?"

"I can't answer that question yes or no."

"Was your purpose to contact the Communist Party of Germany?"

A long moment went by, and then the judge said, "Please answer the question, Mrs. Cohen."

"Yes," Barbara said.

Crombie shrugged. "I have no further questions."

"What was your profession in nineteen thirty-nine?" Kimmelman asked her.

"I was a journalist, a correspondent for *Manhattan Magazine*."

"And you entered Germany as a journalist on assignment from your magazine?"

"Yes."

"Who were Claude and Camille Limoget?"

"They were journalists, friends of my dead fiancé."

"What was their relationship with you?"

"It was a social relationship. They would come to my apartment, and we would have fierce arguments."

"Fierce arguments? But why?"

"Because they were Communists. Marcel and I were not."

"Yet you could be friends?"

"It was that way in Europe, in France anyway."

"And since you were to go to Germany as a journalist, what did these two friends, Claude and Camille Limoget, ask of you?"

"They said that all the connections between the Communist Party of France and the Communist Party of Germany had been destroyed. They wanted desperately to find out whether there was any kind of organized resistance left in Germany. They gave me the name of a professor at Friedrich Wilhelm University in Berlin, and they asked me to try to find out whether he still had anti-Nazi connections."

"And did you find out?"

"No. The Gestapo had killed him."

"Then you never had or attempted any contact with the Communist Part of Germany?"

"No."

"Did you ever have any contact with the Communist Party of France?"

"No. The Limogets were the only Communists I knew, socially or otherwise."

"So the construction that you undertook a mission for the Communist Part of France is Mr. Crombie's invention?"

Crombie objected angrily, and the judge asked Kimmelman to rephrase his question.

"You never undertook a mission for the Communist Party of France in the sense implied by Mr. Crombie?"

"No, I did not."

"Then why did you put your life in jeopardy, as I understand you did, by trying to contact this German professor?"

"Because it was nineteen thirty-nine," Barbara answered tiredly. "Because the whole world appeared to be going down before the Nazis. Because they had killed the man I loved, and because I despised them and everything they stood for."

"That is all. Thank you," Kimmelman said.

Boyd Kimmelman did not believe in long summations, especially in this case, since all through the trial he had sensed the hostility of the jury. There was a thin line between annoying them and touching, somewhere, a nerve of response, a memory of human dignity.

"My client," he said, "is not an ordinary woman, and I would do her a disservice if I pleaded that she was. She is a person of principle, and she has lived her life according to the principles she has cherished. She comes from one of the oldest and wealthiest families in San Francisco. At the age of twenty-six, she fell heir to a legacy of something in excess of fifteen million dollars. She refused this legacy, not accepting any part of it. It became the Lavette Foundation, a charitable institution that supports research in science and in medicine. I mention this only to underline her sense of morality and principle.

"She is a widow. Her husband was killed six months ago, in the struggle for the State of Israel. She has a small child. She earns her living as a writer, and she is recognized as a gifted and a humane artist. Under other circumstances, a grateful government might see fit to reward her sense of compassion, her humanity. She has never done anything of which she need be ashamed. Indeed, her whole life honors the country that gave her birth.

"You have heard her on the witness stand. In no way has she tried to evade her responsibility. She has not denied her action. A question was asked of her. She was asked to give the names of eighteen people who were her friends and who had placed their trust in her. She could no more do this than she could reject her whole existence. She was not defying her government or the powers of Congress; she was not being stubborn or intractable; she was simply doing what had become the very fiber of her being. A great writer once wrote, 'To thine own self be true, and it must follow as the night the day, thou canst not then be false to any man.' Must she be condemned and punished for being true to herself and to the best principles of this nation? I think not, and I beg you to have the compassion and the understanding to bring in a verdict of not guilty."

Crombie was even briefer, as if certainty dispensed with any great need for argument. "We are a nation that functions under law, and God willing, this will continue to be the case. Congress makes the law of the land, and in order to make that law, to frame legislation for the well-being and health and protection of this nation, it is empowered to gather information. He who is subpoenaed before a committee of the Congress of the United States and who refuses to answer a question pertinent to the matter at hand and posed by Congress—he who does that is in contempt of Congress. Do away with this power of Congress, a power before which the mightiest must bend his head, and you do away with democratic government.

"At what point does so-called principle become arrogance? Are we to believe that only Mrs. Barbara

Cohen is possessed of principle? Are there no principles in our government? In our Constitution? And what is principle? Is anyone who defies the Congress of the United States entitled to wrap himself in this so-called principle—and insinuate that we ordinary folk are immoral, that we have the ethics of thugs?

"I reject such insinuations. And I am not impressed by the fact that the accused comes from a background of wealth. This is a government of the people, not of the rich, and when the rich break the law, they must look for no impunity. This woman, Mrs. Cohen, arrogantly confesses to the act of contempt. She proves her own guilt. There is only one point at issue here: Did she refuse to answer a question addressed to her by the House Committee on Un-American Activities? We have proven that she refused. The rest is up to you."

Judge Meadows' instruction was equally concise. "You have heard the evidence," he told the jury. "Mrs. Barbara Cohen, the accused, is charged with having committed a contempt of the Congress of the United States. The act of contempt, in a congressional inquiry, is the refusal to answer a question that is pertinent to the inquiry at hand. Now as far as the accused's refusal to respond to the question is concerned, the evidence given leaves no room for equivocation. The question was asked. She refused to answer it. By her own testimony today in this court, she specified and concurred in that refusal.

"This leaves only one point to be decided by this jury: Was the question pertinent to the function of the House of Representatives' Committee on Un-American Activities? In its original establishment, under the chairmanship of Congressman Martin Dies of Texas, this committee was constituted to conduct investigations into Nazi, fascist, communist, and other organizations termed 'un-American in character.' Today we group its purpose under the broader label of 'subversive.' The purpose of such investigations is to frame appropriate legislation for the protection of the people of the United States.

"The evidence has been presented to you. You are not to be swayed by emotional considerations. The question of the guilt or innocence of the defendant rests upon one single issue: namely, was the question asked of her pertinent to the appropriate function of the House committee. Should you find that to be the case, you have no choice but to bring in a verdict of guilty as charged."

Soaking in her tub at the hotel, Barbara decided that no civilization that provides an unlimited supply of hot water can be all bad. I am now a condemned criminal, she thought, yet I don't feel very much different. In fact, I feel relieved that this stupid mockery of a trial is over with.

It had taken the jury all of twenty minutes to come to a unanimous decision that the defendant was guilty as charged. Then Boyd Kimmelman had taken her back to the hotel while Baxter remained to talk to the judge in his chambers.

"I want a bath," she said to Kimmelman, "and then I want to change my clothes because I feel dirty and uncomfortable and nasty. Suppose we meet in the dining room at seven."

"Barbara," Kimmelman said, "I feel rotten. I let you down. I feel stupid and useless, but most of all I feel that I let you down."

"Boyd, I am being very serious now. I think you're one hell of a lawyer. When you summed up, I wanted

to crawl into a hole, I was so embarrassed by your
description of me. I hope you realize that not one
word of it is true. Nevertheless, I appreciated its rhetorical quality. You know, daddy used to tell a story
about a lodge meeting, a memorial to one of the members who had died. The speaker went into an emotional description of the suffering and misery of the
deceased member to the point that everyone in the
audience was in tears except for one man, who sat unmoved and stony-faced. A lodge member sitting next
to him asked whether the speaker's account was not
moving enough to wring tears from a stone. 'Oh, yes
indeed,' said the stony-faced man, 'but I'm not a member of the lodge.' You see, Boyd, none of them is a
member of the lodge—not the judge, not the jury, not
Mr. Crombie. We've had our day in court, and a part
of me is rather satisfied. I'll join an interesting group
of writers whose books have led them into a prison
cell."

"For heaven's sake, Barbara, you are not in a prison
cell yet. And you won't be if I have anything to say
about it."

"You're a dear." He was just short enough for her to
lean forward and kiss him on the forehead. "Now I
want my bath."

Before she got into the tub, she called home. It was
three o'clock in the afternoon in San Francisco, and
Jean had just returned from the park with Sam.

"How are you, Bobby?" Jean wanted to know.

"Just fine. What about you and my son?"

"Your son is in fine fettle. I am exhausted. Child
raising is for the young. But we had fun. How is that
stupid trial going?"

"It's over. I'm guilty."

"Oh, no, Bobby."

"Now don't get upset. For the moment, nothing is going to happen. I haven't even been sentenced yet, and even if they do sentence me to jail, Harvey says that the appeals can take anywhere from a year to three years. So I won't be going to the pokey for a while."

"How can you joke about it?"

"Mother, how can I be serious about it? I felt like Alice being tried by the king and queen of hearts. Harvey was provoked with me because I kept giggling. He and Boyd were great. They really are good lawyers, and they are so miserable now."

"Darling, when will you be home?"

"Tomorrow, I hope. But then I have to find out when the judge decides to sentence me. I'll keep in touch with you. And please don't worry about me."

Jean's notion of Washington inclined toward the social side, and she had persuaded Barbara to include a short black chiffon evening dress. Barbara put it on now, with black high-heeled evening shoes and sheer black stockings. Her lack of despondency pleased her; she applied make-up carefully and lightly and piled her hair on top of her head. When she appeared in the dining room, only twenty minutes late, both Baxter and Kimmelman rose and stared at her.

"It's no occasion for mourning," she assured them. "We are bloody but unbowed, and very hungry."

"You're beautiful," Kimmelman said.

"How very nice of you, Boyd. I don't know about you two, but I want a large, cold martini." Then she added, "There'll be no talk of law and order and courtrooms until we've finished our drinks."

It was after the drinks and after they had ordered dinner that Baxter told her of his talk with Judge Meadows. "I pointed out that California was a long distance away and that it made no sense for the government to shuttle us back and forth. He agreed to sentence you tomorrow morning."

"How thoughtful of him!"

"What was his attitude?" Kimmelman asked. "I mean, how did he appear? Friendly?"

"Very cold, I'm afraid. He doesn't like us—either because we're from California or because he thinks we are all redder than a rose."

"Oh, Harvey, not you," Barbara said. "Anyone who'd think you were a radical is dense."

"I don't know whether that's a compliment or not."

"Did you talk to him?" Kimmelman insisted. "Did you at least build Barbara's character?"

"I tried. He annoys easily. He told me that it was improper for me even to suggest that I might influence him."

"If you cut him, he'd bleed ice water."

"Or vinegar," Barbara said. "Please don't worry. Whatever will be will be."

"The thing to remember tomorrow," Baxter said, "is that it's only the beginning. We'll take this to the Appellate Division, and if they don't reverse him there, we go to the Supreme Court. I think his whole charge was in error."

"What is the best I can hope for?" Barbara asked.

"A suspended sentence and a stiff fine."

"And the worst?"

"God only knows," Baxter said. "A week ago I would have said that no sane judge would give you a prison term."

"The Hollywood people got prison terms."

"Yes, I know."

At ten o'clock the following morning, Baxter, Kimmelman, and Barbara sat in the court, alone except for two attendants. They waited for fifteen minutes before Judge Meadows entered.

"All rise!" the bailiff called.

Meadows seated himself and stared at Barbara. Then he glanced at the black man, who lifted this morning's iceberg while the judge wet his mouth with ice water. "At a moment like this," Meadows said, "one thinks of contrition. I don't regard you as an ordinary criminal, Mrs. Cohen, but as a product of these difficult times. I have taken into consideration that you are a mother and a widow, and therefore, before I pronounce sentence, I am going to ask you whether you will express a willingness to purge the contempt. You can do this by appearing before the House Committee on Un-American Activities and answering whatever questions they feel necessary to ask. Will you agree to do this?"

"No, I'm afraid not," Barbara said.

"Then you leave me no choice. I sentence you to pay a fine of five hundred dollars and to serve six months in a prison to be designated by the federal Department of Correction. Your attorneys have already filed for an appeal, so the court will allow your present status of bail to continue until the results of such appeal are determined."

PART FIVE

Punishment

Sitting in the park with her father, Barbara watched Sam circle around and back and forth on his tricycle. Tall for his age, well knit and competent, he handled his small machine with ease and grace.

"How old is he now?" Dan asked. "I lose track."

"Two years, nine months. He'll be three in December." She looked at her father curiously. "Daddy, do you mind this? I mean just sitting here in the park?"

"Mind it? What's to mind?"

"Oh, I don't know. It just seems peculiar, Dan Lavette sitting in the park with nothing to do."

"You're not telling me to take off?"

"Daddy!" She took his hand. "I love having you here. I love having you with me. Have you ever tried a conversation with sparrows? Or sea gulls? The sea gulls are better. And I'm bored to tears with reading. I've just finished *The Seven Story Mountain*, Merton's book, and it would be so nice to be religious if I could only work up some enthusiasm for it. Now I'm into the Kinsey report, and it's just dull, dull."

"The Kinsey report? What on earth for?"

"I suppose it's a substitute for sex."

"What in hell good is a substitute? Why don't you go out, Bobby, meet people? Jesus, you're young and beautiful, and no Lavette was ever cut out to be a monk or a nun. We're a horny tribe."

"I love you."

"It's a year and a half since Bernie died. How long can you mourn?"

"I'm not mourning, daddy. Mourning is guilt, and I have no guilt about Bernie. I have sorrow when I think of what could have been if he had only been willing to accept his life and live it."

"That kind of a man can't accept life and live it. You wouldn't have looked at him twice if he had."

"Perhaps. I don't know. But we were talking about you—Dan Lavette sitting in the park with his grand-child."

"He's a damn fine kid."

"You're through with the empire syndrome? No more shipping lines, no more airlines?"

"Bobby," Dan said, "I built three damned empires. That's enough. It's a fool's game. Either you're crazed by a hunger for money or you're sick for power. That's your brother's disease. I'm very content. I draw plans for a yawl I'll probably never build, and I've finally accepted the fact that the most beautiful woman in San Francisco, who happens to be my wife, actually loves me. That's not bad for a kid from the Tender-loin. As for their lousy rat race, they can have it."

"Talking of the most beautiful woman in San Fran-cisco, where is mother?"

"Making the rounds with a real estate agent. She claims there isn't one decent art gallery in San Fran-cisco."

"She's probably right. But don't tell me she's going to open another gallery?"

"As a business this time. She's still hell-bent on con-verting the city to modern art. It's a good idea. It'll fill in her days, and she always has been devoted to painting. Maybe I'll learn something if she lets me be her assistant—I mean for the heavy work. She's taking in Eloise as a partner, but I doubt that Adam will relish Eloise spending her days in San Francisco."

"You two," Barbara said, "you and mother, you're like a couple of kids. You're absolutely wonderful. You really adore each other."

Dan smiled ruefully. "It wasn't easy. It took forty years of tearing our guts out. We have more scars than a pair of professional fighters. The only thing we had going for us is that we were crazy about each other. Crazy is a better word than love. But if anything happened to her—" He shook his head. "Well, that's hardly to the point. We were talking about you."

"You're forgetting, daddy. I have a date with a federal penitentiary. The last thing I want to do is to get involved with anyone now."

"Well, what in hell are they doing? I called Harvey last week. The case hasn't even been argued at the Appellate Division yet."

"I'm in no hurry, daddy, although sometimes I wish it were over." She leaped up and ran to head Sam away from the street, and Dan, watching the grace and ease with which she moved, wondered, as he had so often before, how he had produced her out of his loins. When he looked at Barbara this way, thoughtfully, really looking at her instead of simply accepting her, it always brought May Ling to mind. There was more of that slender, incredible Chinese woman in Barbara than there was of Jean; and it gratified him that he could think of both of them, May Ling and Jean, without guilt or sorrow. He was not inclined to live in the past, but there was so much of his past that he could never wholly escape. He felt a strange kind

of perverse gratitude for the heart attack. He had
looked at himself during that passage with death, and
he had done so with the realization that he had never
truly been able to look at himself before; and looking
at himself, the whole structure of desire and power
had collapsed. It had almost happened this way once
before, when he had been a jobless derelict on the
docks at San Pedro in 1930, but then it had been at a
moment of misery and defeat and hopeless despair.
This time, in the hospital, realizing that he might die,
there was no defeat and no despair. He had turned to
himself and discovered he was not afraid. He had es-
caped from desire. It was not that he didn't want to
live—he wanted very much to live—but if he had to
die, that would be all right. In a sense, it was the answer to the question Barbara had asked him, but he
had no words at his command in which he could
frame that answer and explain to her why he had lost
any taste for wealth or power.

She returned and sat down beside him again and
said, "Daddy, what is prison like?"

He looked at her and smiled. "I don't think you're
going to prison."

"Nobody thinks so, except me."

The next day, Barbara received a royalty report from
her publisher. Her new novel had been published six
months before, and the sales had not been exciting.
The royalty statement informed her that half of the
advance she had been paid was still unearned, and
the accompanying letter from her publisher was part
apology and part explanation. "It's a damn good
book," Bill Halliday wrote. "Nothing has happened to
change my opinion on that score. But it's a very quiet
book, a very gentle book, and you've made your repu-

tation with two books that were anything but quiet and gentle. You only have to look at the best-seller list to see what the public is eating up today. On the one hand, *The Naked and the Dead*, and on the other hand, a piece of tripe by Lloyd C. Douglas called *The Big Fisherman*. We have a problem trying to figure out where your little book fits in and how to sell it. The story of a returned soldier in San Francisco falling in love and marrying a perfectly ordinary girl and making a decent life out of it is probably one of the most difficult things to bring off; and how you've done it so well, considering the hellish experiences you've undergone while writing it, I don't know.

"But I do not want you to think that we've caved in under the pressure and that we're not trying to sell the book. And there is pressure. I am not denying that. Some of it is very subtle, some isn't. Two FBI men paid me a visit. Very polite. They simply said it was their practice to interview the employer of anyone convicted of a federal crime. I said that I couldn't think of any crime you had ever committed, and they said that the record showed otherwise. Then they wanted to know whether I intended to continue publishing your books, and I told them I had every intention of doing just that.

"The more subtle pressure comes in the shape of returns. The cartons in which some early orders were shipped have been returned unopened. I am only itemizing these things because I don't want you to feel that we have just dropped your book by the wayside. I think I can say with a touch of pride that there is still no blacklist in publishing, as there unquestionably is in network television and in films. We have every intention of continuing to publish your work."

Barbara put the letter down with a wry smile.

There was no blacklist in publishing, but there was no mention in the letter of an advance for her next book or even a note of curiosity as to what she might be working on. It was a full year since any magazine had asked her to do a piece, and an unsolicited article she had written about her experience in Washington had been turned down by every magazine she had sent it to. When she followed it with a story about Saudi Arabia and places where no other American woman had ever been, that too was rejected.

Well, she would manage. She had her salary from the foundation, and she still had a substantial amount of money in the bank, money that her mother had banked for her as trustee of Barbara's inheritance from her grandfather. She would not starve or have to turn to her father for money. At the same time, to feel a sort of invisible net tightening around her was not pleasant.

Yet she would not indulge her anxieties. To create her own company of ghosts in a self-manipulated nightmare was the way of madness. She remained cheerful not because she consciously created a mask of cheerfulness and not because she was indifferent to her own fate, but simply because she was alive and in good health and because the sun rose in the morning and set at night. If it was not the best of all possible worlds, it was one that provided no alternative.

Speaking in Wheeling, West Virginia, Senator Joseph R. McCarthy said, "The reason why we find ourselves in a position of impotency is not because our only powerful, potential enemy has sent men to invade our shores, but rather because of the traitorous actions of those who have been treated so well by this nation. It has not been the less fortunate or members of minority groups who have been selling this nation out, but rather those who have had all the benefits that the wealthiest nation on earth has had to offer—the finest homes, the finest college education, and the finest jobs in government we can give. This is glaringly true in the State Department . . . In my opinion the State Department is thoroughly infested with communists. I have in my hand fifty-seven cases of individuals who would appear to be either card-carrying members or certainly loyal to the Communist Party, but who nevertheless are still helping to shape our foreign policy."

It is held by many that November is the best month of the year in Southern California. The summer heat is gone. The hot Santa Ana desert winds have ceased to blow. The air takes on a delicious crackling quality, the sky is as blue as anywhere in the world, and very often the cool Pacific wind liberates the Los Angeles basin from its coat of smog.

All this was in the mind of Alexander Hargasey as he drove west on Sunset Boulevard from Hollywood to Beverly Hills. He opened the windows of his Rolls-Royce, breathed deeply, and reflected on the best of all possible worlds.

It must be said in Hargasey's favor that he never forgot his origins, which is more than could be said of most of his colleagues. He was born in the slums of Budapest, apprenticed at the age of fourteen to a primitive filmmaker, drafted into the Hungarian army, captured by the British in 1917, and at last he found himself in Hollywood in 1922 with no capital except his wits. Now, in 1949, he was regarded as one of the bastions of the film industry in its defense against the increasing encroachment of television.

In Beverly Hills, Hargasey turned left onto Rexford

Drive and then into the driveway of a handsome
home, built after the manner of a French château. A
Chicano maid opened the door, and a voice from upstairs called out, "Is that you, Alex? I'm up here.
Come on up."

He climbed the stairs and entered a bedroom that
was thirty feet square and decorated in blues and
pinks and pale greens. Flowered chintz and expensive
brocade—Sally Lavette's taste was nothing if not catholic. She was sprawled on a chaise longue reading a
script. She wore blue jeans and a blue work shirt, and
her long yellow hair was tied with a ribbon behind
her neck. She wore no make-up, a plus in Hargasey's
opinion and an indication of the complexity that confronted him.

Once in an interview, in reply to a question about
what he considered his greatest achievement, Hargasey had replied, "An understanding of the psychology
of the movie star." His reply was taken as facetious,
but it was not so intended. For twenty-five years,
Hargasey had witnessed and frequently manipulated
the elevation of boys and girls from Nebraska, New
York, Kentucky, Utah, Texas, and a dozen other
places into stardom. He had seen shy, small-town,
high school graduates turned into rapacious monsters;
he had seen simple, hard-working, ranch hands become egomaniacal tyrants; he had seen soft, apparently gentle and pliant men and women become hard
and vicious; and he had seen people who once never
drank become alcoholics in the space of months. He
had seen virgins turn into promiscuous women, and he
had seen seemingly decent men turn into brutal wife-
beaters. It was not a nice process. There were excep-
tions, but these he could count on the fingers of one
hand and still have a finger or two to spare, and his

only consolation was that each case was sufficiently different for him always to hope for an exception to the rule.

Certainly, Sally Lavette was different, but in what way Hargasey was as yet unable to say. At least she was not stupid or insensitive. Stupidity and insensitivity were the two aspects of a human being that Hargasey dreaded most. They worked to set up an impenetrable wall, against which neither reason nor emotion could prevail. Quite to the contrary, Sally was bright and sensitive. Unfortunately—as a part of Hargasey saw it—she had starred in two films that were both brilliant successes; the other part of him found her success both fortunate and rewarding. There are people who cannot act. Years of dramatic school, the best of coaches, the best of teachers, leave them untouched. There are others who fall into acting as if some mysterious gene had transmitted the talent at birth, and it was in this latter category that Sally belonged. A suggestion was sufficient; Hargasey had only to indicate what he desired of her, and she could do it and even carry it a step further. She had that very necessary thing for a great actor, an instinct for what was right, and she gave Hargasey that rare feeling of creation and triumph that comes to a director who discovers a natural in the art.

Now she tossed the script aside, rose, and kissed him lightly. "Dear Alex—what brings the mountain to Mahomet?"

"So now you're Mahomet? A small mountain I have always been. I'm here because you don't answer your telephone."

"Because an unlisted number doesn't remain unlisted for ten minutes in this stupid place. Why don't you sit down instead of standing there and glaring at

me? You make me feel more uncomfortable than my
mother does, and that's going some."

"Am I glaring?"

"You're glaring. Sit down."

He was aware of the change in position. There was
a point where it always happened, where the pupil
became a star, and then the pupil became the master.

"Glaring is thinking," he said. "I am thinking about
the script on the floor over there. Expressive is when
you're not acting too. You don't throw a script on the
floor you have regard for."

"Alex, I love you and I love your syntax. Don't be
angry at me."

"Have I ever been angry at you?"

"I can remember once or twice."

"All right. So what about the script?"

"Do you remember what you said to me fifteen
months ago when I came into your office after I sent
you my screenplay? You said it stinks. This one stinks.
It's a rotten screenplay. I could do better."

He remained judiciously silent, thinking that the
screenplay she had just thrown aside had an overwhelming male lead. He didn't have to remark on this;
she was entirely aware of it.

"Well? No comment, Alex?"

"Comment? What's with a comment? We try something else. We find something you like."

"You're angry."

"I'm not angry, Sally."

"I know you by now. When you sit like that without
even crossing your legs, with your arms folded, you're
angry."

"I'm not angry. I'm unhappy. Where's Joe?"

"Oh, Alex," she said with annoyance, "why don't
you stop that shit and stop treating me like a little

girl. You know damn well where Joe is. He's in the
clinic where he always is, and at night he sleeps on a
cot in his office, and if you think that makes me
happy, you're crazy. And do you know how I know
that you know where Joe is?"

"No, tell me," he said mildly.

"Because Joe came here to see May Ling yesterday,
and he told me the whole story about how you went
over to Boyle Heights and tried to give him five thousand dollars for his clinic. He was burning. My God,
Alex, that was a stupid thing to do!"

So a girl of twenty-three who I pick out of nowhere
is telling me I'm stupid, Hargasey thought. Well, that's
the way it happens. It happens.

"Why was it a stupid thing to do?" he asked. "Joe
is doing something wonderful. So I appreciate what
he's doing. I don't have a heart? I can't put some money
there?"

"If you had thought twice about what you were
doing, you would have known that Joe's first response
would be to decide you were trying to buy him off."

"Buy him off from what?"

"From me!"

"What? What are you telling me? Joe thinks we're
having an affair? I don't play with children!" Hargasey's voice rose. "I won't even tolerate an insinuation
to that end. You know me more than a year. Have I
ever—"

Sally went over and put her arms around him.
"Alex, stop that. I won't have a fight with you. Joe
thinks I've turned into some kind of superbitch. I
will not have you thinking that." She stepped away
from him, her pale eyes intense and angry. "He does
not think I am having an affair with you because I
told him I was not, and in no uncertain terms. I told

him I was having an affair with no one. You know
that! You know what kind of filthy gossip this industry feeds on. Has there been any gossip about me?
Have you seen me make a play for anyone? Do you
really think I want any of those pretty-boy, brainless
studs? What do you think has happened to me? Don't
you know? Can't you understand that when you pay
someone who grew up on a farm in the Napa Valley
half a million dollars in a period of fifteen months, it's
going to do something to them? I'm not suffering. I
love this. I love being a star. I love acting. I don't
know whether I'm happy. There are times when I'm
just miserable. But I'm always alive, and when I lived
in that wretched little house at Silver Lake, I was
never alive."

Listening, watching her, Hargasey could only think
of a performance. What a splendid performance! But
that was the nature of it; that was why she was what
she was.

"I don't want to divorce Joe," she told him. "I don't
want to. I love him. I've always loved him, since I was
twelve years old. But he has this cursed poverty complex. And then, God help us all, I earned the money.
If he had earned the money—well, I don't know. But
for him to live in a house that I bought with my
money—oh, no, he has his pride, that disgusting
bullshit pride that goes with having a pair of balls.
And don't look shocked, Alex. I was swearing just as
eloquently before I ever met you and Paramount Pictures."

"Can't you understand how Joe feels?"

"Alex, what is this to you? Why should you give a
damn about what happens between Joe and me? Do
you know anyone in this business who makes it and
stays married to the one who was there first?"

"You think that's good?"

"I think it stinks. But what do I do? Tear up my contract with you? Burn down this house? Buy a house in Boyle Heights? I've been writing poetry. Does that surprise you? I've written over fifty poems this past year, and I'll have them published. It's a gesture of largesse on my publisher's part. They will pay me an advance of one hundred dollars, and over the next few years I'll earn another hundred. I am not going to get down on my knees to Joe and plead for forgiveness. What have I done?"

Hargasey sighed and spread his hands. "All right. This is something talking don't help and talking don't solve." He took a script out of his jacket pocket. "I brought you another one. Girl in the French Résistance." Sally's eyes widened. "Captured. German concentration camp. Escapes. Gives her life so the man she loves can live and dies with a German firing squad singing 'The Marseillaise.'"

This time Sally did not dispute his syntax or remark on the ambiguity. She threw her arms around him and hugged him. "Alex, I adore you. You never heard me sing. I'm not great, but I'm all right. I mean, I do carry a tune."

Judge Hampton Fremont telephoned Harvey Baxter and asked him to stop by his chambers at five o'clock that same afternoon.

"What do you suppose it is?" Kimmelman asked when Baxter told him about the call.

"God knows! Possibly he's heard something from the Appellate Division."

"If he has, wouldn't it be unethical for him to tip you?"

"I don't think so."

"How did he sound? Good? Bad? Depressed? You know he's rooting for Barbara."

"I don't know, just said he wanted to see me."

"You could have asked him whether it's good or bad news."

"For heaven's sake, Boyd, you don't ask a judge a question like that. I'll go over there and then I'll know what he has to say. And don't say anything to Barbara. Don't get her hopes up or down."

Fremont was pleasant but serious. "Sit down, Harvey," he said. He finished signing some documents; then he looked up and stared at Baxter unhappily. "You lost," he said. "The Court of Appeals upheld Judge Meadows. I just learned about it. You'll know officially tomorrow."

Baxter nodded forlornly. "I was afraid of that."

"I called you in to find out whether you intend to go to the Supreme Court?"

"Absolutely."

"Good. Take the steps immediately, and we'll continue Mrs. Cohen at liberty. That may give you another six months. Not that the Supreme Court will hear your arguments. They'll never grant certiorari."

"Why not? We have a tremendous issue here. It goes far beyond the question of a simple misdemeanor."

"That's just it, Harvey. We've let these two lunatic committees drive us into the most ridiculous and obscene bind the federal courts ever fell into. Never in my memory has the issue of contempt been used to punish people of principle. Well, we've dug our own hole. You see, any challenge in these cases becomes a direct challenge to Congress' right to enforce its subpoenas. If the court hears one of these cases on a constitutional issue—and there are some—it faces a pretty predicament. If it decides for the government, it vitiates the Bill of Rights. If it decides for the defendant, it vitiates the power of Congress. Perfect horns of a perfect dilemma, and the answer is usually a denial of certiorari. But they'll brood over it and talk about it and examine their conscience, and that will take time, maybe three or four months, maybe a year if their calendar is heavy, and in that time who knows what can happen? We might even come to our senses, God willing. I hate to see that woman go to prison. It offends me, not only because she's Dan Lavette's daughter, but because she is something. So just hang in there, Harvey, and give it the full run."

"You can count on that, your honor."

"And remember that I'm here. There's not a great deal that I can do, but if worse comes to worst, I can ease it over some of the rough spots. I like that girl."

"So do I," Baxter said.

Barbara found herself unperturbed by the news. The telephone had rung while she was writing, and she found herself resenting the interruption. Harvey Baxter went into a long explanation, telling her that Judge Fremont was continuing her freedom on her own recognizance, that she was not to worry, and that he and Boyd Kimmelman were working on their brief for the Supreme Court.

"What on earth is certiorari?" she wanted to know.

"Just a fancy name for the Supreme Court's willingness to hear a case. If they grant certiorari, they will hear our plea."

"Good. Carry on, Harvey," she said almost indifferently.

Then she went back to work. The morning hours were best, and she treasured them. Sam had been entered in nursery school from nine to two in the afternoon, and that left the morning hours free. Barbara was well aware that she lived in two worlds: the specific, controlled world she created on blank sheets of paper, and the real world, uncontrolled and seemingly created by madmen. Fourteen years had gone by since she had begun to write as a professional, and she frequently felt that it was only because she could lose herself in this managed world of her own creation that she had been able to survive. Out of the real world, the day before, had come a letter from David Ben-Gurion, the prime minister of Israel.

"My dear Mrs. Cohen," he wrote. "The sacrifice your husband made for our freedom has only now come to my attention. I realize that nothing I can say will lessen your grief. I am writing to tell you that we will never forget, and that his name, along with the names of so many others fallen in the struggle, will be enshrined not only on a monument to their memory but in our hearts as well."

It was a small country. But in spite of the fact that the prime minister had signed the letter himself, it irritated her. She did not enjoy condolences. In her mind, she composed a reply which she never sent: "My dear Mr. Ben-Gurion. I know you bear no responsibility for my husband's death, but since you have written to me, I shall now tell you how I feel about the matter. I do not think that there is any such thing as a noble death, a heroic death, or a good death. I have lived most of my adult life around the sound and smell of war, and it is a smell that reeks of all the filth that man has created. Since I am a woman, I give myself the privilege of being an outsider. I stand at the rim of a lunatic asylum called civilization, and I listen to the obscenities of so-called leaders. I don't know why I am saying all this to you. God knows, the Jews have suffered enough. But my own suffering is very personal. I want my husband here beside me, and my husband is dead. Nothing will change that."

Brooding after Harvey Baxter's telephone call, she wondered whether indeed the world in the pages she created could be different from the reality? It was not her nature to bog down on the problem of who she was and where she was going; she felt she knew exactly who she was and sooner or later she would be going to prison; but the pages she wrote presented other problems, and the work came slowly and painfully.

"But at least it's different," she told herself.

At lunchtime she ate scrambled eggs and practiced her Spanish with Anna. After her years in France, Barbara spoke French like a native, but her Spanish was kitchen talk and no better. She had been trying to teach French to Sam, but he was more adept with the Spanish he picked up from Anna. The result was confusing, to say the least.

"I'll get Sam if you want me to," Anna said, "if you want to go on working."

"No. The work has become totally pointless, and when that happens, it's best to leave it alone for a while. I'll pick him up, and then we'll wander over to Grant Avenue, where my strange mother has rented space to open an art gallery."

"But she had a gallery on Russian Hill."

"Ah, no. That thing on Russian Hill was a museum. My mother is always a step ahead of the world, but it doesn't appear to catch up with her. She decided to establish a museum of modern art, but San Francisco never worked up any enthusiasm about it. The legend that we're really cultured is only a legend. Under the white collars and the umbrellas, we're still a frontier town. This project is actually a business, an art store, only when it's an art store, Anna, it's called a gallery. There never has been a truly fine gallery in town, but mother intends to change all that."

Jean was changing it in a second-story floorthrough on Grant Avenue, just off California Street. Barbara entered with Sam, who wrinkled his nose at the smell of fresh paint and looked around in amazement. Dan, in jeans and a blue work shirt, was painting the walls dead white while Eloise, also in jeans, was working on a repainted Louis Quatorze chair, trying to remove the paint with sandpaper and solvent. Jean, who was preparing tea, welcomed them, hugged Sam, and informed them they were just in time to eat. "I want to paint like grandpa," Sam demanded. Dan climbed down from his ladder and handed his paintbrush to Sam.

"Have you lost your mind?" Jean cried.

"It doesn't matter. The walls are white anyway."

Sam, under Dan's guidance, began to smear an unpainted part of the wall while Jean and Eloise put out tea things on a bridge table. Barbara, somewhat awed, watched the proceedings in silence.

"Don't judge it the way it is now," Jean said. "We have three gallery rooms right through the building, front to rear. The rear room has a skylight. The floor will be carpeted, pale tan, just a shade darker than cream. Spots to light the pictures. The office is off the middle room."

"It's going to damn well be the classiest gallery west of the Rockies," Dan said.

"More paint," Sam said.

"We deal in only the Moderns," Jean went on. "Nothing farther back than the Expressionists. They are going to look at Pollock, Rothko, Ajay, Klee, Calder, Kandinski, and Marin, and they are going to like them and appreciate them and buy them, and the Philistines will be vanquished."

"Whatever that means," Dan agreed.

"Will he eat oatmeal cookies?" Eloise asked.

"He loves them."

"I see it, but I don't believe it," Barbara said, removing the brush from Sam's hand and trying to wipe the paint off his face while he protested violently. "Only because we're going to have oatmeal cookies," she explained to him. "Or would you rather paint? Paint or cookies?"

"Cookies," Sam decided instantly.

"Takes after his grandfather," Jean said. "What don't you believe, Bobby?"

"Dan Lavette painting walls. Jean Seldon in jeans—I'm not trying to pun—and work shirt. Who was it said, there is no San Francisco society without Jean Seldon?"

"But I'm not Jean Seldon. I have been Jean Lavette, Jean Whittier, and now we're giving Jean Lavette another try. It's a whole new ball game; as your old man would say. We're having more fun than any of us ever dreamed of having, and who knows, we may make some history."

"But, mother, you can't sell those artists in San Francisco. You know that. Oh, they might buy a Georgia O'Keeffe, if it's a bona fide buffalo skull that they can recognize, but Calder and Klee? Never."

"We shall educate them, shall we not, Eloise?"

"We'll try."

"And how does it work? Are you all three partners?"

"Only the ladies," Dan said. "I'm the janitor."

"And what about your boat, daddy? And the days

you and mother are going to spend sailing the bay?"

"That's not out. I'm doing a whole new set of plans.
I'm not sure I want a yawl. I'm not completely sold on
it, so now I'm designing a cutter. Don't you worry.
Another year, and Sam'll be able to sail with me. Between him and Freddie, I have me a crew. What
about it, Eloise, will you let me teach Freddie how to
sail a boat?"

"Why not? He's seven now. And Joshua's a year old.
You won't exclude Josh because he's not your grandson?" she asked.

"Absolutely not."

"Is he a year old?" Barbara asked in surprise. "What
happens to us?"

"A great deal happened to you," Eloise said. "You
know, he was born so soon after Bernie died."

Barbara closed her eyes and shook her head.

"What is it, Bobby dear?" Jean asked her. "Are you
all right?"

"Perfectly all right. It's just that people are strange.
I'm strange. Harvey Baxter called me today to tell me
that the Appellate Divison had turned down our appeal and supported Judge Meadows—and do you
know, I had forgotten all about it."

"By those who know it exists," Lucy told her husband,
"the club is called the establishment. That's a British
term."

"I know," Tom said somewhat petulantly. "I have
been there you know." He resented Lucy when she
became too didactic, yet he always listened and he
was constantly amazed at the things she picked up,
and the people she knew.

They were having breakfast in the solarium of the
old Sommers mansion on Pacific Heights. Alvin Som-

mers had died of a stroke three months before, leaving
his home and everything else he owned to Lucy, and
she and Tom had moved into the house a few weeks
later. It was a magnificent graystone structure of
eighteen rooms, one of the first great homes to have
been built on Pacific Heights and only four lots from
John Whittier's house. That did not perturb Tom.
Whittier had cancer and was dying in the hospital.
Tom did not desire him dead, but at the same time he
recognized that this way he would be spared the un-
pleasantness that could develop from having him as
a neighbor.

They no longer built houses with solariums, and
Tom was not too comfortable with an indoor jungle,
but Lucy would not touch it. It had always been their
breakfast room and tea room, and since it meant so
much to her, Tom was content to let it be. His old
home had been rented out. He could have pressed
Lucy to live there, but in all truth he preferred the
archaic grandeur of the Sommers place.

"Tom, I'm not trying to be superior," Lucy said gently. "I would never dream of marrying a man who was
my inferior in any way, and it's time you accepted
that. It's just that the English use of the term fasci-
nates me. They accept the fact that a small group of
men exercise control, that it always has been that way
and that it will continue to be that way. We delude
ourselves into thinking otherwise."

"Some of us do and some of us don't," Tom said.

"Of course," Lucy went on, "they do not refer to
themselves as the establishment. They would consider
it pompous and gauche, and these men are neither
pompous not gauche. They are very practical, down-
to-earth people."

"Go through it again," Tom said, his eyes half

closed. He remembered the names only too well, but a
request like that pleased Lucy. Tom was not conscious
of the mother-and-child game they played, yet he fell
into it partly out of his own need and partly because
of Lucy's response.

"Joseph Langtrey, First New York Trust."

"He's the only Easterner. That's odd."

"He keeps a place in Sonoma County. He has three
thousand acres there. He raises grapes and horses."

"I suppose their equivalent exists in the East," Tom
said. "Probably in Chicago too."

"Not precisely the equivalent. All right, we have
Mark Fowler, newspapers; Ira Cunningham, steel;
Louis d'Solde—how would you describe him?"

"Submarines, tanks, chemicals—it goes a long way. I
don't know how far."

"Geoffrey Culpepper, very quiet. You know, there
is almost nothing about him. I know he has a place in
La Jolla, down near San Diego, but apparently no one
knows where. Electronics, communications, that sort
of thing. He's very big in television manufacture, Culpepper Electronics, but that's only the tip of the iceberg. Diodes, microwaves. A lot more that truthfully I
don't understand. He also controls a string of radio
stations and three television stations. Well, so much
for our mystery man. The last of the group is Oscar
McGinnis."

"And all one has to say is oil, which just about sums
it up. The question is, Lucy, where do we fit in?
These are giants. We have a net worth in the neighborhood of three hundred million."

"It's not too bad a neighborhood."

"It's still very small potatoes. You say they call
themselves the club?"

"Just that. The club. When Mark Fowler asked me

to lunch with him, I had no idea what he wanted. He was an old friend of my father, and I thought it was simply a gesture. Actually, I had heard rumors of the group, people calling it the Bayside establishment. But no one really knew who they were. Fowler simply laid it all out for me. Oh, nothing earthshaking. Six important, influential men of affairs who meet once a month to discuss the country's economy and political direction. Of course, that's euphemistic. Men like these do not hold debating sessions or gossip to hear themselves talk. But he stressed that there is no formality, no minutes, no notes taken. He mentioned that he trusted my discretion almost in passing, but it sank home. In the same way, he suggested that you might like to join them at their next meeting, at Langtrey's place."

"Why didn't he come to me directly?"

"I suppose that would have formalized it. I imagine they eschew anything that smacks of formality. I'm the daughter of an old friend. It could come off simply as an expression of interest. I mean, that's actually what Fowler said, 'Tom Lavette, interesting young man. We'd like to chat with him.'"

"That's all?"

"Isn't it enough? I know it's a cliché to say that one doesn't see the forest for the trees, but the Seldons and the Sommers too have been fussing with the trees for a hundred years now. First there was the bank, and then Dan Lavette's shipping line and his property and the airlines, and then the combination of both, and then the taking over of the Whittier interests, and now your father's fleet of tankers—and you keep yourself engrossed with each little bit of it, like someone putting together a jigsaw puzzle without knowing what the picture on the puzzle is. But the plain truth

is that today we are a power on this coast. Giannini,
Hearst, Crocker, Hughes—none of them has the diver-
sity of influence that we can exercise. And it's been
quiet. Except for that idiocy on your sister's part,
we've kept our heads down, and I imagine the club
likes the display of prudence and good taste."

A week later, Tom drove out to Joseph Langtrey's
sprawling adobe ranch house in Sonoma County. Tom
had been born into a very wealthy family, had been
educated at Groton and Princeton, and had spent time
with wealthy relatives in Boston and in London, yet
the manner of entertainment at Langtrey's ranch was
subtly different from anything he had ever experienced. It was opulently simple. The servants were
Chicanos, dressed in white, and they anticipated his
every desire. The living room was a huge barn of a
room—tile floor, beamed ceiling, great fireplace, over-
stuffed furniture. Langtrey, tall, slender, gray-haired,
greeted him easily, as if they were old friends. He had
met the short, stocky Fowler before. Cunningham was
an undistinguished man, pince-nez, thin, sandy hair
over a balding skull. Louis d'Solde wore a mustache,
long saturnine face, impeccable clothes. McGinnis
was huge, enormously fat, two-hundred-dollar cowboy
boots under gray flannels; and as if in calculated contrast, the mysterious Culpepper was a small, elegant,
scholarly looking man in his mid-forties, his voice soft
and modulated against McGinnis' booming Texas explosiveness.

Dinner in a dining room with whitewashed walls,
decorated only with two very large Remingtons, was
simple and good. The wine was explicitly native California vintage. No soup, a large, roasted joint, carved
to choice from a silver cart, potatoes and vegetables,
followed in the old-fashioned manner by a savory, and

then pie and coffee and brandy. It was hardly the kind of dinner Tom would have served to important guests—or to unimportant guests, for that matter—but he recognized and appreciated the reverse snobbery that went into it. It was an evening for men. There were no women visible anywhere, nor was there any talk of women. The cigars passed around at the end of the meal were three brands of the best Havana. The conversation during dinner was knowledgeable and catholic in breadth. Langtrey and, surprisingly, McGinnis had been to the opening of *Death of a Salesman* in New York. Langtrey had enjoyed it; McGinnis called it hogwash. There was a good deal of talk about Korea. D'Solde was quite certain that there would be civil war there within months and that the United States would be in it, as he put it, "lock, stock, and barrel." Culpepper was worried about China, fearing that there was no way they could become involved in a Korean war without Chinese intervention. "You might sound out Truman on that," he said to McGinnis.

The conversation moved from subject to subject, the easy talk of men who had access to people and places without limit, but there was no direct reference to Tom's presence or the reasons for it. They brought him into the conversation quite naturally, but during dinner it was simply conversation. They asked him questions about the redwood reserves, a subject on which he was well versed, but that too was simply conversation. It was not until they were once again in the living room, sitting in front of the fire with cigars and brandy, that Culpepper said to Tom, "We hear you've been seeing Drake?"

Tom nodded. "Yes, I have."

"What do you think of him?" McGinnis asked.

Tom had the feeling that they would measure him by his answer, and he considered the question for a moment or two before he replied. "He's not profound, but he's cunning. He's almost demoniacally directed, and he's very ambitious. He's also possessed of the poor-boy syndrome. He worships money and wants it very badly."

"What of his manner?" Langtrey asked.

"He can be very ingratiating."

"Why did he let that charade with your sister go through?"

"It's the same poor-boy syndrome. He worships money, but the hostility goes with it."

"That was before you met him?"

"Yes."

"I imagine he's willing to let your sister purge herself," Culpepper said, "but she won't if I read her right. I admire her. She has guts."

It came as a surprise to Tom. He nodded slowly and waited.

"Do you trust him—Drake?" Fowler asked.

Tom shrugged. "Once he's sold what he has to sell, I don't see that he has much choice."

McGinnis was studying Tom thoughtfully. McGinnis was a well-hidden man. There was more there, Tom decided, than one would surmise from the cowboy boots and the enormous girth.

"Could he win a big election?" McGinnis asked slowly.

"I think he could if he were properly coached and directed. He has a quality that appeals to people who don't think. Most people don't think. And he has no principles as far as I can make out—except power and money, if you think of them as principles."

"What would you think of him as vice president?" Langtrey asked, smiling slightly.

"He's not a fool. It would have to be a stepping-stone."

McGinnis stared at Tom and nodded. Then Fowler changed the subject, questioning Tom about the tankers he had ordered from Germany.

When the evening broke up, Langtrey said to Tom almost indifferently, "We get together about once a month for food and talk, Lavette. We'd like you to join us."

"I'd be delighted to," Tom said.

When Joe Lavette telephoned Barbara and told her that he would like to fly up to San Francisco and talk to her, she invited him to dinner, suggesting that he stay overnight and catch an early plane back in the morning. Barbara cooked dinner herself. She was a good cook, and she enjoyed it; and while her skill had come in part out of her years of living in Paris, there was also an instinct that separates the natural cook from those who follow recipes and breathe prayers. She prepared a clear, jellied soup, a veal stew with mushrooms and noodles, and for dessert, fruit and cheese. Joe ate hugely of everything, with the apology that he had not tasted food like this in months. He had lost weight; his cheeks were sunken, his facial skin drawn tight, and while it was in a curious way quite attractive, it intensified his Oriental appearance. Looking at the two of them, they would hardly be taken for brother and sister, Barbara with her light skin, her gray-blue eyes, and her honey-colored hair, and Joe with his dark eyes and black hair and brown skin; yet bodily they were much alike, tall and long-limbed, with wide, straight shoulders. Joe was nervous and uneasy, with the manner of one who constantly rehearses his words and as constantly leaves them unsaid. He praised Sam, gave him a wind-up fire engine he had brought, played with him, and then after the child had been put to bed, talked about Barbara's session with the House committee and what she might expect.

As to his reasons for coming, he explained apologetically to Barbara that he intended to approach the Lavette Foundation for another grant. "We just can't hack it anymore, Bobby. I hate to come to you because I know you can't refuse me, but we need our own decently equipped operating room and at least six beds. We've had three people die on us because of red tape and problems with admissions, and it just kills me to see it."

"Joe, of course."

"It's not small. It means another wing. We need a hundred and fifty thousand dollars."

"Don't worry. The foundation has plenty of money. Joe, you didn't have to come here for that. You could have filed a formal application."

"I wanted to see you."

"And you haven't said one word about Sally."

"What's to say?"

"What's to say? For God's sake, Joe, what's wrong with you? According to what Eloise tells me, you want to divorce her."

"Well, that's the way it is."

"What is? Will you talk sense? Is she in love with someone else? Are you?"

"I've never looked at another woman."

"Oh, yes, I do love an answer like that. If you never looked at another woman, you ought to have a colleague examine your gonads."

"You know what I mean. I love Sally. So tell me how to handle it. She's a film star. She earns half a million dollars a year. She bought this huge barn of a house in Beverly Hills, new Thunderbird in the driveway, Chicano maid, nurse for May Ling. Every time I open the newspaper I see her name. I work in a clinic in Boyle Heights. Can you put the two together? Can you? Just tell me that."

"Are you legally separated?"

"No. I wanted that. She won't have it."

"I hear you live on a cot in your office. Is that true?"

"It's true."

"You sold the house at Silver Lake?"

He nodded.

"I don't have to ask what you did with the money. You put it into the clinic."

He nodded again.

"What would you like me to do, Joe? Give you a silver star for nobility? Do you remember when Sally was a little kid and so crazy about you, she would say, 'Joe is wonderful, only he's dumb.' She was right. Only I don't think you're so wonderful."

"That's great. I need this."

"Maybe you do. Sleeping on a cot in your office! If I read that in a book, I wouldn't believe it. You take a bright, wonderful, exciting young woman and you try to turn her into a brainless drudge."

"All I asked her was to be a wife and a mother."

"That's not what bugs you, my brother. She is a wife and a mother. You can't face up to a wife and mother who is famous and who earns a half a million a year. If the situation were reversed and you were a Beverly Hills doctor earning half a million a year or whatever a Beverly Hills doctor earns, you'd expect

Sally to be the happiest woman on earth. What kind of a crazy game are you playing, working eighteen hours a day, sleeping on a cot in your office. My father, who is also your father, happens to be a millionaire."

"I can't go to him for money."

"I'm not talking about that. I'm talking about your mind, what there is of it. This Jesus syndrome of yours makes me ill. You can afford a decent apartment, and you can afford to live like a human being, and no patient at the clinic would be an iota the worse for it. Tell me, if you lived with Sally in Beverly Hills, would the clinic suffer? I know your pride would. Would the clinic?"

"I couldn't even pay half the upkeep on that place."

"Could Sally pay half the upkeep on the Silver Lake place out of what she earned with her poetry? And by the way, she is a hell of a good poet. Did you ever think of that? Did you ever stop to think of what it is to be a woman, Joe? Try it. Just clear your head, clear your mind, and say to yourself, I, Joe Lavette, am not an oversized male stud, a sort of saint in Boyle Heights whom everybody loves because I'm a doctor and can help them. I'm none of that but a lonely, helpless girl whose dreams have been shattered, and there isn't one damn thing I can do about it."

"You've got it so pat, Bobby. It's all my fault, right?"

"I'm not talking about fault. Joe, Joe," she pleaded, "try to think of one man you ever knew in your life who understood what it is to be a woman. I go upstairs every night to that stinking cold bed alone, because I fell in love with a man who remained what most men are, a kind of bright, idiot child, and when he went off on his own version of the Jesus syndrome, he never gave two thoughts to what it might mean to

Sammy and me if he got killed. I'm not accusing you of anything. There's no viciousness in playing the man's game in a man's world. That's just the way it is. But Joey, you're a decent, kind, and gentle human being. Try to see it the way it is."

Time passed. The threat of prison receded to the back of Barbara's mind. It was there, but it was something she no longer lived with from day to day, only remembered from time to time. She worked on her new book, writing and rewriting. It was the story of a man who was very much like her husband, so much so that at times it was as much Bernie as she could make him. She had decided to tell the story in the first person, a way, she realized later, of attempting to make him live again through herself; and to place herself inside a man's body and thoughts was the most difficult thing she had ever attempted. Time had blurred her grief but had not removed it. The two men she had loved, Marcel Duboise and Bernie Cohen, were too much a part of her for her ever to be rid of them. They were woven into her thoughts and her dreams, and sometimes, writing of the one, she would find herself slipping into patterns of the other. She had heard of men and women who had gone through three, four, even five marriages, but it was something beyond her comprehension. There was a drying out, an inner emptiness, that she did not believe could ever be filled.

Dan and Jean plotted and arranged dinner parties, as did other friends. She was introduced to divorced men, to widowers, to single men who had never married. Most of them were utterly enchanted by the tall, lovely, knowledgeable woman—and a good many of those enchanted were also intimidated. A few asked for second dates.

. "I'm sorry," Barbara would explain. "I'm not up to dating."

"You can't do that," Jean pleaded. "You can't live the rest of your life alone."

"I'm not alone. I have friends and I have a family. But I can't sit through an evening and exchange inanities with these men, and most of all I have no desire to be pawed by someone I don't care for and be told that the price of a dinner entitles some boob to go to bed with me. I've been through that route, mother, and I don't want to travel it again."

"What then?" Dan asked Jean. "Does she go on like this alone?"

"It's not the worst thing in the world. She's a very superior woman, and a superior woman has a rotten time of it in your male world. She's too old and she's been through too much to pretend. Anyway, what's so desperately important about marriage?"

"I find it important," Dan said.

"Still and all, if it weren't for you, I'd settle for being single."

But Barbara had not settled for any state, single or married. For the moment, she was content to live from day to day, or in a larger sense from book to book. A new book became a postponement of life. "Until I am finished," she told herself, "I don't have to make any decisions. Or until I go to jail," she added.

Sam was growing up with almost terrifying speed. It was only yesterday, Barbara thought, that he had communicated with grunts and tears. From there he progressed to words, and she had been delighted to discover that among the various genes that she and Bernie had bestowed upon him, there was one that embraced vocabulary. Now the words had become sentences, and he said to her one day, "You have a daddy. Why don't I?"

"You did have a daddy," Barbara told him, wondering just how to continue, and deciding finally that the only way was to have it straight out.

"In school," Sam said, "everyone has a daddy."

"You had a wonderful father," Barbara said, picking him up and holding him in her arms. "He died. He loved you very much, but he died."

"I saw a dead cat," Sam said seriously. "Is he dead the same way?"

"No. Not exactly. He died far away, in another country, fighting for the freedom of his own people."

"Who are they?" Sam asked.

She was getting in deeper, but she clung to her cause. "The Israelis," she said, feeling that she had gone wrong there.

"What is dead?" Sam wanted to know.

"It's what happens to people when they get very, very old."

"Was my daddy very, very old?"

"Quite old." She nodded. Sam clutched her and began to cry. "You're old," he whimpered.

"Not old enough to die. It will be a long, long time before I die."

"Will I die?"

"When you're terribly old. But that's so far away I can't even imagine it."

"I don't want to die," he sobbed.

"Of course not, of course not," she whispered, rocking him gently. "Nothing bad will ever happen to my beautiful little boy. You will grow up and become a fine handsome man and marry a beautiful princess."

He stopped crying and looked at her with interest. He had his father's pale blue eyes.

"With yellow hair?" Sam asked her.

"If you wish."

"I like your hair better."

"All right, brown hair."

"Tell me a story about the princess."

"Very well. Her name was Daisybelle, and she lived in a castle made of five varieties of cookies, but mostly ginger cookies."

Sam began to chuckle. "Don't make castles of cookies."

"I admit they're unusual, but so was Daisybelle. She was given to gowns of spun sugar, which made it perfectly natural for her to live in a castle made of cookies . . ." She went on with the story of Daisybelle, and in a little while, Sam was asleep in her arms. It was an effort to stand up, and she thought wryly that the story of the man who began by lifting a colt, lifting it each day until finally it was a horse, had no validity at all.

The guard at the gate to the Paramount Studio found his name on the list and repeated it, "William Clawson? Right?"

Billy nodded.

"O.K. You'll find Mrs. Lavette on Stage Four. Park over there, and then follow the yellow line to the first cross alley, on your left. Or ask someone. They're shooting in there, so if you see the red light outside flashing, you don't go in until it cuts off."

Billy nodded, parked his car, then walked onto the studio grounds. Outside the huge, hangar-like building that was Soundstage Four, the red light was flashing. Billy waited. He had abandoned the turtleneck and jeans for today. He wore gray flannel slacks, a blue blazer, a white shirt, and a tie, and curiously enough, he was uncomfortable in the clothes, as if he were in costume for a role that ill suited him. It took something like this to make him realize how totally he had fallen into the life of the barrio, how absorbed he had become by the work in the clinic. Yet dressed as he was, tall and slender, with what Sally had once called his "damn upper-class good looks," he drew admiring glances from girls passing by. Physically, he was compatible with the place.

The red light went out; Billy opened the door and entered. Inside was a dark wilderness of cables, flats, and equipment, and toward the other end of the great building, a concentrated blaze of light. He picked his way toward the light, his eyes gradually becoming accustomed to the darkness, and he came to the edge of a circle of men and cameras. The set looked like a large sewer sliced in half, wet and dripping, an inch of water at the bottom. Sally, barefoot and wearing a shapeless gray sack of a dress, stood in the water.

A short, fat, bald man was pleading, "Once more, Sally, please."

"Christ, Alex," she shouted, "you've done six takes! It's one lousy, simple scene. I've done it. I've had it."

"Darling, darling, please. It's so simple, it's impossible." He turned to a good-looking, well-built man, shirtless, wearing a pair of soaking wet pants. "Once more, yes, Walter?"

"If it's O.K. with Sally, sure."

"See, see," the fat man pleaded. "It's O.K. with Walter."

"All right. Get it over with. We've been in this miserable sewer all afternoon."

"Positions!" the fat man shouted. "Lights!"

The big kliegs blazed on the scene. The shirtless man took his place at one side of the set. A make-up man poured a scarlet fluid that looked like blood or catsup onto his shoulder so that it dripped over his chest.

A young man, holding a scissor-like contraption on which was lettered SCENE 42, TAKE 7, HARGASEY, stepped out in front of the set. "Camera," Hargasey said. The young man snapped his contraption together and then retreated. "Action," Hargasey said.

The man in the wet trousers, his chest now covered with the fake blood, staggered into the scene. He saw Sally. Tense and rigid, Sally saw him. She tried to speak, but the words would not come. Billy found himself drawn into the scene. The agony on Sally's face was so real that for an instant he forgot his surroundings. The man tried to take another step toward Sally. His knees gave, and he crumpled into the water. Sally bent over him, reached out one shaking hand to touch him.

"Cut!" Hargasey shouted. "Oh, beautiful, darling. Beautiful. We wrap it for today and do the close-ups tomorrow."

"Thank God," Sally said.

The kliegs went off. The man with the blood was toweling himself dry. Sally came off the set, and as she was about to pass him, Billy said, "Hey, Sally, I'm here." He spoke uncertainly, as if to suggest that if she desired to ignore his presence, why, that would be all right too.

She paused and stared at him, then her face lit up and she ran to him and threw her arms around him. "Oh, Billy, Billy, how good to see you! Only who could ever recognize you, you look so absolutely divine." She linked her arm in his. "Come with me. Oh, I'm so glad to see you."

Her dressing room had a tiny sitting room attached

to it. "You stay right there so we can talk while I change. It's been so long. I know that Boyle Heights and Beverly Hills are two different worlds, but they're not a thousand miles apart. And you're only here now because I practically dragged you here by sheer force because I made you think it was some awful crisis. It isn't. But I do want to talk to you."

She had changed into a pleated skirt and a cashmere sweater, and she looked like a schoolgirl. The make-up was gone. "Now look at me, Billy," she said. "Am I so different?"

"You look splendid. How's the baby?"

"Not a baby at all. May Ling walks and talks a blue streak. You'll see her, because I want you to come home with me."

"I thought I might take you to dinner."

"Dinner is waiting at home. You have your car here. I'm on Rexford Drive in Beverly Hills, which is very easy to find. You just stay on Melrose until you hit Santa Monica, and then turn right off Santa Monica onto Rexford. I'll write down the address. We'll go straight there, and we'll have time for drinks and a good talk."

At home in Beverly Hills, Sally paraded him through the house, with May Ling running back and forth, chattering on with her own commentary. Billy, charmed by the child, decided that she looked like a Chinese doll.

"She does take after Joe," Sally said. "Or after his mother, perhaps. Well, Billy, what do you think of my house?"

"I like it. But I can understand why Joe wouldn't feel comfortable here. I've lived in a house like this. He hasn't."

"And I haven't—until now. I will not talk about Joe.

He's impossible. Impossible! Oh, I wish I were in love with someone else! Sometimes I'm ready to say to him, All right. Divorce me and get it over with."

"Does he really want a divorce?"

"How can anyone know what Joe really wants? He doesn't know. He thinks it would be noble to divorce me. He and his shitty nobility. Oh, I'm sorry. You always look so hurt when I use gutter talk. But it's perfectly natural with me, Billy. I was always that way."

"Joe is a wonderful guy. I hate to see either of you hurt."

"Who is he wonderful to? If he could only find two hours a day to be wonderful to me and his daughter, we'd make out fine. No, let's not talk about that. We'll have dinner and we'll talk about Higate. Do you ever go up there? Eloise's new baby is delicious. Now, there you are. She has two kids, and still, Adam never blinked an eyelash when Eloise and Jean became partners in the new gallery."

Billy smiled. "I don't think Eloise could do anything that Adam would disapprove of. He adores her."

"Supposedly Joe adores me."

"It's different. Raising kids up there in the valley is different from raising them here in Los Angeles."

"I grew up there, so I ought to know."

After dinner, the baby asleep, the house quiet, sitting with Billy on the couch in front of a gas-log fire in the living room, Sally said, "I simply had to talk to you. If I don't talk to someone about this I'll go out of my mind. I can't talk to my mother and father. I mean, they have no notion of this industry. Pop had a sister, whose name was Martha. She wanted to be in pictures, and she came down here to Hollywood, where she was taken by a couple of cheap swindlers. I don't know the whole story exactly. Maybe it was dope and liquor or something like that. Anyway, she ended up by killing herself. Drove off a cliff up on Mulholland Drive, so you can imagine how much sympathy they have for the movie business. I'd talk to Barbara, because I love her so and she's such a great person, but she's Joe's sister and she has her own misery, and anyway, Billy, you are a clergyman, sort of, and you're the only clergyman I know, and you must have solved a lot of problems, all those years in the Pacific."

"Sally, darling, I'm not really a clergyman. I can't tell you what to do. Anyway—" He stopped and shook his head.

"Well, go on. What were you going to say?"

"I haven't any right to say it."

"To say what? Oh, I hate people who do that!"

"All right. I can't tell you what to do because I love you. You know that. I've loved you ever since that day we met in Joe's office."

"Is that so awful?"

"It's awful. Joe's my friend. I suppose I worship Joe in a way." Sally shook her head hopelessly. "Not only that," Billy went on, "I never made out with women. Oh, God, I don't know what's wrong with me. Funny, you coming to me for answers."

"If you think you love me," Sally said slowly, "why don't you do something about it? Why don't you kiss me? Why don't you take my hand? Why don't you touch me?"

He took a while to answer, and then he said, "Because you're you. You're Sally Lavette. You're Joe's wife. You're a film star." He added lamely, "I'm an Episcopal priest."

She began to giggle.

"Don't laugh at me, please."

"Still? I mean, are you still an Episcopal priest? You haven't done any priesting for a long time now. Isn't there a statute of limitations or something? Actually, I don't know a thing about Episcopal priests, except for that silly story about the two Irishmen standing in front of an Episcopal church, and the priest comes out, and Pat says to Mike, 'Will you look at him, with five children, and he calls himself father.'"

"Now you're laughing at me again."

"Oh, no, no. I'm trying to make you laugh. Billy, you're so kind and gentle, and you're very good-looking. One of the grips thought you were a star from another studio, honest. So why can't you touch me? God won't strike you dead. Billy, I haven't slept with Joe for a year and a half—and not with anyone else either, if you're convinced that actresses are whores in plainclothes."

"Oh, no. I don't think that at all. I'm not an idiot."

"I'm sure you're not. But you do act like one at times." She moved close to him. "Look at me, Billy." He turned and stared at her. "Now kiss me."

He leaned over and kissed her gently.

"There. It wasn't too bad, was it?"

"Please don't laugh at me again, Sally. I couldn't stand that."

"I won't laugh at you."

He put his arm around her, and she laid her head against his chest. "I guess," he said, "I'm as happy now as I've ever been."

"But you still think it's sinful."

"No. No, Sally. I gave up on sin a long time ago. Once, in the Solomons, I took the confession of a kid who was dying. He thought I was a Catholic priest, and I let him think so because he was all shot to pieces and there was no time to find a Catholic chaplain, even if I had known where one was, which I didn't. The kid was a murderer. He had stuck up a gas station and shot the owner, and now he was dying with such fear and terror that you can't imagine. He died in my arms. I suppose if it made any sense I'd send in my resignation. Take my name off the books. I'm not a priest anymore. Only it doesn't matter. I just stopped thinking about God. It's too confusing. I'm lucky because I have enough money not to have to work at a job, so I can help people at the clinic. It's the only thing that makes me feel good. Until tonight. This makes me feel good, sitting here with my arm around you. I feel guilty and rotten, but I also feel good."

"Do you want to go to bed with me?" Sally asked softly.

"I've wanted to from the first day I saw you."

"Then come upstairs with me, and we'll make love, and then we'll sleep. I'm starved, Billy, starved. You were never cut out to be a priest, and I make a lousy nun. It's almost nine o'clock, and I'm up at six and at the studio at seven."

The earth turned, and day followed night. At the corner of Market and Fifth, four armed men gunned down a police officer. In the heavy fog off the Golden Gate, a navy hospital ship sank after colliding with a freighter. There was a day when seven hundred and forty-two young Americans became casualties in Korea. Foreign Minister Robert Schuman of France and Foreign Secretary Ernest Bevin of England began discussions on the prospect of rearming Germany. There was a day when an advance post of sixty-three Americans was wiped out in Korea, and the dead lay with their eyes open and their bodies

shattered. Mohammad Reza Shah Pahlavi of Iran
went home after telling the people of San Francisco
that their city was a jewel in the crown of this mighty
nation. A six-year-old boy in Ingleside shot himself to
death with his father's pistol. Queen Mother Nazli of
Egypt visited San Francisco. Your city is like a jewel,
she said. In the most powerful and secure of nations,
Arthur W. Wallander, director of civil defense for the
City of New York, put the city on a twenty-four-hour-
a-day alert. "We don't know when it will happen," he
said. Fire burst out in the dome of San Francisco's
City Hall, and there were suspicions of arson. General
Douglas MacArthur came to San Francisco. General
Douglas MacArthur came to New York City. The
President had fired him with deep regret. Prime Minister Yoshida of Japan arrived in San Francisco. At
ceremonies held at the Opera House, he signed the
peace treaty that formally ended World War II. General Douglas MacArthur broke his silence and said, in
an address to the Congress of the United States, "It
has been said, in effect, that I am a warmonger. Nothing could be further from the truth." Jerome David
Salinger wrote a book called *Catcher in the Rye*. It
was called the best book about a young boy since
Mark Twain.

Barbara was reading *Catcher in the Rye* when Boyd
Kimmelman rang her doorbell. She had been expecting him. He had called, oddly enough, on a Sunday
morning, asking whether he might drop by and spend
a few minutes with her. When he came into the house,
Barbara said, "You catch me at my worst moment,
Boyd. Do you know what my worst moment is? It
happens when I read a book that absolutely delights
me, and I say to myself that I wish I had written it,

and then I have that awful feeling of knowing I never could have written it, not in a hundred years." She held it up. "Have you read it?"

"Not yet, no."

"Well, you'll like it, I think. You don't have to buy it. I'll lend you my copy when I'm finished. Now come on in and sit down. I sent Sam out to the park with Anna so that we might talk in peace. Sam gets larger and more obstreperous by the day, and I shudder to think of where it might end. With an oversized mother and an oversized father—well, who knows?" Kimmelman was nervous and unsure of himself. Barbara chattered away to put him at ease. "Come on, now, Boyd, sit down and make yourself comfortable. I think this is the first time you've ever been in my home. Now isn't that awful? We've had a hundred meetings, at your office and at the foundation, and this is the first time you've ever been here. I feel so ashamed. It's tiny and vertical, but that's the way all these old Victorian houses are. But it is nice, don't you think?"

He sank into a chair, nodded, and stared at her.

"For heaven's sake, Boyd, you must know by now that I don't warrant kid glove treatment. You call up and ask to see me on a Sunday. I know only too well that the Supreme Court decision comes down on Monday. It is that, isn't it?"

He nodded again. "An old law school buddy clerks for Douglas. I asked him to telephone me first thing with whatever might come down. He called last night. They're denying certiorari. God, how I hate to have to sit here and tell you this after all this time."

"Which means that finally they have decided that they will not hear argument on my case."

"Nine miserable old men who haven't got the guts to face up to that stinking committee. I feel so frustrated I could bust a gut—guts, that's all it is, guts. If they would only hear argument! No, this is the easy way. Sidestep it, pass the buck."

"Is this the end then, the final word?"

"I'm afraid so, Barbara. Oh, I could go to Washington, and I think my old buddy could get me in to see Justice Douglas, and he might be able to delay it for a while, but so far as legal opportunities are concerned, this is the end of the road."

"Then I don't want it postponed. When will the public announcement be made?"

"Tomorrow."

"And when do I go to jail?"

"That depends on how much time you need to clear up your affairs. Thank God for Judge Fremont. I can get a week, even two weeks, before you have to surrender."

"And where will I serve the time?"

"Well, we can be grateful it won't be Alderson Prison in West Virginia. The usual practice would be to book you in Washington and then send you to West Virginia, where they have this women's prison. But they've opened a new prison for women on Terminal Island off San Pedro, and Judge Fremont has seen to it that you'll be booked at the federal courthouse here and then sent to Terminal Island. I hear myself saying it, and I don't believe it. Jesus, Barbara, I think I'd give my right arm if this didn't have to happen to you. I look at you, and I don't believe it. It's just that it's you—" He shook his head hopelessly.

"Boyd, it could be worse, it could be a year. It's only six months. You can't keep blaming yourself."

"I have a feeling I did everything wrong, straight from the beginning."

"There was no right way to do it. Now listen to me.

Tell me exactly what I have to do. I don't want two weeks. I want to get this over with just as soon as possible."

"You don't want us to try for a rehearing?"

"Is there a chance in the world?"

"No. I have to be honest."

"Then I don't want it. Today is Sunday. I need two days, Monday and Tuesday. I'll surrender on Wednesday. Tell me exactly what we do."

"I'll come by Wednesday morning. It will have to be early, say seven-thirty. I'll go with you to the courthouse, and they'll book you. You will have to be fingerprinted, or perhaps that takes place on Terminal Island. I'm not certain. Then they'll either drive you or take you by plane to San Pedro. I would guess you'll drive. There will be a woman marshal with you. I'm not trying to make light of it, but in the lexicon of prisons, the federal prisons are the best in the country—if you can think of a prison as being better or worse. I hope you won't be too frightened."

"Boyd, believe me, I am not frightened. If anything, I'm curious, and a little sad. I'll admit that. To go six months without seeing Sammy is more than I want to think about."

"You don't have to. He can visit you. Specifically, they have five visiting days a month for adults, once a month for the kids. But then you can spend the whole day with Sam."

"In a prison? Oh, no. There's one memory I don't want to put on him. I don't want him to see me in prison and then have to carry that around with him the rest of his life. That would be too cruel."

"Well, that's up to you."

"What do I take with me?"

"Nothing, Barbara, only the clothes on your back."

"No toothbrush, soap, things like that?"

"No. Just your clothes. Yes, I'd take a purse, with whatever you normally carry in your purse. And your wristwatch. Take about fifty dollars in cash. They let you draw a certain amount each month for cigarettes and candy, which is just about all you can buy."

"I don't smoke, Boyd. You know that."

"Well, then for candy or whatever."

"Can you and Harvey come to see me?"

"Of course. We're your attorneys."

"Who else?"

"It's limited to family except by special request. But that's not too hard to work out. The thing to remember is that you're not cut off. You may get the feeling that you are, but you're not. Harvey and I are here, ready to do whatever has to be done. Then there's your mother and father. Your brother, Joe, lives down there in Los Angeles, so he's close by."

"Boyd," she said a bit impatiently, "stop being so damned Pollyannaish. There are things you do alone. You give birth alone and you die alone and you go to prison alone, and it doesn't matter who's standing by. All right, I seem to have it all now. I'll be waiting for you Wednesday morning at seven o'clock."

He nodded bleakly and rose to go, departing just as Sam came rocketing into the house. Barbara prepared lunch for the two of them, reading to Sam from A. A. Milne while they ate. After he had stretched out for his nap, she called her mother.

"What do you and daddy have going for this evening?" she asked Jean.

"Nothing very important. We were going out for dinner."

"Could you stop by afterward. I think we have to talk."

Later that evening, after Barbara had spelled out the expected course of events, she said to them, "I want you to know that I'm glad you're the way you are. I couldn't bear it if you made a fuss about this."

"I would if I thought it would do any good," Jean said.

"Well, you always gave me my head. I appreciate that. And when you come to think of it, I've been through just about everything. The main thing is Sam. Make him feel loved and treasured."

"We'll manage that," Dan agreed. "The boat is almost finished."

"You're a good sailor, aren't you, daddy?"

"Just about the best."

"I don't want you to bring him down to the prison."

"It's six months, Bobby. That's a long time for a little boy."

"I know, but I think this way is best. If I change my mind, I'll let you know. Isn't it crazy, my going to prison on Terminal Island? The same place," she said, "where my father built the biggest shipyard in the world."

"Well, not quite the biggest."

"Big enough. Big enough for Admiral Land to say you changed the course of the war. I was there once, in forty-one, I think."

Dan nodded. Jean sat silently, watching the two of them. She didn't trust herself to speak offhandedly; she had to think of her words and measure them, spacing them properly and unemotionally. Barbara was the one thing she had done right and well, even from the beginning.

"I don't remember the prison," Barbara said.

"It was a military compound then, a finger of land that sticks out of the island to the west."

"Then you can see the ocean?"

Dan nodded.

"And ships?"

"Yes, they pass by when they make port at San Pedro or Long Beach."

"That will be nice. Well, we can't sit around and talk all night, can we?"

"What shall we tell Sam?" Jean asked slowly.

"He knows I've been a correspondent, that I've had to travel all over the world for stories. He knows that I make my living from stories—and incidentally he's been spoiled by them. You can't just put him in front of a TV set. He wants stories, so I'm afraid you'll have to raid the bookstores and read to him. I'll tell him that I must go away for a while, and you back that up. That's all. I'll have all his things packed. It might be a good thing if you could come by on Wednesday as early as possible."

"We'll be here before you leave," Jean agreed.

"Good. Anna will stay here in the house, and Harvey's office will take care of the bills."

"For Christ's sake, if you need money," Dan began vehemently.

"No, daddy, I don't need money, and if I do, I'll ask you. I think Sam will be all right up there on Russian Hill, and it's only six months."

On the way home, Jean said nothing. It was not until they were in the house that she began to cry. She sat in a chair, her hands folded, weeping quietly. Watching her, Dan realized that this was the first time in all the years he had known her that he had ever seen her weep.

The marshal who drove the government Buick was named Buck Gedding, and he wore a spectacular old-fashioned revolver strapped to his waist. The woman marshal, Sadie Thomas, rode in back with Barbara. "We won't bother with handcuffs, dearie," she told Barbara. "I didn't need Judge Fremont to tell me that handcuffs were out. Good heavens, I never gave it a cotton-picking thought, I did not. We are not barbarians—although I can tell you this. They are not all like you; no siree, sir, they are not, not by a long mile. I had women in here would claw your eyes out, and there was one little filly had a knife on her. She pulled the knife on me, and I'll bear the scars to show it until my deathbed day."

"Sadie, will you can it," the driver said. "You can talk anyone deaf, dumb, and blind. Furthermore, conversation is not permitted, which is something you know as well as I do."

"Oh, that is just fine, Buck Gedding, but if you expect me to sit here next to this poor woman for four hundred miles in dead silence, you got another think coming. So I suggest you drive the car and allow me to tend to the prisoner."

The prisoner was lost in her own thoughts, and in time Sadie Thomas wound down into silence. Barbara was in a muted state of shock. She had allowed herself only the smallest portion of emotion that morning, going through a scene she had rehearsed in her mind a hundred times. It was an instinctive condition of the professional writer to write a scene mentally before it was played. Everything had to be in place; everything had to fit and everything had to function, each sentence and paragraph worked into a specific balance. Barbara could recall a time in Burma when she witnessed an attack of Japanese fighter-bombers on an American installation. They darted in, swooping down one at a time, each dropping its load of small, hundred-pound bombs. She stood covered to her waist in a slit trench, ignoring the pleading of a sergeant who was trying to get her down without actually manhandling her, standing there like an idiot in a forest of unfolding, deadly rosebuds, seeing the whole display in the third person and turning it into words as she watched. It was not a writer's trick, it was a writer's sad destiny; and she had done the same thing today, divorcing herself from herself, even cold inside as she held Sam in her arms and kissed him. Dan was not a storyteller; he clutched her with an agony that transmitted itself. She could feel it in the hard muscles of his body, and she felt belittled by the fact that one part of her mind could wonder how it felt for a father to see his daughter go off to prison.

Jean looked at her out of a face suddenly old. Never before had Barbara thought of her mother as an old woman. Sixty-one is not old, but now that fine, aristocratic face had crumbled. Barbara was almost glad to get away.

"Terminal Island," Sadie Thomas was saying, "is by no means the worst place in the world, dearie. The air is good, and that's more than you can say of Los Angeles. No smog there. I don't know how people live in Los Angeles. Well, each to his own."

They stopped for lunch at a roadside stand. "Government buys you lunch," Gedding said, dispensing largesse as its present representative. "Two sandwiches and coffee. What would you like? You stay in the car."

"And suppose she has to use the ladies' room?"

"You go with her."

"You got to use the ladies' room, dearie?"

"Yes," Barbara said, "but I'm not hungry. I don't want any lunch."

"The government buys it."

"I'm sorry, I'm not hungry. I'll have coffee."

"We're going to the ladies' room," Sadie Thomas said, "and then we are going to sit down inside like civilized people."

Barbara sat at the counter flanked by the two marshals, sipping her coffee and thinking that she was not very good at this. It had barely started, and here she was totally depressed. She could remember no time in all her life, not even when the news of Bernie's death came, when she had been overtaken by such a feeling of total hopelessness and despair. She had been removed from everything she loved, cherished, and depended on. She was alone and powerless. She realized full well that the world was full of people who lived their lives alone and powerless, but that had never been her case. In the past, no matter what had happened, no matter where she was, she could reach out to people of power and influence who loved or respected her. Even in Nazi Germany her connection with the power circles of the United States had been noted and respected. Now, for the first time, she was totally cut off; the connections with her life, her past, her family, and her friends had been severed. Two people, sitting on either side of her, owned her body and soul. If some lunatic impulse should cause her to bolt out of the roadside stand and run for freedom, this large, heavy man called Buck Gedding would be justified in drawing his gun and shooting her down. Or at least so it appeared to her. All the rights and privileges that any American citizen takes for granted had disappeared. It no longer mattered what her crime had been; all the discussions of whether her crime was in all truth a crime had become academic, rhetorical games. To everyone she

would encounter during the next six months, she was
a criminal.

Back in the car, driving south again, unable to bear
the chatter of the woman marshal, she pretended to
be asleep, lying back with her eyes closed. The night
before she had slept for only an hour or two; now the
pretense became fact. Curled into one corner of the
back seat, she slept for the next two hours.

It was almost twilight when they reached San Pedro
and rolled slowly onto the little ferry that would take
them to Terminal Island. "You stay in the car," Gedding said to her, and Sadie Thomas nodded her agreement. "It's the rules, dearie." They locked the doors.

On the island, they drove past the shipyards, idle
now, the old ways empty, the buildings boarded over.
They drove past the Customs House to Seaside Avenue, flanked on either side by empty lots and ware-
houses, and then down Seaside Avenue to the end of
the island. Now Barbara could see the harbor waters,
a flat, crowded, ugly port, a mass of fishing boats,
tugs, rusty freighters, so different from the great,
windswept expanse of San Francisco Bay that it
brought tears to her eyes.

The car pulled up in front of her place of exile,
board buildings like army barracks, a ten-foot fence of
heavy linked metal, and guard towers. Sadie Thomas
pointed to a quadrangle of brick buildings. "The
men's prison. Yours is better, dearie, believe me. We
go in here, so just try to make a good impression right
from the beginning. It pays off."

They entered the building set between the woven
wire walls. A matron-officer in a blue prison uniform
signed Gedding's papers and signed a receipt for Barbara's purse. Then two marshals left. Barbara never
saw them again.

* * *

The officer behind the admissions desk emptied Barbara's purse and spread the contents. There was a billfold of money, which she counted carefully. She was a broad, solidly built woman in her middle years, with a thick neck and a small pug nose. "I'm Officer Hurley," she said. "I'm counting the money in front of you, so pay attention. One hundred dollars. You can seal it for your release or you use it against your purchases in the commissary. Which do you want?"

"I'd like to use it while I'm here," Barbara said softly.

"Speak up!"

"I'd like to use it while I'm here."

"That's better." She was studying the folder Gedding had left with her. "Barbara Cohen. Contempt of Congress, six months." Her eyes examined Barbara from head to foot, the pale brown hair caught in a bun behind her head, the gray flannel suit, the white blouse. She fingered the purse. "You're one of a kind here, Mrs. Cohen. This is not exactly Alcatraz, but neither is it the Fairmont. Just mind your P's and Q's." They were in a long, narrow room, a counter running its length, and behind the counter, cubbyholes in the wall.

"We'll begin with your fingerprints, Barbara," Officer Hurley said. "Just step over here, and let's have your right hand."

Barbara stepped to the counter. Officer Hurley rolled ink onto a glass plate, took Barbara's hand, and then, finger by finger, into the ink and onto a card.

"Left hand."

Again, each finger was rolled in the ink and then rolled with the same motion onto a card. Then she gave Barbara a towel. "Wipe off the ink."

The outside door opened, and a man in prison garb of shapeless blue entered, carrying a camera on a tripod.

"Set up," Officer Hurley told him. "Be with you in a minute." The photographer was staring at Barbara hungrily. He couldn't take his eyes off her as he set up his camera. Officer Hurley took a slate with a string attached to each corner and on it chalked Barbara's name and a number. She came around the counter and put the string around Barbara's neck so that the slate hung in front of her like a breastplate. "Stand right here," she said, pushing Barbara back against the wall. "Eyes open. Look directly into the camera." She said to the photographer, "What the devil are you waiting for, Sweeney?"

He squeezed his flash. The light blinded Barbara. "Don't move," he said. "I need a second shot."

Her eyes were clenched tight.

"Please open your eyes, miss."

The camera flashed again.

"All right. Take it away, Sweeney."

He departed reluctantly, his hunger and need trailing after him.

Hurley went behind the counter, found a meshwork metal tray, and pushed it toward Barbara.

"Take off your clothes, Barbara, and put them in here. They'll be cleaned, courtesy of the government, and they'll be held for you."

Barbara stared at her.

"I said take off your clothes."

"Here?"

"That's right. Here."

"I don't understand."

"What do I have to do, draw you a diagram? Now

you listen to me, Barbara. This is just the first step.
But learn now. You do what you're told to do."

"I'll be naked."

"That's right. You won't die and you won't catch
cold. You're in a federal House of Correction. You
come in with those clothes and you go out with them,
but while you're here, you wear what we give you. So
sit down in that chair and strip down."

Still Barbara stared at Officer Hurley, who nodded
coldly. Barbara took off her jacket and handed it to
her. Then her skirt, her blouse and her petticoat. For
a long moment, she stood in her brassiere and girdle,
feeling humiliated and ridiculous. Then she sighed,
kicked off her shoes, pulled off girdle and stockings,
unhooked her brassiere and stood naked.

"Pick up your clothes and put them in the tray."

Barbara did so.

"Now go through that door and sit down in there
and wait."

The door Officer Hurley pointed to led into a small
locker room with a single bench down the center.
Two other naked women were sitting on the bench,
and they looked at Barbara mutely as she entered.
Neither of them spoke. One was a tall, well-built
black woman. The other was a slight, skinny white girl,
twenty-one at the most, who sat huddled over and
shivering, trying to cover her pubic hair with one
hand and her tiny breasts with the other. Barbara
stood uncertainly, looking at them and trying not to
look at them, conscious of their nakedness and her
own nakedness in a way that she had never been conscious of nakedness before, until finally the black
woman grinned and said, "Sit down, honey. There
ain't no telling how long them motherfuckers will

keep us here. And that goddamn stone floor is cold, cold."

Barbara sat down next to the white girl, who shivered and cringed and whimpered softly.

"Are you sick?" Barbara asked.

"No, she ain't sick," the black woman said. "She's a doper. She just started climbing the shitpile. Two, three hours from now, she be screaming like a lunatic."

"Oh, God," Barbara whispered. "Can't they do anything for her?"

"Here it is cold turkey, honey. You're not a doper?"

"Thank goodness, no."

"You think those bastards would give us a little heat here. My name's Annie Lou Baker."

"Mine is Barbara Cohen."

"What brings you here, sister?"

"Something called contempt of Congress."

"What?"

"Yes, it's a crime," Barbara said.

"Shit, in the slammer for having contempt? Honey child, that would put me away two dozen times a week—"

Whatever else she might have said was interrupted by the opening of the door opposite to the one through which Barbara had entered. Past this door, Barbara saw a brightly lit, tiled shower room, and through the door came a woman in a bathing suit, a pail in one hand and a scrubbing brush in the other. "On your feet, girls," she called out. "I'm Officer Davenport, and this here pail is filled with a solution of soapsuds and DDT. We welcome you, but not whatever bugs, maggots, or lice you bring with you. We run a clean sanitary house. So get your backsides under those showers, and once you're wet, I'm going to wash your hair."

"Ain't nobody going to wash my hair with DDT," Annie Lou Baker said.

"No? Well, listen, child, either you get under that shower in ten seconds, or I call in a couple of male guards to hold you while I wash your hair. Now which is it?"

The black woman grinned. "Either way, it got points. Hell, what's the difference?"

She walked into the shower room. Barbara followed, hardly enthralled by the prospect of having her hair washed with DDT, yet falling into the realization that here one obeyed. There was no appeal. One obeyed. She was sure there were various punishments for disobedience, but the one single punishment that mattered was the loss of time off for good behavior. That she knew about. In her case, good behavior amounted to a reduction of her sentence by a day each month, six days out of the sentence; and even now she was determined that not one minute of those six days would be sacrificed.

The white girl held back, crouched and shivering. "How long since you had a bath?" Officer Davenport demanded, grabbing her by the arm and pulling her under the shower. "Come on, kid. You're going to kick it no matter what, and a good shower won't make it any worse. Now all of you, use the soap and scrub."

Ten minutes later the showers went off, and Barbara took the towel Officer Davenport handed her and dried her body and hair. Her hair was still damp and smelled of the soap and DDT concoction, but hair dryers had not yet made their appearance in federal prisons.

Davenport wrapped herself in a terrycloth robe and

sang out, "All right, girls. Follow me, and we'll get some clothes on you."

The women wrapped the towels around their waists and followed her into the next room. The prison clothes were stacked on a table, and two women prisoners did the dispensing. They each wore a shapeless gray wraparound dress that fell halfway between the knee and the ankle and flat-heeled black shoes.

"Give her your sizes," Officer Davenport said. "Bust size, dress size, and shoe size."

"Not that it matters," one of the prisoners said.

"We'll do without your advice, Suzie."

Barbara pulled on the gray dress and tied it at the waist. "You're a big girl," Suzie said, "so we got problems." She was a sharp-eyed, tight little woman of about forty. "What size shoe?"

"Nine."

"Jesus God! I don't know if we got any nines." She called to the other, "Billy, you got a nine?"

"Nine and a half?"

"They're kind of loose," Barbara said apologetically.

"I got an eight, but that'll mortify the hell out of you."

Barbara settled for the nine and a half. The three women dressed themselves, and Billy and Suzie stacked three piles of clothes and toiletries on the table.

"Now this is yours," Officer Davenport said to Barbara and the others. "It's government issue, so you don't mess it up. You're responsible for your possessions. Now here each of you has pajamas, bathrobe, uniform, underwear, toothbrush, tooth powder, comb, brush, deodorant, shower cap, and jacket. Take care of it."

Another woman entered the room while she was

speaking, a tall, thin, gray-haired woman of fifty or so wearing the uniform of a prison officer.

"This is Officer Skeffington," Davenport told them. "She'll take you to the isolation cells, where you'll spend tonight and some of tomorrow. This is only for your isolation period, so don't get too nervous. You won't be living there." She nodded at Rosalie. "She's the doper."

Trembling, Rosalie pleaded, "Help me, help me, please."

"We're helping you more than anyone ever helped you, so just pull yourself together. Now come along, girls," Officer Skeffington said. "Pick up your stuff and bring it with you."

"Do we get fed?" Annie Lou demanded. "Lady, I'm starving."

"You address me as Officer Skeffington. If you don't know the officer's name, you will address him as 'sir' or her as 'madam.' And nobody starves in here. You will be fed."

She led them down a corridor, around a corner, and then into another corridor, where there were five wooden doors. Officer Skeffington unsnapped a ring of keys from her belt and opened the first door.

"In here," she said to Barbara.

"Could I have a pencil and some writing paper?" Barbara asked.

"You'll have all that tomorrow when you're assigned to your quarters. I can't give you any here."

Barbara nodded and walked into the cell. The door closed behind her and the key turned in the lock. She looked around the room. There was an overhead light with a pull cord, an iron cot of army issue, a bottom sheet, a pillow and pillowcase, two blankets, a wooden chair, a sink, and a toilet. The floor was con-

crete and the room smelled strongly of disinfectant.
There was also a small table.

Barbara put her possessions on the table and sat
down on the chair. Happily, there was no mirror in
the room. She had no desire to look at herself. Her
hair was still a damp mass, lying moist and uncomfortable on her neck and shoulders. She took one of
the two cotton towels that were folded on the sink
and tied it around her damp head like a turban. It
helped.

"So this is it," she said to herself. "I am finally in
jail. If I had only come here when I walked out of the
courthouse in Washington it would be over now, long
over. Too late now. I have six long, dreary months of
this wretched place, of being submissive, of being ordered around, of being bored and humiliated, and for
the life of me I still can't put my finger on what kind
of a crime I have committed."

A key turned in the lock. The door opened, and a
pretty little black woman carrying a tray entered the
cell. She wore an inmate's uniform, the same shapeless
gray smock, but she carried it with style, and she wore
a colored hand-embroidered belt. "Got you some eating food, sister. It ain't soul food, but it ain't bad either. This here's just pickup. You be eating better tomorrow. My name's Ellie. Why don't you just stack
your junk in the corner and I put this on the table."

Barbara cleared the table and Ellie put down the
tray. "I pick up tomorrow," she said. "So you take
your time, sister. See you in jail."

"Thank you," Barbara said.

The black lady left, locking the door behind her.
There had been something so kind, so gentle, so en-
dearing in her manner that it brought tears to Barbara's eyes. She had now been in prison for almost

three hours, and nothing that had happened had been in any way like what she might have expected; but then, she realized, prison, like war, can be neither imagined nor anticipated. It can only be experienced, and during the three hours she had been here she had learned more of the nature of prison and prisoners than in a lifetime of reading. Well, someday, she told herself, she would write of all this, and at least she would know whereof she wrote.

She turned to the tray. Until this moment she had felt no pangs of hunger. They had taken away her watch with her other possessions, but she guessed it was almost nine o'clock. She had not eaten since seven in the morning, and then it had been only dry toast and coffee. Now, suddenly, she was ravenously hungry. The tray contained two thick sandwiches of ham and cheese on white bread, a dish of coleslaw, a piece of brown cake, and a mug of coffee. There was evaporated milk in the coffee and it had been sweetened. She ate everything—the sandwiches, the coleslaw, and the cake. The single utensil on the tray was a spoon, and she found herself licking it clean.

What a difference a full stomach makes, she thought. Who was it said that revolutions are not made on full stomachs? Well, perhaps it applies to worry as well. Her head was nodding in spite of the coffee. She undressed and put on the pajamas. Apparently Suzie had decided that nothing would do but the largest pair in stock. The sleeves covered her hands, the trousers her feet.

"Oh, the hell with it," she said. She pulled the light cord, crawled into bed, and a moment later she was asleep with the sleep of utter exhaustion.

She slept more soundly than she had in days due to the cumulative effect of tension and exhaustion, and

she awakened to the sound of a knock at the door.
The tiny cell was filled with morning light from a
high window, and for a moment or two, so deep had
her sleep been, Barbara was unable to remember
where she was and experienced a momentary surge of
panic at the sight of the tiny room. Then the key
turned in the lock, and Ellie entered with another
tray.

"Breakfast, sister," Ellie said. "How you sleep?"

"Like a log."

"Good. Now you clean up and put yourself together. Then you make up the bed. You fold everything at the foot of the bed—sheet, blankets and pillowcase, nice and neat. This here's your breakfast, so
you eat this first, and I take away your other tray."

"Are you a prisoner, Ellie?"

"I sure enough am. Honor prisoner. Sister, I been
incarcerated seven long years."

"Good heavens, for what?"

"Murder," Ellie said indifferently. "I been married
to this no good sonofabitch who beat up on me and
my two kids day in, day out, and one day I just
couldn't stand no more of it, so I took his gun, and
said, you touch me, you bastard, I kill you. That's
what I did. I kill him." She shrugged.

"But this is a federal jail."

"He was a soldier, sister. So here I is. Now never
mind all that. Long done and gone. You eat and clean
up, and then the physician's assistant going to come
by and talk to you."

"Ellie," Barbara asked, unable to restrain her curiosity, "they give you the keys to these cells?"

"That is right," she replied, shaking the key ring.
"These here cells ain't really cells, just isolation rooms.
Suppose you get out of this cell? Then you is locked in

the building. Suppose you get out of the building? Then you is behind the gates and the walls, with the man up there in the tower with his gun. Suppose you go over the wall? Then you is on an island, sister, and you know something, thinking about escaping is like taking stupid pills."

Barbara laughed. "I'm certainly not thinking about escaping."

"Good. That laugh is very nice to see. When I see you last night, you got a face like death warmed over. Poor sister, what you do? Kill someone, peddle dope, pass bad checks? You sure enough don't look like no floozie."

"I committed a contempt of Congress."

"You committed a what?" Ellie shook her head. "Someday you tell me. Right now I got my work."

After she brushed her teeth, Barbara sat down to eat. There was a bowl of oatmeal, covered with sugar and already cold. Barbara had a few spoonfuls and then gave up. There was a roll, buttered, that she ate with her coffee. Then she washed her face, combed her hair, dressed herself in her prison clothes, and made up the bed as instructed. There was no nail file in the toiletries, not even a scrap of paper that she could fold into a triangle to clean her fingernails.

"This is ridiculous," she said aloud. "I'm in jail, and I stink of DDT and disinfectant and my hair is an unholy mess, and I'm worrying about dirty fingernails."

A knock at the door again. Ellie's voice asked, "You decent, sister?"

"I suppose you could call it that."

The door opened, and a dark man with thick eyebrows and sloping shoulders entered the cell. "I'm Gallo, the physician's assistant," he said. "I take your history, and then you go for your physical. Sit over there on the bed." He dropped down at the chair and opened the folder he had with him.

"Name?" He had hardly glanced at her.

"Barbara Cohen."

"Married?"

"I'm a widow."

"Then Cohen's your husband's name. Maiden name?"

"Lavette." She spelled it.

For the first time, he looked at her thoughtfully. "I'll want your home address and the address of your next of kin." She gave them to him. "Name and address of family physician, if you have one."

"Dr. Milton Kellman, Mount Zion Hospital, San Francisco."

He paused and studied her again. "You're an odd one. Nothing to do with this history, but may I ask what you're in here for?"

"Since it appears to be a common question that pervades this place, I don't mind. I'm almost used to it. Contempt of Congress."

"Oh? Wait a minute, Barbara Cohen. I remember. But that was ages ago."

"Like the mills of the gods, the mills of justice grind slowly, but they grind exceeding fine."

"No doubt. Contagious diseases. I'll name them. Just say yes or no. Chicken pox?"

"Yes."

"Measles?"

"Yes."

"Diphtheria?"

"No. I was inoculated."

"Whooping cough?"

"No."

"Mumps?"

"Yes."

"Syphilis?"

"No," she said softly.

He looked at her again. "I have to ask. Gonorrhea?"

"No."

"It's a jail, Mrs. Cohen, not the YWCA."

Angry suddenly, she said, "Why the hell don't you get on with this and stop apologizing to me! I know damn well I'm in jail! What do you think I'm here as, a social worker?"

He paused with his pen in the air to stare at her.

"I'm sorry. I don't often lose my temper."

He shrugged. "Let's continue."

When he finished, he closed his folder and walked out of the cell without another word, slamming the door behind him. A few minutes later, Ellie returned.

"You burned the man's ass, sister. You watch your step, huh? Now we go for your physical."

"Do I take my things?"

"No. You leave your stuff and we pick it up after they assign you a room. This here building is Administration and Orientation, and you is three weeks here before they assign your permanent quarters. But not in the cell. You get a decent room, which ain't much but better than a cell. But right now you get undressed and put on your bathrobe."

The doctor was thin, aseptic, and coldly impersonal. His name was Sutter. He wore a white laboratory coat, and Barbara noticed that his collar was dirty and that there were dark moons under his fingernails.

He poked at the scar on her abdomen and said, "What's that—a section?"

"Yes."

"The child born alive?"

"Yes."

"Get on the table there and lie down."

"Why?" Barbara asked.

"I'm going to do a pelvic."

"You mean a vaginal examination?"

"If you wish to call it that."

"I don't want it," Barbara said.

"What do you mean, you don't want it?"

"I don't want it. There is nothing wrong with my vagina. I'm not using it as a receptacle for dope, if that's what you're after. I'm here for six months, and I can't see why on earth that has to include a vaginal examination."

"Suppose you let me decide that." He exchanged looks with the nurse, a stout blond woman.

"It's a prison rule," the nurse said.

"I don't want it!" Barbara said emphatically.

"I'm not going to force you," Dr. Sutter said, regarding her unpleasantly. "This is not a concentration camp. But it goes on your record. This is your second day in here. You're making a bad start, Barbara, I can tell you that."

She was back in her cell, putting her things together, when the door opened and a tall, dark-haired woman with striking blue eyes, wearing an officer's uniform, entered, closed the door behind her, and stood looking at her. "I'm Captain Cooper," she said. "I understand you refused the pelvic. Why?"

"Because I'm not an addict or a dope peddler," Barbara replied. "I'm here for contempt of Congress. That gives you the right to lock me up. It doesn't give anyone the right to poke around in my vagina."

"You're pretty damn sure of yourself, aren't you?"

"Oh, no. No, ma'am, I am not. I am depressed and lonely and miserable and frightened. I am also damned angry, because I did nothing criminal—"

"You can can that right now," Captain Cooper interrupted. "I am not a judge or a jury. I am an officer in a federal House of Correction. Now you listen to me, Barbara. You've done a stupid thing on your second day in jail. For this I could dock your time off for good behavior. I will not tolerate troublemakers. There are rules. You run a prison with rules. You're no fool. You're an educated woman, and you should understand that. Now this time I'm going to let it pass, and count yourself lucky. I am not impressed with your background or your contacts. The next time you step out of line, I'm going to lay it on you with all my weight. By now you've seen enough of this place to know that we run a civilized institution, but we deal with criminals. We have solitary confinement when it is necessary, and we have other ways. Now take your things and follow me."

Barbara picked up her possessions and followed Captain Cooper down the hall, past the isolation cells. Women in prisoners' dress passed by, glancing at her curiously. Here were open doors to small rooms, each room about eight by ten, with a cot, a small chest of drawers, table and chair. Each room had a window that was unbarred. Captain Cooper pointed to one of them.

"In there. This will be your room for the next three weeks. You will keep it neat and clean; make your bed immediately upon arising, see that no dust or dirt accumulates. The door is never locked. This is the orientation period, when you will learn the rules and regulations of this institution."

"Thank you," Barbara said.

The officer looked at her, and their eyes met. "We'll see," Captain Cooper said.

A loud bell announced lunch. Annie Lou Baker, in

the room next to Barbara's, met her in the hall. "Now this ain't bad, honey," the black woman said. "I been in lots worse places."

"Where's Rosalie?" Barbara asked her.

"They got her back in that cell we been in, screaming her head off. That kid kicking it hard, hard."

Ellie came along and told them to follow her. They were joined by about a dozen women in the orientation section, and Ellie led the way to the dining room, which was in another building. It was a welcome shock for Barbara to step out into the open, to feel the cold, clean wash of the sea air against her cheeks and to glimpse the great stretch of the Pacific in the distance. Films of prison life had prepared Barbara for the tiers of cell blocks, the long, narrow tables where prisoners sat side by side, the bleak misery of bowed men in striped suits. To her relief, the dining room resembled nothing as much as the dining room of a somewhat shabby girl's school. The tables seated four, and the food was served cafeteria style at one end of the room. The inmates apparently sat where they pleased; that is, except for the new prisoners, who were confined to one section.

There was ample food. Lunch consisted of frankfurters, sauerkraut, potatoes and green beans, bread and butter and coffee, and Jell-O. Ellie whispered to Barbara and Annie Lou, "Don't take more than you can eat, sister. They don't like for the food to be thrown away."

"They can't cook up more than I can eat," said Annie Lou. Barbara felt no desire to eat, but she forced herself to get through a frankfurter and some green beans. Everywhere in the dining room the inmates were talking, many of them laughing. It's not awful, Barbara thought. It's demeaning and degrading to be here, but it's all right. I'll learn things I could never learn otherwise, and it's not forever.

After lunch, the women who were segregated for orientation had a half-hour to themselves in the yard. There were no gates or barriers on the sea-wall side of the prison. Barbara watched a big white cruise ship sail by, out of Long Beach harbor. It was strange and incredible to be here, locked up on this finger of land, not mistreated, but controlled, manipulated, deprived. Long, long ago, during the bloody San Francisco longshore strike of 1934, Barbara had worked in a soup kitchen that served the strikers. No one had known who she was. She had spent all of her allowance on food for the kitchen. Many of the longshoremen liked her, but one of them fell in love with her. His name was Dominick Salone, and one day, in anger, he said to her, "It's easy for you. You walk into this and you can walk out of it. You make a game out of life. You make a game out of being poor. For me it's not a game. There are no exits for me."

Now she came finally to understand what he had meant. There were no exits here. It was valid, and terrifying in its validity. This was something she would not be able to explain to anyone, not inside the prison, not outside. Because, she was beginning to realize, everyone in this prison had lived lives without exits. Prisons were for the poor, the truncated, the hopeless, and the desperate; there was no way she would ever be able to communicate to those outside what it meant to be poor. She was not sure she knew, but she was sure that before she left here she would know, for already she sensed that it was not a matter of money alone; it was something that reached into the mind and the heart and the soul.

During the afternoon she sat in a room with Annie

Lou and took intelligence and aptitude tests—ridiculous tests, the very taking of which diminished and humiliated her.

After dinner she was given paper and envelopes, and she sat down in her tiny room to write her first letters from prison. The first was to Sam. "My dear, darling Sammy," she wrote. "Grandma will read this to you, and it will be just like me talking to you. I have my work to do here, so it will be a while before I see you again. But I have decided that each week I'll write a special story, just for you, and send it to you. I know that won't be nearly as good as telling you a story that I make up as I go along, because when I make it up as I go along, I have you there to direct me.

"But if you teach granny how to do it, I am sure she can change the stories properly. I think of you all the time because I love you so very much. I can close my eyes and see you quite clearly, and you must do the same thing. Just close your eyes and think—and then you will see me. It takes a little magic, and you have always been very good at magic. I send you love and many kisses."

To Jean and Dan, she wrote: "Here I am, facing my second night in prison. It is by no means as awful as I had imagined it would be, and I am sure that compared to the Los Angeles County Jail—note a conversation daddy and I had awhile ago—this is a very civilized place. The letters are censored, and I have been told that I must not write in specific terms about the prison. Well, I'll try to keep it general. We are not in cells but in rooms, and we are not locked in at night. The food is edible institutional food, and I don't foresee any difficulties much worse than boredom and loneliness in the coming months. In the short time I've spent here, I've already heard the expression 'building time.' Apparently that is the great hurdle everyone faces in a prison. At home, when I write, time runs away from me. There is never enough time for anything. Here the whole thing is reversed. Time is your enemy. Time is endless. But why do I go into this? Good heavens, you have enough to worry about.

"As for Sammy, I am enclosing a letter to him. I don't want you to lie overtly to him. At the same time, I don't want him to know about this now. He can't handle it yet. When he can, I'll tell him. Meanwhile, just keep up the illusion that I am working elsewhere, a place I can't take him to.

"Now for requests. I would like a subscription to the *Chronicle*. You are allowed to provide that for me, and I can receive the newspaper each day. At least it will be a link to the home town. Also, I would like to read Faulkner's new book, *Requiem for a Nun*. That must come to me from the publisher, so you will have to send them a check.

"When I learn all the details about visiting hours and rules, I'll send them on to you. Meanwhile, I guess the only other thing I can ask for that the rules allow are letters, so you might pass the word around to anyone who might care, especially to Sally and Joe and Eloise and the others at Higate. Also, write me in great detail about the new venture that is to bring the finer things in modern art to the philistines of the Bay Area. And for daddy: coming here, we drove by your old shipyard. It has the look of a sad, abandoned place. And for both of you, all my love. I don't know what I would do without you."

The following day, Barbara was called into the office of Mrs. Roberts, the case manager, a small, rather severe-looking woman, whose small, dark eyes studied her carefully. "Cohen, Barbara," she finally said. "Are you Jewish, Barbara? I ask you that because we do have church services, and although we have no Jewish inmates in the present population, we have a visiting rabbi available."

"My husband was Jewish. I'm not."

"I see. You're a widow? Or divorced?"

"A widow."

"Well, the chapel is elective. You can go or not, as you wish. Many of the girls find spiritual comfort there."

"I understand."

"This is a work prison, Barbara. According to your record, you are an educated woman, and I am sure you can understand that it would be a woeful waste of the taxpayers' money to bring people to an institution like this and then permit them to become demoralized by idleness. Here, everyone works, with the hope that work habits will find a permanent place in the prisoner's character." While she spoke, she was going through a folder on her desk. Without looking up she said, "You test very high. Unusually high. You're down here as a writer. What do you write?"

"I was a correspondent during the war. Since then, I've been writing novels."

"Under this name?"

"No, I use my maiden name, Barbara Lavette."

"Barbara Lavette." Mrs. Roberts wrinkled her brow. "No, I don't think I've read any. Well, the obvious place for you would be the education department. We have such difficulty finding qualified inmate assistants. But that wouldn't do. We have instructions from Washington. No reds in the education department."

"Reds? Mrs. Roberts, I am not a red."

"This is not for me to decide. Personally, I simply

cannot imagine how anyone in his right mind would want to overthrow this government by force and violence, but as I said, it's not for me to decide."

Barbara sighed and kept her peace.

"Somehow I don't see you at a sewing machine. Can you sew?"

"Not very well, no."

"Do you know anything about gardening? We're just about the only federal prison without a farm attached to it, but we do have a small truck garden and a greenhouse, and we're a bit shorthanded there. The girls are not fond of gardening."

Barbara knew absolutely nothing about gardening—she simply watered her house plants when they required it—but the thought of being able to work in the open, in the Southern California sunshine within sight of the ocean, was so exciting that she lied without hesitation. "Oh, yes, of course. I'm a very good gardener. As a matter of fact," she said, embellishing it, "I took a course in college," hoping that no one would inquire of Sarah Lawrence, since she was quite sure they had never given a course in any branch of agriculture.

"Vegetables?"

"Oh, yes. Vegetables."

"Indeed. It sounds promising. I'll take it up with the board. Meanwhile, you have a few more days in isolation before we assign you to a work unit."

"Can I use the library?" Barbara asked. "You do have a library?"

"A very good one. Ask Ellie to take you there. She's the little colored girl in charge of isolation."

In the library, Barbara found three books on gardening. She read each one from cover to cover. Two days later, at breakfast, Ellie said to her, "You report to the truck garden today. Sister, you will have one sore back."

Sally Lavette awakened with a splitting headache and with a mouth that tasted like leather soaked in vinegar. She sat up in bed and stared in bewilderment and then in disgust at the man sleeping beside her. She rammed her elbow into his side, and when he came awake with a squeal of distress, she snapped at him, "Who the hell are you?"

He sat up in bed, naked under the sheets. "For Christ's sake, Sally. Jerry Donner. Last night—"

"I don't give a damn about last night!" she shouted. "You get your clothes on and get your ass out of here in the next thirty seconds, or I call the cops and tell them you raped me!"

"Are you crazy? Have you gone nuts?"

She pulled open the drawer in the night table next to her and took out a gun and pointed it at him. "I'm counting to thirty. I want you out of here and downstairs and out of my house, or so help me God, I'll commit justifiable homicide. And the way I feel right now, it would be a relief."

"All right, all right—take it easy. I'm going." He pulled on his pants, stuffed tie and socks and undershorts into his pockets, pulled on his shirt and jacket, stuck his bare feet into his shoes, and stumbled from the room. She heard him going down the stairs. She had reached twenty-two. She stopped counting and flung her daughter's water pistol across the room in disgust.

"Oh, God in heaven," she whispered. "What has gotten into you, Sally? That creep! That disgusting, spineless, little sonofabitch! Why? Why? Tell me why!" She felt sick and dirty and crawling with hatred of herself. From somewhere Groucho Marx's line flashed into her mind. "I wouldn't want to belong to any club that would have me as a member." And she paraphrased it for her own need: "I wouldn't want to be caught dead with anyone who would crawl into bed with Sally Lavette."

"No, I would not," she said.

She douched and showered, washed her hair, and then sat under the dryer, wondering whether she should go to her doctor and have a Wasserman test. She had wrapped her last picture two nights before, but she had a conference with Hargasey and her agent scheduled for eleven o'clock today, and after that, lunch with Fay Killens, who did the Hollywood gossip column for United Press. She had no idea what time it was. The blinds were closed, the drapes drawn. While she was under the dryer, Jovida, her housekeeper, came in and parted the drapes and tilted the blinds. The sun blazed in.

Sally turned off the dryer and asked in Spanish, "What time is it, Jovida?"

"Ten. Mr. Hargasey called. He doesn't want you to be late."

"The hell with Hargasey. What went on here last night?"

"Big party."

"Was I very drunk?"

Jovida shrugged.

"Where's the kid?"

"In her room, playing."

Sally closed her eyes and nodded. She shivered slightly. May Ling had become a very quiet, withdrawn child. She was only four and a half years old, but she was strangely adult, quiet, almost joyless, a slender little girl with straight black hair and ivory skin that was almost translucent.

"Here is the mail," Jovida said.

A letter in an armed services envelope with a Korean postmark caught her eye. She threw the other letters on the bed and tore it open. "Dear Mrs. Lavette," the letter read. "There is no easy way to write a letter like this. William Clawson, who was chaplain with the 4th regiment of the 7th Divison, died of his wounds this morning in our hospital. I promised him that if he died, I would write to you and convey to you his very deep and sincere affection for you. I did not know him, but he appeared to be a very decent and honorable man. I do not know what else I can say." It was signed "Major L. V. Cotton, M.D."

Sally held the letter in trembling hands. She wanted a drink very desperately, and just as desperately she desired not to drink. She had not seen Billy Clawson since that night at her house, and that was so long ago. Everything was so long ago. How long was it since she had been to Higate or seen her father and mother or spoken to Eloise or Adam? Everything had stopped. Her life had been shattered into timelessness. Her eyes blurred as she tried to read the letter again. She put it down and wiped her eyes. Then she read it once more, and after that, she went to the telephone and called the clinic. A part of her mind remarked that she was not weeping, and she answered it by saying, "Tears come from the heart. My heart is cold as ice, so don't ask me to cry."

Frank Gonzales took her call. "Hello, Sally," he said somewhat strangely, as if she were a stranger.

"Is Joe there?"

"No." Hesitation. "No, Joe went up to the Napa Valley to be with the family. Billy Clawson died. He was killed in Korea."

"Why didn't you tell me?"

"We only got word yesterday."

"Yesterday was yesterday. Today is today. What kind of bastards are you, both of you!"

She slammed down the phone, tears finally breaking through. Then she wiped them away, dressed herself, and pulled a suitcase out of the closet. With the suitcase half-packed, she broke off, picked up the phone, and called Pacific Coast Airlines. They told her they could put her on a twelve o'clock flight.

She ran to the door and shouted for Jovida, who came running up the stairs. "Pack a few things for May Ling—nothing fancy, just play clothes and some sweaters. Put them in that suitcase over there. We're going up north to Napa."

"For how long?"

"I don't know."

"What shall I tell Mr. Hargasey?"

"I don't care. Tell him I don't care what you tell him. Tell him anything."

On the plane, May Ling said, "I like to go to Higate. I'm glad we're going there." She sat very primly next to Sally, a well-behaved little girl with black hair cut in bangs.

"I didn't think you remembered."

"I remember," May Ling said. "Will daddy be there?"

"I'm not sure. He went yesterday, and he's a very busy doctor. So I don't know whether he'll be there today."

"I hope he is."

Sally did not reply to that. She didn't know what she hoped. She felt that Joe would be on his way back to Los Angeles, and that would be better for everyone concerned. She had not seen Joe for six months, and when she saw him before that, they had nothing to say to each other. They were strangers who were married.

At San Francisco airport, Sally rented a car and drove to Napa. Over a year had passed since she had been home, and strangely, she could not remember why she stayed away. Her whole life now defied her memory. In America next to being President, the most was to be a movie star, and maybe it was, more than being President. Those were the gods and goddesses of the times, and like gods and goddesses, they huddled in their shrines and hid from the worshipers. Otherwise, they moved to an accompaniment of whispers and swiveling heads and other acts of worship. Now she was here, back where she had been before, and bit by bit, she began to remember who she was. She drove through the city, across the Golden Gate Bridge, through Marin County, with the round, dark hills cradling the road, and then through Sonoma.

"It's very pretty," the small dark girl by her side said. "Isn't it pretty, mommy?"

Long, long ago, before May Ling was old enough to understand words, Sally would write little poems to her, silly little poems. She tried to remember one of them, "Sally's baking cake. I don't care to bake, so I merely sit and watch her, making sure she doesn't botch her—job—no, that's not it."

"That's nice," May Ling said.

Today was the longest they had been together, side by side, in months, years? Sally tried to remember, then shook her head hopelessly. "We're in the valley now," she said to May Ling.

"I know."

Did she know? She was a wise little Chinese child. Yet she was only one quarter Chinese, and the rest was everything under the sun, English and Scotch-Irish and Italian and Jewish and French—all of it mixed up in this small, serious little girl.

She drove through the gates of the winery. May Ling got out of the car and stood in front of a big Airedale, unperturbed by the fact that the dog licked her face. Sally walked into her mother's house and into the kitchen. A moment later she was in Clair's arms. Was Joe still there?—telling herself that it was so simple if one can remember, if one can feel oneself. Clair said yes, he was still there. He was not leaving until tomorrow. Her grandchild watched the two of them.

"You and Billy," Clair asked directly, "were you to-gether—in love—how was it?" She had always been that way, direct and without embellishment.

"I think he loved me. I don't know. I don't seem to know much about anything. Where's Eloise?"

"In her house."

"I'll leave May Ling with you."

Sally went to Eloise.

"They all die," Eloise whispered. "The world is so sick. He was my brother and I hardly knew him. I cried a lot, but I cried for the little boy I remember."

"I know."

"What was he like? Isn't it sad? I have to ask you what he was like."

"I suppose he was the most decent man I ever met," Sally said. "He was a stranger here. Do you know what I mean?"

"I think so."

"He was a stranger on earth, and he made the best

of it. I don't know how else to put it." Sally began to cry, and the crying turned into racking sobs.

Eloise waited. "I didn't even know he went back into the army," Sally sobbed. "He walked away, and then the whole world forgot me. Why did they forget me? I didn't want to hurt anyone."

Only half aware of what lay behind her misery, Eloise cradled her and comforted her. Sally was alive. The dead didn't suffer. Eloise had hardly known her brother. Even in the years between the two wars she had seen him only twice. People laughed at him.

She asked desperately, "Why did people always laugh at Billy?"

"I never laughed at him," Sally said.

"I always felt that he was running away."

"Yes, he was."

They sat without speaking for a little while; and then Sally said she had to wash her face.

"Joe is here," Eloise said through the sound of running water.

"Yes, I know." She toweled her face, rubbing the skin fiercely.

"You look lovely," Eloise said, feeling she had to say something, that she could not stand there with Sally in silence. "You don't need make-up. I suppose you do when you make a movie."

She was not Sally; she was a film star. All the disconnected thoughts of Eloise, all her grief and half grief and guilt—all of it was skewered by her being alone in her house with a famous film star. Death had bewildered and upset her, and this thing upset and bewildered her even more.

"I'm Sally." It came almost harshly. "I'm your sister-in-law. I don't give a damn about movies!"

"You're angry. Did I make you angry? I'm sorry."

"Oh, no, no, darling. Not you, ever." She threw her arms around Eloise and kissed her. "You're like Billy, and Adam is the luckiest man in the world. I sometimes think he's the only lucky man in the world."

"So is Joe," Eloise said lamely.

"Why? Because he's married to a bitch?"

Eloise couldn't cope with her. Sally shook her head. "Can't I help?" Eloise pleaded, and suddenly Sally was overtaken by a mixture of envy and anger—envy mostly—of someone like this gentle, yielding woman who could not bear to see someone else in pain or frustration.

"No, I'll be all right, love, believe me. It's coming home that's so damn terrible, but you wouldn't understand that and I can't explain it. I have to be with myself for a little while, and then I'll be all right."

"But you'll stay? You won't go back right away?"

"I don't know," Sally said.

She almost bolted from Eloise's house. It was the house that Adam had built for his wife, quarry stone to match the old buildings of the winery, furniture upholstered in flowered chintz, curtains of dotted Swiss, hooked rugs on the floor—a house built to conform with everyone's notion of a muted American dream. Yet Sally forced herself to condition her contempt and confront it. Eloise was no fool. She probably knew more about modern art than anyone Sally had ever known, more than Jean, who had been her teacher. "Then what is it?" Sally asked herself. "Am I jealous? Am I afraid?"

She had not seen her father yet, nor did she want to see him right now. Jake and Adam were in one of the buildings of the winery. Sally began to climb the hillside between the rows of new-leafed vines. Back down below her, she could see Clair and May Ling and Eloise's two children. She thought her mother was calling her, but she wasn't sure; she ignored the drifting sound and climbed higher and higher toward a clump of eucalyptus that Jake and Clair had planted almost thirty years before. When she reached the cluster of trees, she saw Joe sprawled on the ground, his back to one of the trees.

She was amazed to see him. Somehow she had put it out of her mind that he was also at Higate; but to Joe it was even more of a surprise, and he stared at her speechlessly, as if she were not real and any word or response on his part would cause her to vanish.

She walked over to him. "Hello, husband," she said. Still Joe seemed unable to speak. "I took the plane to San Francisco and drove up here when I heard that Billy was dead. I brought May Ling with me. She's down there with mother."

Joe nodded dully and clambered to his feet. Sally noticed how bad his color was. He was pale and drawn. He had lost weight. "Did Frank call you?" he wondered.

"No, I got a letter from the doctor who took care of Billy. Billy asked him to write to me," she said deliberately. "Oh, this is great. We don't see each other for months, and it isn't even hello, Sally, I'm glad to see you."

"I am glad to see you."

"Now that I've prompted you." She turned on her heel.

"Where are you going?"

"Back down there. To collect the kid and go home. I don't belong here."

"Please—please wait," Joe said. "Please. Let's talk a little. Don't confront me like this and then run away. I can't stand that. Please don't."

She hesitated, wavered.

"Please, Sally. I love you more than anything on earth. If you walk away from me now, my life walks away. I'm not just saying that. I'm telling you the truth, and you know how hard it is for me to talk like this."

She didn't move. He went over to her and touched her very gently, very tentatively. Then he put his arms around her and she pressed her body against him, whispering, "Oh, Joey, you sweet dumb bastard. You never did a bad thing to me except screw up my whole rotten life."

"I guess that's the truth," he admitted. He held her, and they were both silent for a while, and then he said, "Let's sit down here and just talk a little and see if we can make some sense out of all this."

He sat down again with his back to a tree, and Sally leaned against him, pulling his arms around her. But the talk didn't come, and they sat there quietly as the afternoon light faded and a chill crept into the air.

"I keep saying it in my mind," he said at last, "but I know you can't quit."

"I don't know what it is, Joey. I keep trying to explain it in my mind so I could say it, but I can't. All I know is that when I go to the studio in the morning I'm alive, and I have to be alive. Other people don't, but I do. I don't give a damn about the rest of it—the idiot fans, the hoop-la, the fame. Believe me, I don't. It's reading a script and seeing it in your mind and knowing you can turn into the person they're writing about—and everything else stinks, and Beverly Hills, you can have it—but, Joey, I love acting so! I do love it!"

"Do you want to divorce me?"

"No. Oh, you're dumb, dumb. I love you. I want us

to live together and go to bed together and make love together, that's what I want."

"In Beverly Hills?"

"Joey, does that make any difference? Will one patient in your clinic suffer because you live in a house in Beverly Hills?"

"Where you pay the taxes and you pay the help and you pay the mortgage. Sally, I take a hundred dollars a week out of the clinic's funds. Frank takes the same. Do I let you support me?"

"Would that be so terrible? They pay me half a million dollars a picture now, not because I'm worth it. You're worth ten times what I'm worth, but that's the way it is in this crazy business. I could give half of what I earn to the clinic and still have enough to live on. I don't need money. I wear Levi's and work shirts, and they dress me at the studio—"

"And you live in a hundred-thousand-dollar house."

"Will you give it a try, please, Joey?"

"Let's stay here a few days and get to know each other again. Will you do that, Sally?"

"Yes."

"And then we'll see."

It was toward the end of her fifth week in prison, a few days after the first visiting day, that real depression set in, a thing Barbara had never experienced before. There had been times during her life when she had been depressed, anxious, overwhelmed by grief, but none of it had been like this. She ate only enough food to stay alive; she stopped caring. A core of indifference took over her being, and the world around her became totally bleak and meaningless. During the hours when she was not working in the garden or the greenhouse she lay on her cot, staring at the ceiling.

On the second day of this, Annie Lou Baker came into her room and pulled a chair up next to her bed.

"Honey child," the black woman said, "you got stir sickness, you got heavy time on you, and you got to come out of this or you never gonna build no time. Always comes with the visitors. God be praised, ain't no one gives a fuck about me. Trouble is, you been fighting your time ever since you come in here. I seen it. You don't build no time by fighting it. You got to look at them motherfuckers and say, They is the man and I is me. Don't make no difference them dry cunts sweettalk you and come off like ladies. They ain't no ladies. Hell, sister, what would a lady be doing in this shithole? Trouble with you, Bobby girl, is you never had your ass peeled before. You got class, and that makes doing time a heavy, heavy thing. But honey child, you done knocked five weeks out of the six months already. Six months. I could build me six months standing on one foot, but then, I is a nigger and you ain't, and that makes a difference. Another thing, you got to stop feeling you been put on. It eats you up. Me, I could figure the same thing. I get a call from this pimp to bring three floozies out to Vegas, and it is a federal rap for transporting working girls across the state line. Is that a pisshole thing or not? O.K., so I am here for two years. I need a rest. Don't work on it, girl, just don't work on it."

"I'll be all right," Barbara said.

"Only if you let yourself be all right. Who come to visit you?"

"My father."

"Big sonofabitch with white hair?"

"Yes."

"That's what does it. Every time."

Annie Lou left, and Barbara lay on her cot, wondering whether Annie Lou was right. She didn't realize that Annie Lou had struck a chord, that her own mind was occupied, and that the pit into which she had plunged was beginning to lighten. It was not what she thought about or what she wondered about, but simply that she could think or wonder. She thought about the visiting day and her increasing excitement as it approached. Ellie had warned her, "Sister, visiting days are like the man. They lean on you. They don't help." Barbara rejected the thought. She couldn't sleep the night before the visiting day, she was so eager to see her father, to talk to him, to hear all the news from his lips, to have him tell her how Sammy was, how her house was, how the city was—how, indeed, the world was.

And then the reaction and the depression began to set in even before Dan arrived, and when she finally did see him, all she could think about were the empty shipyards. The whole thing flashed into her mind as a formed symbol, the great, sprawling shipyards where Dan Lavette had built ships that saved the Allied cause, and now on the same island, in the same place, his daughter crucified. Of course Barbara did not consciously deal with it in that manner. She was sensible enough to know that the war would have taken much the same course even without Dan Lavette's shipyard, and that if the ships had to be built, someone else would have built them, nor was she sufficiently self-indulgent to see herself as a martyr crucified; nevertheless the symbol came and went, leaving its shadow, and when she saw Dan, she was so overwhelmed with self-pity that she had to fight to keep back her tears, and while she told herself that the pity was for her father, it was in fact self-pity, pure and simple, and it began the period of depression.

Dan and Barbara sat together in the visitors' room. That was not too bad; she could hold his hand in hers, touch it and examine it.

He looked at her sharply. "Are you all right, Bobby?"

"Yes, just fine, daddy."

"Is it awful?"

"No, it's pretty decent. Better than I could have imagined."

"How's the food?"

"Good. Quite good."

Afterward, back in San Francisco, Dan said to Jean, "The awful thing is that she didn't ask me anything."

"Didn't she ask about Sammy?"

"When I opened it up. When I told her how he was. Like when I told her about you or Joe. It kills me. Jean, it kills me! What the devil is wrong? What's happened to her? What have they done to her?"

"I don't think they've done anything to her, and from what you tell me, it's not a place where they do awful things to people. I think Barbara is very unhappy and quite depressed, and I can't say that I blame her. Poor child. I want to go down there, Dan, next time. If only she would let us bring Sam to see her."

"I'm not sure that would do any good."

It began with the visiting day, worsened day by day, and finally Barbara didn't go to work but lay in bed. Officer Davenport came into her room. "You're not sick, Barbara. The doctor says you're not sick."

"The doctor's an idiot," Barbara muttered.

"What did you say?" The heightened pitch of Officer Davenport's tones caused several inmates to pause by the open door and listen.

"I said the doctor's a fool."

"And I say you're shirking."

"Oh, get out of here and leave me alone."

"What!" Officer Davenport spread her legs, placed her hands on her hips, and faced Barbara. "Now you listen to me, you society bitch! If there's one thing I hate worse than reds, it's rich reds, and we have had just about enough of your classy, nose-in-the-air superiority. This is not a debutante stable," she said, mixing her metaphors, "so either you shape up or else."

To which Barbara replied, "Oh, fuck off!"

The gathering gallery in the hall burst into applause and laughter. Davenport exploded. Barbara's depression broke, and Captain Cooper said to her, "There is no way out of it this time. You want punishment, Barbara, and you'll find I can handle the situation very nicely."

For the next two weeks, Barbara cleaned toilets and took grim satisfaction in the work. For one thing, compared to being trapped in a deep depression, this was delightful. Of course, compared to other kinds of work, it was far from delightful. But on the other hand, there were certain fringe benefits that derived from her depression, from the incident with Davenport, and from her current status as toilet and shower room stewardess—namely, a new respect from the other inmates. Until now, only Annie Lou and Rosalie Conte had been relaxed and friendly with Barbara. The other inmates kept their distance. They were suspicious of her; she was a foreign creature, the way she moved, the way she spoke, the way she combed her hair. Even her crime was singular and defied their understanding. Now her encounter with Davenport cracked the walls that separated her from the others, and the way she cheerfully and without complaint scrubbed the porcelain pots and burnished the faucets in the toilets earned her respect. Toilets were the most hated job in the prison, yet day by day as she cleaned the toilets, Barbara's spirits rose. And it did not happen again. She emerged from the depression with the horrible memory of having been low and miserable enough to have taken her own life. It burst the bubble of the tremendous self-assurance that had been with her all her life.

Then one of the inmates discovered that the Barbara Lavette who had written a book that actually existed in the prison library was the same Barbara who here in jail was known as Barbara Cohen, or by the honorific TQ, toilet queen. It was Barbara's first book, the story of her experiences in France and Germany, and the book was passed from hand to hand and read until it began to fall to pieces. Her fellow prisoners might have been diffident or hostile or uneasy in approaching an actual author, but Barbara's position vis-à-vis yellow stains on the inside of a toilet bowl both complicated and simplified the place of a writer in the prison population. She began to realize more and more clearly that some light brushstrokes of modern penology do not change a prison into a girls' boarding school. Barbara was the only inmate charged with contempt of Congress; and it was her own small, personal triumph to be accepted and trusted by the murderers, thieves, whores, madams, forgers, and dopers.

If anyone had told her a year before that she could be in a position where she would suspend all the moral judgments of civilization, where acceptance by criminals as an equal and a friend would delight her, she would have rejected the notion as unlikely at best. It was many years before the women's movement burst upon the world, and even if Barbara had been preoccupied—which she had not been—with the role of women in society, she would have had no knowledge or any understanding of women who were criminals. She had never lived in or could have imagined a society where a third of the population was black, another third Mexican or Chicano, and still another third Caucasian, and where all had emerged from poverty and deprivation and ignorance.

Officer Davenport searched for additional toilets. She found one that had been abandoned for years. "I want this place to shine," she told Barbara. It took four hours, and Barbara left it shining. What with harsh detergents, cleanser, disinfectant, and the weeks of digging in the garden, her hands were red and rough, the nails broken, the skin toughened; but she had triumphed over the toilets. Captain Cooper returned her to the garden. "But walk carefully," Cooper said to her. "You pegged yourself as a troublemaker. I still haven't decided whether to dock your good time. What do you think?"

"I think it's up to you," Barbara said. "At this point, I truly don't give a damn. You can't hold me more than six months."

"I wouldn't be insolent if I were you. It doesn't pay off."

"I'm not bucking for honor status," Barbara said, "and I really don't give a damn what you do to me. I'll clean the toilets or mop the floors—whatever you say. That's up to you."

"What's eating you?" Captain Cooper asked. "This is a damned good institution. As jails go, it's as good as any in the world."

"That doesn't say much for the world, does it? Five thousand years ago, they discovered that if someone does something the top dogs don't like, you build a cell and lock them up, and in all the time since then, we haven't improved on it or found another way."

"Do you know a better way?"

"No, I don't. But I know this way stinks."

Barbara received a letter from Sally. "Joe tells me you don't want visitors," Sally wrote, "and I can't understand why. I want so much to see you. Joe and I are trying desperately to work things out, and we're living together again in the house in Beverly Hills, but it isn't easy. It seems so inane to even mention our problems to you when your own problem is so much greater. Anyway, we do have some hopes and we are trying. I'm on another picture now, and I'm trying to set my mind to give it up after this. But I don't know if that will work, Bobby, I'm so selfish." The letter went on for five pages of closely written script. Reading it in the evening in her tiny room, Barbara tried to feel it, to have a sense of Sally and Joe and their difficulties, but it was all so far away. Sally wrote of Billy Clawson's death, and Barbara felt sick with the waste of it, the hopelessness of it; yet she had hardly known Billy Clawson, and knowing him the little she had, had misjudged him. How many people she had misjudged! How very little of anything she had known, with all she had seen and all of her travels!

The night before, a woman named Reba Fleming, who was in prison for forging her endorsement on someone else's Social Security check, had slipped into Barbara's room after lights out and crawled into her bed. Reba was a buxom blonde of about forty-five. Barbara did not particularly like her, and for that reason she had bent over backward to be pleasant to her. Not too many of the inmates were pleasant to Reba, and she lived in a mournful envelope of self-pity. Now

Barbara, asleep a moment before, awakened to find Reba in her bed, caressing her and pleading with her to make love and be made love to. A month before, Barbara would have reacted with annoyance and disgust. Now she found herself wishing that she could satisfy this stout, dull woman's desperate need for sex and love and sympathy.

"It's all right, Reba," she said, holding her. "Just lie here. It's all right."

She thought of this, sitting with Sally's letter. She would have to answer it—but not now, not tonight. Tonight she had to write to her father and mother, who were insistent that they both come to see her.

"It's so hard for me to say, don't come," she wrote. "I don't really know how to explain that I don't want any more visitors. When I first learned that I would have to go to prison, the most important thing I could think of was whether I would be allowed to have visitors. There are women here who never have visitors, and it's a heartbreaking thing, they're so sad and unhappy over it; but the real cause of their sadness is that they have no one outside to visit them. That's the root of it. I'm different. I have so many people outside who love me, and I think both of you know how much I love you, so you will not think I don't love you when I ask you not to come here. Being here is something I must do alone and get through alone. Visitors make it so hard. I try to forget the outside world." She paused in her writing, then added, "I have made many friends here. As strange as it may sound, I have never been closer to women. I don't know if any of it can survive outside, but in here it's good."

As time went by, the inmates turned to her more and more frequently. She was their neutral ground, their umpire, their adjudicator; and the more Barbara became the butt of the officers' venom and resentment, the more trusted and resorted to she was by the prison population. Very slowly, bit by bit, the women in the prison came to realize that Barbara was there because she wished to be there, that her freedom could have been purchased at the price of a few words. It was nothing she ever explained or referred to, yet it percolated through the population. They needed no complex explanations of the role of the informer. They understood it only too well. They brought their sorrows to her, their fights with each other, their dreams, their guilt, and their stories. After all, she was a writer, and as a writer, they decided, it was her obligation as well as her vocation to listen.

And listen she did—to an endless, sordid tale of poverty, of human souls squeezed dry, of love given and betrayed, of love given and rejected, of women beaten by their husbands, of women once children and beaten by mother and father, of prostitution, of pimping, of murder, of every conceivable form of brutality—and she listened.

Her marvelous, youthful beauty faded. At thirty-five, she still had the bloom of twenty-five; at thirty-six she looked her age. Her face, burned brown by the sun from her hours in the garden, leaner, the first lines marking it, the first tiny wrinkles around her eyes. She was healthy. She was never sick after that initial bout of depression; and if she was not happy, she was for the most part content.

Jean held that she was at an age, considering her life, where nothing could surprise her, but she admitted afterward that she was taken entirely by surprise when her son's wife, Lucy Sommers Lavette, walked into the gallery. Eloise, sitting at a tiny table and working on their catalogue, looked up and saw Jean's expression; she said later that if there had been sound to accompany the look, she would have been certain that the second earthquake had arrived. Fortunately, Dan was not present; he was over at Fisherman's Wharf, where he and Sam were polishing the brass on Dan's new boat—or at least so Jean thought, not knowing what else they could do for hours in a boat tied to a mooring. Dan had not seen either Tom or his wife since their encounter in Tom's office, and Jean was not at all certain how he would react if he came face to face with either of them.

She had to admit that Lucy's appearance had changed for the better, thinking that it could hardly have changed for the worse. Her hair had been cut short, her make-up was professional, and Jean recognized her beige cashmere as a valid Balenciaga.

Jean greeted her pleasantly, with just the proper slight touch of condescension, as if to remind her that in the old days, a Sommers might associate with a Seldon during business hours, but a social relationship would be unlikely. "What brings you here, Lucy?" Jean asked her.

"Curiosity, I suppose. And paintings. Everyone's talking about your gallery."

"And what are they saying?" Jean asked.

"I'm afraid people feel you're ahead of your time."

"But that's rather nice, to be ahead of one's time. Are you looking for a painting, Lucy?"

"Well, Tom and I are only beginning to acquire things. We thought it would be nice to have a Picasso. Or a Cézanne."

Jean and Eloise exchanged looks. "I'm afraid we don't have a Cézanne," Jean said. "There are very few of them, you know. You might find one for sale in

New York or Paris, although I haven't heard of any. We do have one interesting Picasso—I believe he did it in nineteen twelve, when he was working with Braque. You know, around that time, he and Braque were composing pictures that consisted of flat areas superimposed upon a diversified surface. It was very experimental but quite beautiful if you know how to look at it. If I'm not mistaken"—she turned to Eloise— "they did invent the collage, didn't they, Eloise?"

"As far as I know, they did. They laid the groundwork for the Dadaists, who followed them."

"Why don't you bring it out?" Jean suggested.

Eloise went to the back and returned with the painting, which measured about twenty-four by thirty inches, and placed it on the easel.

Lucy stared at it for a few minutes, then asked, "What is it? I mean, what does it represent?"

"I don't think one sees it that way," Jean replied tolerantly. "One sees it in terms of space and color, arrangements of space and color—" She paused to glance at Eloise.

"Very much in the style of Braque," Eloise said pointedly.

"Oh, yes, very much in the style of Braque. Of course, Lucy, it's very much in the eye, the tutored eye and the untutored eye. I would certainly not try to sell a picture like this to the wife of some nouveau whose husband would turn on her in wrath. But Tom was brought up with good paintings, or so I like to tell myself. Of course, my instinct would be to give it to you, but unfortunately Eloise here is my partner— you do know Eloise?"

"I don't think we've ever met," Lucy said stiffly.

"In any case, it's a splendid painting."

"And how much are you asking for it?"

"Three hundred thousand dollars," Jean said blandly.

Eloise turned away and clasped her hands tightly.

"You can't be serious!" Lucy exclaimed.

"Oh, I am, indeed."

"I don't understand this, Mrs. Lavette. I really don't understand it at all, unless you take me for an utter fool. I was reading only last week where they sold three Picassos at Parke-Bernet in New York, and the highest price was thirty-seven thousand."

"My dear, there are Picassos and Picassos."

"Well, I certainly have no intention of paying three hundred thousand for that ridiculous painting."

"I understand," Jean said gently. "One should never purchase a painting one doesn't love, and since I know your reaction to it, I'll be the first to say no, Lucy, it's not for you."

After Lucy had marched out of the gallery, Jean and Eloise stood and stared at each other. Finally Eloise said, "Oh, you're wicked, Jean. You are so wicked."

"Ha!" Jean exclaimed. "I am wicked? If ever there was a case of the pot calling the kettle black! Who was it marched back there so calmly and came out with that silly Braque collage?"

"Only because I expected you to explain to her that we don't have a Picasso and that Braque was a close associate of his in those days."

"Eloise, your golden locks will turn purple if you lie like that. Did you say it was a Braque?"

"You're the senior partner. Jean, after all, you did go into a detailed explanation, and it was you who told her the price was three hundred thousand. Suppose she had bought it? Suppose she had said yes? Would you have sold it to her?"

"What are we asking for it?"

"Fourteen thousand. But hold on; my dear Jean, didn't you tell me to go back there and bring out the Picasso?"

"We're neither of us to be trusted, are we? Would I have sold it to her? I think I would have—just to see what would happen when, as Dan would put it in his own inimitable manner, the shit hit the fan. Ah, well, perhaps we're better off this way. We don't have the three hundred thousand but we do have our integrity."

It was a night when Barbara could not sleep. She had not imagined that she would be nervous when this night came, but the others had warned her. "It is a bad night," Annie Lou had said to her. "It is a night when you is sure you is going to die." And it was. She was afraid to sleep; if she slept, she could die sleeping and never know.

The hours were endless. For months time had been her enemy; now time, in its last spasm of anger and resistance, stood still; and Barbara cringed, surrendered her defiance, and pleaded for the night to be over. With surrender came a sort of half-sleep, and when she awakened, the first gray of dawn was in the sky. She rose, made her bed for the last time, washed, combed her hair, and walked quietly through the dark barracks out into the open. She walked across the exercise ground to the sea wall and stood in the misty dawn, watching the sunrise. A tugboat came steaming by slowly, dragging a barge behind it. A man on the barge waved to her, and she waved back. The sea breeze was cold and clean on her face. In the light of day, her fears were dissipating. She examined her hands. She had cut her nails carefully; they were short but clean. The red soreness had worked out of her hands; they were hard and brown. The day before, the girls in the beauty salon, where they were taught hair dressing and skin care, had done her hair. On her little finger was a silver ring, a gift from Ellie, who had pleaded with her to accept it.

She heard a step and turned to see Captain Cooper, who joined her at the sea wall and stood looking out over the harbor. After a moment, Cooper said, "Well, Barbara, it's not the worst place in the world, is it?"

"It's a prison."

"So it is. We have prisons. There's nothing you or I can do about that. I like to think that it's better than most."

"I imagine it is."

"It's been a strange experience for you, hasn't it?"

"Very strange."

"It's an odd thing for me to say, Barbara, but I will say it. I'm glad they sent you here and not somewhere else."

"Thank you."

"Have your breakfast. Then go to admissions. They'll give you your clothes and your paycheck."

"Paycheck?"

"We do pay wages, not much but still something. We're not a slave labor camp. Is someone coming for you?"

"My father. I asked him to be at admissions at ten o'clock."

"That will give you enough time." Cooper thrust out her hand, and Barbara took it.

Barbara picked up her basket of clothes at the admissions desk and walked slowly back to her room. A cluster of inmates were waiting for her, ignoring Officer Hurley. "Break it up!" Hurley was saying. "Come on now, break it up, or I'll put you all on report."

They were embracing Barbara. "Bug off with that shit, Hurley," Annie Lou whispered, hugging Barbara. "What the fuck do I do without you, honey child? You are the only black white woman in the joint."

"Now this is the last damn time I tell you to break this up!" Hurley shouted.

"Oh, I am going to miss you, Officer Hurley, you and Officer Davenport," Barbara said. "But I shall dream about you. You'll be right there in all my nightmares."

It was a poor joke but they loved it, and they broke away laughing and giggling. "You don't give up, do you?" Hurley said to Barbara. "Jailhouse smartass right to the end."

"Right to the end."

"Well, don't ever forget that you've been here, lady bountiful. You can tell that to your classy San Francisco friends."

"Oh, I shall," Barbara agreed, and unable to resist, she added, "And do you know what else? I shall tell them that while I am gone, you, my dear, are still here—with a life sentence." Then she fled into her room, slamming the door behind her, upset because she had allowed herself to be provoked. But the mood passed, and she was overtaken by a sort of melancholy. "Good God," she said aloud, "I really think I'm reluctant to leave this place, and that is absolutely crazy." Yet she knew that she had found something there that she had never found anywhere else. "Well, it's over. That's the main thing."

She stripped off her prison clothes for the last time and stuffed them into her pillowcase. Then she dressed herself in the same white blouse and gray flannel suit that she had worn when she arrived. The clothes were loose. According to the scale, she had lost only a few ounces, but her whole body must have tightened up. She wondered whether her shoes would fit after months of wearing oversized clogs. The shoes were tight but not too uncomfortable. The heels, however, were strange, and they took some getting used to.

Looking at herself in the mirror, she faced a stranger. "Barbara," she said very seriously, "you will simply have to get used to the way I am now. I have served my time and paid my debt to society. I have no apologies to make."

Dan was in the waiting room at admissions when Barbara entered, and he took her in his arms.

"Poor daddy," she whispered. "I never gave you an easy time of it, did I?"

Driving to the ferry, Dan said, "This is a rental. We drop it at the airport and make the noon plane. Sammy is with Jean, waiting in your house. That's the way you wanted it, isn't it?"

"Just the way I wanted it, daddy. It couldn't be more perfect."

At a few minutes past two o'clock, Barbara opened the door of her house on Green Street and walked into the living room. Jean had been reading to Sam, who was seated on the couch next to her. When he saw Barbara, he leaped off the couch and started toward her. Then he paused, staring at her. His face wrinkled and the tears started. She went down on her knees and embraced him.

"You won't go away again?"

"Never," she said, "Never, never, my darling."

PART SIX

Memory

Some say that since the nature of God is unknowable, He takes visible form in terms of worship. Norman Drake paid off his taxicab and stood in front of Tom Lavette's residence, the old Sommers mansion, in an attitude of respectful obeisance. In all truth, it was less the house that he worshipped than what it stood for. His wife, however, would have been quite content with the house.

His wife was not his most enthusiastic admirer. When the business of Barbara Lavette had first occurred, she had said to him in no uncertain terms, "You are a fool. With the whole country to choose from, you pick the Lavette family."

When he dined with Tom and Lucy and reported back to her, she said, "Are you an idiot? Why didn't you tell them that you would drop the whole thing?"

"They didn't want me to. The truth is, he doesn't give a damn about his sister."

"Coming from anyone else, I might believe that."

He had undertaken, in the course of years, two plaintive liaisons with sympathetic women in Washington, a city with no shortage of sympathetic women, and in each case, he had evaded divorce with the plea that it would destroy his political career. Then he

gave up sympathetic liaisons for a tolerable relationship with a blowsy woman who worked in his Washington Office. His wife found out about it. "Can you
give me one good reason why I shouldn't divorce
you?" she demanded of him.

"One, yes—I think," he begged her. He could be
humble and beseeching.

"Just let me hear it, and if it concerns your political
career, you can take it and stuff it. I am past giving a
damn about your political career."

"I don't think you should say that," he pleaded. "I
mean, it is my political career, but it goes beyond
that. I think I have a chance to be vice president."

"You are out of your mind."

But he was able to convince her that he was not
entirely out of his mind, and tonight, standing outside
of the Lavette mansion, he was a good deal closer to
the incredible goal of vice president. His wife might
have asked herself with some cynicism why they had
chosen him; for himself, he could find reasons. He felt
he had resources that had never been tapped, a
breadth of understanding he had never put to use,
and above all, imagination. He felt certain of that. He
did have imagination.

Well, this was not the time to indulge in dreams.
Whatever the decision would be, whatever Lavette's
hints would lead to, tonight would provide him with
definite answers. He had been assured of that.

He pulled the iron chain that hung from one jamb
of the ornate doors and heard the gong echo throughout the house. No cheap electric doorbells here. A
butler opened the door and took his hat and coat.

"The gentlemen are in the library, Mr. Drake," he
said. "They are expecting you."

He followed the butler, swallowing nervously, and then trying not to swallow. His doctor had warned him that this nervous swallowing of air was the chief cause of his flatulence, and flatulence was the last thing he desired tonight.

Tom Lavette rose to greet him as he entered the library. Seated comfortably around the room, some with cigars and brandy, were six men.

"Good of you to come and join us, Drake," Tom said, as if there had been an alternative to his coming there tonight. "I'll introduce you. This is Joseph Langtrey. Congressman Drake." Langtrey nodded without rising. "Mark Fowler," Tom said.

"Evening, Drake," Fowler said. They knew each other. Fowler rose slowly, offering his hand.

"Ira Cunningham," Tom said.

"Just so you know where the chips are stacked, young feller," Cunningham said, "I am president of Lakeland Steel. Mr. Langtrey runs the First New York City Trust Company, and Louis d'Solde over there has a finger in half the chemical companies in this country."

"I think you know Mr. Culpepper and Mr. McGinnis," Tom said.

If he didn't know them personally, he knew very well who they were and what they represented. He took the seat that Tom indicated. He accepted brandy and a cigar, which he left unlit. And he waited.

McGinnis was talking about Kuwait and its oil resources. He had four hundred million dollars invested there, and he was wondering how the new State of Israel was going to affect the whole balance of oil and nationalism. Drake followed the conversation that came out of this, waiting from moment to moment for them to ask his opinion. But they didn't, and finally Culpepper turned to him and said, almost casually, "Lavette here thinks you'd be a good bet for the vice presidency. Do you want the job?"

"Yes, sir, I do. But then, won't it depend on who'll be President. I mean, who'll be the candidate, his choice?"

"Our choice," said McGinnis.

"How clean are you?" Fowler asked. "I don't mean women or little peccadilloes. I mean fraud. How clean are your campaign funds? I'm not going to ask whether you ever took a bribe. What is there on paper? What kind of bank deposits are there that you can't account for?"

"I've been scrupulous about my bank deposits, and there's nothing on paper that could be embarrassing."

"What about Internal Revenue?" Langtrey asked him. "Do they audit you?"

"Not for the past four years, no, sir."

"Well, you will request an audit. As soon as possible. Providing you can come out of it clean."

"I can. No problem in that direction."

"You have a safe deposit box?"

"Yes, sir."

"What do you keep there?"

"I have some bonds and stock certificates."

"No cash?"

He hesitated, then nodded. "Yes, some cash."

"How much?"

"About eighteen thousand."

"Get rid of it."

"How?"

"How the devil do I know? Give it to your wife. Spend it. Spread it around—a few hundred here, a few hundred there. Buy her a fur coat."

"What's the situation with your wife? Do you get along?"

"Oh, yes, it's a good marriage."

"And your kids? No fancy escapades?"

"Oh, no. They're fine kids."

"Now understand us," Fowler said. "If we win the election and you stand in as Vice President, it's a dry run, so to speak, a test run. The future will depend on how you conduct yourself, and the future means the top job. Do you follow me?"

"I think so."

"As far as this House committee of yours is concerned, we've had enough of it. It's meaningless and nonproductive, and the same goes for McCarthy's shenanigans. You'll change the image. I think the less subpoenas from here on in, the better. Now there are certain things we are interested in, not only for our good but for the good of the nation. McGinnis there wants to unlock the offshore oil. We need it. Louis is deeply interested in the advancement of the space program. Lavette wants transcontinental and European franchises. Cunningham is worried about the growing bias against new aircraft carriers. These are only indications. There's no point in going through a detailed list tonight. Plenty of time for that. The only thing we are really interested in this evening is an area of understanding. Do we have it?"

"I would say we do," Drake agreed.

After Drake left, Fowler said to Tom, "I do hope your judgment stands up, Lavette. I don't like that little sonofabitch."

"I think," Tom said, "he has the quality of loyalty that you would find in a well-trained whipped dog. I can't think of anyone else down there in Washington who could be purchased as completely. Also, for reasons I must confess I don't understand, he is one hell of a vote-getter. Apparently the people who do the voting love him."

"I don't love him," Culpepper said. "When I think of that man as potentially President of the United States, I wonder what in hell this country is coming to."

That night in bed, having given Lucy a blow-by-blow account of what had taken place in the library, Tom said, "After all, Lucy, we haven't done too badly, our little combination of Lavette, Seldon, and Sommers. We're still the smallest apple in the basket, but we're in there, aren't we?"

"It goes further than that, Thomas. We shall one day have shares in the man who runs the most powerful nation on earth. It's not simply owning a politician—it's owning the whole beautiful thing." She reached out and touched him tenderly. "That is power."

Suddenly, he was away from her, lost in his own thoughts.

"Tom?"

"Yes." He stared at her.

"Ugly little beast, but he's all ours."

"Yes."

"What on earth—you are pleased, aren't you?"

"I suppose so."

"What's eating you now?" She was irritated. It was her triumph. She wanted it to be his as well.

"It doesn't matter."

"Dan Lavette?" she asked softly.

"He's my father."

"Tom, we've been all through that. He had to find out. Anyway, he doesn't mean a damn thing to you."

"You really believe that?"

"According to you," she said. "According to you.

And as for Barbara, you didn't send her to prison. That was her own choice."

"In all my life," Tom said tiredly, "in all my goddamn stupid life, there was only one thing I wanted and couldn't have. I had all the rest—everything except a nod from that cold bastard who calls himself my father. If once, if only once he had looked at me and spoken to me the way a father does to a son—"

"Oh, stop it." Lucy was annoyed. "It's been a good day. What are you doing to it?"

"I don't hate him."

"You're being a damn fool." She turned off the light and rolled over on her side.

Tom lay awake, a line putting itself together in his mind—the last line of some book he had read long, long ago, when he had been at Princeton: "Of such is the kingdom of heaven."

Alexander Hargasey was taken ill on the set of a film he was directing, and four hours later he died. He was overweight and in poor physical condition, and he was struck down by a massive coronary. By the time Sally arrived at the hospital he was dead, and Sally sat in the hospital waiting room and wept as she had never wept before. She was in the third month of pregnancy. She had loved Hargasey. He had been surrogate father, confessor, teacher and good friend. Whispering to herself that boy or girl, this child would be called Alexander, she surrendered to a grief that was real and unadorned with any of her romantic trimmings. She had never truly faced life and she had never confronted death as it must be confronted, as the end of something, as a cruel hole in her mind that could not be evaded or healed.

Joe went with her to the funeral. He had his own

memories of the director, a fat, bald comical character; he listened to Sally's estimate of the man, and not without a degree of awe and shame. "He was a good man," Sally said. "It was a kind of decency that I don't even understand because I don't have it. Not a shred of it."

"I liked him," Joe pleaded, reminding Sally that he had met Hargasey years before, when Hargasey had commissioned Dan Lavette to build him a yacht. She was thinking that he blamed Hargasey.

"I will not make a picture with anyone else. Never. I'm through. So it doesn't matter what you think of Alex Hargasey. I'm through with it."

Joe took her home and went on to the clinic. Later that day, at six o'clock in the evening, he returned to the house in Beverly Hills and found Sally sitting in the semidarkness of her bedroom.

"Are you all right?" Joe asked her.

"Sure. I've been thinking."

"Did you mean what you said before? About never making another film?"

"I'm pregnant."

"What!"

"It's all right. It's perfectly normal. I'm in my third month."

"Are you certain?"

"Yes, I'm quite certain, Joe. I went to Dr. Brimmer at the studio. I've had the tests."

"Do you want the baby, Sally?"

"It's my baby. What do you think?"

"I think it's good. But I don't understand about the movies. God, we've talked so much about it and what it means to you. How can you stop something that means so much to you?"

"Because it doesn't mean that much anymore." Then she began to cry again.

"Sally, please, don't cry."

"I'm not crying for Alex now," she managed to say. "I'm crying for myself. Oh, I feel so rotten, Joe, so lost and so frightened. I'm here, and I don't know what I'm doing here. I don't know how I got here. Joey," she said pleadingly, "I want to go home."

"Sure. We'll go up to Napa for a few days. If you want to, you can stay there for a few weeks with May Ling."

"I don't mean that. I want to go back there for good, and I want you to come with me. Please, please, Joey. You can open an office in Napa. Or in Oakland, if you want to. There are just as many poor, sick people in Oakland as there are here. But I can't stay here. I want three or four kids. I want to be a human being. I want to be able to walk down the street without everyone turning to look and whisper about me. Please, Joey."

"What about the house?"

"We'll sell the house. The hell with the house! Don't you understand? My own daughter's a stranger to me. I don't want kids who are strangers."

"I've put so much into the clinic—"

"Joey, let's try to save ourselves. We're part of the human race, aren't we? And the clinic will survive. Just say that you'll give it a try—because if we miss out now—"

He shook his head unhappily.

"Please. Just give it a try."

He was broodingly silent. He promised nothing. He simply muttered, "O.K. I'll try."

* * *

Barbara's decision to go to Israel was very sudden, not anticipated even in her offhand thoughts. Simply her having been away from Sam for so long should have precluded it. Jean took it as a whim.

"Why now?" Jean asked her. "Oh, I know you must be restless after those hideous months in prison. But haven't you been separated from Sam long enough?"

"It would only be ten days at the most."

"Why?"

"I don't know why. Maybe to lay a flower on Bernie's grave. Maybe to see what my husband died for."

Or to find an answer when she didn't know the question. In New York, at Idlewild Airport between planes, she was ready to cancel her passage to Europe and return to California. But she talked herself out of that, and instead she telephoned San Francisco and spoke to Sam. "Am I going to live with granny always?" Sam asked plaintively.

"No, no, no, darling. I'll be back next week."

"But you promised me you wouldn't go away again. You promised. You know you did."

At that moment she almost decided to take the next plane home. But she did not, and the following morning she was in London. Just before noon, she took off in an El Al plane on the final leg of her flight to Tel Aviv.

The man sitting next to Barbara struck up a conversation with her. An Israeli, he was in his seventies, urbane, spoke excellent English, and he introduced himself as Aaron Cohen. He informed her that he owned a bookstore in Tel Aviv, and when she told him that she was Barbara Lavette, he responded with recognition and pleasure. "Of course. I should have recognized you from your picture. I sold a good many of your books."

"In Hebrew? I wasn't translated into Hebrew."

"Oh, no, in English. We sell a great many English books. But there's no reason why you shouldn't be translated into Hebrew, and I can do something about that. But what brings you to Israel? Curiosity? Or are you working on a book about us? You're not Jewish, are you?"

"No. My husband was. His name was the same as yours."

"It's a common Jewish name. Is this your first trip to Israel?"

"Yes."

"You say 'my husband *was*.' Are you divorced? Or a widow?"

Barbara told him what had prompted her trip, insomuch as she knew what had prompted it. Cohen listened thoughtfully, then nodded.

"I think I understand," he said.

"Do you, Mr. Cohen? I'm not sure I do."

"Well, it's not a very pleasant thing to say, but death is a finality. Or it should be. Life must go on. You're a prisoner of your husband's death. I think you must free yourself."

"That's a strange thing to say."

"Have I hurt your feelings?"

"I'm not sure. I'm not sure of very much at all, and the truth is I'm not really sure what brought me here. Every step of the way I was on the edge of changing my mind."

"Where is your husband buried?" Cohen asked.

She opened her purse and took out her notebook. She remembered the name; it was the pronunciation she was unsure of. "It's called Kiryat Anavim."

"Oh? Yes, I know the place. It's a kibbutz on the

road to Jerusalem—that is, on the Tel Aviv road to Jerusalem. You do know what a kibbutz is?"

"A sort of commune?"

"Yes. This one, Kiryat Anavim, is rather old and large, and I think they do have their own military cemetery, but you know, that would be only for their own people—I mean for the boys of the kibbutz who were killed during the war. You say your husband was killed somewhere to the east of Haifa?"

"On the road to Megiddo? I'm not sure."

"In forty-eight?"

"Yes."

"Well, things were very confused then. I've never seen the cemetery at Kiryat Anavim, but it can't be very large. It's a pleasant place. But then, I'm biased. I feel that the Judean Hills are the most wonderful place on earth."

"How will I get there?" Barbara asked him.

"It's very simple. We're a tiny country. Just take a taxi outside your hotel. Where are you staying, by the way?"

"I have reservations at the Dan Hotel."

"Yes, very nice. On the shore. There will be taxis outside of the hotel. From the hotel to the kibbutz, it's about an hour and a half. If you don't plan to stay too long, the driver will wait."

Like most people, Barbara had her preconceived notions of Israel. Knowing that Tel Aviv had been founded by a handful of Jews on the sand dunes of the Mediterranean shore less than half a century before, she was more prepared to see a tentative, frontier sort of place than the enormous, throbbing, modern city that greeted her.

After she had unpacked her single small bag,

bathed, and changed clothes, she left the hotel to walk. It was still only noontime, and it struck her that she could hire one of the taxis in front of the hotel and complete her mission before the day was over. But now that she was here in Israel, her mission appeared to her to be meaningless and she could make no sense out of the fact that she had come eight thousand miles to look at her husband's grave.

Walking down Frishman Street from the Dan, she came to Dizengoff, turned left, and walked along the broad avenue with the whole world meandering along around her, boys and girls and young soldiers with rifles slung over their shoulders, old men and old women, black people and white people, Jews, Arabs, Christians—every face mankind had ever made for itself, short, tall, fat, thin, everything that was human—an easygoing, unhurried mixture not quite like anything she had ever seen anywhere else.

She bought a frankfurter in a roll and a bottle of Israeli beer and sat down at a small wrought-iron table in one of the many cafés that line Dizengoff. The beer was good, and suddenly ravenously hungry, she ate a second frankfurter.

Better now, her hunger gone, Barbara sat there on Dizengoff and tried to have a sense of this place, a feeling of this place. Like so many white Protestant Americans, she granted Jews and being Jewish a peculiar position in her thinking. The thinking was always prefaced by a denial: "I am totally indifferent to whether someone is Jewish or not." Only it was never just someone. A Pole or a Russian or a Hungarian or even an Englishman could have been someone. Jews were specific. Jews were the reality of what she had experienced in Nazi Germany. A Jew was the man

who had shared her bed and who became her wedded
husband. A Jew was her father's partner. Jake Levy
had been Jewish. Sally was part Jewish. If she saw her
life as a fabric, it would be woven through and
through with Jewish threads. Barbara's mother had
conquered her own anti-Semitism by ceasing to refer
to anyone as Jewish. She simply Christianized a whole
people and left it there; sitting in Tel Aviv, Barbara
began to giggle at the realization. Jean was wonderful. Why couldn't she be like her mother? But suppose,
she asked herself, Jean was here, recognizing that this
was a Jewish country? Ah, well, Jean would solve it.
Jean solved things. Tom solved things. Even Sally and
Joe came to a working arrangement. That left Barbara. Barbara solved nothing, finished nothing, concluded nothing. Was her father the same way? she
wondered. Did the two of them sit on the edge of the
world looking at it, the way she now sat at a table on
Dizengoff?

For the tenth or twentieth or fiftieth time, Barbara
asked herself why she had come and what she was
doing here. Surely she was in no need of an emotional
bath, and the picture that arose in her mind's eye, the
picture of herself kneeling by Bernie's grave and placing flowers on it, was so sentimental and fraudulent
that she turned away from it in anger and exaspera-
tion. She got up, paid her bill, and walked with long
strides back to the Dan Hotel. She was now self-
confessed, she felt, and whatever scales had clouded
her eyes had fallen off. She was entirely occupied by
a fine liberal rage at all of those who fracture the
world and mankind into nations and races and reli-
gions. She herself would not stoop to it. She had seen
enough of war and death and suffering to abhor this

whole business of Jew and Gentile. She had married a
man. He was a man, a member of the human family, a
tall, easygoing, capable human being. In some way
she could not entirely comprehend, he had understood
her and had been able to give her some moments of
great happiness. Now he was dead. That too was a
part of existence. She was not the only widow in the
world. But in his case the mythology, as she saw it
now, of this place, this Israel, was the force that had
killed him. Well, whatever it was, she would not indulge it. She had made a mistake in coming here; she
would not add to the mistake by performing the sentimental journey to the cemetery. She would return to
the hotel, pack her things, and go back to America
where she belonged. And without guilt. She had done
her share to make this snake pit men called civilization a little more tolerable. She would not succumb to
guilt.

She was back in her room at the hotel, packing her
suitcase, when the door opened and the chambermaid
entered with fresh towels. She was a small, wizened
woman who smiled tentatively at Barbara and said,
"Are you leaving? But you just came." Her English
was heavily accented, and it occurred to Barbara that
it was a French accent rather than Israeli. Looking at
her more closely, Barbara noticed the number tattooed on her forearm.

"Yes, I'm leaving," Barbara replied.

"You just come—this morning."

Angry with herself, with the whole world, provoked
at herself for succumbing to a sentimental notion that
took her away from her son after being separated
from him for six long months, Barbara found herself
resenting the intrusiveness of the chambermaid. They

were like that, aggressive, pushy; and where else in
the whole world would a chambermaid pry into the
business of a guest she did not know? And then the
thought itself sickened her. How, how could she think
in such terms? What was wrong with her? All this little woman had done was to reach out to another human being with a question, and in her mind Barbara
had rejected her, condemned her in terms of the most
vulgar racism. It did not matter to her that she had
not spoken the words. The thought was sufficient to
make her feel that she should beg the chambermaid's
forgiveness; yet if she did that, it would only make
matters worse.

The chambermaid put the towels in the bathroom.
She was turning to leave.

"Please don't go. Stay a moment," Barbara said.
"Can you?"

The chambermaid paused and stared at her.

"Are you all right, miss?"

Barbara dropped down onto the bed and clenched
her hands. "Yes—yes, I'm all right."

"I bring something—maybe a cup tea."

"You're French," Barbara said.

"Yes. How you know?"

"Your accent." And in French, Barbara said, "Can
we talk in French? It's so long since I've spoken to
anyone in French?"

The wrinkled face broke into a smile. "How very
nice to see a Frenchwoman here. We don't get many
French guests in the hotel."

"I'm not French. I'm American," Barbara said.

"But your French is perfect."

"No, hardly. I lived in France for years. But I'm
rusty now. Can you stay a moment or two? I want so
much to talk to someone, and that's the worst of it

when you travel alone. There's no one to talk to. Can
you stay a few minutes?"

"Yes. Surely."

"Please sit down," Barbara said. "My name is Barbara Cohen."

The chambermaid nodded eagerly and seated herself on the edge of a chair, sitting very straight, as if
to take the edge off the intimacy of sitting down. "I'm
glad. My name is Annette Tilman. I mean I'm glad
you're Jewish. Or American. I don't feel warmly toward the French."

"I'm not Jewish. My husband was Jewish."

"Oh."

"You don't like the French?" Barbara asked. "But
you're French."

"I'm Jewish. Now I'm Israeli."

Barbara didn't know what to say to that, and for a
moment or two they sat in silence. Then, suddenly,
the chambermaid said, "How old do you think I am?"

The question was a trap. Barbara felt defensive and
bewildered. Why was she sitting here talking to a
chambermaid? Why wasn't she arranging for her passage on the first plane out? She felt that she was
being ensnared, and there was a touch of something
woeful in her face as she stared at the chambermaid.
How old was this woman? The face was seamed, and
next to the chin was a row of welts, scars. Had she
ever been a beautiful woman? The face was battered
and broken and as wrinkled as old leather. Only the
pale blue eyes staring out of it made it something else
than ugly.

"I don't know, really—I can't guess ages," Barbara
said, thinking that the woman was at least sixty, but
at the end of sixty years of suffering.

"Yes, you have a heart, Madame Cohen. You are

very young and beautiful. I'm not envious. I am alive.
My health is not bad. I live here in the land of Israel.
I enjoy my work, and each day my Hebrew improves.
I shall tell you how old I am. Twenty-nine years. You
don't believe me? Credit the Gestapo. I don't speak
about these things, ever, but you appeared so upset,
so astonished because I said that I do not feel warmly
toward the French. We lived in Rouen. I had a husband, two children, a mother, a father, three sisters,
and a brother. I also had two nephews and a niece
and a very old grandmother." She held up her hand
and began to count on her fingers. "We count. Myself,
but I am alive. We count with my husband, one, two,
three, four, five, six, seven, eight, nine, ten, eleven,
twelve, thirteen. All dead, turned in by our good
French neighbors to the Gestapo. So I hate the
French with all my heart. But that is stupid, isn't it? I
don't understand people, even myself, because all I
can think about right now is how pleasant it is to sit
here and talk to a nice lady like you in my own language. And meanwhile, who does my work?" She
leaped to her feet. "I do my work. Who else?"

She smiled apologetically and left the room. Barbara sat on the bed, staring at the door. Then she unpacked for the second time, and went downstairs and
had some dinner.

At eight o'clock the following morning, dressed in
an old gray flannel skirt, a sweater, and comfortable
shoes, Barbara asked the doorman of the hotel which
of the cabs had a driver who spoke English.

"All of them," said the doorman. "You take from the
front of the line. I don't play favorites."

The driver at the front of the line said, "My name's
Sol Katz. Where to, lady?"

"Can I take you by the day?"

He looked at her thoughtfully, then nodded. "Twenty-five dollars, American." He was about fifty, slope-shouldered, with heavy belly, purple growth on his shaven cheeks, heavy brows, and curly black hair. "Get in," he said. "Where to?"

She told him.

He got into the driver's seat, twisted around to face her, and said, "You're sure that's where you want to go? Kiryat Anavim? It's just a kibbutz."

"I'm sure."

He pulled out into the traffic. "You got relatives there?"

"No."

"I didn't think so. You don't look like nobody got relatives there."

"I guess not. You're American, aren't you?" she asked him.

"If you call Bensonhurst America?"

"Where's Bensonhurst?"

"In Brooklyn, with everything else. Well, I been here since forty-eight. I came over to help out and I stayed. What are you, miss, newspaper lady?"

"Sort of."

"You going to write about Israel?"

"I write about most places where I've been. I suppose I'll write about Israel."

Barbara had no desire for conversation. She wanted to look at the countryside, to let it impinge on her, to feel what her husband might have felt about this place. It was like nothing she might have anticipated. In all her travels as a wartime correspondent, she had missed this tiny sliver of land. The very fact of her husband's commitment had caused her to erect her own wall against anything Israeli. It had been her rival, the single contender for the man she loved, and in

the end it had won, and he who had been her man lay
not in her bed but in the soil of this place. It was a
place that for her had never had a real existence. Her
religious upbringing had been perfunctory at best.
Dan Lavette had been born a Roman Catholic and
had put aside his religion to marry her mother. Sunday school classes in the proper Episcopal precincts of
Grace Cathedral on Nob Hill taught the mythology of
a place called the holy land. That holy land was a
place where a man who was a god walked on the waters of the Sea of Galilee, where He dragged a cross
along the Via Dolorosa, where the dreams and hopes
of mankind had been nailed to a wooden cross, and
where Roman soldiers ruled a people who were
shrouded in the uncertain mists of antiquity. None of
it bore any relationship whatsoever to the teeming
streets of Tel Aviv through which Sol Katz expertly
steered his taxicab, leaning on his horn and shouting
at other drivers in that strange, throaty language
called Hebrew. The older, broken-down sections of
Oakland made a more familiar equation.

Out of the city, they drove along a two-lane asphalt
road past villages, junkyards, and factories; then there
were the farms and the meadows. She sought for com-
parisons and recalled places in Ohio and Illinois that
were not unlike this. It was a cool, lovely morning, the
sky wonderfully blue, the air as sweet as honey.

They came to a place where the land swept away to
the north in a great, beautiful unspoiled stretch of
meadowland, like the rolling meadows she remembered from the south of England, and Sol Katz called
back to her, "Miss, out there"—he pointed—"out there,
that's where King Saul fought his big battle with the
Philistines. They came up from the coast, around Tel
Aviv, and he came down from the hill."

So it was not lost entirely, the myth of Grace Cathedral, even with a cab driver from Bensonhurst. Her eyes were wet, and she fought against the tide of emotion taking hold of her. "It's an illusion," she told herself. "This is simply a place, a part of the earth. We are people, and wherever we are is equally sacred, and if we can't learn that, then nothing is any use. And I will not give in to the dreams and battle cries that took Bernie away. I am going there because I am here already. I'll see it and get it over with."

They were climbing into the hills. Here, too, it was unlike any of her imaginings. The hills were covered with young green trees, cedar and pine and the air was sweet with pine fragrance. Now it evoked New England out of her memories.

"We planted them," Sol Katz said.

"What?"

"The trees, miss. Every one of them. We planted them."

"But there are thousands. The hills are covered with them."

"That's right. Used to be nothing but bare rock and grass. That's something, ain't it?"

"It certainly is," Barbara agreed.

"There's Kiryat Anavim," he said, pointing to a cluster of white, red-roofed houses in the distance. The kibbutz lay in a little valley against a hillside, the buildings climbing the hill above orchards, fields, and cultivated terraces.

"Who is in charge of a place like that?" Barbara asked after a moment.

"Miss—say, what's your name, lady? We're spending a day together, I should call you something beside miss."

"Barbara Cohen."

"All right, Miss Cohen—"

"Mrs. Cohen," Barbara said.

"All right, Mrs. Cohen. A kibbutz, it's usually run by a committee. There's a secretary or a president or someone like that."

"Will they speak English?"

"Someone will. You got to remember, Mrs. Cohen, we were occupied by the English for a long time."

Then they were at the kibbutz. There was an asphalt parking place that held a collection of old cars, trucks, and two tractors. Beyond it, an open shed of a machine shop, where men, stripped to the waist, were working on a third tractor. The road from the parking lot wound up the hillside to a stone and stucco building. The place clung to the mountainside and climbed it, and along with the stone walls and buildings, blazing red ramblers climbed and tumbled everywhere. The morning sun was hot, the air still. Honeybees buzzed over the flowers, and a huge black and yellow butterfly paused for a moment on Barbara's shoulder. A young woman in shorts came down the road, glanced at her curiously, then got into one of the trucks and drove off. A mongrel dog came up to her and licked her shoe.

Sol Katz walked around his car, observing the tires. "Nice place," he said. "You don't know anyone here?"

"No one, I'm afraid."

He called out in Hebrew to the men working in the machine shop, and they shouted back at him. He got the information he desired, and he said to Barbara, "I'll take you to the office. The secretary's name is Sarah Perez. They say she's there now. How long do you think you'll be here?"

"No more than an hour."

"All right. I'll be by the car. If you want to, we can drive up to Jerusalem. It's only a few miles from here."

"I'll see."

Barbara followed him up the road to the long stone building. "In there," Katz said. "They tell me she talks English, so you won't have no trouble."

He left her and went back to his car. She had a feeling that it made him nervous to be away from his taxicab. Evidently it was the central focus of his life. She opened the door and went inside. A hallway with doors opening off it and all the signs in Hebrew. She knocked at the first door to her right, and when a woman's voice responded in Hebrew, she opened the door and went in. The room was furnished with a plain wooden table, several wooden chairs, and some filing cabinets. Behind the table sat a thin, dark woman of about forty. A ledger was open in front of her.

"I'm looking for Sarah Perez," Barbara said.

"Myself, yes. What can I do for you?"

"I'm an American. My name is Barbara Cohen."

"Please, sit down." She pointed to a chair. "You're a journalist?"

"No."

"I thought you were because you know my name. Sometimes they send journalists here to write about a kibbutz."

"I'm a journalist, but that's not why I'm here." Then, as best she could, Barbara explained what had brought her to Israel.

"To see your husband's grave?"

"I don't know. Perhaps. Or perhaps I simply had to come."

"But I don't know why you should think your husband is buried in our cemetery. We have a small military cemetery, but it is only for the boys from the kibbutz who fell in the war. Your husband was never a part of this kibbutz, was he?"

"No. But they told me—"

"Wait, don't be troubled," Sarah Perez said kindly. "I have the register here." She went to the filing cabinet and found a notebook and began to thumb through it. While she was doing this, a slender, white-haired man, pink-cheeked, in his seventies, with a small white beard and mustache, entered the room.

"Ah, Shimon!" Sarah Perez said, adding to Barbara, "He will know. He remembers everything."

"Not everything. Even God, He doesn't remember everything."

"Shimon," she said, "this is Mrs. Cohen from the States. Her husband was killed near Megiddo in forty-eight. She was in the States. She was told that he was buried at our kibbutz."

The old man looked at Barbara, and then he said something to Sarah Perez in Hebrew.

"He offers you compassion," she said. "He says you are a good and beautiful woman."

"I suppose I am old enough to tell you myself. What was your husband's name?"

"Bernie—Bernie Cohen."

He stood for a moment with his eyes closed, and then he nodded. "Yes, I remember. There was some confusion because one of our boys named Cohen was in the north. Then the body was sent here, then his papers were sent here. He was American." He shrugged. "Why not here? It's a good place, a very ancient place. Are you unhappy for that?"

Barbara shook her head.

"You want the body exhumed and brought to your home?"

"No. This is what he would have wanted. To lie here."

"Then you just want to look at his grave?" the old man asked her.

"Yes." It was senseless, to leave her child again and come all the distance for this. To look at a grave. Now, sitting here, in the bleak office of the kibbutz, facing the two strangers, she felt not only foolish but inwardly shattered, purposeless, as if overcome by a growing sense that prison had left her empty, her life meaningless.

"If you wish, I take you to his grave," Shimon said.

"Yes, please." She stood up. "Thank you," she said unhappily to Sarah Perez.

The old man led her out into the sunshine, along a narrow dirt road that led up the hillside. "The dead still guard us," he said strangely, pointing up the mountainside. "Up there, just beyond the crest, is the border of old Judea, which the Jordanians still hold. It's quiet now, but still we live on the edge of eternity. That is not an easy way to live, is it?"

"No, I don't think so."

"You are not Jewish, are you?"

"No."

"And now you are here in this strange place with these strange people. It must be very hard."

"No, it's not hard. I suppose I'm trying to understand why I came. Whatever lives of my husband is inside me, not here."

"Why not here?" the old man asked. "Ah, here is the cemetery. Not very big, only a few hundred graves, but from one small kibbutz, for us it was a terrible bloodletting. The flower of our children."

The graves ascended in steps up the hillside, and each was finished with loving care, each with a small headstone inscribed in Hebrew.

"I can't read this," Barbara said plaintively.

"I'll find it."

A young man and a young woman, both in shorts and browned by the sun, were cutting and fitting stone, building an ornamental staircase to ascend the hillside between the graves.

"You know," Shimon said, "I grew up in Canada. We are most of us from somewhere else, and my memory of cemeteries is of cold, bleak places. Why should that be so? We thought this should be a different kind of a place. That golden stone they are cutting and shaping comes out of our own mountain. It is the same golden stone that old Jerusalem was built out of."

They were climbing higher and higher, and now, ahead of her, at the end of the path, Barbara saw a small stone building, like a crypt, perhaps eight feet square and windowless.

Shimon touched her arm. "Here, Barbara."

She paused. He pointed to a grave alongside of where they stood. "That's it. Your husband's grave."

She looked at it. No different from the other graves, simply a grave with some Hebrew lettering on the headstone and below it, the dates: 1906–1948. She felt nothing, only empty, dry, dry as the dust. She stood that way for perhaps five minutes, pleading inwardly for something that was nameless and undefined and perhaps nonexistent.

Then, in a voice as dry and toneless as her inner feeling, she pointed to other headstones upon which small bits of fieldstone had been placed. "What do those small stones mean?"

"It's an old Jewish custom. When you visit a grave, you leave a stone on the headstone. Some say it's an indication that you have been there, and you leave something to stay with the dead. That's a sentimental notion, and I'm not sure it has any validity. It's a very old custom, and I don't think anyone knows exactly what it means."

"And there, in that little house?" Barbara asked. "Is it a crypt—for ashes?"

"We don't cremate people in our faith. No, it's not a crypt."

"What then?" she asked, not really interested but not knowing what else to say.

"Why don't you step inside."

"It doesn't matter."

"Perhaps it does."

Then, feeling petulant and put upon, Barbara strode over to the tiny stone house, flung open the door, and stepped inside.

The stained glass of the roof let a blazing shower of light into the small room. On the walls to her left and right, from floor to ceiling, each in a Plexiglas, airtight frame, each about six inches square, were the photographs of the men who were buried in the military cemetery of Kiryat Anavim. Only they were not men. They were boys. They were children. They were laughing, delighted children. These were not posed photographs but snapshots lovingly gathered from parents and relatives.

She found herself going from picture to picture, from laughing face to laughing face. "Oh, my God," she whispered, "I am looking for Bernie." But they would have no picture of him.

Then the dry dam within her broke, and she collapsed on the floor, sobbing hysterically. She had wept in the past, but never had she let go of all emotional holds and barriers and let collapse the walls that surrounded her and protected her.

The old man waited outside. He heard the sound of her grief as did the two young people who were cutting stone, but when they wanted to go inside to answer what they felt was a cry of agony, a plea for help, he pushed them away.

"Leave her alone," he said. "Leave her with the dead. This is her time for such things."

The dam broke, and after the first great surge, the water lessened. Gasping, Barbara found that she could breathe. The tears stopped finally, and she was able to open her purse and take out a handkerchief and wipe her face. She rose shakily, feeling not so much faint as lightheaded, and then she went outside.

"Are you all right?" Shimon asked her.

"Yes. I'm all right."

"Shall we go back?"

"Yes."

But after a few steps Barbara said, "I forgot something."

Shimon watched as she walked back up to Bernie's grave, took a small stone from the ground, and placed it on his headstone.

The light breeze was just enough for headway, just enough for the rudder to respond to the wheel as they ran north into San Pablo Bay. Jean, wearing old Levi's and a big white sweater, sprawled on cushions in the cockpit and watched Dan.

"Well, old girl," he said to her, "how do you like it?"

"I'm getting used to it."

"Slow learners, both of us. Half a century to get you into a boat, half a century to civilize me."

"I don't know about the civilizing process, but you're forgetting that in the old days I made three trips to Europe."

"Ships, not boats. There's a difference, my girl."

"Oh, Danny," she said, "do you remember? The first time you came to our house, the big old pile on Nob Hill, and you had that argument with old Grant Whittier, and then you explained the difference between a ship and a boat. I thought you were so wonderful—"

"Come on."

"I did. Even if you didn't know what fork to use."

"My God," he exclaimed, "you noticed that?"

"Of course I did. You thought you were so clever. Whenever a dish was served, you didn't touch the silver until someone else showed the way. You just sat there, watching the whole thing like a young hawk."

"Come on, Jean, that was over forty years ago."

"I'm not senile, old man. My memory still works."

"I'll be damned if I know what you saw in me. I was just a young roughneck who had a taste of the world and wanted the rest of it."

"That's what I saw in you."

"Take the wheel," he said to her. "The wind's going. I'm going to take in the sail and start the motor. We'll head back. How about dinner at Gino's? I been thinking about spaghetti all day."

"Ever the flatterer," Jean said as she took the wheel. "Out on the bay with a pretty girl, and all you can think about is spaghetti. You're getting fat."

"Well—maybe a little. I'll work it off."

She watched him as he took in the sail, a big, white-haired man whose face was grooved with lines and wrinkles, his skin burned dark, his long-fingered hands strong and capable. He wore jeans and an old

sweatshirt, and he was easy in those clothes; and she
felt good watching him. That's part of it, she told herself, to feel good and easy about a man and to have no
doubts.

He started the motor. "Bring her about nice and
gentle," he said. "Head for the point. Do you mind
staying with it?"

"Whatever you say, boss."

He stood holding on to the mast, watching her. "You
are a damn beautiful woman," he said with appreciation.

"I'll be sixty-four next week."

"Either that means something profound or you're
worried I'll forget your birthday."

"It means I celebrate your flattery but doubt your
veracity and your eyesight."

"Nothing wrong with my eyesight. The thing about
Gino's," he said, "is that we don't have to change. We
can tie up the boat and walk there."

"You can't get your mind off spaghetti."

"Mind, hell. It's my stomach, woman. I am starved."

Two hours later, Jean eased the boat into the mooring, and Dan made the lines fast. With his arm around
her waist, they strolled over to Gino's Italian restaurant. It was onto twilight, with the fog beginning to
settle on the bay.

Dan paused suddenly and turned her toward him.

"If you're thinking of pawing me," Jean said, smiling, "you should have done it on the boat."

"Don't think I didn't think of it. Do you know, we
never made love on the boat. That makes no sense at
all."

"You are incredible, mister."

"Yeah. But all I want to do right now is kiss you."

"Here?"

He took her in his arms and kissed her, oblivious to the glances of people passing by.

"I suppose it's our age that makes them nervous," Jean said, "and we're dressed like a couple of bums. Ardor is supposed to cool."

In the restaurant, after they had eaten and were finishing a bottle of red wine, Dan said, "You know, I used to come here a lot with May Ling."

"I know that."

"Did you ever love another man, Jean? During the bad years? I don't mean going to bed—I mean really love another man?"

"No. Not even for a day, Danny."

"Funny. I loved May Ling. But she always knew that you were there, inside of a part of me. I've had a strange, crazy life, Jeanie, and how I ever came out of it on top of the heap, I'll never know. But I want to tell you this. I think I love you as much as a man can love a woman—well, as much as I can. And I want to thank you with all my heart. That's all."

Jean filled their glasses. "To us, Danny."

On the day Sam went back to school, Barbara put on an old sweater and a comfortable pair of shoes and walked down Powell Street to the Embarcadero; and then, turning right, she set out toward Market Street and the old ferry building. It was a fine, cool morning, and as she walked she was filled with a sense of being home in this place, which had its beginning with her family's beginning. No other place she had ever been gave her the same feeling of security, of rightness. It didn't matter that so much was wrong with the city, the state, and the country; enough was right to fill her with a feeling of well-being.

Walking for miles was essential to her work. Only

when she walked was her mind completely clear, and then she could evoke the images, the memories and the impressions so necessary to a writer. Life is the fact of being, and this moment in the life of Barbara Lavette Cohen was full of a sense of being. It was nothing explicit, certainly nothing more explicit than the salty tang of the sea air, the wind blowing out of the Pacific, out of China and Japan and the Spice Islands.

She was alive and home and free. And she was hungry. She had reached Battery Street, and now she swung around to walk back to Fisherman's Wharf. It was past eleven o'clock, a proper time for hunger. Barbara bought a loaf of the good San Francisco sourdough bread at the bake stand on Jefferson Street, and walked out onto the Hyde Street Pier to sit on a stanchion and eat the bread and throw bits of it to the gulls. She remembered sitting here with Bernie twelve years before, when they met for the first time after the war, but there was no pain in the memory. Ahead of her was the dancing, whitecapped surface of the bay, flowing with the tide through the Golden Gate and out into the endless sweep of the ocean. Behind her, piled up on its lilting hills, the strange, wonderful city that had been built by the Seldons and the Lavettes and the Levys and the longshoremen and the bricklayers and the carpenters and the steelworkers and a million others.

And here was a wide-winged gull to snatch a crust of sourdough bread.

She took a last bite of the bread, savoring its taste, threw the rest to the gulls, rose, and breathed deeply.

"It's all right," she told herself. "It's just as it should be."

She saw them turning the cable car, ran for it, and

swung onto it just as it began to move. She stood on the running board as the car climbed Russian Hill, feeling the cool wind on her face and smiling slightly. If there was any thought in her mind at that moment, it was simply an acknowledgment. She was there, with herself, and all was well.

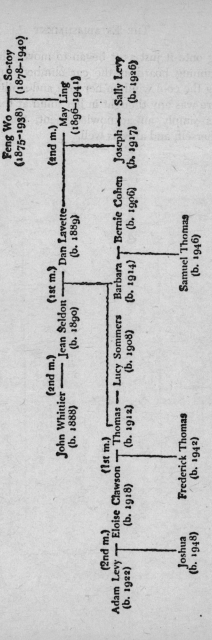

THE LAVETTES

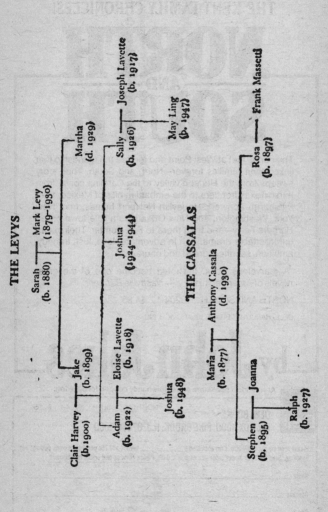

THE LEVYS

Sarah (b. 1880) — Mark Levy (1879–1930)

Clair Harvey (b. 1900) — Jake (b. 1899)

Eloise Lavette (b. 1918) — Adam (b. 1922)

Joshua (b. 1948)

Martha (d. 1929)

Joshua (1924–1944)

Sally (b. 1926) — Joseph Lavette (b. 1917)

May Ling (b. 1947)

THE CASSALAS

Maria (b. 1877) — Anthony Cassala (d. 1930)

Stephen (b. 1895) — Joanna

Ralph (b. 1927)

Rosa (b. 1897) — Frank Massetti

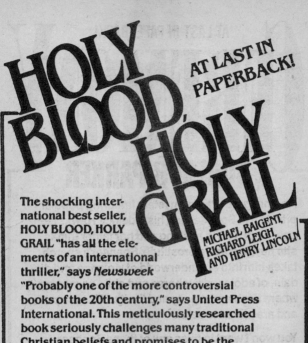